DRAGON SAGA

BOOK THREE

THE SONG OF THE WIND

NICOLETTE ANDREWS

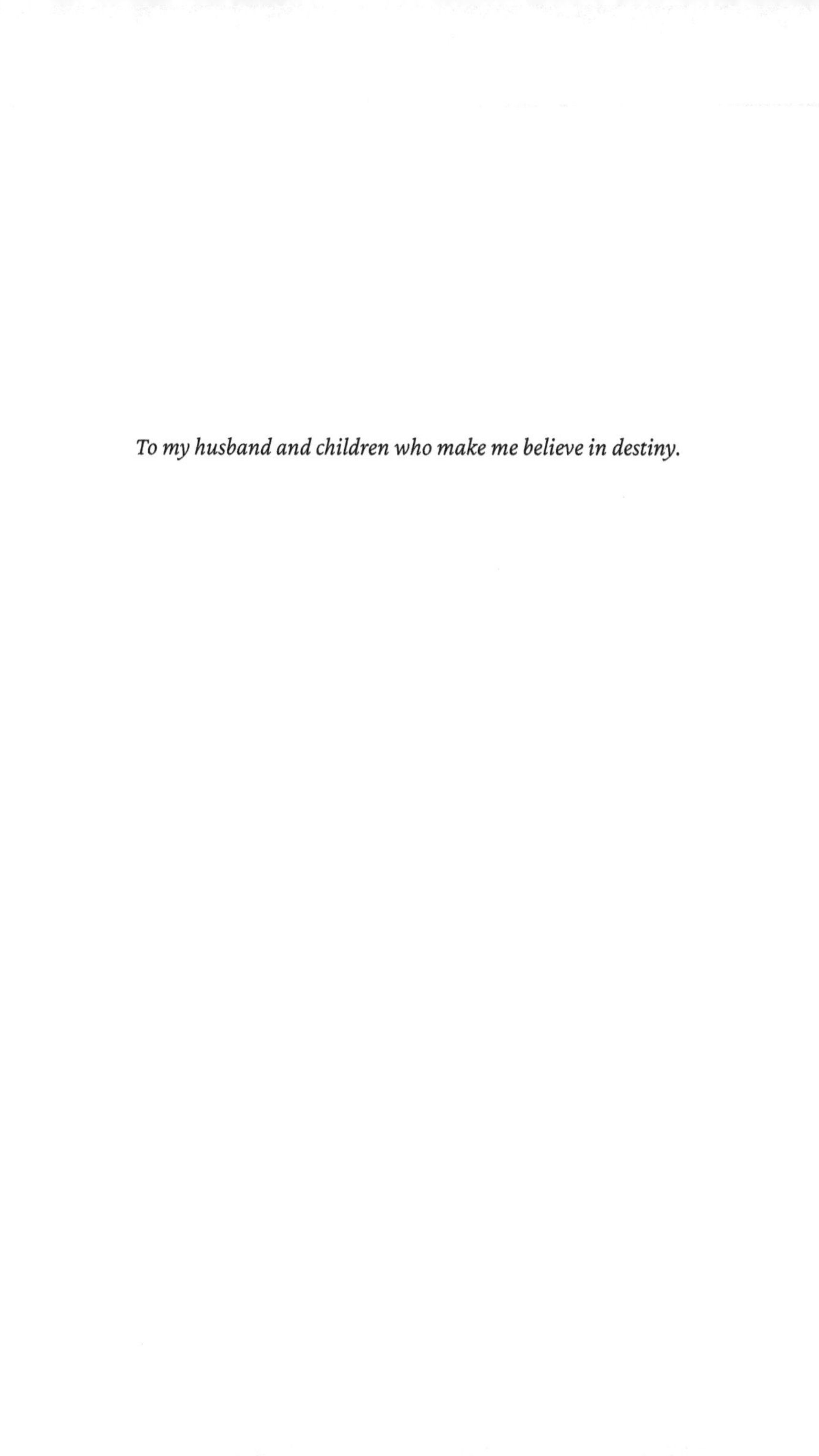

To my husband and children who make me believe in destiny.

THIS EDITION MADE POSSIBLE BY MY INCREDIBLE KICKSTARTER BACKERS

EXTRA-EXTRA SPECIAL THANKS TO:

ARTHUR DIXON, BUBS MARTINEZ, CHRIS-ANDRÉ PEDERSEN, COURTNEY R. DELGADO, DIANA BRITTON, HEIDI Z., NATASHA WIMMER, SEAMUS SANDS

EXTRA SPECIAL THANKS TO:

AMANDA ESCHMEYER, ASHLEY, AURORE MOREL, CHRISTINE HAAS, DAPHNÉ MELANSON, DR. CHARLES E NORTON III, ELIZABETH FRAZIER, ELVINA PATINO, EMILIE GARNEAU, EMMA FLAWS, FRANCHESCA CARAM, JESSICA JOHANSEN, JOHN CALLAHAN, JONAH PAVLICEK, KAREN BULGARELLI, KASEY OVERSTREET, KASS M., KATHERINE MALLOY, KATIE PAWLIK, KIM HILLMER, LEIA, M.W. M. COSGROVE, MARY LIVINGSTON, MOON THEIASDOTTIR, NEREIDA GREEN, NICOLE HAARSTAD, TAYLOR PRINCE

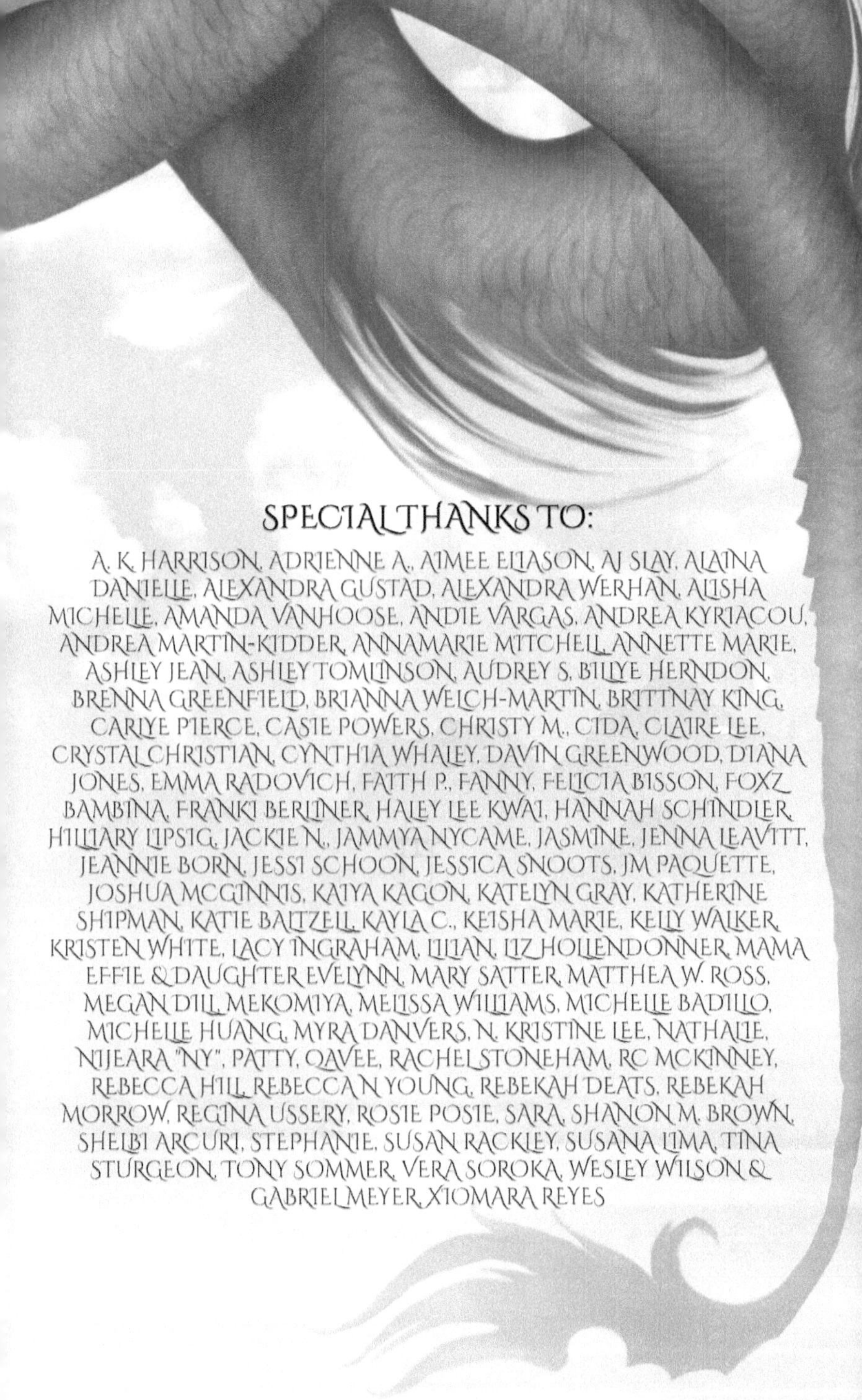

SPECIAL THANKS TO:
A. K. HARRISON, ADRIENNE A., AIMEE ELIASON, AJ SLAY, ALAINA DANIELLE, ALEXANDRA GUSTAD, ALEXANDRA WERHAN, ALISHA MICHELLE, AMANDA VANHOOSE, ANDIE VARGAS, ANDREA KYRIACOU, ANDREA MARTIN-KIDDER, ANNAMARIE MITCHELL, ANNETTE MARIE, ASHLEY JEAN, ASHLEY TOMLINSON, AUDREY S, BILLYE HERNDON, BRENNA GREENFIELD, BRIANNA WELCH-MARTIN, BRITTNAY KING, CARLYE PIERCE, CASIE POWERS, CHRISTY M., CIDA, CLAIRE LEE, CRYSTAL CHRISTIAN, CYNTHIA WHALEY, DAVIN GREENWOOD, DIANA JONES, EMMA RADOVICH, FAITH P., FANNY, FELICIA BISSON, FOXZ BAMBINA, FRANKI BERLINER, HALEY LEE KWAI, HANNAH SCHINDLER HILLIARY LIPSIG, JACKIE N., JAMMYA NYCAME, JASMINE, JENNA LEAVITT, JEANNIE BORN, JESSI SCHOON, JESSICA SNOOTS, JM PAQUETTE, JOSHUA MCGINNIS, KATYA KAGON, KATELYN GRAY, KATHERINE SHIPMAN, KATIE BALTZELL, KAYLA C., KEISHA MARIE, KELLY WALKER KRISTEN WHITE, LACY INGRAHAM, LILIAN, LIZ HOLLENDONNER, MAMA EFFIE & DAUGHTER EVELYNN, MARY SATTER, MATTHEA W. ROSS, MEGAN DILL MEKOMIYA, MELISSA WILLIAMS, MICHELLE BADILLO, MICHELLE HUANG, MYRA DANVERS, N. KRISTINE LEE, NATHALIE, NIJEARA "NY", PATTY, QAVEE, RACHEL STONEHAM, RC MCKINNEY, REBECCA HILL REBECCA N YOUNG, REBEKAH DEATS, REBEKAH MORROW, REGINA USSERY, ROSIE POSIE, SARA, SHANON M. BROWN, SHELBI ARCURI, STEPHANIE, SUSAN RACKLEY, SUSANA LIMA, TINA STURGEON, TONY SOMMER, VERA SOROKA, WESLEY WILSON & GABRIEL MEYER, XIOMARA REYES

Lord of the Sea's Palace
Kaito's Palace
Namahane Village
Hidden Temple
Mt. Kuriyama
Aiko's Forest
Mt. Iwaki
Temple of Mt. Iwaki
Kaedemori Clan House
Mountain God's Shrine
Tengu Mountain
White Palace
Sun Temple
Osaka
Kaito's Palace

ONE

The only light was a smattering of stars across the inky black sky. Suzume's lungs burned from exertion, each breath coming out in a painful wheeze. The bamboo forest that surrounded them was growing denser, closing in on her and obscuring what little light she could see by. As they plunged deeper into the forest, the group found themselves in near impenetrable darkness. A creeping sensation persisted and sent cold shivers down her spine. She searched behind her for a pursuing yokai, but all that she could see was the faint glint of Naoki's blades. Just behind him, Tsuki flashed her a toothy smile. *He would be having a good time.* Suzume returned her attention to the path ahead. Her only guide was the flickering flames of Rin's multiple tails as she led them through the twisted maze of the bamboo forest.

Rin turned a corner and Suzume was left to fumble in the dark, using her hands out in front of her and what little she'd memorized of the path ahead. The hairs on the back of her neck prickled. She hadn't been imagining it—there was a powerful yokai nearby. Its spiritual pressure pressed down upon her. Her ability to sense these things was growing stronger all the time, and she could sense it as if were a scent, or as if she were touching something tangible. Neither of those senses quite described the feeling. It was much more of a queasy churning of her stomach. Gooseflesh rose all along her body, and the spark of flames traveled up her veins. It was getting closer.

A ferocious roar pierced the silent night. Suzume's head whipped around, searching for the source, but she couldn't see anything beyond the canopy of black above. The bamboo was so dense nothing should have been able to see her either. But she still got this sense of eyes watching her. She was so preoccupied that she did not notice Rin had stopped in front of her. The priestess collided with Rin, who was in her true form of a fox with multiple flaming tales. Suzume rubbed her nose, which had smashed into the giant fox's backside.

"You could have warned me we were stopping," Suzume grumbled.

"He's getting closer," Rin said, putting a damper on any more complaints Suzume might have.

"I gathered as much."

The group fanned out around her, reaching for their weapons. Suzume clutched at her staff, palms sweaty. The fire was right there at her fingertips, ready to be unleashed to wreak havoc upon any foe. She could do this. She had done it before. But after what she had done, knowing what dwelled inside her, she held back from reaching out to it. The ground beneath Suzume's feet trembled, the vibrations traveling up her body. It was getting closer.

From out of the dark shadows, a figure dressed all in black emerged. His eyes glowed green in the darkness as he sang a song. Suzume could feel the power rising off him, igniting every cell in her body. Her throat itched to join in with him, to feel that power course through her, but she clamped her mouth shut instead and just watched Makato, or Hikaru, which was his real name.

The notes of his song faded into the night and he turned to the others. "That should give us sufficient cover for now."

"It won't last forever. We better hurry," Rin said in a rumbling voice.

They continued through the twisted maze of the bamboo forest, and the creeping sensation would not leave Suzume. Maybe it was because the nights were turning colder, but the chill continued to grow. A small spark of her flame would both warm her and give her something to see by. But with her power, it wasn't always that simple. One little spark and the next thing she knew she'd be consumed by Kazue. Instead she followed the dim light Rin emitted and rubbed her palms against her arms, trying to keep warm.

"How much farther?" Akira asked, her voice floating from somewhere in the darkness behind Suzume.

It was a disorienting feeling, being surrounded but having no real way of seeing any of them. It was as if they were all lost in darkness.

"Almost there," Hikaru replied. His disembodied voice echoed around Suzume.

As if summoned by his words, the bamboo forest came to an abrupt end. The night was still and the only sound was the chirp of insects.

"I think we lost him," Suzume said, with an audible exhale of relief.

"Wait here, just in case," Rin said before stepping out from the archway of bamboo.

Rin lifted her fox head, sniffing the air. After a few cautious moments, she gestured for the others to join her. Outside the forest there was nothing but a long stretch of rolling hills, nothing to disguise them for a league. Suzume hurried across the space, wanting to be back in the shelter of treetops as soon as possible. Her gaze kept drifting to the cloudless night. If something was flying overhead, they'd see it in an instant.

Halfway across a cloud passed overhead, casting a long shadow over them. Behind her she heard the clink of a sword being drawn. The long serpentine shadow was directly over her and she tilted her head back to see a flash of blue scales against the dark sky. She squeezed her hands into fists to suppress the sparks that already threatened to ignite all over her body.

Maybe he didn't see us. But how could he miss them, when they were out in the open?

An ear-piercing roar shook Suzume to her core.

Or he did.

The others closed into formation around her, weapons drawn. As if they could protect her from what was coming. Suzume reached for her staff, but feared drawing it. If she fought now, the power would only leap to her defense and she feared the consequences if she did. So she dropped her hand to her side instead, relying on her friends for protection.

The dragon took a dive from the sky, on a crash course with their group. He skimmed over the tops of their heads. The rush of the wind as he passed tossed Suzume's hair back, and she whipped her head up to watch his progress as he landed a few feet away.

In a puff of smoke, he transformed from a serpentine dragon to something more human. From a distance, Suzume could see his icy blue eyes. He stormed toward them, one hand extended, partially transformed, and tipped with razor-sharp claws.

"Out of my way," Kaito growled at Naoki and Tsuki, who stood directly in front of her.

"Not gonna happen I'm afraid," Tsuki said. Even though she couldn't see his face, she imagined he had a grin.

"Then I'll make you move."

The dragon lunged for the two swordsmen, claws clashing with blades, the sound ringing out into the night. The two of them circled the dragon, whose face had partially transformed into something dangerous and beastly. Elongated fangs protruded from his mouth, his face was covered in scales, and his eyes were a dangerous blue. He spun slowly in a circle while the swordsmen held up their weapons, on guard.

"I do not wish to fight you," Naoki said.

"Too late for that," Kaito said as he lunged once more for the swordsman.

Even in a fight of two against one, the odds were in Kaito's favor.

Suzume's hands were slick with sweat as she gripped her staff. She let it go though, she wouldn't use it against him. Not at the risk of hurting him once more. She stepped out from the protective barrier Rin and Hikaru had put between her and the dragon.

"Stop!" she shouted.

Kaito froze, his hand in the air prepared to slash at Tsuki. His piercing blue eyes caught hers and narrowed.

"What are you doing?" she said to the dragon, hands on hips, arms trembling. She'd wanted to make a clean break. But knowing the dragon, that was never going to be possible.

Kaito lowered his hands to his side. "Excuse me?"

"Why did you follow us?"

He shook his head and stalked over to her, grabbing her wrist and yanking her close to him. "Is this a joke? You snuck away in the middle of the night. What else was I supposed to think other than you were kidnapped?"

Sparks danced between them as her fire could not be suppressed against the threat of his icy grip. It would be so easy to fall into old habits, let him lure her back in with an argument that he would inevitably win. She had left without a goodbye for this very reason. She yanked her hand away.

"You knew I wasn't kidnapped." She glared back at him.

A few errant sparks sputtered out and died, fading into the dark. Kaito glared at the space between them.

"You have a knack for trouble," he said but the old joke was half-hearted at best.

"Well you see that I'm fine, so you can leave now." She turned to walk away. If she looked at him, she might still give in and stay with him. Not because she thought he'd ask her to stay, but because she was afraid her own resolve would crumble. It would be so much easier to fall into his arms and become his pet, kept hidden away forever. But that's not who she wanted to be.

Kaito balled his hand into a fist. "What are you hoping to prove?"

She turned around to face him once more, her face flushed with anger. "Do you really not get it?"

"I see that you're still too reckless for your own good. I'm bringing you back before you get hurt."

He reached for her once more and she picked up her staff, blocking him with a flaming barrier that she had not intended to use, but was grateful for just the same. Ice coated his hand as he grasped the staff.

"Do you want to know why I can't go back there?" Suzume asked as she knocked the dragon backward. He skidded back a step or two. She was lucky that time. He'd not expected her to go on the attack. But before he could recover, she lunged toward him, swiping her staff at him. He dodged her attack, rolling out of the way. She felt her power swell inside her, a raging inferno that was just waiting to be unleashed—Kazue's flame, the power of the kami. Whatever it was, it wanted more than anything for Suzume to prove to Kaito just how strong she had become.

He had to feel it as well, the rise of her spiritual pressure. But he was pretending not to. He only saw her as a fragile princess, a woman incapable of protecting herself, but she had become so much more. She swung at him again, letting rage guide her steps. But Kaito was much faster than her and he was behind her in a heartbeat.

He wrapped his arm around her torso, pressing her staff against her body and pressing her back against his chest.

"I don't care what your reasons are. I know what's best for you."

Her anger rose in her like the tide, and flames burst out of Suzume, turning her into an inferno. Kaito jumped back and away from her before he too was burned. She turned to face him, and saw the flame reflected in his eyes and she saw his fear. The scales receded on his skin and he reverted to a more human visage. She thought Hikaru had broken the spell that caused her to steal Kaito's energy, but the bond was not broken. They were still connected and the longer they remained together the more she would hurt him and herself.

The thought sobered her and she let the flames die out. Kaito was left nearly bent over, clutching at his stomach.

"This is why I'm leaving," she said, gesturing toward him.

Kaito stood up again, as if he had not almost been brought to his knees by Suzume's brief show of power.

"You don't have to use your power," he growled. But she could see the strain on his face and the cracks in his veneer, which showed his real fear of her.

"That's what you don't get. I don't want to give it up. If I have to choose between you and my power, then I choose my power." It was a lie, of course. She didn't want this destructive power, but she didn't want to be a kept woman either.

She turned to walk away, hoping that she'd made her point clear and he'd let her walk away once and for all. But before she could even take a few steps, Kaito chased after her. He grabbed her but this time she didn't feel any of the frost in his touch. It was warm and firm.

It was so difficult not to turn around and beg him to protect her. She was terrified of the power inside her. So scared that she would lose control again, and hurt someone else.

She wished she could live the ideal life he wanted for her—living protected and comfortable, a similar version of the life she had once had back at the palace. But that Suzume was gone, burned away and nothing but ash.

"Let me go," she said, softly.

As if he was a puppet on a string, Kaito loosened his grip. It shocked her that he listened. His entire body was tense, clenched and angry.

"Do you think I'm going to let you go that easily?" he asked.

"Is keeping me like your pet going to change the past?"

"You're mine." His voice was a growl.

She shook her head. "No, I'm not."

She took another few steps and he followed. "Just stop!" she shouted.

Kaito froze in his tracks. "This isn't funny," Kaito growled.

Suzume turned to him once more. "I'm not trying to be funny."

"Then whose spell is keeping me from moving?" he snarled.

Everyone had the same confused expression on their faces. Then she remembered how after she'd taken Ai's energy she had been able to control her. Could it be she had the same control over Kaito?

"Pat your head."

Kaito's arm moved stiffly to his head and he tapped it once and then twice.

Suzume covered her mouth with her hand. *He has to listen to me.* There were so many evil thoughts running through her head, all of which would only lead to trouble. As much as she wanted to tease him, and fall back into the same routine they used to have, she knew there was only one command she had to give.

"I'm going to walk away and you cannot chase after me. Do not search for me. I never want to see you again."

"Do you think I'm going to listen to a mere human?"

"You don't have any choice. We're bound together and you have to obey."

Two

It had been five hundred years since Kaito had gazed upon this shoreline. While he had been sealed away, his dreams at times had brought him back here—seated at the head of the great hall, his subjects feasting while the sounds of music and laughter filled the room. The palace had been full of life and color, his people as varied as the islands over which he ruled. When he closed his eyes, he could almost hear them again. But when he opened them, the sky overhead was gray, and his once vibrant palace had been stripped of color, hardly distinguishable from the sky and sea. Everything was one muted canvas.

The palace long ago was a shining jewel set on the ocean's surface. At the height of his power it had been a testament to his strength. Now all that remained was a bleak island, buffeted by waves. At first glance, it appeared to be nothing but crumbling stone. To any passing human eye, that was exactly how it seemed. But Kaito saw beyond that, to the crumbled walls which once fortified his palace. The beautifully painted tiles which once covered his roofs were cracked and bleached by the sun.

Raindrops pattered onto his face and Kaito tilted his head back to let them roll down his neck. Perhaps the clouds overhead were reflective of his mood, and the sea's raging against the sandy shore fueled by his anger. There was no denying it now, time had almost wiped away the last traces of him and his kingdom. Nothing was how it was supposed to be. First he lost Suzume, and now this.

"You are back where you belong," Ai said. Though childlike in appearance she had at one time been one of the most powerful of the first children. Beloved daughter of the Lord of the Sea, and Kaito's one-time mistress. She had insisted on joining him on his quest to return home, rather than remaining in the underwater palace which had once been her prison.

The two of them had lost everything, taken by Kazue. But if he had known what awaited him here he would have held back on returning. He would have gone to search out allies first, prepare himself. After everything he'd lost already—his pride, his rulership. He had hoped this place would remain the same as so many other palaces had. But this was just another cruel twist of the knife.

"It can be rebuilt," Ai said, reading his mood.

Kaito lowered his gaze to the horizon once more. Water blurred his vision as he held up his hands. Thunder rumbled overhead as lightning cracked through the sky. The sea grew still, recognizing its master. The waters parted, and from the depths of the ocean arches rose. Seaweed was tangled around their tops, but the color had not faded and the bright crimson shone like a flame against the bleak landscape. Following the arches, a stone pathway emerged from the sea floor and crabs scuttled across it, heading back to the water they'd been so rudely removed from. Everything fell into place with a shuddering halt.

"I am home."

He strode beneath the arches, heading for the doors which clung to the remains of the outer walls. The massive wooden doors hung loosely on the hinges, battered by the wind and sea for centuries. They were mostly rotted. Beyond the main gates the central courtyard greeted him. Seabirds had made nests in the eaves of the outer buildings. Broken shells and the skeletons of fish littered the ground. Kaito's feet crunched on shells and bones as he crossed it. He made a mental note of everything that would need to be returned to its former glory.

"This is a mess," Ai said, hiding her face behind her large sleeve. Everything stank of rotting fish.

Kaito continued up the main stairs through the outer ring of buildings, where in times past the lesser of his court dwelled. These buildings had taken the brunt of the ocean's torment. All that remained was the skeletal structures jutting from the foundation. Sea life had taken up residence and barnacles clung to stones and walls.

Into the second and third rings the damage was less, though age and neglect showed in the damp decay that clung to everything. Kaito stopped before the double doors, which had once led into his audience room—the place where he had ruled over Akatsuki. The double doors, shielded from the elements, seemed untouched by time. Unlike the outer reaches of his palace, this place still held some of its spiritual energy due to spells woven into the fabric of the place and his own essence which had seeped into it from hundreds of years of residence. He brushed his hand against the wood, but as he did a jolt went through him. His spells had been contaminated with unfamiliar energy.

He pulled his hand back. It was most likely scavengers who had come while he was away. Once word of his defeat had spread, the yokai would have thought little of his possessions other than to take it for themselves. That was a matter for later, however. Kaito pushed open the doors and they creaked, protesting their use after five hundred years of stillness.

As soon as he opened the door, raucous laughter drifted outward.

"Someone is here," Ai said, stating the obvious.

He felt the shift in her spiritual energy as she channeled her power to defend him. Not that he needed it. He was more than strong enough to fend off a few squatters. Likely it was some low-level yokai who had moved in while he was gone. He wasn't surprised, but he wasn't pleased either.

The audience hall was long, lined with numerous supporting beams, and the ceiling was high—at least five times his height, to accommodate all types of yokai. At the far end of the room was a raised dais, where he had once presided over his court. A fire flickered just at the foot of the dais, casting long shadows onto it and the surrounding pillars and walls. A figure sat where Kaito once sat. These were very presumptuous squatters.

It was exactly the sort of distraction he needed, knocking around a few yokai might help calm the rage which churned around in his gut. The small band of yokai were seated around the fire. Kaito and Ai kept to the shadows, hiding behind the pillars as they crept closer to the group. A yokai with garish blue hair and curling horns sprouting from the top of his head lounged on the dais, his head resting in the lap of a beautiful yokai, whose blue-green hair fell to the ground behind her. She stroked his head, running her long fingers through his hair.

There were no more than ten of them in the room. A quick scan of the surrounding area revealed there were no more about. All of them had the same sort of appearance—jewel toned hair and horns on their head. Though their appearance was nothing like any yokai he had seen before, he was surprised to find they were dragons. Who would willingly assume these ridiculous forms? *I thought I knew all the dragons in Akatsuki.* He assessed them another moment, trying to discern if he had met them before and did not recognize their current chosen forms. But after careful probing, in which none of them so much as flinched, he determined they must be some lesser beings closely related to dragons.

The group was so busy drinking and laughing, none of them noticed him until he was in their midst.

"I return home and I find my palace infested with vermin," he said.

The group jumped to their feet, some half-transformed, curling clawed hands into fists. Others reached for rusty, beaten up swords and blunt objects, as if any of it would stand a chance against him. The only ones who did not react were the woman and the man at the front of the group. The reclining dragon remained with his head in the woman's lap, eyes closed.

"Who are you to enter the great dragon's domain?" the dragon asked without even bothering to turn his head toward Kaito.

Kaito threw his head back and laughed. His laughter echoed through the chamber and sounded like the crack of thunder. "Not only do you steal my palace, you dare to impersonate me?"

The dragon opened one eye as he turned his head to peer at Kaito. "Who's impersonating who? You come into my throne room unin-vited, interrupt our party..."

"You insolent ruffians, Ai shall teach you for speaking that way about one of the first children," Ai piped up, but her childlike voice and small stature did not leave much of an impression and the dragons all laughed uproariously.

"Perhaps you should put your lapdog on a leash," said the dragon nearest to them. He was a towering creature, at least a head taller than Kaito and three times as thick. He would have thought it all an illusion but his spiritual energy matched his outer physique.

"Ai is not a lap dog." Her eyes shifted to all dark pupils and her hair transformed into a myriad of tentacles whipping around behind her.

The dragon only continued to laugh until the moment one of her tentacles reached out, wrapped around his throat and lifted him off the ground. His legs kicked, useless beneath him, while his hands clawed at Ai's tentacle, trying to break her grip.

The other dragons approached and Kaito transformed, bearing his own claws, his arms covered in blue scales.

"I am the Great Dragon, born of the first children, created by the Lord of the Sea, and the ruler of Akatsuki."

The dragon sat up at last, swung his legs around so they were dangling over the edge of the dais, and leaned forward to stare at Kaito.

"It's been a long time since we had a challenger," the dragon said with a devious smile.

He leaped down and strolled over toward Kaito, who stared at him with arms crossed over his chest.

"Have your dog let go of my man and let's have a real fight."

Kaito nodded slightly toward Ai, who dropped the dangling dragon. He fell to the ground on all fours and gasped for breath. One of his comrades went over toward him and helped the big man to his feet while glaring at Kaito.

The leader held out his hand and another of his men handed him a sword. Unlike the other swords, this had a carved pommel in the shape of a dragon made of jade.

"I'll have you know I've never lost a challenge."

"Neither have I," Kaito said with a smile.

The leader grinned at him. He was cocky and had likely risen to a position of power as a result. Among yokai appearing strong meant almost as much as being strong. But that was only half the battle, and they were all about to see what true power meant. Kaito unfurled his spiritual energy, which until now he'd kept contained. It swept over the room, filling the space, causing the entire hall to vibrate with it.

The leader's smile faltered. They had felt it, all of them had.

"Let's begin," Kaito snarled.

They took their places. It had been a very long time since Kaito had fought a challenger, or would this make him the challenger? No matter. He hadn't been posturing when he said he'd never lost. He'd won the right to rule by being the strongest and he'd kept his position for the very same reason.

It was no surprise when the dragon attacked first. He lunged at Kaito, striking with precision. Kaito could have dodged it easily, but he let the blade graze his side. Bright red blood splattered onto the ground. He knew how to handle a blade, so it wasn't all talk. But when his smile widened, Kaito knew the ego that lay beneath that skill. It would be his undoing.

"First blood," the watchers chanted.

They'd been quiet up until now, perhaps uncertain how their leader would fair against someone with as much spiritual energy as Kaito. But by letting him have the first blood, they grew more confident. They jeered and stomped their feet. And they were not the only ones growing more bold, their leader was as well.

"How do you expect to beat me with just your claws?" the leader taunted.

"A true yokai needs nothing else."

They continued to circle around one another and the dragon struck again. This time Kaito dodged. He'd let him wet his blade, but he would not let him land a blow again. Kaito led him on a chase around the circle, letting him believe he had him on the run.

After a few minutes of back and forth, Kaito had his back against the edge. His opponent was closing in. When the dragon arched his arm backward to land what would have been a killing blow, it left his left side exposed. Kaito made his move, slashing upward, raking his claws from hip to armpit. It tore his kosode and left a ragged gash down his side.

More importantly, it caught the dragon by surprise. Real fear flashed in his eyes, but to his credit he did not even reach to staunch the bleeding. He did leap backward and away from Kaito's dangerous claws.

"You're better than I thought. All the others fell within a few minutes."

"I should say the same for you."

The dragon's smile grew wider. "I've never had to do this before."

His rival's body transformed—his arms growing in size, his height lengthening—as his spiritual power unfurled from within him.

It was enough to shock Kaito. This was not some minor yokai, or a bastardized dragon. He'd only done a cursory check of his opponent's spiritual energy. But as his true power was revealed, Kaito knew exactly who he was dealing with. He had changed his appearance but he was still the same.

Kaito threw his head back and laughed. "It's good to see you again, brother."

THREE

His brother smiled at him, baring his canines like a feral dog. "I'm surprised you did not recognize me straight away," he said.

They continued to dance around another in a slow circle, neither attacking as they watched one another warily.

"It was hard to recognize you without your face in the mud," Kaito taunted.

The dragon lunged for him with the sword, and Kaito raised his hand to block it, his palm encrusted in ice to save him from the blow. They stared at one another over the blade.

"I thought you were dead."

"Is that why you decided to take my palace? Since you could never win it from me in a fair fight?"

His brother leaped backward and away from him. The dragons were still cheering and stamping their feet.

"There was no need, since you were defeated by a mere mortal woman."

Kaito felt his hackles rise and he lurched forward, letting his temper get the better of him. An icy spear formed in his hand and he jabbed it at his brother's torso. Before he could embed it in his gut as he would have wished, his brother leaped out of the way.

"It's true then, you were brought down by a woman?" He threw his head back and laughed.

Kaito launched a second attack, attempting to put him off balance. But as he had done before, his brother danced just outside his reach. Kaito wanted nothing more than to claw that smug smile off the bastard's face. Because he was not thinking clearly, he left himself open to the same trick he'd been trying to drag his opponent into and when he swung too wide, his brother struck him hard across the back, bringing Kaito to his knees.

Ai gasped and attempted to rush forward and help him, but as soon as she did, the dragons around them put out their arms to stop her.

His brother stalked around him with that same smug smile on his face.

"That's her, our master's favorite. You went crawling back to her." He looked scornfully toward Ai, who only glared back at him. His brother turned to Kaito again. "You were free. You had everything and the moment you lost it you went back to them." He threw his head back and crowed. "I always knew you were a fool, but not this much of one."

"And what about you?" Kaito growled, between gritted teeth. "What have you done besides drink and waste your time in my rotting castoffs?"

Anger flashed in his eyes as he raised his sword, prepared to cut Kaito's head off. But before he could land the blow, Kaito pierced his shoulder with another spear made of ice that came up from beneath him. His brother was propelled forward, and his weapon fell from his grip as blood gushed from the wound.

Pressing his advantage, Kaito stalked toward him, throwing in a couple punches while his opponent was still disoriented. His brother swayed on his feet for a moment. The blood loss and the ice protruding from his shoulder would take a lot of energy to heal, giving him enough time to make his final blow.

As Kaito swung downward, his brother caught him in his grip. He glared into Kaito's eyes. "You left. Someone had to protect them." He seethed.

Kaito headbutted his brother and knocked him square on his rear. His brother laid sprawled on his back, and Kaito pressed his foot against his throat.

"I have returned now."

The dragons that surrounded them all fell silent. The stomping had ceased, and all that remained was the ragged breathing of the two. The odd collection of yokai in the room was not the court he had left behind, but it was a start.

He turned to face the group without taking his weight off his opponent's throat. "I am the true Great Dragon. Follow me now and you shall all have a place in my court. We shall return this place to the glory it had once been."

The group took a moment to process his words before they broke out into uproarious cheers.

"I will spare your life, but if you pretend to be me again, I will destroy you."

He removed his foot from his throat and his brother sat up rubbing his neck.

He scowled at him but Kaito paid him no mind and let the group surround him. Their voices overlapped with numerous questions and congratulations. That was the way of the yokai, they were a fickle bunch. His brother, their former leader, was all but forgotten.

The woman yokai with the long green hair brought Kaito a bottle of sake. He took a deep drink from it, quenching his thirst, before he threw it down onto the ground, shattering the bottle to pieces. The dragons roared their pleasure.

"Please, take a seat of honor," the woman said, pointing to the dais where once he had proceeded above his court.

But he knew his place in their group was tenuous as of yet. They did not trust him and he did not trust them. He had earned a place on his throne in the past, but that was over now. This was in many ways like starting over.

"I would rather drink with you," he said and placed himself in the center of the circle.

The dragons looked around at each other as if they couldn't quite believe what he was doing. But after a few minutes of awkward staring they sat down as well. The bottle of sake was passed around. The only one who remained separate from the group was his brother, who lingered at the edges of the group with a sour expression on his face.

Once the liquor was flowing and the conversation became less stilted, the dragons relaxed, talking and laughing and including Kaito as if he was one of them. Kaito took a swig of sake from the jug. It took a lot to get him drunk but at this pace he just might. His stomach buzzed pleasantly. He passed the jug to Ai who held it away from herself as if it was a disgusting insect.

"Tell me, how did you come to dwell in my palace and pretend to be me?" Kaito asked with a laugh and a nod toward his sulking brother, to make it clear he felt no ill will toward him.

"After you were defeated by a human-" his brother began. Kaito glared in his direction but did not stop him. He would resist the urge to be petty, for now. It only made his brother seem like the lesser man.

He looked back at the group and laughed. "Someone is still bitter he lost."

The group joined in on the joke, and another took up the tale. The speaker was a female yokai with purple hair cropped short, just long enough to tuck behind her ears. She had a clever face and a mouth meant for smiling.

"In the years after you disappeared, there was a struggle for control of Akatsuki. Everything was chaos, many died. But when the dust settled four rulers emerged, each taking over different domains in Akatsuki."

"Who rules these domains?"

"They're gone now," his brother said, arms crossed over his chest like a child. His stance reminded him of Suzume when she was being stubborn. The reminder was unwanted and he had to turn away before he let bitter memories sour his victory.

"What happened to them?" he asked.

The dragons all shared a look and Kaito raised his brows in question. "No one knows for sure. Perhaps a hundred years after the wars, the

Lord of the North went missing," said a slender yokai with crimson hair that was short and spiky.

"And two hundred years later, the Lady of the East. But everyone says it was her brother who tried to take her rule," said the big yokai who Ai had tried to strangle.

"Until he disappeared without a trace."

"One by one all the strongest yokai have fallen until there were none left," his brother said, turning to face them now. The light from the fire cast his face into deep shadows, making him appear almost skeletal.

Kaito looked across the group. No one would meet his gaze. "And no one took control of the island after that?"

They shook their heads. "There were those who tried," said the purple-haired dragon. "But anyone who came up on top was quickly defeated."

"By who?"

"That's the thing, it was always different. The Lord of the South, for example, they say it was his son who betrayed him. He rules but only over their clan. None of the yokai of the region would trust him or swear allegiance after that," said one dragon.

Another chimed in, "Mhhm. And the spider's empress was killed by the leader of the neko and they've been warring ever since."

They continued to babble on about the rise and fall of power, but it was all things he'd heard before. When he was sealed his absence of rulership had plunged the world into chaos.

The jar of sake had come back around to Kaito. He held it in his hand for a moment, spinning it around. When he'd first broken free of his seal, he'd gone to visit the swamp guardian. He had said that no one ruled, that clans of yokai kept to themselves. But he had also mentioned rumors of a powerful shape-shifter absorbing yokai. He'd assumed it was Hisato, but according to Suzume he was only recently freed. It didn't explain hundreds of years of power shifts. What if there was something even more powerful out there? Someone had to have broken Hisato free.

Kaito took a long swig of the bottle before passing it on once more to Ai. She took a dainty sip this time, but even as she did, she pulled a face and passed it to the laughing dragon to her right.

"I've heard rumors of a shape-shifter who absorbs yokai."

There was an uncomfortable silence as the dragons around the circle looked everywhere other than him.

"You've heard it as well."

"It's why we've come together," his brother said, glaring at Kaito as if challenging him to argue against such a measure, or to call them cowards for doing so.

The dragon with the purple hair spoke, "All the yokai have splintered into different clans. We have to look out for our own. It only made sense to use the old dragon seat of power as our place." She met his gaze, not so much a challenge, but begging to be understood.

Kaito waved his hand in a gesture that said he forgave them. It was good to see someone had put the place to use.

"What became of my other brothers and sister?" Kaito asked, turning his attention to his brother.

He kept his back to Kaito for a moment, before saying in a very low voice, "They've fallen, all of them. We are all that remains."

He had feared as much. Kaito was quiet for a moment, thinking of how many of his friends had been lost. How many more remained or were in hiding?

"I am sorry to hear that," Kaito said.

His brother turned only to glare at him. Perhaps he blamed him for disappearing. It was true he would never have let this happen had Kazue not sealed him. Kaito laced his fingers together and leaned forward to look at the rag-tag group of dragons before him. They were lower-level dragons, deities of streams and local bodies of water. It was a sign of the times to see them gathered here away from where they should have been worshiped and adored, as they had in the old times.

"I can understand banding together, but why leave your posts?"

"The humans no longer respect us as they once did. The shrines are disappearing. And any whose power is too great come under suspicion and are hunted."

"Are you such cowards that you cannot stand against humans?"

No one would meet his eyes.

Kaito sighed. It was the woman dragon with the long blue-green hair who spoke for the first time. "We cannot fight against them. The yokai have grown weak. Without our powerful yokai to protect us, the lesser are left at the mercy of the humans who grow stronger every day. We need a strong leader to protect us, to guide us."

She batted her long lashes in his direction, and he took a moment to assess her. She was beautiful, he could see why his brother had taken her as a lover. It had been a long time since he'd taken another dragon to his bed, but he remembered his last one well, and he could see the lust in her eyes.

Ai stood up, placing herself between the two of them. "She is right," Ai said, glaring at the woman for daring to look upon him. "It is time we gathered your kingdom back together, brought back the rule of the yokai."

"I agree. But it will not be simple. With the island divided, and my court flung to all ends of the earth, I will need yokai who are willing to serve."

The dragons leaped to their feet, the hunger in their gaze was plain as day. They wanted to serve him, they needed to serve him. As if they'd been waiting their entire lives for this very moment.

"What can we do?" the purple haired dragon asked. She was the most eager of all. Kaito could see it in her eyes.

"I appreciate your enthusiasm. It gives me hope. For tonight, let's drink and think of better days."

The dragons cheered together. Memories of his old friends were brought to mind. He shook his head. He was not going to be caught in sentimental memories, not again.

They drank long into the night, and when the night was over, Kaito, not quite drunk but close enough, stumbled down the hall toward where he remembered his bedchambers had been. It had been a long time since he drank so much and perhaps a bit too much, because the floor swayed dangerously under his feet. He leaned against the wall for a moment, catching his bearings before continuing down the hall.

He found his chamber door open, as if he had just stepped away the day before. It was as if no time had passed here, as if his five-hundred-year imprisonment was nothing but a bad dream. Either way, he was glad to be back in his bed. He laid down on the futon, burying his face in the mattress. When he rolled over however, he found he was not alone.

He raised his head to see the beautiful woman dragon smiling at him, her long, blue-green hair artfully placed to cover her naked breasts.

FOUR

K aito's eyes grazed over her exposed skin. The firm globes peaked out from beneath the curtain of her hair. She shifted slightly, revealing more of herself to him.

"Well, I wasn't expecting this," he said, still a little foggy from the sake he had drunk.

"I thought you might be lonely," she said, leaning in. She pressed her lips to his. His hands snaked around the back of her neck, tangling in her long hair as he explored her mouth with his tongue. As ruler of Akatsuki, he'd met women like her that used their sexual appeal to climb the social ladder. It was clear that was her intention with his brother, and now that he'd taken over control, she'd attached herself to him. They were fun for a night, and he was just drunk enough to not care.

Her hands roamed over his chest, pulling at the hem of his hoari, signaling him she was ready to take it further than kissing. They broke apart, and he knelt on the bed in front of her as she pulled at the edge of his clothes. When she was bent forward in front of him with only the top of her head visible in the dim light, her blue-green hair was almost black. And for a moment he thought of what it might be like to have a different woman in his bed.

Kaito's entire body tensed. *I must be drunk to be thinking about her.*

To rid himself of such thoughts, he pulled his hoari off. As soon as his skin was exposed, she kissed a trail up his stomach. Kaito closed his eyes and indulged in her ministrations, but instead of enjoying the pleasure this woman had to offer he thought of Suzume's face and the moment she had walked away. Anger welled up in him.

When the dragon reached his neck, he'd had enough of play and pushed her back so she laid sprawled on the futon. Her hair fanned out around her and her eyes were half-lidded. But he didn't see the beautiful yokai. Instead he thought of Suzume that morning he'd woken with her in his arms.

Kaito growled and dipped down to kiss her once more, but the honeyed taste of her lips had turned to ash in his mouth. Her hands snaked around the back of his neck, pulling him closer. She tugged at him and pulled him to straddle her. But anger and the conflicting images in his head made continuing less than convenient.

Kaito closed his eyes. *Now is not a good time.*

"Something the matter?" she asked.

"Nothing at all." He dipped down to kiss her, hoping if he could focus on the feeling of her lips everything else would disappear.

But those pesky thoughts would not leave him, no matter how much she stroked and teased him. All lustful thoughts were thrown from his mind. Kaito climbed off the she-dragon and turned his back to her, running his hands through his hair.

"I think I may have drunk a little too much."

She crawled up behind him, pressing her breasts against his back. "I can help with that." She wrapped her arms around him, her hands dipping lower.

He pushed her away from him and stood.

"Have I done something to displease you?" she asked.

He turned to her as she leaned on one shoulder, her body artfully draped with the blanket. When he had been the ruler of Akatsuki, he had any woman he wanted. There had been a countless string of women, both human and yokai. Sometimes multiple women in his bed at a time. But that was before Kazue. There had been no one since her. And it would have been one thing if it was thoughts of her. But Suzume? That smart-mouthed brat? She had chosen to leave him behind. She'd banished him from her side. He shouldn't care if she lived or died, and yet he couldn't get her out of his head.

Kaito shook his head. "You are-" His eyes glanced up and down her body. "You are exquisite. But I've had a long journey and I am tired. For tonight, I think it would be better if I slept."

She pulled a face and rose up off the bed. She picked up a robe off the ground, hastily covering herself. She shook her head and headed for the door, then turned to face him.

"You know I've heard the rumors about you. Everyone says you got a taste of human and never looked back."

His eyes flashed blue with his displeasure.

"Get out." He pointed toward the door, and she stormed out without a second glance.

Once she was gone, Kaito flopped back onto his cushion and laid staring at the ceiling. Why had she filled his thoughts in that moment? He told himself that it was over. If she would go so far as to banish him from her sight then he didn't need her. Let her deal with Hisato and all that came with it. All he needed was his kingdom, to get back the life he had before Kazue. And here he was turning away, perhaps the most beautiful creature he'd seen in centuries.

"What a fool I am," he said to the dark.

In the morning, Kaito strolled into the audience room with a smile on his face. Not because he was in a particularly good mood, but because he didn't want to give the impression anything was amiss. A trio of dragons was standing beside the fire which doubled as a cook-fire. Fish had been put on spits and were roasting over the flames.

When he approached, they stopped whispering. So much for hoping she'd keep her mouth shut. They'd been talking about him. He could smell it in the air. The she-dragon was nowhere to be seen, but he could see from the look in their eyes.

"Anything wrong?" he asked.

It was the purple-haired dragon. He had learned last night her name was Hana. "Is it true you were sealed by a human priestess and that's why you disappeared for so long?"

He felt his anger rise. "Who told you that?"

The three wouldn't meet his gaze, but averted their eyes to everywhere but him. Kaito glared at them, willing them to speak.

"My brother was sealed by a priest," the big yokai, Kenta, said sheepishly to Kaito.

He felt his anger cool. It wasn't so much an accusation, but a way for them to bond with him. He decided to take his advantage while he had the chance.

"Yes, it was a priestess who sealed me."

"I knew it," the smallest dragon, Arata said. "These humans have grown too powerful."

"Was it the one they called Kazue?" Hana asked, her eyes wide as a child's. His nightmares were nothing more than fanciful stories to them.

"It was," Kaito replied flatly.

"I heard she killed hundreds of yokai," Arata said, shaking his head.

"Do you think she has anything to do with the attacks?" asked Kenta.

"What attacks?" Kaito asked.

"There's rumors of a priestess who wields fire killing yokai all over the island."

"It's not her." Kaito clenched his hand into a fist. It seemed he couldn't escape reminders of Suzume.

The trio turned, blinking at him in surprise. "How could you know? You were sealed."

Kaito realized too late they were talking about things of the past. Things he'd have no way of knowing.

Before he could explain himself, his brother, Jirou, as he called himself now, said, "Because he was in love with her." The she-dragon followed close behind him.

Kaito narrowed his eyes at him.

"That's not possible. You wouldn't love a human—they're beneath you."

"But he did. That's what brought the great dragon crashing down. He fell in love with a human woman."

Now he knew where the she-dragon heard about his fall from.

"It's early to be challenging me, brother," Kaito said, turning to him, posturing.

The wounds Kaito had inflicted the day before had healed over, but Jirou's pride it seemed would take longer to heal. He didn't want to have to kill him. There were so few remaining of the first children and he needed his strength. If only he could see past his bitterness.

His brother came closer to him, glaring at him. "A weak dragon cannot lead. If you can be brought down by a human, how can we trust you?"

Kaito flexed his claws, displaying the power in him and unfurled his full power, letting his brother know who was the stronger of the two of them.

"If you want to fight me, then do so."

"We want the truth. Did you love a human?" the she-dragon asked from behind his brother.

Kaito narrowed his eyes at her, but all the dragons were watching him and waiting for an answer. If he told the truth, he'd lose the little respect he'd gotten thus far. He wasn't going to lose his palace to a bunch of low-life yokai.

He threw his head back and laughed. "Don't mock me, brother. I may have made a mistake and been trapped, but I am back now. And nothing will stop me from taking what is mine."

His brother wasn't willing to back down just yet, however. "How do we know you're not going to make the same mistake again?"

The other dragons rumbled in agreement. Everyone wanted proof. But what proof could he give them? Even if he ripped out his beating heart to show them that would never be enough.

Kaito narrowed his eyes at him.

But before he could answer, Ai answered for him. "What if he were to take a bride?" He had not even heard her approach until she was already in the middle of them.

Kaito glared in her direction, but the dragons fed on her idea.

"If we allied ourselves with another of the first, we would be strong enough to take back our land," Hana said, balling her hands into fists.

"It could bring all the clans back together," Arata said, excitement glowing in his eyes.

Kaito seized on their enthusiasm. "We shall return to the glory of our former kingdom. With all of your help we can get back what was lost."

And all eyes were trained on him, shining with excitement. Kaito turned to his brother with a smug expression.

"Why wait? Let's start by ridding ourselves of those vermin on the coast."

"Yes, they've kept us trapped in this decaying castle for far too long," Kenta said, pumping his fist into the air.

"What vermin?" Kaito didn't like the glimmer in his brother's eye.

"Humans have settled along the coast, fishing in your sacred waters. They are using priests to drive away all the yokai. We've done what we can to keep them from this place, but every few decades they attack again. We should rid ourselves of them before they attack again. With your power we will be strong enough."

Jirou had trapped him without meaning to. If Kaito tried to stop an attack then it would make him appear weak. But he wasn't going to slaughter humans for no reason.

"I think we should wait until we are stronger before we can attack," Kaito said.

His brother seized on this as he feared he would.

"Why not now, unless you love humans?" he said, danger lurking in his gaze.

He was prepared for this. "You've already said it yourselves, the humans have gotten stronger. They know how to fight us. I, the strongest in Akatsuki, was sealed for five hundred years by a human. If we rush in and fight without a plan, we will all fall. I did not rise from the dead to be struck down once more."

The group growled in assent, seemingly appeased. "First, we must rebuild our fortifications and gather more soldiers to us, then you will have your revenge. Then the yokai will rise again."

"And you will take a wife?" his brother asked, a twisting smile on his face.

Kaito glared back at him. "I will do whatever it takes to protect my kingdom."

The dragons cheered but his brother only watched him with hooded eyes. The others gathered around him, all chattering at once. They didn't see as his brother slipped out the back, murder in his gaze. But Kaito did, and he would have to keep an eye on Jirou.

Five

"You look like you could use a rest," Tsuki said, as he walked backward in front of Suzume. It had been a grueling two weeks since they'd left Kaito behind. Her feet hurt from walking. Her entire body hurt for that matter. But knowing Tsuki, this wasn't about her comfort.

"I'm not in the mood for your jokes," Suzume grumbled.

"I'm serious. We've been going non-stop, it's time we indulged a little," Tsuki said. "There was an onsen somewhere nearby here if I remember correctly."

"You haven't been here in hundreds of years, brother. How can you be certain it still remains?" Akira said, using her brother's form to scold him. Most of the time she didn't bother to take control of the body they shared to do so.

"Well, I haven't gotten out much in the past five hundred years."

"Is there really a hot spring?" Suzume asked. Despite her intention to ignore him, he'd piqued her interest.

"Would I lie to you?" Tsuki flapped his hand in her direction.

"You do, frequently. Remember those berries you told me were safe to eat?" She scowled at him. She thought she'd never stop vomiting.

Tsuki knocked her accusation away like a buzzing insect. "How was I supposed to know it wasn't safe for humans?"

"That's kind of an important point!"

"Finding shelter would be wise," Naoki said, stopping their argument before it could begin.

"Then it's settled." Tsuki clapped his hands together. "This way." He gestured for them to follow him.

"Nothing is settled!" Suzume called after his retreating back. Hikaru shrugged his shoulders in Suzume's direction before following after Tsuki, and Rin followed her husband. Suzume remained stubbornly behind, while Naoki waited for her.

"Fighting will not fill the void," Naoki said.

"I don't know what you're talking about."

She hated how well Naoki could see through her. Ever since they'd left, she'd been unconsciously trying to get back what she had lost. She never thought she would miss arguing with someone. Naoki followed after Tsuki and Suzume was forced to join the group.

They took a winding path through the forest. At first it seemed like it was a trick after all. There was nothing but a sea of dark trees. Then a paper lantern appeared, hanging from a tree branch, illuminating a pathway. More paper lanterns were hung down a meandering path from the forest toward a group of buildings nestled against a mountainside. Even from a distance, tendrils of steam could be seen rising up from the outdoor baths.

"So you weren't lying," Suzume said, impressed Tsuki had not led them on a wild goose chase.

"I told you so." Tsuki grinned as he almost ran down the pathway.

Excited by the prospect of a warm bath, Suzume chased after Tsuki down the pathway. As they got closer however, the tingling sensation she related to yokai grew stronger and as she looked around sensing a potential attack, a few things failed to add up. The lanterns were not hung on branches as she previously thought, but floated in the air.

"Wait a second," Suzume said, stopping in her tracks. "Why is there an onsen in the middle of the forest?"

Tsuki turned to face Suzume with a cheeky grin. "Oh, did I forget to mention? It is a yokai onsen."

"Are you crazy? I can't go in there. I'm a rare delicacy to yokai." She gestured toward the building in the distance.

"She's right," Rin chimed in. "A human cannot just walk into a yokai place."

"I know this place. She'll be fine," Tsuki said, waving off their concern.

"It is not wise to invite trouble," Naoki said.

"He's right." Suzume pointed with a flat palm to Naoki.

"We'll disguise her," Tsuki said with a shrug.

"How can you possibly disguise me?"

"Do you think your fox magic could disguise her?" Hikaru asked his wife.

"You agree with them?" Suzume stared at Hikaru incredulously. Of all people she thought he would see reason.

But he did not bother to respond to her complaints, nor did Rin who replied to him, "If you can weave your spiritual powers with my illusionary magic, I think we can make a passable disguise. As long as no one looks too hard at her."

Hikaru nodded his head in agreement. "Yes, like that time when we fought the Nyobo."

"That's what I was thinking." Rin smiled.

"No way. This is stupid. I'd rather camp in the wilderness." Suzume turned to walk away. She had not gone even a few steps when another distant roar rolled through the nearby mountains. Suzume turned on her heels and returned to the others. "On second thought, maybe this won't be so bad."

Tsuki bit his lip to stifle his laughter. Rin and Hikaru turned away from her, presumably to hide their own amusement. The two of them deliberated for a few moments, before Rin presented what appeared to be an ordinary leaf. Then without ceremony she slapped it onto Suzume's forehead.

Suzume rubbed her head. "Did you have to hit so hard?"

Rin ignored her complaint and said, "The physical transformation will fool most yokai."

"A leaf on my head? That's going to trick them?"

"Look." Rin nodded toward a nearby stream. Suzume walked over. The reflection was poor but what stared back at her was not human.

She screamed and stumbled backward. She felt her face; her eyes, nose, and mouth were all in the proper place. Cautiously, she peered into the water once more. Her head was covered in bright red fur, and a pair of fox ears were on top of her head. She also was sporting a long muzzle, that when she tried to touch it, only felt like her own flat human nose. She touched her face in the reflection and her hands had turned into paws tipped with pointed yellow claws.

"This is amazing." Suzume had a new admiration for the Kitsune.

"The illusion will only remain if there's no interference from your spiritual power. So you have to keep your temper in check," Rin chided.

"Won't they sense my spiritual energy?" Suzume asked.

"My spell will misdirect anyone who tries to look too closely at you. It should give you an extra blanket of protection. But draw attention onto yourself and they will know," Hikaru said.

"Keep my mouth shut, I got it." Suzume glanced at her reflection once more, turning her head from side to side as she admired her fox appearance. This might actually work. And perhaps she'd get a bath out of the deal.

"Are you certain you can handle that?" Tsuki asked while trying to hold back his laughter.

Suzume glared back at him in response.

As they approached the inn, Suzume heard the raucous laughter from within. The laughter sounded almost human, and as much as she tried to convince herself that this plan would work, her heart continued to race. She took a deep breath and followed Tsuki inside as he pulled back the fabric hangings onto the dark interior.

The main room was filled with tables that were crowded around with an odd assortment of yokai. A pair of tanuki, raccoon-like creatures wearing human clothing, were very focused on a board game in front of them. Five river otters were drinking sake together and laughing at some joke. Apart from the cute and furry occupants, there was a small man with red fur and a loin cloth as his only clothing. He watched their group cross the room with a single eye in the middle of his head. Not far from him, a woman used her long black hair to feed a mouth at the back of her head.

Everyone stopped what they were doing as their group walked past. The laughter and talking died away, leaving behind only the sound of their footsteps. At the back of the room was a counter and a single man stood behind it. He was facing away from them. From the back he seemed to be almost human, wearing plain clothes and his dark hair was tied up in a top knot.

Tsuki leaned on the counter. "Me and my companions are in need of a room."

The man turned around and Suzume audibly gasped. The man had no face. Where his face should have been was smooth, featureless skin.

"We don't have any vacancy," the innkeeper said in a growling voice.

On the wall behind him were several markers with numbers. Suzume presumed they were for the rooms. The main chamber was only a quarter full. They could not be without any vacancy.

Tsuki laughed. "Perhaps you remember me. I am—"

"I know who you are."

A ball of fear clenched at Suzume's chest. All the yokai in the room had stood up. They reached into sleeves for hidden weapons, or extended pointed claws and revealed sharp teeth.

Suzume reached for her own staff, strapped to her back. *I knew this was a bad idea.*

Tsuki held up his hands in a placating gesture as he backed up. "I see my reputation precedes me. I'm flattered really."

"What did you do?" Suzume hissed at Tsuki. A nearby tanuki squinted in her direction. Suzume scooted to the side, hiding behind Naoki.

The innkeeper stepped out from around the counter, and reached for a weapon behind his back. "You have a debt, Tsuki. And now you're going to pay."

The crowd of yokai closed in around them. Suzume's hands trembled as she squeezed the staff into the palm of her hand. The flames were starting to spark along her body and the fear was setting in. She saw the leering faces of the yokai, with their pointed, yellow teeth and their dark, hungry eyes watching her.

The faceless innkeeper came out from behind the counter and slammed a token onto the table. "You skipped out without paying your bill."

Tsuki laughed and shook his head. "Hyoshi, that was five hundred years ago. I can see you're just as much a miser as you were back then."

All around them the room burst into laughter and Suzume was left searching the room, wondering how she had missed the joke.

The innkeeper slapped Tsuki hard on the back. "Where have you been?" he asked.

"I've been a bit tied up you could say." Tsuki smiled as the crowd of yokai pushed their way forward to crowd around him and ask him questions.

Suzume could only watch, dumbfounded, as the yokai offered up strange coins, laying them on the counter to pay not only for Tsuki's debt, but to give them the best room in the inn. They were led in a whirlwind of activity and happy chatter between the innkeeper and Tsuki to an enormous room with a private garden.

It wasn't until the innkeeper shut the door and the group was alone once again that Suzume said, "What was that?"

Tsuki laughed. "I told you I knew this place."

"You don't just know this place, all those yokai paid for this room. Why?"

"My brother has a bit of a reputation," Akira said cryptically.

Suzume narrowed her eyes, hoping the force of her glare would be enough to draw a confession out of them but neither of them elaborated on what that meant exactly.

"Why don't you all enjoy the baths?" Tsuki gestured broadly to the room. "Tonight is on me."

Not one to turn down a hot bath, Suzume decided to let it slide. The group headed out the door toward the bath but Tsuki stayed behind.

"Aren't you going to join us?" Suzume asked.

"My brother cannot be trusted in the woman's bath, and I would rather not have to endure the men's," Akira said as she took control of the body she shared with her brother.

"Unless you want me to join you this way," Tsuki said, using his sister's face to speak.

"No thanks." Suzume rolled her eyes.

Suzume, Rin, Hikaru, and Naoki headed toward the baths. The entrance was divided by gender and the group was forced to split apart. It was hard to imagine the stoic Naoki soaking in a bath, but they entered anyway.

After disrobing, and scrubbing off the worst of the travel dirt from her skin, Suzume entered the bathing area to find the pool was large and blissfully empty.

Suzume stepped into the water. She could feel the warmth creeping through her entire body the moment her toes touched the water. She waded into the water until it was breast height and then sunk into the water up until her neck.

"I could get used to this." Suzume sighed.

Rin followed after Suzume and swam around a bit. "I can't remember the last time I just relaxed." She sighed before leaning against a nearby wall.

Suzume swam a few laps before joining her. She tilted her head back and let the warm water course through her. She had almost fallen asleep when she heard voices of yokai coming to join them in the bath.

Suzume's eyes shot open at the sound of girlish laughter. A trio of neko, cat yokai, sauntered into the bath area. They were talking amongst themselves as they joined Rin and Suzume in the water, so they hardly gave them a glance. They were too absorbed in their conversation.

"I heard he's searching for a bride," said one of the neko.

"Didn't he take human lovers? I could never be with a yokai who's been with a human." She made a gagging sound.

"But can't you just imagine being the bride of the most powerful yokai in Akatsuki?"

"He *was* the most powerful yokai in Akatsuki. Where has he been for the past five hundred years?"

Suzume's ears pricked up. They couldn't be talking about Kaito could they? And what was this about a bride?

"I heard he's gathering together powerful yokai, making an army. Whatever the reason he left, he's back now and I plan on getting in his good graces."

"You have no shame." The other yokai laughed.

Rin placed a hand on Suzume's shoulder. She had not even realized she was staring at the yokai. She stood up abruptly. She needed to get away.

"Suzume." Rin said her name but she only shook her off and climbed out of the water. She wasn't in the mood for a bath anymore.

Six

"It was me and the oni, face to face. It was perhaps ten times my size..." Tsuki threw out his arms as the crowd around him gasped in horror.

The same neko that Suzume had overheard talking about the dragon in the bath had her arms draped around Tsuki's neck. She was starting to get an idea of what sort of reputation Tsuki had at this onsen.

"And the dragon did nothing to help you?" One of the neko asked Tsuki.

Tsuki shook his head slowly. "You've heard the rumors about him, right?"

The group stared at him, eyes wide with anticipation. Tsuki glanced around the room for dramatic effect and his eyes came to rest on Suzume who had just entered the main hall of the inn.

She glared at him. *What rumors?*

Tsuki looked away and smiled at the neko. He grabbed her chin and tilted her head up to face him. She blushed and averted his gaze. "He's not as powerful as they say." Tsuki leaned back in his chair.

Suzume, already sick of hearing talk of the dragon, went to the far side of the room where she wouldn't have to hear about Kaito. She thought leaving him behind would mean never having to hear mention of his

"

name again, but she should have known the dragon would not be so easy to escape.

She pushed her way through the crowded room. Unlike when they first arrived, the room was now bursting at the seams with yokai of all kinds. They were moving about the room drinking and gambling.

As Suzume tried to make her way toward an empty table, a yokai bumped into her back, forcing her into another yokai seated at a nearby table.

"Watch where you're going," Suzume snarled. When she turned around she came face to face with a massive yokai with blue skin and a trio of horns on top of his head. On his hip was a large cudgel, which could easily squash her like a bug.

"Who are you talking to?" he said in a grumbling voice.

Immediately she felt the flames rise to her fingertips. The last thing she needed right now was for her powers to expose her true nature. Suzume stumbled backward and the person who she had run into at the table stood up. She could see nothing but the back of his head. He had dark hair that was tied in a top knot and he wore a fine silk hoari.

"You made me spill my drink," the man said to the yokai.

"This kitsune-" The yokai gestured at Suzume, who was still disguised as such, but before he could finish the yokai said, "Pardon me, I didn't know it was you." He bowed his head to the man and walked across the inn as far as possible from him.

Suzume glanced at the back of the man's head, wondering who this strange yokai was that had come to her rescue, but just as he was about to turn and address her, someone tapped her on the shoulder.

"Can I get you something, miss?" Suzume turned toward the speaker and screamed, surprised by the faceless innkeeper standing beside her.

Suzume covered her mouth and then after taking a second to compose herself she said, "No, thank you."

"Are you certain? Tsuki is paying for everyone's drinks tonight." The innkeeper gestured toward Tsuki, who was still drinking with the others.

And how is he going to pay for it, I wonder? Someone else's coin?

The man tilted his head, presumably waiting for her to make an order, though it was difficult to say what the man was thinking without a face to read.

"I'll take a bottle of sake," she said.

The innkeeper disappeared through the crowd. Suzume turned to look for the man who had stood up to the yokai for her, but he was gone. She shook her head, if something as fearsome as that yokai ran from him, maybe she didn't want to know who he was. She certainly didn't want to be in anyone's debt.

She found an empty seat in the corner of the room and sat with her back against the wall and looked around. Rin and Hikaru were likely back in the room. And knowing Naoki he was probably hiding in the shadows nearby. It felt safer to be in a crowd like this. To these yokai she was nothing but another kitsune, a nobody, and perhaps for the first time in her life she preferred it that way. The innkeeper returned with a bottle of sake and a glass for her to drink out of. Suzume poured herself a drink. Never before had she been much of a drinker, but she didn't want to draw any suspicion for not at least having a drink in front of her.

Something about that man's voice and his clothes seemed almost familiar. *What, are you hoping Kaito disobeyed your command and followed you anyway and now he's watching you from the shadows?* She scoffed at her own thoughts. *He's forgotten all about me. The dragon is busy rebuilding his kingdom and searching for a bride.* She gulped down the sake in front of her. It sent a burning sensation that spread from her throat radiating outward and through her limbs. It was different than her fire; it was much, much better.

I don't remember sake being this good, she thought as she stared at her empty glass. She'd indulged in on different occasions but this sake was different. The effects were almost immediate and very pleasant. She poured herself another drink and downed that as well. And then another. Across the room, Tsuki must have told a joke because everyone was laughing uproariously. It didn't stop her from thinking about Kaito as she had hoped it would. Suzume glared into her cup. *Maybe I shouldn't have banned him from searching for me.* She shook her head. This was a dangerous road to wander down. She took another drink and slammed the sake bottle down.

A neko at the next table looked up at her as she did so. He looked her up and down before standing up and coming to join her. The edges of the yokai were rather hazy. When she moved too fast her head spun. *I can't be drunk. I only had a couple of glasses.* The creature was mostly animal in appearance with the head of a cat. One eye had a thin bald patch over it, from an old cut.

"Mind if I join you?" he asked as he took the jug and poured himself a drink.

"I'd rather you didn't." She lunged for the bottle but came up short.

"Come now," he said as he held the bottle just outside her reach. "A pretty kitsune like you shouldn't be drinking alone."

"I'm not a kitsune," she slurred, forgetting for a moment the disguise that Hikaru and Rin had put on her. "I like being alone," she amended.

A devious smile curled the neko's lips. "You don't have to pretend here. This is a safe place."

"I still don't want company." She snatched the bottle off the table, bringing it close to her before pouring herself another glass. She threw back her drink, letting the fiery liquid ignite her insides.

It burned less this time, but a pleasant numbness spread through her body. Her cheeks flushed with heat, and she pressed her cold hands against them.

"I'm the kind of company you want to keep." The neko leaned in close to Suzume, his hot breath stank of rotting meat. "It's dangerous out there."

Suzume scoffed. "How so?" She leaned forward in what was meant to be a mocking way, but from the way he smiled she feared he misconstrued her actions. She shot backward, putting space between them.

The neko glanced around the room, as if he feared someone would be listening in. "The emperor has been sending out yokai hunters. They're everywhere. You can never be too certain who to trust."

She narrowed her eyes at him. She was finding it difficult to focus on him. "Thanks for the advice." She stood up to leave.

"Where are you going?" He grabbed her by the shoulder.

She shrugged away his advance, and flames burst between them. "I said leave me alone!" she shouted. The room went silent as everyone stared at her.

"Is that a human?" one of the yokai asked.

"Not a human, a priestess!"

There was a clatter of screeching chairs and overturned tables as many yokai stood up at once. Tsuki was trapped behind a wall of bodies and could not reach her. Suzume's head swiveled from side to side, the room was spinning and she couldn't keep her feet.

The yokai closed in, hands and claws grasping for her. It only agitated her flames more, which burst between her and the crowd, forcing them backward.

"Let me help you." The neko grabbed onto one of her arms, pulling her backward as a few brave yokai chased after.

Suzume struggled against her captor, but either his grip was too tight or her reflexes were too slow. Her fire did nothing to deter him it seemed.

"Let me go!" she shouted as they dragged her out of the main room, down a dark hallway, and out into the night. The cold air outside hit her like a slap to the face. The thundering footsteps of yokai followed them out.

"You want me to leave you to that crowd then?" he asked.

He flung her over his shoulder and darted off into a sprint, into the woods. After a few moments the sounds of her pursuers faded away.

"They've stopped chasing me now. Let me go!" She beat on his back.

"Did you think I was rescuing you?" He laughed. "There's a lot of yokai who will pay a good price for you."

Panic rippled through her. She hadn't been thinking straight. Of course he wasn't trying to rescue her. *I cannot believe I'm being kidnapped again.*

Just then a figure stepped out from the forest in front of them. He was human in shape, backlit by the moonlight.

"Good evening," he said, his voice refined and somehow familiar.

"I don't want any trouble," the neko said.

"I'm glad to hear it. Let her go and you leave with your life."

"That's not going to happen." He dropped Suzume onto the ground where she fell like a sack of vegetables.

She didn't wait for them to fight. As soon as he let her go she leaped up and ran in the opposite direction. Her head was spinning from too much drinking, and she didn't get a few feet before tripping and tumbling onto the ground. Footsteps approached behind her and she felt the spiritual pressure of a powerful yokai.

Suzume turned, ready to defend herself with fire if necessary, despite her better judgment. But when she saw a handsome face crouched beside her, holding out a hand to help her, all the fight drained out of her. Well, most of it.

"Are you alright?" he asked.

She refused his help, instead climbing to her feet on her own with some difficulty. Getting up too fast made her head spin again, and she reached out for something that would keep her from falling, which turned out to be her rescuer.

The man caught her and for a single moment she leaned into him before remembering this was a stranger. She lurched backward and almost fell once more and then righted herself. She squinted at him. Maybe it was because she'd had too much to drink, but he seemed familiar.

"Do I know you?" she asked.

The man helped her stand upright. "I do not believe I've had the plea-sure," he said with a smile that could only be called charming.

A handsome and heroic stranger. There had to be something wrong with him. "Who are you? Why did you save me?"

"Let's just say, I don't like seeing women in danger."

"I'm not some sort of woman in need of saving."

"Clearly."

He turned as if to walk away from her, leaving her in the middle of the forest. She should have let him go, she was lucky he didn't ask for anything. Perhaps it was the drink but she felt compelled to follow him. She chased after him.

"I'm not buying it. No one does anything without getting something for themselves."

A smile pulled at the corner of his lips, it was cheeky and dangerous. "Yokai liquor is much too strong for a human."

"Who are you?"

"My name is Ryuu."

"That's not what I meant and you know it. You're not like the others." She nodded in the direction she assumed the inn was.

"No?"

She scowled at him—it was just like a yokai to be intentionally vague. "Are you working for the dragon, did he send you to spy on me?"

Ryuu laughed softly. "Can't say I've ever met him."

She narrowed her eyes at him. She wasn't sure what to think of him.

"Let me give you some advice," Ryuu said, "Don't mention the dragon. He has enemies everywhere. Your connection with him will only put you in danger."

Suzume frowned and was preparing a retort when Tsuki and Naoki came running up from behind Ryuu. They had their weapons drawn, but as they approached Ryuu held up his hands in the sign of surrender.

Tsuki and Naoki placed themselves in front of her, blocking her from Ryuu.

"Are you hurt?" Naoki asked.

"You're a little late for the rescue." Suzume rolled her eyes. "Not that I needed rescuing."

"She had everything well in hand when I arrived," Ryuu said, feeding into her lie.

She frowned in his direction.

"We got caught in that mess you made back at the inn," Tsuki said. "We didn't even realize you'd left right away."

"I can see you're in good hands. Goodnight, Suzume," Ryuu said, interrupting their conversation. He bowed his head toward her before strolling away. She wanted to chase after him. She wasn't done asking him questions. But Naoki placed his hand on her shoulder and gave a small shake of her head. *How did he know my name?*

SEVEN

Too long had he been away from his domain. It had been even longer since he'd allowed himself to fly in his true form. Thick, white clouds surrounded him, cloaking him from any casual observer's view. Though any mundane human who might have seen him would have convinced themselves it was nothing but the trick of the eye. The sea beneath him sparkled like thousands of diamonds. At times he would dip down, letting his legs skim the surface of the waves. Sea spray fell onto his scales and fed his spiritual power. He had almost forgotten what it felt like to be this powerful, to be where he belonged. As he indulged in this euphoric sensation of freedom, of rightness, the toxic anger that had been gnawing at his insides started to lessen.

All of Akatsuki had been his dominion before, but this coastline was his home. He took his time re-familiarizing himself with his surroundings. It felt as if both no time had passed and too much time had passed all in one. The landscape had changed dramatically in his time away. The mouth of the river which poured into the bay had gotten wider. Cliff faces had eroded, collapsing into the sea and leaving large gouges in the land. In some places he did not recognize anything at all, but some permanent features such as the mountains were unchanging.

More than the waxing and waning of nature, was the mark humans had left upon the landscape. There were more human dwellings than ever before. Since he'd been freed he'd seen glimpses of their swelling numbers but it was much more evident here at the coast. He'd been faintly aware of their quick reproductive cycles, but their numbers had doubled and tripled, while the yokai numbers continued to dwindle. He could not help but wonder how the world might have been had he not been sealed. Seeing human towns so close to his own palace rankled him a bit. It showed just how little respect they had for his kind—just as the dragons had said.

Though they had numbers, their strength could not rival that of a true yokai. Of that he was certain. Humans were just as weak and stubborn as before, and they didn't know what was best for them. The anger he'd been trying to release bubbled up in him once more.

In need of a distraction, Kaito stretched out his spiritual energy and let it roll over the land, searching for more like him. The time was coming when he would need to summon them all to his palace. Already repairs were underway to return his home to its former glory, but he wanted to get a sense of who was close at hand.

He traveled along the coastline for miles and miles, but he found not a single trace of a powerful yokai. The only thing apart from humans he sensed was the occasional low-level yokai—mindless creatures who were little more than animals. He felt almost nothing and was growing discouraged until he got to the mouth of the river. It was the largest river and not far from his palace.

He felt energy there, an intense diversity of human and yokai. It was so powerful he could not untangle one from the other. The place vibrated with energy and he was drawn in by it, as if under its spell. He hovered overhead in the clouds. He was not so reckless that he would fly straight in without thinking. But there was something about this place. It felt familiar, though he had known no towns when he had ruled here. All he had remembered being here was a single shrine—oddly enough one that had been dedicated to him. This place could not be the same.

Kaito flew down to get a closer look. Upon closer inspection it was a town of relatively large size. The town was nestled between the ocean and the mouth of the river. Along the seaside, ships of varying sizes were lined up. On the riverside were docks and more ships, presum-ably ones that took goods inland.

Hundreds of humans bustled up and down the streets trading and visiting different establishments. Apart from the waterways, there were roads leading into the town as well. He was intoxicated by the sights, sounds, and smells of the place and decided to go in.

Kaito landed and transformed into his human visage. He was reminded of the old days, when he had been curious about humans and had disguised himself as one of them. He walked into the town, eyes casually grazing on everything. The place was filled with sounds —horses neighing, men haggling, and in the distance he heard street musicians playing.

The human town was alive. Pulsing with spiritual energy, it seemed to be woven into the very fabric of this place. *How odd*, he thought. It was hard to tell where the shrine that once stood here had been, since the landscape had changed so much. *I wonder if I should be offended that they took it down?* But he couldn't bring himself to be offended. This place had a certain charm that was hard to deny.

As he strolled down the street he spotted a woman standing at the door to a building shouting at the passing crowd.

"Good food and drink here." She flirted and winked at men passing by who were drawn in by her good looks and then, hooked by the scent of fried food coming from within, took seats at the myriad of tables. He stopped to watch her, amused by her charms. There was an energy about her, her voice was melodic, like a song and the spell it wove brought people in by droves it seemed. The restaurant was bursting at the seams.

"Sir!" She waved at him when she caught him staring, and Kaito found himself being drawn in by her spell as well and walked over.

"A nobleman like you shouldn't be out in this heat." She gestured toward the sky. In fact, it was rather a pleasant day. But he wasn't about to tell her otherwise.

Kaito's lips curled into a smile. "Perhaps I could have a drink." He gave her a flirtatious smile. She flushed prettily before ducking beneath the hanging cloth over the entrance to show him to a table.

The space was an open area beneath a roof hung with lanterns and raised up above street level. Almost all the tables were filled. Humans from all walks of life drank and ate, their voices overlapping and becoming a low-level buzz. Kaito was shown to a table along the edge of the covered space, giving him a view of the street beyond where he could watch the people ambling by. The pretty young woman set a glass in front of him, setting a bottle of sake on the table without asking.

She poured him a drink. "I'll bring you some food." He didn't even have to order. She seemed to know her job well. He had no real interest in human food, but rather to learn more about this town. He sipped the sake as he listened to the chatter around him.

"The army is on the move again," one middle-aged man said. He was balding on top but he was trying very hard to disguise it by combing his hair over.

Another man with a round belly and fine clothes sat at his table. "I hear there's trouble in the capital. They say the general turned on the emperor."

"I heard the mother of the emperor's fifth son wants to put him on the throne," said a third thin man with a narrow little beard on his chin.

"Those Kaedemori are all power hungry. We'd be better off without them," said the balding man.

Kaito shook his head. The humans were no threat to him when they continued to squabble amongst themselves, just as they had five hundred years ago. They were so worried about grasping for power in their short pointless lives that they could not conceive trying to attack the yokai. Kaito took another sip of his sake. It was weak and watered down. Perhaps not surprising given the nature of this establishment.

The humans were not the threat to the yokai. The real threat was Hisato, out there somewhere. He needed to build up his army to stop him. But how could he make the dragons understand that without making himself seem sympathetic to humans?

The woman returned with food and drink, and set them down with a smile. It occurred to him he didn't even know the name of this town. Or how it had gotten here. The girl moved so fast she was turning to leave before he could even form a question. He grabbed her by the wrist to stop her.

"What is this place?" he asked.

"This isn't that sort of place." She yanked her arm away from him and for a moment he felt a spark of spiritual power in her. The sensation reminded him faintly of when Suzume's powers reacted to him. But this was different. It was a much weaker feeling. It explained her ability to lure in customers.

He shook his head. "Not this establishment, this place." He made a wide wave toward the street.

She scrunched her nose up, thinking he was a crazy person. "Eat your food."

She marched away and Kaito let her go. He didn't need to be shamed by some human woman. He glanced down at the plate of food. What had smelled delicious outside looked limp and unappetizing on his plate. He had no intention of eating, but instead listened more to their talking. Eavesdropping was the best way to gather information. Perhaps one of these people would say how this town had come to be erected on a shrine ground.

A man came and sat down across from him. He wore a straw hat pulled down low, so Kaito couldn't see his face. But he sensed his energy as soon as he came close.

"This town is Osaka," he said, reaching across the table to take Kaito's sake bottle and pour himself a drink.

Kaito scowled at the man. His spiritual energy was strong, but he could not get a clear read upon him. Kaito wasn't certain if he was human or yokai.

"This used to be a shrine to the great dragon," Kaito said as he tried to discreetly see beneath the man's hat.

The man laughed. "It has not been a shrine in centuries. Not since the Great Dragon disappeared. Now this is the main port between the capital and the south."

He peered sidelong at the man. "Who are you?"

The man turned away to take a drink of his glass. He set down the glass with a quiet thump. "Just a lonely merchant looking for some company."

Kaito scowled. He was tempted to reach across the table and tear off the hat he was wearing. But decided against it.

"Do they still worship the dragon?" Kaito asked casually.

The man chuckled. It was a deep, hearty laugh. "Oh yes. They attribute all of their wealth to the great dragon."

Kaito smiled to think of it. The shrine had been a favorite of his. When the local fisherman prayed here for calm seas he'd always listened to their prayers and they had often left him offerings. It was good to see it was still the same.

"It is too bad the dragon is gone," the man said as he lifted his head so Kaito could see his mouth curl into a mischievous smile. And the dragon caught a glimpse of the man's storm gray eyes. Deep lines were carved into his face. He was not yokai, that was certain, but he wasn't a normal human either. There was something almost familiar about him.

"Perhaps his blessing still remains on this place, despite his absence," Kaito said as he attempted to probe the man's spiritual energy for answers. But it was a locked box he could not break open.

"And I hope it remains that way." The man set coins down on the table. "Thanks for the drink."

The man stood and Kaito did as well. He had more questions for him. As he tried to pursue him however, a strong wind blew through the restaurant and the woman carrying a tray of food had it knocked from her hand by the gust. The platters and jug of sake fell to the ground with a crash. Kaito turned to see what had happened.

When he turned back to the man he was gone. Kaito leaped out onto the street to search for him. The wind blew through the streets, almost removing hats from heads and sending door coverings flapping in the wind. There was no sign of the strange man and people walking down the street gave Kaito a wide berth, watching him as he stared. That energy, not human but not yokai either. It was very similar to... he shook his head. He didn't want to go down that path.

Kaito tried searching for the man but his search was in vain. After spending the better part of the afternoon looking, he headed back toward the palace. As he was reaching the edge of town, he felt a yokai presence following him. At first he pretended not to notice anything, and continued at a leisurely pace. There was a nearby gap between buildings, and he walked down it, listening as footsteps followed him. Then without warning he turned on his follower. He launched into him, pinning him against the wall of a nearby building. Jirou gave him a devious smile.

"How did I know I'd find you here?" Jirou said, revealing his pointed canines.

Kaito bared his teeth back at him. "You were following me?"

"I came looking for you, brother. You were gone a very long time."

"Don't you have better things to do?"

"Not since someone took my place." He laughed as if it was all a joke, but he could see the resentment in his eyes. They'd always been rivals, but time had only made it worse. And his recent defeat could make him dangerous. Kaito would have to watch him.

Kaito let go and stepped back. "If you wanted to come drink with me you should have told me," Kaito said, laughing off the tension.

Jirou dusted off imaginary dust from his clothes. "In a human town?"

"Why not? They're harmless enough."

His brother glanced around the village, his nose crinkling. "I don't know how you can stand the stench."

He was trying to bait him, but Kaito wouldn't rise to it. "Better than how you smell."

His lips curled into a smile. "Have you always loved humans or was it just once you sheathed your sword in one?"

Kaito bit down on the rage that was threatening to bubble up inside him.

"Why did you really follow me?"

He strolled over to a nearby cart and stole a piece of fruit from it. "I came to warn you. It would be better if you distanced yourself from the humans."

Kaito balled his hand into a fist. "Is that threat?"

"Remember your kind, brother. The others may not know all the details but I do. I know you loved that woman, and you'd give your life to protect her."

"She's dead," Kaito growled.

"I wasn't talking about Kazue. I was talking about Suzume."

Eight

The shrine was a palace unto itself. A long walkway of multiple bright red torii arches separated the outside world from the holy place of the divine beyond. Hikaru stared at the long pathway. It twisted slightly and the red arcs blurred together to make a long red tunnel. For the past twenty years this place had been home for him. This place had also been his prison and he had not even known it. Trapped by his own forgotten past, he'd been cut off from the woman he loved for more than two decades.

As if reading his thoughts, Rin squeezed his hand. He turned to his wife. They'd spent centuries together, been through it all. But leaving her behind again after such a short reunion was the hardest thing he'd ever do.

"I lost you for twenty years, I will live for a few nights we are apart," she said, seemingly reading his thoughts.

He tugged on her arm, bringing her close to him. He rested his chin on the top of her head, inhaling the scent of her, burning it into his memories. *How could I have forgotten her for even a moment? Every breath I took while we were apart should have been dedicated to finding her again.*

"But how will I survive without you?" He ran his hand over her head, tangling his hands in her hair. Rin tilted her head back, a mischievous smile on her face.

"If you're not careful I might not let you go."

"Is that a threat?" He leaned in close, capturing her lips in a kiss. How he had missed this feeling. There had been an ache in him for so long that he could not fill. And it was this, feeling her hands around his shoulders, his lips against hers.

They pulled apart a little breathless and a little disheveled.

"I better let you go before things get out of hand." She smoothed down his hair and straightened his hoari for him.

"Come with me," he said, prolonging the inevitable.

"You know I would join you but the wards are too strong. Yokai cannot enter the temple grounds."

"Then use your fox-fire and burn the arches to ashes. We'll storm in there and demand answers." He grinned.

Rin pulled on his ear gently. "Don't do anything reckless. You're not Suzume."

"I suppose I'm not." He cupped her cheek, and Rin leaned into it. Neither of them wanted to go, but he was wasting time. The sooner he finished this, the sooner they could start their lives over again.

"Please don't do anything foolish. Whatever you might learn, it's not worth your life."

"You know me. I'm always cautious. What about you, have you settled in?"

Rin smiled. "Yes, we're staying at a human inn for now."

"It won't take long. It will be a few days at most, and then we will be together again." Hikaru kissed her lips and shared one last lingering embrace before she pushed him away gently.

"Go before I change my mind." She slapped him gently on the arm.

Hikaru walked backward a few steps, and Rin watched him with a half-smile tugging at the corner of her lips. Eventually he was forced to turn around and focus on the path ahead.

Questions had been burning in the back of his mind ever since he had regained his memories. Well, most of his memories. How did I become like this? It was why they had traveled to the shrine. Why Suzume had left Kaito behind. They had to know why Kazue's soul was inside them. Perhaps finding that out could help them better understand how they could defeat Hisato. As they were, they couldn't harm him without hurting themselves.

At the end of the tunnel of arches, Hikaru was greeted with a barren courtyard. It was late in the day and the priests of the temple would likely be in meditation. The courtyard was a sparse open space, swept free of even a single leaf. The only decoration was a giant gingko tree in the courtyard center. A string of ofuda was strung around the center of the massive trunk.

As always, Hikaru found himself drawn to the tree. He walked over it and pressed his hand against the rough bark. He could feel the pulse of the tree, the slow ancient thoughts, the energy force that ran through it. If he wished it, he could bend it to his will. For the past twenty years he had thought he could feel the tree, but he had convinced himself that it was all in his head. No human had that sort of ability. That was what the head priest had told him, but he wasn't human. Not really. And his attachment to this tree was due to his imbalance of earth in his soul.

He rested his head against the tree, letting its energy flow into him, rejuvenating him, bringing him back to life and giving him the motivation he needed to see this task through. *Thank you, my friend,* Hikaru said, and a tingling sensation brushed down his spine as if an invisible hand had caressed down his back. He had no doubt it was the tree's way of acknowledging him.

"You've returned at last," said a raspy voice behind him.

At first Hikaru thought it was the voice of the tree, but when he turned he saw it was the ancient head priest who smiled at him.

Without thinking, Hikaru fell into a deep bow. Twenty years living in the shrine had ingrained in him a need for ceremony. In some ways being here brought him closer to the man he was when he was just Makato and not Hikaru—the man he had been before Kazue's soul was put into him. It felt almost as if there were two versions of him. Two sides with independent memories warring for dominance within him.

The head priest gave a dusty chuckle. "Have you come back to pay penitence?"

"I came for answers, master."

He laughed again. "I'm sure you have." He gestured for Hikaru to follow him, and with his hands folded in the small of his back, he walked slowly toward the nearby shrine building.

Hikaru followed just behind him, head bowed, as was fitting someone of his rank. They passed by the main shrine building, an ornate structure. The eves and support beams were painted a brilliant red, and a complicated series of carvings decorated it. Just in front of it was an offering box, and deeper within the recesses of the building was the shrine proper, where the kami dwelled. Hikaru found his gaze lingering on that space. If Kazue had sealed the kami, then that space was nothing but an empty sham.

"Strange rumors have been going around since you left," the Head Priest said.

"Many strange things have happened since I left," Hikaru replied, turning his attention back to the priest.

The old man nodded his head in reply, but said nothing more. He led Hikaru past the shrine building to the dormitories of the higher-ranking priests and then to the Head Priest's office. The Head Priest's personal assistant was waiting for them and he opened the door while kneeling on the ground. Hikaru waited outside until the Head Priest had made himself comfortable. The assistant closed the door after them.

The Head Priest sat on a thick pillow covered in red fabric. When Hikaru had first arrived at the shrine, the head priest had been the second-in-command to the then Head Priest. He'd been quick to smile, and loved to spar. He'd always been more militant than the wise and deep-thinking Head Priest back then. Time had ravaged his body, and the once spry man had difficulty moving. Pain in his joints limited his ability to do much of anything at all other than to meditate and contemplate the world's mysteries. Perhaps that was the cycle of man.

Hikaru knelt down in front of the desk. The priest leaned forward and steepled his fingers as he regarded him.

"You left your post," he said, not as an accusation, but more of a question. The Head Priest trusted him. They trusted each other.

"It was the emperor's orders."

"Ah."

The question he needed to ask was lodged in the back of his throat. Not because he was afraid to ask it but because his desire to adhere to tradition forced him to remain silent.

"You had a question?" the Head Priest prompted after a few painful minutes of silence.

"How did I come to this shrine?"

The Head Priest's expression was wistful. "How long has it been now?"

"Twenty years."

His sharp gaze turned to Hikaru, and he appraised him. "And you have not aged at all since then." He laughed to himself.

Hikaru continued to stare without response. He was avoiding the question.

"You were the second then, so you must remember who brought me here." He left off his more pertinent question—'And why.' He doubted the head priest would know their motives.

The Head Priest sighed heavily. "They all come for different reasons. Their families cannot feed them, exceptional ability is discovered at a young age, or other tragedies..." He stared down at his desk, which was cleared of any clutter or paper.

"But I'm different."

The Head Priest nodded his head. "You are not like the others. Your ability has always far exceeded that of even myself." He smiled at Hikaru, attempting to draw a smile out of him as well.

But Hikaru could not return the gesture. The priest was avoiding the question. Hisato had returned all Hikaru's memories of the past, of Rin, who he had been. All of them calculated to manipulate Hikaru into doing his bidding. But he had not returned to him why he was this way. According to Suzume, Hisato had not been free from Kazue's spell until Suzume was born. Which would have been after Hikaru had been brought to this shrine, and that meant someone else had done this to him.

When Hikaru did not return the friendly gesture the Head Priest offered he shook his head. "I was the second at the time, and the emperor was always calling me away." He waved his liver-spotted hand in dismissal. "You still cannot remember your past?" He raised a single white brow in question.

Hikaru shook his head. "Perhaps you could consult the records? Each acolyte's history is recorded there."

"Those years are in the hall of records." He rubbed his chin, pulling at the loose skin there, something Hikaru knew he did when he was nervous. "I would have to request it brought here. And the records are incomplete since the fire. We may not even find what you are searching for."

"It means enough to me that you would try." Hikaru bowed his head to show his gratitude even though the Head Priest had not agreed to do this favor.

The Head Priest stopped tugging at his chin. "Why are you curious about this now?"

"Is it wrong to wonder who I am?"

"All men who come here give up who they were before. It is better for you that you cannot remember."

"But our pasts shape our future."

The Head Priest stared off into the distance as if he was contemplating the weight of Hikaru's words.

Without looking at Hikaru he said, "There are rumors going about, dangerous rumors, that you've left the emperor's side."

"I would never betray the emperor," Hikaru replied, perhaps a little too quickly.

The old man turned to meet his eye. "Be careful. You do not want to make enemies here."

Hikaru nodded. "Let me know when you have the records."

The Head Priest bowed his head in acknowledgment, and Hikaru saw himself out. The assistant was still in the hall when he exited and he too bowed his head as he passed by.

If only he could go to the inn where Rin and the others were staying, but with the Head Priest already on alert and rumors flying he could not risk it. All it would take would be for the Head Priest to inquire with the emperor about Hikaru's mission and then he would be exposed. Hikaru headed to his chamber. Over the past twenty years it had been his sanctuary, a place where he could escape from the horrors of his day to day.

Though his simple futon would not be the same as the embrace of his wife, it would be satisfactory enough. He was weary from weeks on the road. Even though he was not human, he still fatigued. They'd tried to move quickly to the White Palace, especially after Suzume's dangerous run-in with the yokai, they thought it best they get to a human place.

He turned the corner in the dormitories approaching his chamber, and saw that there was a gap in his door, as if someone had entered and not closed it all the way. He may well have left the door open himself the last time he was here. But his intuition told him otherwise. Hikaru crept closer toward the door, drawing a dagger that he hid on his calf.

As he got closer, he heard thumping sounds from inside and the low murmuring conversation of two men. He peeked through the crack in the door to see two palace guards turning over his futon and digging through the drawer where he kept all his letters.

Hikaru stepped back slowly. If the palace guards were searching his room, it was already too late. Before he could get two steps away however, the door was slammed open and the guards came out into the hall.

"Stop right there!" they shouted.

He ran for the opposite direction, taking a sharp turn around the corner. But what he had not anticipated was more palace guards waiting to intercept him. Hikaru skidded to halt and turned around to see two more guards had joined the first two. He was surrounded. Though he did not want to use his spiritual power against humans, he had no choice.

The song rose up in his throat, but before the first notes could even leave the tip of his tongue a competing chant bound his power, tying his tongue to the roof of his mouth.

Without his song to protect him, he was powerless. The men swarmed him, but he did not put up a fight as they bound his hands behind his back.

"Makato, you are under arrest for treason against the emperor."

NINE

Normally Suzume was the one being kidnapped, and being on the other side of the rescue plan was a surreal experience.

"They were waiting for him," Rin said. Her voice shook only for a moment, then she straightened her back. "I had a bad feeling as soon as we arrived, so I waited and hid just outside the temple grounds. Not long after Hikaru entered, I saw him being dragged out by guards. I followed as closely as I could. They took him to the palace prison."

"We have to go and save him," Suzume said, ready to jump into action.

Rin shook her head. "He wouldn't want us to put you in danger."

"I don't care what he wants." Suzume threw her arms out to make her point. "If the emperor has him it must mean we're on the right track."

"I'm going alone to save him," Rin said.

"What are you going to do against the emperor's army? Or the warrior priests? You can't face them on your own."

"He's my husband."

"Let us help."

"What are you going to do, Suzume? You can't even control your fire." Rin's words were like a slap across the face and Suzume took a step back. It was true, she couldn't control it and more than that, she was terrified to use it. But her pride wouldn't let her admit it. How many times had the others come to her rescue? It was her turn to do the same.

"You don't know what I am capable of," Suzume countered.

"I know exactly what you're capable of. You almost killed Kaito with your selfish actions and if I left you to your own devices you'd probably get the rest of us killed," Rin shouted, her chest heaving with each breath.

Suzume glared at her. She couldn't find the right words to express how she felt, but she didn't have to because Rin was the first to storm out of the room, slamming the door after her.

Suzume stood in the center of the room, her hands balled into fists.

Naoki came up behind her, but did not touch her. She knew that the fire was coursing over her body, turning her into a flame, proving to Rin that she had no control over her body. She'd come here with Hikaru in search of answers, to find out why she was this way. To figure how to better control it. But nothing had changed. Rin, Hikaru, all of them saw her as nothing but an incompetent fool.

But Suzume would show her. She knew the palace better than any of them. She knew how to get Hikaru out.

Suzume headed toward the door.

"Where are you going?" Akira asked.

Suzume didn't even bother to look at her, and instead she grabbed her staff from where it was propped against the wall. "I'm going to rescue Hikaru," she said as she strapped her staff to her back.

"You heard Rin. It's better if you stay behind."

"No one knows the palace like I do," Suzume countered and proceeded out the door.

Instead of trying to stop her like she thought they would, Akira and Tsuki joined her.

"I was getting bored waiting around in this place anyway," Tsuki said with a mischievous grin.

Suzume glanced over her shoulder at Naoki, who was following behind as well. It was good to know they had her back at least. Whether they thought she could do it was another story. They might be following her just to make sure she didn't get herself killed.

Getting through the city was the easy part. No one paid any mind to a priestess and two armed men. She was feeling confident, having mapped out the beginnings of a plan in her head. But it wasn't until she was faced with the palace guards and two armed guards that her conviction wavered.

The common folk did not enter the palace for any reason. And with her clothes, and lack of proper conveyance, the guards were not going to just let her walk in. These weren't your typical guards either, but warrior priests. She could feel their spiritual energy as she got closer. Her palms were sweaty with nerves. It was through sheer will that she didn't burst into flames.

"I don't know if I can persuade a priest," Akira said as they paused just out of earshot of the warriors.

"There's no other way in. Unless you think we can scale the walls." They were several feet high and guards patrolled along the top. Even if she could somehow scramble to the top, she would be shot before she ever reached it.

Akira nodded and they approached the guards. As soon as they got close, she saw the guards come to attention. They would sense their spiritual energy, surely.

Akira approached first and the guard held out his weapon. "Stop right there."

Suzume's heart leaped into her throat. Maybe this had been a reckless plan after all.

"Who are you? What business do you have at the White Palace?" the guard asked.

"I am Lady Kana," Akira said smoothly. "I am here to visit the princess by her request."

The guard glanced over their group. He didn't seem to believe a word of it.

"Give him my letters," Akira said, gesturing for Suzume to hand the man a blank piece of parchment she had scrounged up. As she handed the priest the fake document their hands brushed against one another and Suzume felt a spark run down her spine. The priest yanked his hand away. His brows furrowed as he examined the blank paper and then looked up at Suzume once more.

"What is this?" he asked.

"Something the matter?" Akira asked, pulling in closer. She touched the man's arm, an intimate gesture any real lady would never have done. He looked down where she had touched him. His suspicious gaze darted from Suzume to Akira.

"Is this some sort of joke?" But he didn't shake Akira's hand away. Instead he was staring into her eyes.

"The princess is in desperate need of my company. Won't you let us enter?"

His eyes didn't glaze over as she'd seen others do who'd fallen prey to Akira's power. This wasn't going to work. Suzume reached for her staff, hidden beneath the cloth on her back. The man continued to stare into Akira's eyes. The rest of them may as well have disappeared. But Naoki clutched his sword, ready to draw, just in case.

"Go ahead." The guard stood aside, allowing them in.

Suzume let go of the breath she'd been holding, while Akira bowed her head to the man and gave him a smile as they headed into the courtyard beyond.

Once they were away from the guard, Tsuki took over control of the body he shared with his sister.

"That was a close one, wasn't it?" he said.

"Too close," Akira agreed.

"At least we got inside."

"I'm just worried about how we get out," Akira said.

As soon as they entered the palace grounds, Suzume's head was swiveling back and forth, taking in all the things she thought she'd never lay eyes on again—a cherry tree which had beautiful blossoms in spring, the courtyard where festival celebrations were held, and in the distance, the palace dwellings where she had grown up. It was the place where she and her mother had resided before her exile. *Focus, now is not the time. We have to save Hikaru first.*

"The palace prison is this way." Suzume waved for them to follow, for once taking the lead.

It was not as simple as strolling through the palace to the prison. They had to be stealthy. Akira, Tsuki, and Naoki had the advantage of being invisible. Suzume had to keep everyone at a distance and pretend to be a priestess going about the business of a priestess.

They walked the long way down a series of garden paths, which were barren of any occupants. This late in the season, the trees were stripped of leaves. The air was too cold for garden readings of poetry or musical performances. It made the perfect way to sneak about the palace.

Everywhere she looked Suzume was filled with fond memories. She passed the maple tree where she'd received her first confession of love, the pond by which she'd sat and listened to music. It all felt like a dream to be here again.

As Suzume was distracted wandering the grounds, she did not hear footsteps approaching from the other direction.

"Someone is coming," Tsuki said.

She saw the figure approaching, and the only way to avoid being seen was to hide behind a nearby boulder. Suzume jumped behind it and crouched down low. The man approached and stopped just on the other side of the boulder.

"Is someone there?" he called out.

Suzume's skin turned ice cold. Beside her Naoki was already drawing his blade. She did not want to kill innocent people, but she also didn't want to get captured either.

"What is it, Akihiko?" The second voice sounded very familiar. *Please do not let an old suitor find me hiding in the garden.*

"I thought I saw someone walking in the garden. But when I got closer they disappeared."

"It must be your imagination." There was a slight pause, perhaps where the courtier was peering around trying to catch sight of her. Then the second voice said, "Counselor Takahari is looking for you."

"Oh, is he? I better go then."

Suzume listened as the first man's hurried footsteps faded away. But the second man had not moved.

"Is he gone?" Suzume mouthed to Naoki.

She couldn't stay crouched down in the bushes forever. This man couldn't linger in the garden forever either. She slowly peeked around the corner to see who he was. The man was tall, but she could not say who he was. He turned to leave and Suzume caught his profile. As she did, she tumbled backward. It was Tsuki's quick thinking that stifled her cry.

Ryuu, the man who'd saved her at the inn peered in their direction. But after a quick glance, he shrugged and walked away.

They waited a few moments in silence to be certain he was gone before getting back up again.

"What is he doing here?" Suzume pointed in the man's direction.

"You know him?" Tsuki asked.

"He's the one who saved me from the neko back at the inn."

"Are you sure?"

"I'm positive."

"We don't have time to waste," Naoki reminded them.

He was right, of course, and they resumed their trek. Prisoners were held in a special compound at the far reaches of the inner palace. Though she'd heard whispers about the place her whole life, Suzume had never been there herself. It was enclosed by a courtyard with a single gate and two guards were always on duty—or at least they should have been. When they arrived the guards were incapacitated.

Rin beat us here.

Naoki took the lead and led their group into the courtyard beyond. Several more guards were lying on the ground. A battle had taken place here surely. The doors leading into the building were open and scorched. Naoki peered inside before gesturing for Suzume and Tsuki to follow him.

Many of the cells were empty except for the very last cell on the end. Just outside it, Rin was kneeling and reaching through the bars.

When she saw Suzume running toward her, she stood up.

"I told you to stay behind."

"It doesn't matter now. I'm here so let's get him out."

Hikaru was lying on the ground inside the cell unconscious and covered in bruises. A single line of blood had dried on his forehead.

Rin fumbled with a key she had presumably stolen from one of the guards and threw open the door. Suzume glanced around. It had all been too easy and in her experience, that was never a good sign. Rin picked up Hikaru, carrying him in her arms like a baby.

Tsuki and Naoki waited at the door, eyes scanning the courtyard. Once they were outside, Suzume drew her staff. They weren't going to get out of here without raising some suspicion, not with a bloody, unconscious man.

"How'd you get in here?" Rin asked.

"Through the front gate."

Rin chuckled. "I should have known. How do we get out?"

It was the first time she'd asked her for advice. But there wasn't time for any feel-good moments. They had to get out of here.

"There's a lesser gate where deliveries are made. If we can get there we can overpower any guards."

"Sounds good to me." Rin nodded.

Suzume led the way, with Naoki not far behind her. In truth she knew of the gate's existence but it had been years since she'd been anywhere near it. She'd only ever visited it once as a girl on a dare from her older half-brothers.

Once they exited the prison, Suzume made a guess as to where it might be. But as they rounded the corner, they were confronted by a retinue of many armed guards.

"Run!" Suzume shouted. They turned to go the other way but as they did, they found themselves blocked off by another group of soldiers.

Everyone closed in around Rin who was carrying Hikaru, weapons drawn.

"We're outnumbered," Rin said, panic in her voice.

"I like those odds," Tsuki said, rushing forward, sword swinging, just as Naoki did.

Neither of them heard the faint croak of "Don't" from Hikaru.

Suzume felt the priests' spiritual power rising like a wave, crashing over her just moments before their song rang out. It called to her, begging her to join in their song or better yet to take their power for her own. Suzume clamped her mouth shut, fighting the urge to indulge in the destructive power that was threatening to overwhelm her. She placed her hands over her ears.

Rin set Hikaru on the ground, joining Tsuki and Naoki, who were struggling against the warrior priests' spiritually endowed weapons that wounded yokai and prevented them from healing.

Hikaru reached for Suzume's hand and squeezed it. His right eye was so swollen he could barely open it. "Don't give into it," he said. What part she could see of his iris was glowing green.

The temptation was drawing both of them in. *I can control this. I am in control.* She chanted inside her head to drown out the draw of their song.

As the others fought, they did not see the intricate circles on the ground, which were glowing faintly with power. The soldiers pushed them backward, forcing them into the circles. Then the song changed to the song of binding. Suzume clutched at her staff, if she unleashed her power she could stop them. But even while she was trying to suppress her destructive urges, she was drawing from Hikaru, and unless she could learn to control it, she would draw from everyone here, maybe even kill them.

She fell to her knees, doubled over, as she fought within herself on what to do.

Then as suddenly as it started, their song ended. All that remained of her friends were three stones in the center of the circle.

Ryuu stepped forward from the crowd. Suzume stared up at his face, not sure she was seeing things correctly.

"Take him back to his cell."

Two soldiers jumped to do his bidding. They grabbed Hikaru by the shoulders and dragged him away.

"Let him go!" Suzume finally found her voice and jumped up ready to attack. But before she could land a single blow, Ryuu caught her by the wrist, stopping her. She fought against him, but his grip was incredibly strong.

"What are you doing here?" she demanded.

He ignored her question and directed his men to depart, pulling her away behind him.

"Are you Hisato?" she demanded. Why hadn't she thought of it before? It would be just like him to use a handsome face to deceive her.

He yanked her harder down a pathway, not toward a prison but toward one of the palace buildings. She knew this place, but he could not be bringing her there.

"Answer me."

"It's better if you don't ask questions," he said.

Inside servants were waiting. They bowed to them as they opened a series of doors leading down a short hallway. At the end of the hallway was a room lit by golden candlelight. It was mostly bare except for the tatami floors and a reed screen that divided a dais from the rest of the room. A shadowy figure sat on the dais, his face invisible behind the screen. She did not need to see the face of the man to know who was waiting for her.

The door behind her was slammed shut. She was alone with the emperor.

TEN

In her lifetime, Suzume could count on one hand the number of times she had been summoned to stand before the emperor. She had never seen his face and he had only ever spoken to her through a screen, that same screen that separated them now. Suzume fell into the deepest bow possible, pressing her head against the tatami mat, her hands flat against the floor. As much as she'd like to give him a piece of her mind, she was at a disadvantage here. He'd captured her friends and she was powerless by herself.

Being back in this room again made her feel like a little girl. On the rare occasions she'd been summoned to the emperor's presence, it had always been with other family members—most often her mother and younger brother, or her half-siblings. Kneeling in front of the emperor without anyone else to take the focus off of her was uncomfortable. She felt the weight of his stare, even if she could see nothing but a silhouette of his form through the screen.

"It has been a long time, Suzume."

Her tongue was glued to the top of her mouth. One did not speak to the emperor, not without permission. Unless you had a death wish. And she figured that after breaking into the palace prison she probably wasn't in his good graces right now.

"Please rise," he said.

Suzume moved into a seated position but kept her gaze glued onto the floor. She had to wrestle with her desire to sneak a peek at his face. As a child it had been a game between her and her siblings to try and see the emperor's face. Seeing it without his permission was considered treason. As a child of his second wife, Suzume was not of the same ranking as his children with the empress. All of his children with his other wives were considered inferior. Trying to see his face as a child would have resulted in a scolding, but now it was much more dangerous. She was no longer considered his child. But the temptation remained. *Why did he bring me here?*

"You must be wondering why I brought you here." Suzume's head shot up without thinking. Could he read her mind? She could not see anything with the screen between them but just to be safe, she looked back down again.

Am I supposed to answer that or is it a rhetorical question?

The emperor stood up, she knew by the soft footfalls on the tatami. This had to be his tactic—intimidate. It was a favorite of her mother's. Wield your power like a weapon to harbor fear and uncertainty. Silence was the most dangerous tool in her arsenal—the person who spoke first lost. Even knowing all the tricks, Suzume could not stop herself from falling right into them. Her mind whirred with questions.

The screen clunked and rattled as it was drawn up. His footsteps got closer. *Don't be afraid. He wouldn't have brought you here without reason. He could have just as easily thrown you in prison.* Despite her attempt to calm her nerves, her entire body trembled. She'd faced the most heinous of yokai—monsters ten times her size, creatures that could tear her apart limb by limb, or creatures that could trap her in nightmares as they slowly drained the life out of her. She'd face a hundred more of all of them a hundred times over to escape this room.

"You do not need to fear me, daughter."

A cold chill ran down her spine. *This is a trick.* Never once in her life had her father directly addressed her, nor could she think of a time he had shown her fatherly affection. This had to be Hisato in disguise. But she couldn't just make that accusation, what if it was the emperor? She balled her hands into fists, clinging the fabric on her legs. Faint sparks scorched the fabric as fear overrode her control of her power.

"Look at me," he said, gently.

Even spoken kindly it was a command, and she lifted her head. It was disappointing how average he was. If she had passed him in the hall, she would have overlooked him entirely. The only thing that would set him apart was his clothes. Gold embroidery covered every inch of his hoari, which was draped over a red hakama. Even the hat atop his head had embellishments in gold and a chain of office around his neck indicated his station—emperor of Akatsuki.

"Are you really the emperor?" she asked, emboldened by just how human he appeared. Wouldn't it be just like Hisato to use an average face to lure her into a sense of security?

He chuckled. When he smiled the corners of his eyes crinkled, just like her little brothers. "Yes, it's really me."

It didn't bring her any comfort. But she doubted Hisato would have the forethought to include that sort of detail into a disguise. She'd always imagined her father as someone much more imposing. This benign man was nothing like the visions of her childhood. It was disappointing to say the least.

"You brought me here for a reason." She glanced around the room, expecting Hisato to make his appearance at any moment.

He motioned behind him to the dais, where he had been sitting when she entered. A banquet had been prepared with two seats.

"I'd like it if you'd join me for dinner."

He held out his hand for Suzume. She reached out to take it but when she saw her tanned and scarred skin beside his, she pulled back. Before today she would never have dreamed of seeing his face, so touching him with her calloused appendage seemed a crime in itself. He noticed her hesitation and took her hand in his, pulling her to her feet.

She whipped her head toward him, a chastisement on her lips, but then she spotted the guards lingering in the shadows of the room and remembered her place and where she was. She lowered her gaze to the floor.

He led the way back to the dais and Suzume followed one step behind him, falling into old habits without a thought. This had been her place before. She'd left just enough room for the emperor's first family—his three sons by the empress, the heirs to the throne.

She waited to take a seat until he had sat down first. When he sat down it was with dramatic flair, tossing back the tails of his hoari before gently resting his palms on the table in front of him.

Across from him was a single silk pillow, and Suzume slowly lowered herself onto it. As she dropped her eyes to the table, the scent of food made her stomach gurgle. She covered her stomach to hide the offending noise.

If he noticed, the emperor did not say anything. A servant came forward with silent footsteps and ladled food onto the emperor's plate. She felt his sharp gaze watching and assessing her.

A second servant came and offered Suzume food as well. Despite the enticing scent of the food, she wasn't sure she could make a morsel pass her lips.

The servant gestured to the plates, silently asking which she would like. Suzume chose a fish cooked in sauce, just to avoid offending the emperor by not eating.

The servant filled her plate with more than just the fish, also adding on rice and other side dishes. Suzume stared at her full plate. It smelled like home, and as much as she wanted to eat, she couldn't with the emperor's eyes on her.

The emperor skewered a bite and placed it into his mouth, chewing slowly. When he was finished, he said. "You do not need to wait for me. Enjoy." He gestured grandly at the massive spread between them. It could easily feed a dozen people or more.

She knew no one else was coming. This was just his way of showing his wealth and power. Her mother had used the same technique countless times. What else had her mother learned from the emperor?

Suzume pushed food around her plate to pretend to be eating as she devised a plan. There was still a chance she could free the others.

"I must apologize for the hasty meeting. When Ryuu told me you had arrived, I could not wait to speak with you."

He acts as if this was intentional and his guards didn't just capture me and my friends. But she was willing to play his game.

"It is good to be back," she replied.

They ate in silence. Or rather, the emperor ate in silence while Suzume pretended to eat. When the emperor was finished, the servants cleared away the plates and a bottle of sake was brought out. Each of them were poured a glass. Just looking at the jug made her want to retch. After drinking the yokai sake she'd had the worst headache and had not been able to keep any food down for a day.

The emperor drank his in one gulp and Suzume felt obligated to at least put on a show of drinking. She took a tiny sip and had to fight the gag reflex. She turned away and pretended to drain the cup, before discreetly setting the almost full glass down again.

"You look so much like your mother," the emperor said.

Suzume froze. *Is that a good thing or a bad thing?*

She decided given the fact that her mother had betrayed him, it couldn't be good. "I am sorry if I bring you painful memories."

He chuckled softly. "It was a compliment, child. Your mother is renowned for her beauty."

Suzume's brows shot up, but she turned away to hide her expression, playing into the role of demure princess. It was one she was very familiar with.

"You're too kind, your majesty," Suzume replied, glancing at him from the corner of her eye.

The emperor leaned forward. "There's no need to pretend with me, Suzume."

Suzume's heart raced in her chest. He was bluffing. It was shocking he even knew her name. It wasn't possible he knew anything about her. "I don't know what you mean."

"Izume taught you well. But your tricks won't work on me."

"Forgive me for saying so, your majesty. But you hardly know me." Her words were a little sharper than she intended.

"I have eyes everywhere."

There was no use pretending then. Suzume turned and faced the emperor head on. "Then let me be frank."

"Please." He gestured toward her. His expression was impossible to read.

"What do you want from me?"

"You are my child. Is it not right for a father to worry about his daughter's wellbeing?"

"You've never taken notice of me before now."

"It was a mistake I am trying to rectify."

Staring into the face of this powerful man was something akin to facing Kaito when he was angry. But instead of his spiritual pressure trying to suffocate her, it was the weight of his presence. When he was seated directly across from her, in the dim light of the chamber, she could feel the power and confidence radiating off of him. This was a man who ruled the country, who played and always won. Suzume inhaled deeply. She did not believe for a moment that the emperor had sought her out because of fatherly love. He knew about her power and she wanted him to admit it out loud.

"I don't believe you."

"Excuse me?" His tone rose. She'd overstepped her bounds.

The reckless part of her didn't care. To him, she was nothing but a tool. The sensible part of her corrected her statement. "I am sure you care for me. But you would not have met personally with just any of your children."

He folded his hands together. "You are more like your mother than I thought."

She stared back at him, her expression blank, but on the inside she was screaming. *That was close.*

"I know about your power. How your mother hid it from me for so long, I do not know. All that matters is I need your help."

She knew exactly why he wanted her now. "For the war against the yokai."

The emperor smiled, he seemed impressed. "That is well in hand. I have a more particular concern in mind. It seems there is a dangerous creature terrorizing Akatsuki in my name."

Suzume's eyes grew wide as she stared at the emperor. "Hisato," she said in a hushed whisper.

"You know of him." He chose his words carefully, leaving Suzume to give her own version of events.

"I do."

"Then I too shall be direct. We need your help. There are rumors you have a great spiritual power."

Suzume sat very still. "How do you know?"

"As I said, I have eyes everywhere."

"If I agree to help you, then what's in it for me?"

The emperor smiled faintly. "You are bold. What is it that you want?"

"You have to let my friends go."

"I can't do that. Yokai are a danger to humans. You're better off without them."

"They're bound to me. They have to obey me." She raised her voice without meaning to. She was reaching a point of desperation, and she was out of bargaining chips.

He shot her a look and Suzume shrank down in her seat. She'd forgotten who she was talking to.

"The empire is at stake, this Hisato is killing innocents across the islands, and the people are growing restless. Will you choose your own selfish desires over the good of others?"

His words struck her harder than she realized as she thought about what she had done in her quest for power.

"I cannot help you," she said. Even if he hadn't captured her friends, her power was out of control. She was no good to anyone.

"Cannot or will not?"

She met his gaze without realizing it, and his dark eyes held her in place.

"Help me save our kingdom and I will free your friends."

And those were the stakes. He had captured her friends, forcing her into a stalemate. She had no other choice. For now, she'd have to play the role of dutiful princess.

"I will do as you command." She bowed her head to the emperor.

ELEVEN

A map of Akatsuki was stretched out before Kaito. Hana, who it turned out was knowledgeable of yokai territories in this age, was helping him determine clan lines and locations. Her knowledge, though helpful, was lacking in many ways. Whole sections were blank. Though the landscape was familiar to him, the territory lines were not. And to his dismay, many of his former allies had either been killed or were now in hiding. No one knew where they had gone. It was as if he had woken in a completely different world. Back in the old days they had all taken their immortality for granted.

He'd spent a long time compiling a list of those he wished to recall to the palace to resume their duties as his generals and advisers. There were a myriad of X's on the map and his list, which had dwindled down to only a handful of names. Many, many more had been crossed out. There wasn't enough time to hear all their stories, but Kazue's name had come up enough times for him to realize she had done the bulk of the damage. What had he unleashed on the world when he had fallen in love with Kazue? How had he not seen her intentions right away? Had he never introduced her to the world of yokai, perhaps none of this would have happened.

"What should we do next?" Hana asked, pulling him from his memories.

Kaito sighed. Three names remained—three of his former generals. One of which, while alive, might be impossible to retrieve. "We must summon the yokai here. They must know their master has returned."

She shook her head. "They will not leave their domains. Many are afraid to reveal themselves."

Kaito looked back at the map once more. "Then I will have to go to them."

He looked around the long audience chamber. It wasn't as if the palace was ready for guests anyway. Even now the echo of hammers filled the space as his men worked to repair the rotting palace. If he were to entertain the most powerful yokai in the realm here, they would laugh to see this hovel. It pained his pride to think others might see just how far he'd fallen.

The double doors at the end of the hall burst open, but that wasn't an uncommon occurrence unfortunately. The dragons were prone to stomping and slamming. They were not the cultured court he'd once surrounded himself with. He'd given up on trying to retrain their bad behavior.

"What is it now?" Kaito said, not looking up from the map. He was already planning his journey across Akatsuki to find his generals.

"A dozen priests have arrived at the port human village," the dragon announced, a little breathlessly.

Kaito grit his teeth to keep from snapping at them. Their foolish fear of humans was starting to wear thin. The priests would not be able to find this place, and that was to assume they'd even care they were here at all. He had more important concerns than a group of humans, in a human town. "And for that, you needed to interrupt our strategy meeting?" Kaito said, unable to keep the anger from his tone.

"Jirou and Kenta went out to fight them."

Kaito swore. The last thing he needed was his impulsive brother picking a fight with the humans. It was only going to be a bigger headache. "That fool," Kaito snarled.

Kaito headed toward the door. He would see to this himself. Perhaps if he intercepted them in time he could avoid an even bigger mess to clean up.

"You and you," he pointed at two dragons that were milling around. "Come with me."

They snapped to attention, following him out into the courtyard. After his brother had threatened him outside the human town, Kaito had had him watched. But apparently not close enough. He should have known some loyalty would remain to his brother even after he'd taken control. These young dragons did not know him. They did not know what sort of threat he posed. Well they would learn today who they really must fear. Not the humans, but the great dragon who'd once struck fear into the hearts of all yokai.

He headed straight for the ocean town where his brother had discovered him. The day was sunny and clear, and Kaito could see the village even from a distance. In the bright daylight it shimmered, an idyllic ocean town. When he spread out his senses he found not a trace of Jirou. Some of his fear abated. That was until he got closer, and as he approached the feeling of wrongness started to grow. There was an empty void in the center of the town—the same feeling he knew was a yokai cloaking their energy.

He scanned the horizon, searching for visual confirmation of his brother, and saw nothing. But the feeling remained.

"Search the area," Kaito shouted to his men. They each went in opposite directions, while Kaito continued toward the village. Even from a distance, he could see the villagers going about their day, unhurried and with single-minded purpose that dominated their brief existences.

He should have known it was a false alarm. He turned to recall his men, but then he felt it, a spark of spiritual energy. A volley of arrows were shot from the sky, and he turned abruptly to avoid their attack. His eyes scanned the horizon, searching for the attacker, but they were lost amongst the crowded streets of the town.

Just on the edge of the town he saw the tents erected and the flag which flapped in the wind. The emperor's army. He'd come across them before, and both times had ended badly for him. But if this was the same army, that meant Hisato was nearby and this was a trap.

Flying higher into the sky, he spread out his senses. The strange mixture of yokai and spiritual energy made finding the warrior priests difficult. But as he flew over the tops of the town, he sensed them like candles flickering in the dark. He couldn't fight them like this, not while they remained inside the town. There they held the advantage.

He doubled back, recalling his men to follow him. This would take further strategy. The two dragons, which had been circling the perimeter of the town, joined him.

"Our target is that camp beyond the town. Follow my lead and we attack on my signal."

They nodded their heads in understanding and followed him, making their way slowly toward the camp. The priests had taken the bait, following him toward where the bulk of the army was camped. He'd fallen into Hisato's trap before and he wasn't going to do it again. He would not get close enough for them to harm him.

To give them cover Kaito summoned the storms, raising up the winds and the sea. Fishing boats out in the harbor started to rock on the chaotic seas as the wind picked up. The sky overhead was a steel gray, and as they approached the camp, rain burst forth from heavy clouds. Overhead thunder crashed, and with the benefit of the storm they were able to approach the camp almost entirely unseen.

Kaito gave the signal and as one, the dragons rained down ice upon the tents. Soldiers scrambled about, searching for weapons. While mundane archers shot their arrows toward them, the dragons soared ineffectually past them.

Kaito and his men wreaked destruction upon the camp, and as he hoped, the priests came toward him to stop him. They lined up together, and the hum of their combined spiritual energy was like a beacon in the night. Kaito gave the signal and he and the dragons focused their attacks upon them. Their blows landed ineffectually, fizzling against a barrier they had erected around themselves.

His men, growing bold, dived closer. And that was when a secondary, unseen group of priests hiding behind tents emerged, bows drawn. There was not enough time to warn the others of the attack before the arrows were flying. One dragon managed to veer away in time, but the other wasn't so lucky.

The dragon who was struck flew away, but his movements were like a drunken man, weaving up and down. He was losing altitude fast. His companion went to join him, and he helped the falling dragon by letting him lean against him. But the combined weight of the two brought them crashing to the ground, onto to the sandy shore several feet away.

They'd gone enough distance where they were not in immediate danger from the priests, but all it would take was an intrepid few to cross the distance and finish the job. Kaito redoubled his efforts to keep the priests occupied and away from the fallen dragons, using more and more of his energy to batter them with wind and ice.

Then he felt him, like a jab to his side, drawing his attention. Hisato stood in the center of the camp. Though Kaito was too high up in the air to see him clearly, he could just imagine the smug satisfaction on his face.

There was a shout from down below, and the raining of arrows stopped. The priests maintained their barrier but did not attack. Kaito too halted his attacks, and the two sides were locked in a stalemate.

He wanted nothing more than to finish it here, but he'd learned his lesson before against these warrior priests. Besides, one of his men was hurt and in need of aid. Knowing Hisato this was merely a display of his power, a reminder of who had the greater army. He wanted to toy with Kaito. It bruised his ego, but the wellbeing of his men super-seded his pride.

Kaito turned and flew away toward where his man had fallen. His serpentine body lay sprawled on the ground, covered in sand from his fall and bristling with arrows. His labored breathing indicated the arrows were already doing their work. Kaito remembered the intense pain of the spiritual arrows. They sapped all of your energy, leaving you hollow.

The second dragon was Kenji, he remembered now, and the injured dragon was Isamu. Kenji had resumed a human visage, and his face was blanched white with fear. He stared helplessly at his friend as the spiritual energy upon the arrows crackled and popped.

"Those are blessed arrows. They'll purify him." He looked to Kaito with desperation.

Kaito transformed into his more human form and surveyed the numerous wounds protruding from the young dragon's hide.

"Keep a lookout. I'm going to draw out the arrows."

Kenji stared at Isamu's bleeding wounds. The dragon's body was trying to heal itself but was conflicting with the purifying power of the arrows. His muscles spasmed with pain.

The young dragon appeared to be in a daze. "It was a trap. They were waiting for us."

"Get your head together or he's going to die." Kaito grabbed the other man by the shoulders, just holding back from shaking him.

The other dragon blinked for a moment and then nodded his head before turning to watch the forest which lined the beach.

Kaito knelt down by the wounded dragon. His hands twitched in anticipation of the pain. Something purified by a priest or priestess burned as it purified yokai. If there was a priest or priestess he could trust, he would have had them draw out these arrows. As it was, he wasn't sure he was strong enough to do it himself. But he wasn't going to leave this dragon to die. There were already so few of them left.

There were six arrows in all. He could feel the power sparking off of them. The best defense he could use would be to encase his hand in ice. Bracing himself, he grabbed onto the shaft of the first arrow. His ice didn't stand a chance against the purifying powers of the arrow and it melted, running down his arm. White-hot fire rippled outward from his palm, demanding he let go. But he grit his teeth and pulled on the arrow. It came out with a wet pop.

Kaito tossed the offending object across the beach as Isamu roared and thrashed about, his long serpentine body kicking up sand along the beach. Kaito put his hands upon him, trying to steady him like a bucking beast.

"That was only the first one. You'll have to be strong for the rest."

The dragon's large eyes pleaded with him to end his misery, but he nodded his head that he'd understood. There was a burn on the palm of Kaito's hand, and it would only get worse by the time he was done. Without hesitation, he proceeded to pull out the rest of the arrows. Each one was harder to remove than the last, as each arrow sapped away more of Kaito's energy.

By the sixth one he struggled to maintain a human visage. His body was covered in scales, his hands tipped with claws, and his face almost entirely muzzle.

"One more," he said to the young dragon. They were both gasping for breath.

The arrows had taken much more from Isamu, who closed his eyes in exhaustion, too tired to even thrash against the pain. Kaito grabbed onto the last arrow with both hands and pulled it free, almost tumbling backward in the process.

When the last arrow was removed, Kaito knelt over on the ground. His hand throbbed, and his muscles trembled. Kenji hovered over him, a concerned expression on his face.

"Go and bring the others. We need reinforcements." He couldn't bring the injured dragon back by his own strength. He'd be lucky if he could fly back himself.

Kenji turned toward the town and the forest beyond. Thinking, probably as Kaito was, if Hisato decided now to finish him off, he'd stand no match. As much as it bothered him to be perceived as weak, there were times when pride had to be set aside for the greater good.

"Bring reinforcements, now!" The dragon practically stumbled over himself to do as he was ordered.

Kaito stared at the scattered arrows which were lying on the ground and then the burns on his hands. Reluctantly his gaze drifted toward the shadowy forest. The sun had started to set as he worked and all the while he'd felt eyes upon him.

"Come out and face me," Kaito snarled, as he struggled to his feet.

As Kaito had come to expect of Hisato, he was grinning like a madman. He seemed to delight in his pain and that of Isamu. "How honorable, choosing to harm yourself for your men. Do you think that will buy their loyalty?"

Kaito stood up to his full height and faced him. "Why are you here?"

"I was worried about you when I learned Suzume abandoned you." His words were like knives, meant to prod and provoke him. But he was much too tired to fall for his bait.

"If you're looking for a fight, I'm happy to give you one." Kaito balled his hand into a fist. He hardly felt fit to stand, let alone fight.

Hisato only laughed in response. "I cannot harm you, dragon. I only came to bring you a message."

"I don't want to hear anything from you."

"Is this how you were before Kazue? A crude beast."

"Leave while I'm still asking nicely."

Hisato's smile spread across his face. "Then perhaps you don't want to hear about where Suzume has gone." He turned away from Kaito, but he wouldn't rise to the bait. As far as he was concerned, Suzume was dead to him.

But Hisato wasn't one to drop the subject lightly. "She's joined the emperor in his quest to rid the world of yokai. I wonder what your new friends would think of that if they found out?"

Kaito lunged for him, swiping with a clawed hand. But before he could land a single blow, Hisato disappeared, only to reappear behind him.

"You better watch your back, dragon. You never know who you can trust nowadays."

TWELVE

Kaito headed to the throne room. Even before the double doors were thrown open, the sound of laughter spilled outside. His brother was sitting on the edge of the dais. But his casual disregard for rank was the least of his crimes. He held a bottle of sake in his hand, drinking deeply of it. A group of Jirou's most loyal dragons surrounded him—the dragon who'd tried to seduce him, and the dragon who'd warned him of the priests in the village. There was no doubt his brother had orchestrated the entire thing to make him seem weak.

He did not believe he knew just how much danger he'd put them all in. Now Hisato knew where he was, and there was his cryptic message about Suzume. His anger knew no limits. Kaito marched toward them, and the others laughter died away as he approached. But his brother continued to laugh, pretending that he did not see the anger written upon Kaito's face. He turned after a few seconds, just in time for Kaito's fist to collide with his face. He was knocked backward, sprawling onto his back while Kaito stood over him seething.

"What was that for?" Jirou said as he massaged his jaw where Kaito had struck him.

"Isamu almost died because of that little stunt you pulled."

"I have no idea what you're talking about. We've been here all afternoon." He gestured toward his comrades who nodded, giving validity to his lies.

"Your man told me there were priests in the village and that you went to attack them. You wanted to lure me out there to force me to attack the human village," Kaito said.

He waved away Kaito's concern. "Why would I do that? You said we were to lay low." Jirou raised his brows in question, playing the innocent.

"Isamu almost died!" Kenji leaped forward, glaring at Jirou, his hands balled into fists at his side.

Isamu leaned against Hana. The burns from the holy arrows had not healed yet and his face was covered in purple bruises that could not be disguised even in his humanoid form. It would be days before he was back to normal.

Jirou shrugged. "It wasn't me who lured you out there." He smirked at Kaito.

Kaito grabbed his brother by the front of his hoari. "Do you think this is funny?"

"I think a real ruler should protect his people from a threat. You should be thanking me for this opportunity to show us your prowess."

The dragons around them all stared at him. Those most loyal to his brother smiled, while Kenji continued to tremble with anger.

"If you try anything like this again, I will end you." He let go of his brother and turned his back on him.

Kaito turned to stalk away, but before he could Jirou called out to him. "You cannot ignore this problem. While you slept they've hunted us to the brink of extinction. It is time that we rise again, take back what belongs to us. It was said none who stood against you could defeat you in battle. The reign of yokai has been squashed for too long. It is you who should destroy the human menace."

Kaito balled his hand into a fist, barely controlling his rage. His patience was wearing thin as it was. Between Hisato's taunts of Suzume killing yokai and Jirou's goading him into fighting, he was nearly at his breaking point. He'd fought many battles in his long life. But now he doubted his own ability. His power had been less since he'd been freed from the stone and he did not relish the idea of a war.

Because that was what it would be. A bloody war. One he might not win. The threat of Hisato lingered in his mind.

"You look in the wrong direction to glory, brother," Kaito said, hardly holding in his seething temper.

"We are yokai. This is who we are, or have you forgotten that?"

"I know that I bought this crown through the blood of my enemies."

"Your kingdom is infested."

"I do not waste my time on insects."

"The humans have grown too numerous and too powerful. You are a fool if you do not squash them now before it is too late."

"We will not start a war with the humans," Kaito growled, giving his final word on the matter. His voice echoed through the chamber with enough power to bring them all to their knees. They would not challenge him now, even his brother could not suspect just how little his power was. It was why he had not challenged him outright, but sought to damage his reputation. But if they found out the truth, it would be over.

Most of them wouldn't meet his gaze. He had to stop this uprising and now. The best he could do was move forward with his plans. Once he had the strength of other powerful yokai behind him, his brother and those who remained loyal to him would mean nothing. They were bloodthirsty but they were cowards as well. Power won out, even if it was a false power like his own. The scale was not tipped in his favor. But he'd fought greater odds before and won. He could do it again.

Kaito went back to his chamber. But once more found his room occupied. Ai sat on the edge of his futon, poised like a perfect, porcelain doll. It had been a long day cleaning up the mess his brother had made and he'd hoped to find a couple minutes of reprieve, but it seemed that was not to be.

"Why do I even have a chamber door, if everyone comes in whenever they feel like?" he snarled at her, storming past her to go stand at the open doors which led onto a veranda overlooking the ocean. In the old days this place had brought him peace and clarity. But it only really worked if he was alone.

"Ai needs to talk to you," Ai said, ignoring his surly mood.

"I'm in no mood. Leave now while I am asking you nicely." He kept his back to her. Ai had been scarce these past few days. What she was up to he could only guess at. She was as strong-willed as ever it seemed. Some things never changed, he supposed.

But he wasn't in the mood for any of her plots. Things were falling apart around him and the tension with the dragons was only growing. How much longer could he hold onto his kingdom?

"It cannot wait," Ai said. It was meant to be authoritative but her childlike voice ruined the effect.

Kaito rounded on her, baring his canines. "Leave," he roared, the force of his anger shaking the walls. Outside the sky darkened to gray and the sea churned with his mood.

Ai did not so much as flinch beneath the force of his rage. Kazue's spell had trapped Ai in a child's body but long ago she had been the favored daughter of the Lord of the Sea. As one of the first children, she was extremely powerful in her own right. And she'd never been told no. Even if she appeared weak now, Kaito knew what power dwelt beneath that small exterior. Ai knew it too. Her chin was jutted out in that proud way of hers. For a moment he saw the woman she had been, his mistress, and controller of his fate. But he wasn't her puppet anymore.

"You do not have the command of me, Kai," she said imperiously, losing her childlike way of speaking, if only for a moment.

Whatever he might think, she still saw him as beneath her. And maybe he was. She alone knew just how weak he had become. Just how little he had right now. But his anger only made his pride fiercer.

He stalked closer toward her, looming above her, but she only tilted her head back to maintain eye contact.

"You forget whose court you are in." He turned, flexing his clawed hand as he leaned in, using her diminished size to his advantage.

"Ai has not forgotten. It is you who has forgotten how it got this way."

"Not even for a moment have I forgotten what brought me here," he said through gritted teeth.

"It does not seem so to Ai." She looked him up and down. "You're letting your affection for the human blind you to what must be done."

He threw a punch, swinging past her and slamming it into the bed beside her. For the briefest moment her eyes grew wide, then she snapped her gaze back to him.

"I do not love humans," he snarled.

"Perhaps not all. But you are letting the past affect you."

He stood up to pace away from her before he gave into his impulse to knock her upside her head. The anger was burning in his gut like a thousand twisting snakes. *I cannot close my eyes without thinking I will not wake again, that I will never open them again. That I will be trapped in that nightmare for all eternity.*

He turned to face her. "I will never forget what was done to me. And yet you think I love the humans?" He threw his head back in mocking laughter. "I would be glad if I never saw another one again."

"Then why not get rid of them?"

"I have more important things to attend to." He gestured broadly around the room.

"You're lying."

They stared at one another for a few minutes. No one would dare call him a liar to his face but her. He considered retaliating but it would get them nowhere.

"Get out. I tire of this conversation." Kaito turned back to the window, ending the conversation. Outside the sea was tossing and slamming against the island, reflective of his dark mood.

"Your brother is a danger to your rule."

"He is jealous, he always has been. I can handle him," Kaito replied, trying to sound glib.

"If you do not secure your place, then he will. By killing you."

"He knows his place." He would not tell Ai that his brother's open hostility concerned him. They were not close enough for that sort of honesty.

"He'll use her against you."

Suddenly the pieces fell into place and he turned toward Ai with eyes glowing blue in his fury. In a deadly voice he said, "And how does he know her name at all?"

Ai stared at him without response, her round childlike face was blank of all emotion. But he knew without her admission it had been her. There was no other way.

"You have to let the human go," she said.

Anger vibrated through his body, while Ai remained composed. "Do not speak of her to me," he growled. Just thinking of the way they'd parted, and the fact that he continued to worry for her welfare only made him seem weak. When she sent him away he'd sworn he was done with humans.

"You need an ally," she replied, ignoring his outburst.

But he already knew this was coming. It was why Ai had told his brother about Suzume in the first place, to drive him to this point.

"Like you?"

She sat perfectly poised, a childlike mirror of the powerful woman she had been before Kazue had destroyed her.

"There are those who remain loyal to my father, to me. If you would consider a marital alliance-"

"I've already given you my answer. I will not be your puppet again." He turned his back on her, facing the window once more.

She stood up and her footsteps hardly made a sound on the tatami as she approached him. She placed a hand on his forearm.

"It would not be like before. Things are different. You are different."

"You are desperate," he snapped.

She did not even react to the slight. "I am. I need you, Kai. Akatsuki needs a strong leader. Together we can rebuild without bloodshed."

Kaito gave a ragged sigh and stared out at the stormy sea. For centuries he'd resisted his court's pressure to marry, never wanting to tether himself down to one woman. For a time, he thought Kazue could be that woman, but that had been a mistake. A foolish dream. But he could not deny it, the world had changed and he was desperate, as much as it pained him to admit that even to himself. Suzume was behind him, Kazue was dead. There was nothing holding him back from making an alliance that could secure him his rule again. And yet he couldn't bring himself to agree. Not yet.

He could not face Ai as he said, "Bring your allies to me, and then I will consider it."

A smile spread across her face. "You will not be disappointed, Kai."

THIRTEEN

Suzume woke in the morning and wiped the drool from her face. *I can't remember the last time I slept so good.* She stretched and yawned. *I had the strangest dream I was back at the palace and I ate with the emperor.* Suzume rubbed the sleep from her eyes and looked around her room. A painted screen depicting a mountain haloed in fog divided her futon from a larger room. *I don't remember that being in the inn room.*

Suzume blinked away the sleep from her eyes and her hand fell onto something silky. These blankets were much too nice for an inn. *Oh no. Was I kidnapped again?* She threw back the covers, leaped to her feet, and darted around the screen. An unfamiliar woman in a familiar uniform was kneeling beside multiple plates of food. The scent of it made her empty stomach growl.

"Good morning, my lady," the servant said as she bowed her head to Suzume.

"It wasn't a dream?" Suzume asked her.

The servant only blinked at her in confusion. Just to be sure, Suzume pinched herself hard. "Ouch!"

"My lady?" The servant leaped up and rushed over to Suzume in concern. Or maybe she thought Suzume was insane.

I'm really back at the White Palace!

Suzume disregarded the maid's concern and plopped down on the ground in front of her breakfast, shoveling the succulent meal into her mouth. She could not remember the last time anything she'd eaten had tasted quite so good. After breakfast, feeling full and content, she flopped backward onto the tatami floor and stared at the ceiling. *It wasn't a dream.*

"My lady, it's time to get dressed," the servant said.

With a loud groan, Suzume got up and the maid started the complicated ritual of dressing Suzume in layers of kimono. *Should I go and visit Mariko or Ayame? I wonder if Estuko ever married that lord with the crooked teeth she was so in love with? I think she did. I wonder if Ayame ever discovered who was writing those tragic poems?* Suzume laughed, thinking of the horrid love poems. It felt for a moment as if she had woken from a long horrible nightmare. As if her exile and everything after it had never happened.

But halfway through getting dressed, Suzume's eyes rested on her staff leaning against the wall. And reality came crashing back down upon her. Hikaru was imprisoned, and the others were sealed in stone. The emperor's request to have her help with Hisato. That thought sobered her and all of her previous excitement was drained away. There wouldn't be any time for gossip or the childish pastimes of her old life. She had to rescue her friends. But how?

She'd didn't trust the emperor to release them. Fighting Hisato had to be an excuse for something more. Why choose her to fight Hisato? If he knew about her power he must know she had no real mastery of it. Someone like Hikaru was much better suited to Hisato. But the emperor had imprisoned him. There was more here that she'd yet to discover. No one in the White Palace did anything without motive, and the emperor was no exception. The only option was to get out of here as soon as possible.

Since she was in the White Palace, she'd have to play by the palace rules. When the servant finished dressing her, Suzume asked for parchment and brush to write with.

The servant gave her a strange look, but did as she bid. When she returned Suzume set out to write a letter. Her mother had allies, advisers to the emperor. Perhaps one of them could help her. *But what can I barter with?* She had no money, no influence. She shook her head.

I'll figure out the second part later. First I'll write out a list of people who have enough influence to set Hikaru free and get me closer to where the others have been taken. She dipped her pen in ink and it hovered above the paper.

Black ink dripped onto the paper and it resembled tiny branches spread outward across it. She could not think of a single courtier who had enough influence to sway the emperor. Not even her grandfather, who was a high ranking official. *If I could find Hisato...* She set her pen down abruptly. No, she was not going to make any deals with him.

*That's fine. I'll just..._*She had no allies, and no skills to fight her way out. *How am I going to save them, then?*

"Are you finished, my lady?"

Suzume stood up suddenly, nearly toppling over the ink and paper as she did so. If she couldn't do it the old way, then she'd have to think of a new plan. Maybe she couldn't break them out, but if she could get to Hikaru maybe she could ask him what to do. And hopefully he knew a spell to break the seals on the others. Then that would just leave figuring out where the others had been taken.

Suzume headed for the door. She was better at acting than sitting around making a plan. Before Suzume could open the door, the breathless servant rushed in front of her.

"My lady, allow me."

Suzume blinked at her in surprise. She had forgotten how little she actually did for herself when she lived here. Suzume stepped back and allowed the servant to open the door for her. She peered out into the hall and looked both ways. To her surprise there were no guards at the door. *Maybe they're hiding?* Surely the emperor would want her watched. She'd been brought in as a captive after all, even if it was under the guise of her helping the emperor.

"Is something the matter, my lady?" the servant asked.

"No, nothing," Suzume said and stepped out into the hall. As she walked, she could hear a faint echo of footsteps behind her. Suzume turned quickly, reaching for the weapon she wasn't wearing, only to find the servant following after her.

"Do you need anything, my lady?" the servant asked.

Suzume dropped her arm to her side. *I forgot I was never alone when I lived here. I always had at least one servant with me. He doesn't need guards when the maid will report my every movement to him.*

"It's nothing. I'm just going for a walk," Suzume replied before spinning on her heel and continuing down the hall.

She had forgotten how difficult it was to move in this heavy kimono, and she stumbled a few steps at first. When she'd lived at the palace before, she hadn't gotten out much unless she was being carried in a palanquin. The servant was at her side almost immediately, offering a hand. After a few tentative steps, Suzume fell back into the rhythm of it and continued down the hallway.

Not wanting to waste any time, she headed straight for the main palace gates. The palace compound was made up of several buildings and smaller palaces. The emperor, empress, and their children lived in the main palace. And for now, so did Suzume. She'd been surprised when the master of chambers had brought her to the room in the main palace. As a child, Suzume had lived in one of the smaller palaces on the grounds. She wasn't sure if she should be flattered by this honor or suspicious. Perhaps the emperor wanted her close to keep an eye on her.

Whatever his motives, she'd have to leave the main palace to reach the prison where Hikaru was being kept. She strode confidently up to the gates which were guarded by a pair of soldiers. They stood with their backs against the arches, staring outward. As Suzume attempted to walk through however, they jutted out their spears, stopping her in her tracks.

"Let me through. I have business outside the main palace."

"It is the emperor's orders, princess. You are not to leave the main palace building."

Suzume frowned at them and considered arguing even though she knew it was pointless. "I will have to speak to the emperor then." She turned in a faux huff, pretending to be storming off to speak with the emperor. But she knew her boundaries now, and her suspicion was confirmed. Her friends were outside the palace walls.

When she was out of sight of the guards, she looped back toward one of the gardens that dominated the western side of the main palace.

She'd played here often as a child, and she remembered a tree her oldest brother had pointed out to her when she was small. He claimed its branches could be climbed to escape the main palace. Her eldest brother, the heir to the throne, had never seen the outside of the main palace, she was sure of it. But he had liked to brag about adventures he'd had outside its walls just the same.

With winter looming over the fringes of fall, the garden was deserted. Getting to the garden was harder than she thought it would be. The heavy layers of her kimono pressed on her chest, making breathing difficult and almost as soon as she arrived, she had to sit down. Sweat beaded her brow. The kimono was not meant for moving around. As a princess she'd spent most of her time reclining, listening to poetry, and gossiping.

There was a stone bench under a cherry tree, which had lost almost all of its leaves. A few last remnants still clung desperately to its branches. A cold wind blew through the garden.

"My lady, it's very cold. Perhaps we should return inside," the servant said.

Suzume resisted the urge to wrap her arms around her shoulders. "I think it's refreshing," she said as her breath came out in clouds of vapor.

The wind's icy fingers pierced through the multiple layers of her kimono. "But an overcoat would be welcome," Suzume amended— she needed to shake the maid anyway.

The servant bowed and scurried away. Suzume watched her go and once she was certain she was gone she got up to search the garden. If she remembered correctly, the tree shouldn't be far from here. Finding it took longer than she thought it would, but after several panicked minutes of searching she stumbled on the tree almost by accident. It was not as tall as she remembered and the branches seemed hardly strong enough to hold her weight.

Suzume glanced around to make sure the maid wasn't back yet. Once she confirmed the coast was clear, she reached for the lowest branch. Pulling herself onto it was more difficult than she antici- pated and the long billowing sleeves of her kimono kept getting in her way. The multiple layers also made maneuvers difficult. She had just gotten onto the bottom branch when she felt the outer most layer rip.

Suzume sighed and tore off several of the layers, leaving them in a pile on the ground until she was only in her hakama and one single inner layer. The cold made her teeth chatter, but climbing the tree was much easier this way. The highest branch extended almost all the way to wall except for a small gap between. She stared at that gap for a moment, convincing herself that she was making the right decision and not preparing to fall and break her neck. She took the leap and made it onto the wall. Once on the wall, there was nothing beyond but a large fall. She eased herself over the side, and before she lost her nerve, she dropped down onto the ground below.

She landed hard on her ankle and felt the pain ripple through her leg. For a moment she feared she had broken it. A quick test showed that she could put some weight on it, but not much. She half hobbled across the palace grounds, keeping a watchful eye out for guards. The maid would likely be returning to find her discarded clothes at any moment.

Her progress was slow, hindered by her injury and by the need for stealth. She hadn't made it far beyond the main palace building when she heard voices coming from the opposite direction. The only thing to hide behind was a pagoda that overlooked a small pond. Suzume dove behind it and prayed whoever was coming from the other direction did not see her.

"To think he would turn against the emperor," said a man in a rumbling voice.

Suzume's ears pricked up. That voice sounded familiar. She chanced a peek around the corner of the building she was hiding behind. Three men stood beside the gloomy pool. Two of the men she recognized as counselors to the emperor. Her mother had often entertained the two of them. The third man was younger, and a head taller than both of them. His back was to her.

The first counselor said, "Now that house of Kaedemori has fallen, we may all tumble along with it."

That was her mother's family. They were one of the most powerful in the kingdom, second only to the royal family. They could trace their roots back to the birth of the kingdom. Several generations of women in her family had married past emperors and there had even been a few empresses. Had their star really fallen as Daiki had said? She'd assumed it had been vicious lies.

"Are you so entwined with your master you cannot save yourself from his sinking ship?" said the faceless speaker, though his voice did sound familiar as well.

The men both blustered.

"We've done nothing wrong!" the second counselor said.

"And I make no accusations," the younger man replied.

"You will protect us, won't you, Ryuu?" asked the second counselor. Suzume cringed, remembered what a wheedling worm he was. *I'm not surprised. As soon as his protectors are gone he goes looking for someone new.*

"Perhaps, if you can tell me where Izume is."

"No one knows where she fled to."

Suzume had to clamp a hand over her mouth to stifle her gasp. She thought her mother had been exiled by the emperor but these men made it sound as if she had run away.

"Then I have no need of you," Ryuu said coldly and it sounded like his footsteps were heading in her direction. Suzume's heart leaped into her throat. She could run but if she did she would be spotted for sure.

"Wait!" the counselor shouted and the footsteps halted.

"There are rumors that she went back to the Kaedemori's clan house. Perhaps she is there."

"Did you know her at all?" Ryuu said scorn in his tone.

He spoke as if he knew her mother, though Suzume was certain she'd never seen that man before in her life. As she was considering the implications she did not notice the footsteps that were approaching her until it was too late.

Suzume pressed herself flat against the back of the building, hoping that he would pass by without seeing her.

"She has written to me," said the first counselor. Ryuu stopped right beside her. Suzume fought the urge to look at him, fearing even turning her head would catch his attention.

"What did her letter say?" Ryuu asked.

"She asked for word on the emperor's army. She wanted to know where they were headed."

"You're both wasting my time, be gone with the both of you." Ryuu turned his back to her, presumably to watch the counselors go. Suzume waited a heartbeat and then started to inch away, hoping he would miss seeing her hiding in her underclothes behind the building.

"Were you spying on me?" Ryuu asked without turning to face her.

FOURTEEN

S he had two options—admit she'd been listening to his conversation or run. She chose the latter. Suzume bolted behind the building, where a narrow stretch of land separated the structure from the pool. She ran along that edge, hoping he would not pursue her. But she was wrong. He caught up with her in a few strides, grabbing her by the forearm and yanking her backward and into the pagoda.

She spun around to face him. She was no expert at hand to hand combat but maybe if she assumed the pose she could trick him into thinking she was.

"Why were you spying on me?" he asked at the same time Suzume said, "What do you want with my mother?" Their voices overlapped.

Suzume glared at him while Ryuu assessed her.

"Do you know where Izume is?" he asked after a few minutes of silent posturing.

"What is your relationship with my mother?"

"I think that's between Izume and me."

With arms crossed over her chest, she narrowed her eyes at him. It couldn't be mere coincidence that she'd met him at the inn, and now he was at the White Palace working for the emperor of all people. He had to be Hisato in disguise.

"I know it's you, Hisato. I'm not going to fall for your disguise this time."

His brows furrowed. "Is this your way of distracting me?"

She knew all his tricks and she wasn't going to fall for it this time. She threw her head back in mock laughter. "Let's not play this game. What is your plan for the White Palace?"

"I think you have the wrong idea about me."

Suzume scoffed and placed her hands on her hips. "Do you think I'm going to fall for that?"

"I have no idea what you're talking about, honestly."

But now was her chance. If only she had her staff. If she could stop him now before the war started, then all of this would be over and she could go back to her old life. But what if she tried using her power and lost control again? Though she was hesitant to use her power, this was her chance to end things for good. A ball of flame formed in her hand, coming easier than ever before.

"Pretend all you want, but I'm ending this here." She lunged for him, arching her arm backward, determined to drive the ball of flame straight into him.

As she thrust forward for her attack however, he stepped out of the way. Her flame only caught the edge of the sleeve. Fueled by her spiritual energy, the fire burned fast and hot, traveling up his sleeve. Suzume braced herself for the recoil of pain in her own body, but felt none. She watched in horror as he stamped out the flames with his bare hand, a faint glimmering barrier surrounding his hand as he did so.

She held up her hands as if that would do anything to protect her. "How did you do that? You couldn't do that before."

He came toward her, hand raised as if he would strike her, and Suzume backed away. But getting to the exit meant going through him. Her back collided with the wall and he struck her hard in her right shoulder. Her arm fell limp to her side, the flames on it flickering and dying.

"I'm not Hisato."

She bared her teeth in a show of defiance. "Sure you're not." With her left hand she ignited enough fire to cover her hands. She reached up and slapped him across the face. She closed her eyes and waited for the pain to be reflected in her body. But once more she felt nothing.

Suzume waited a few moments before peeking out from beneath her eyelids to see a bright red mark on his face. He had not blocked her attack but she still had not felt it. As realization dawned upon her, Suzume felt a hot blush burning her cheeks.

He leaned forward so he was close to her but not touching. "Are you trying to make me angry?" he breathed.

His spiritual power uncoiled from him, revealing the depth of his power and strength which until now he'd kept hidden. This wasn't Hisato, but he was someone perhaps equally as powerful. Not one to be trapped, she used the emergency move Tsuki had taught her. She brought her knee up toward his groin, but he anticipated her move and leaped out of the way before she could land the blow.

They stood facing one another, Suzume's right arm dangling and the man's face already healing itself of the fiery slap.

"Did Izume send you here to torment me or are you just particularly frustrating," he asked between gritted teeth.

"I don't know where my mother is."

He shook his head. "I should have known."

"What do you want with her?"

"It's time we take you back to the palace." He grabbed her by the wrist but she yanked her hand away.

"Maybe I should just ask the emperor myself. Perhaps he knows." She stared up at him defiantly.

"Who do you think he's going to trust, me or the daughter of the woman who betrayed him?"

"You're just like the rest. None of you know her." She wasn't sure why she felt the need to defend her mother to this practical stranger. Gods knew she'd blamed her mother for everything that had happened to her thus far. But there was something about him that made her want to prove her mother's innocence.

"I think you're the one who doesn't know Izume."

Once more his words had cut her to the quick. It was as if he knew exactly what to say to wound her.

"Wait until I tell the emperor how you've treated me." She felt like she needed to make that point clear. Not that she was certain the emperor would even care. For all she knew this man had been placed here to catch her.

"What would he think if he found you like this?"

"I'm free to go where I like."

"In your undergarments?" Suzume looked down at the thin layer of inner kimono. She had completely forgotten she'd taken off her outer layers to climb the tree. Her plans to free her friends were all evaporating like smoke.

He grabbed her wrist and dragged her behind him, as she made threats she could not follow up on. At the main gate they were greeted by two very surprised guards, who were smart enough to keep their eyes averted. As he dragged her along, her maid came running toward them carrying the layers of Suzume's discarded kimono.

"My lady," she gasped, seeing Suzume flushed in the face, hair disheveled and being dragged by Ryuu.

Ryuu shoved her toward the maid. "Make sure she gets into some warm clothes before she freezes."

He turned and walked away without another word. The maid threw a kimono around Suzume. It was enough to keep her from being indecent. But if anyone saw her with so little on in the palace they would think her lowly. She needed to get back to her rooms right away. But she was more worried about Ryuu and what he was plotting. It didn't matter if there was a chill in the air, the fire in her gut was burning too hot for her to really feel the cold.

Suzume scowled after him as she shouted, "This isn't the end of this."

He didn't deem it necessary to respond.

They hurried down the hallway, trying to get back to Suzume's room before she was seen. While Suzume's mind was focused on revenge, she wasn't really paying attention to where she was going.

"My lady!" the servant gasped. A crowd of people approached from the other end of the hall. At the forefront was a woman dripping in gold and crimson, her long ebony hair dragging along almost to the floor. The empress, as always, paraded around the palace like a proud peacock.

There was nowhere to go. Suzume stood bedraggled in the middle of the walkway.

"My lady, you must bow," the servant whispered.

Suzume bowed mechanically as she moved out of the way of the empress. She dipped her head and moved aside, allowing the women of higher rank to pass her by. She hoped the empress would glide on past her as if she did not exist at all. But luck was not on her side today, and as she was about to pass her one of her ladies leaned in to whisper in her ear. The empress stopped, and turned to face Suzume.

"You're Izume's oldest daughter?" she said, as if she didn't know Izume only had one daughter.

"Yes, your majesty," Suzume said in her most groveling tone. The empress's temper was legendary, as was her feud with Suzume's mother, Izume.

"I thought you were training as a priestess." She looked over Suzume, eyes narrowed as she assessed and judged every inch of Suzume's body. Her maid had only managed to get one layer on her, enough so she wasn't indecent. But even if she hadn't been under-dressed, Suzume felt her imperfections keenly. She'd gotten tanner and her hair was not as long as it had been. Her hands were calloused and chapped. She folded them close to her body to hide them.

The one thing she had left to her was her words. "The emperor summoned me."

"Then I suppose my husband has forgiven your mother after all," she said, not bothering to hide the scorn in her voice.

"He hasn't, majesty," Suzume countered, boldly raising her gaze to meet the empress's.

The empress narrowed her eyes. "Then what are you doing here, in the main palace no less?"

"Perhaps that is something you should ask the emperor."

The empress reeled back, and her ladies behind her whispered to one another.

"Ask me what, wife?" The emperor approached, having come from the other end of the hall. Behind him were two rows of counselors and servants. Suzume lowered her gaze, knowing that with so many people around it would be inappropriate to look at his face.

"I was just welcoming Izume's daughter back to the palace."

"We are very lucky to have her. She will be staying at the main palace for the time being. I hope you will make her feel welcome," the emperor said to the empress.

She nodded her head. "As you wish, your majesty."

"Suzume, Ryuu has agreed to train you at the palace temple. Starting tomorrow."

Suzume's visceral reaction was to protest, but she choked on the words and instead fell into a coughing fit.

The empress scrunched her nose at her in disgust, while the emperor knelt down.

"Are you unwell? Should I call for a healer?" He placed his hand on her shoulder in a tender and fatherly way. Suzume blinked at him as she caught her breath.

"I'm fine. It's nothing serious."

The emperor stood up again, and the empress was practically red in the face with anger. Suzume had to bite down her amusement at the sight.

"Ah, Suzume, I almost forgot. You will be needing this." The emperor handed her a seal. Suzume took it in her cupped hands. "That gives you unfettered access to me and everywhere in the palace."

Suzume bowed her head low. "You are too kind, your majesty."

The emperor chuckled. "Don't thank me, you've earned it. I am very proud of you."

She dared to peek up at him through her lashes and saw that he was smiling, but the empress looked furious. Her dark eyes were narrowed, glaring at Suzume behind the emperor's back.

The piece of metal felt cold in her hands. The emperor did not give out his favor lightly. She could not help but give a smug smile to the empress.

The emperor turned to his wife whose face transformed in an instant from anger to serenity. The emperor nodded his head at her before gliding on past, his counselors scurrying behind him to keep up.

Suzume could not fight the smile that stretched her features. If only her mother could see her now. This would have pleased her to no end. Her entire life she'd listened to her mother rant about how she'd love to see the empress shamed. It seemed she'd done what her mother had never been able to.

The empress rose from her bow and held out her hand. One of her ladies placed a fan in it. She flicked the fan open and waved it in front of her face.

"You're just like your mother," she said, not hiding her contempt this time. She'd been hearing that a lot lately.

"Thank you, your majesty."

"It was not a compliment. We all know what your mother did. It is surprising that the emperor continues this charade."

She flicked her fan closed and then turned her head away as if Suzume was not even worth gazing upon. She glided down the hall away from Suzume. The crowd of her hangers-on chattered behind her. They were looking back at Suzume, whispering, the beginnings of rumors already in motion. She couldn't have planned it better herself. Soon the entire palace would know Suzume was in the emperor's favor. Suzume's grin only grew bigger. *If only I had known about these powers sooner, how different would my life have been?*

Suzume sauntered back to her rooms, unable to keep the enormous smile from her face. When she had imagined coming back to the palace she had always envisioned returning to the life she had once had. She'd never thought she could come back to something even better than before. The servant slid open the door to her room and stepped inside.

It was rather dark, but she wasn't paying much attention, still replaying the expression on The Empress's face in her mind. Suzume chuckled to herself. Today was going really well.

Just then someone grabbed her from behind, pressing a blade to her lower back.

"Keep quiet and there won't be any trouble," said a raspy voice.

FIFTEEN

"Why is it always me whose getting kidnapped?" Suzume said with an exasperated sigh.

The creature tugged harder on her arm and started pulling her toward the door. He must not have appreciated her commentary because he twisted her arm harder.

"Do you have to be so rough?" she whined, pretending to be a weakling while planning her own counter-attack. The one good thing about frequent kidnap attempts was she knew what to expect.

"Quiet, before I silence you myself."

Suzume rolled her eyes. Every kidnapping was the same. It was starting to get terribly boring. While her kidnapper was focused on dragging her out the door, Suzume was channeling her fire into a single point in her body, onto the arm where her kidnapper grasped her. As the flames grew along her skin, the creature yowled and dropped her. Suzume used the momentary distraction to lunge for her staff which was leaning against the far wall. She had foolishly thought the palace was safe enough where she wouldn't need to walk around armed. Apparently, she'd been wrong.

She snatched the staff up and as soon as it was in her hands she felt the flames coursing through her body. As if being close to the weapon had made her stronger and more confident. Distracted by the sensation, Suzume did not realize the creature had lunged for her until the last second when she rolled out of the way.

Spinning to face her attacker, she swung her staff at the yokai. But it caught the edge of her staff, pulled it from her hand, and flung it across the room. Suzume stared into the eyes of her attacker. A neko with a scar over his eye. It was the same neko who had tried to kidnap her at the inn.

"You again!"

"So you remember me," he said in a purring growl.

His golden eyes narrowed as they faced one another, circling each other. Suzume's best defense was across the room from her. Despite not having a weapon, her hands sparked with flames, and Kazue's fire burned hot in her gut. She didn't need the staff to fight this yokai. She had everything she needed right here in her hands. As they continued their slow dance, Suzume prepared to defend herself in the way Tsuki had taught her.

The neko moved smoothly, his twin fiery tails flicked behind him. If he wasn't going to give her an opening, she was going to have to make one. Suzume feigned to the right and the yokai followed her, attempting an interception and as he did, she grabbed onto any flesh she could, scorching it with burning hands. It lacked sophistication but it got the job done. The yokai screeched in pain as her holy fire ran up his arms. Because it was fueled by her spiritual energy, it would continue to burn him without ceasing. While the yokai tried to put out the flames, Suzume ran across the room for her staff once more.

The yokai was not as distracted as she had hoped and as she ran, he threw something which tangled up her feet. Thrown off balance, Suzume pitched forward. She pivoted in the air as she fell and landed on her shoulder to soften the blow. But that had been a mistake. Landing on hard tatami was not as forgiving as she would have hoped and pain rippled up and down her arm. She ignored the pain and reached for the bindings around her ankles. When she tried to touch it sparks erupted and she jerked her hand backward.

"What is this?"

"I've got tricks of my own, girly," the neko said as he stalked over to her.

Suzume flipped onto her stomach and attempted to crawl away, but she was much too slow. She was a few inches away from her staff. She reached for it, her fingertips nearly brushing against it before the neko grabbed her by the ankles and dragged her backward. She wriggled around and slapped his face with burning hands. She choked on the smell of burning hair as the neko put his hands over his smoking face. Suzume flipped back over and hopped toward her staff. With the staff in her hands she was better able to focus her energy on her ankles, where the fire burned through the bindings and she was able to get to her feet once more.

The neko had put out the fire on his face but the flames had burned away the hair and the top layer of skin, which healed as she watched. Bright, shiny pink flesh covered most of his face, leaving him with a grotesque mask and golden eyes bulging in their sockets.

"You're gonna pay for damaging my face." He growled and lunged toward her.

Suzume struck with the staff, but he blocked her attack and grabbed onto it. The pair of them wrestled over the weapon for a few minutes.

"You look better this way," Suzume mocked.

"I'll tear your guts out and make you watch," he hissed.

His rage burned in his eyes, but it also distracted him and Suzume used it to kick his feet out from beneath him. Since he was still holding onto the staff, and so was she, it brought her tumbling to the ground with him. The staff was tossed aside as the pair of them rolled around, clawing and punching at each other each, each fighting to get the upper hand.

Fire encircled the two of them as Suzume's flames rose up to protect her. As she burned him, however, the wounds healed. Her power was not limitless, and already she could see her flames losing effectiveness. By sheer force of will, Suzume ended up on top of her attacker. She pressed both sparking thumbs to the cat's eyes.

The yokai screamed in agony, a gut-wrenching sound high enough to pierce her eardrums. Suzume leaped off him and ran for the door. Just as she was about to reach the door however, it slid open and guards came pouring into her room. All of them were wearing the uniform of the warrior priests.

At their head was Ryuu, his weapon drawn and his eyes glowing blue. The guards fanned out, filling the space. But when they saw the yokai lying on the ground, burning and in pain, Ryuu held up his hand to halt the advance. He had a curious expression on his face.

"I was coming to your rescue, but it looks like you've got a handle on things."

Suzume panted for breath but she couldn't keep the smile from her face. She wouldn't admit out loud but the compliment pleased her greatly. It was the first time anyone had recognized her ability. "I told you I don't need saving."

"I can see that now." Ryuu gestured to the men to capture the yokai, who had not gotten up again, and appeared to be no longer suffering.

The priests surrounded the yokai, encasing him in a shimmering barrier. The yokai did not fight against them but instead lowered his head as he was led out of Suzume's room.

It dawned on her belatedly that he had shown up just in time.

"How did you know I needed help?" Suzume said, unable to keep the accusatory tone out of her words.

"I sensed a yokai in the palace. I've been tracking him and it led me here."

She narrowed her eyes as she watched him. It seemed like a convenient story. But she wouldn't push him, not yet.

"Aren't you going to seal him like you did my friends?" She gestured toward the open door where the yokai had been taken.

"We need a sealing circle for that. I'm taking him back to the temple," he said distractedly as he paced around Suzume's room, lifting up a destroyed screen with scorch marks on it. The floors were singed as well. And there was a shattered tea set just a few feet away, its broken ceramics scattered across the floor.

"Is that where you took my friends?" she asked, though she didn't expect him to answer.

"The palace is no place to keep yokai," he said as he kicked over the serving tray on which the tea had been brought in.

Suzume frowned as she studied him. His back was to her as if he had not realized she was still there at all. Had he meant to give her that piece of information or was he really that clueless?

"How did a yokai get in here?" Suzume asked.

He turned to her again, his gaze sliding over her face as if she were a puzzle he was trying to solve. "Are you saying you've never seen yokai here before?"

"No," she said, drawing out the o.

He shook his head. "Yokai are more clever than you think. This neko was posing as your maid. I should have realized that was the case when you had a lingering yokai aura about you when we met earlier."

Her clothes were tattered and burned, but she didn't see any aura about her.

"You seem to have a knack for arriving just when I need you."

"And you seem to have a talent for getting into trouble."

Though he surely couldn't have known hearing those words from him soured her mood more. Kaito loved to tease her by saying she drew trouble to herself.

"I know," she said, turning away from him. Now that she was thinking about Kaito she couldn't stop. If only he had seen her fight the yokai, maybe he would have thought she was capable of taking care of herself at last. *Stop. Stop right there. He's gone and it's over. In fact, nothing started. Better to forget about him altogether.*

"You act as if you're kidnapped often," Ryuu probed gently, perhaps sensing her frustration.

"You have no idea." She sighed heavily.

He chuckled. It was deep and attractive. But she didn't want to think of him that way. He might not be Hisato, but that didn't mean he wasn't working with him.

"My lady, we need to get you out of here," a servant said, guiding her out of the room before she could question Ryuu further.

She was removed to a new chamber where a servant fussed over her comfort, bringing her tea.

"This isn't time to be drinking tea. A yokai attacked me in the palace. Can't you see how serious this is?" she asked the servant.

They only kept their heads bowed and scurried out of the room. Suzume tried to sit down but she found her feet restless. What was going on here that she'd been attacked on her second night, by the same yokai who had attacked at the inn, and Ryuu had been involved both times. Outside a voice announced, "The emperor approaches."

Suzume froze and stared at the door, she could already see the silhouette of the emperor approaching. What was he doing here, now of all times? She lunged for the tea setting thinking it would be appropriate to seem relaxed. She didn't want him to know about the attack. But as soon as she sat, she realized that she should stand to greet him. She stood up quickly and knocked over her teacup, spilling the contents over her serving tray. Her maid rushed to clean it up as the emperor strode into the room. A stain splattered across her front and the maid bent over trying to conceal the mess.

Suzume bowed to her father, dipping her head low as was deemed appropriate. She'd at least been able to disguise the flustered expression on her face. The emperor moved across the room in a blink and grabbed her hands into his. Suzume's head shot up, causing her to forget all protocol as the emperor met her gaze.

"I heard about the attack, were you injured?" he asked. There seemed to be genuine concern on his face.

Suzume stared back at him, mouth hanging open. It took her a moment to compose herself and when she did, she shook her head and said, "I'm fine. It wasn't anything too serious." She shrugged off the injuries and turned her head away to conceal a cut on her cheek.

The emperor grabbed her by the chin and turned her to face him. "You are injured." Then to the servant he said, "Call the healer, bring them here."

"That's not necessary. It's just a scratch."

The maid ignored Suzume's protest and hurried out of the room, leaving the two of them alone together. "I came as soon as I heard. If I had known you were in danger I would have protected you better. I've ordered guards to watch you day and night. I will not let this happen again. If this had turned out differently..." he trailed off as he searched her face.

Did he send the yokai to attack me, just so he can put me under guard? But that didn't make any sense. If that's what he wanted he could have done that from the start.

"I can take care of myself," Suzume said, yanking her hands away. Her words were harsher than she intended. After everything that had happened today she forgot who she was speaking to. She bowed her head in apology. "I'm sorry, your majesty. I spoke without thinking."

The emperor placed his hand on her shoulder. "There is no need to apologize. Perhaps I am getting carried away. Ryuu told me you fought the yokai on your own. He seemed impressed." He smiled. "Ryuu is never impressed."

Suzume fought the smile that threatened to spread across her face. This was all part of his manipulation. He didn't really think she was impressive. He was trying to keep her compliant. They were both playing this game, but she intended to win.

"Nonetheless, I would feel better if there was someone on hand to protect you. I have asked Ryuu to be your personal guard."

"What?" She turned to face him. "How can you trust him? Don't you know—"

"Ryuu is loyal to me and he will keep you safe. That is all that matters."

She felt like a petulant child, arguing with him. She'd spoken without thinking. She had not come here to please her father. She had to free her friends first. But this would only make matters more complicated.

Sixteen

Flying through the sky and feeling the wind ripple around his body was a feeling Kaito could lose himself to. Everything fell away up above the clouds. There was no marital alliance, there were no personal betrayals, there wasn't even a kingdom for him to rule. There were him and the endless horizon. It had always brought him comfort—it helped everything fall into place. He didn't have to worry about his brother's ambitions or the fractured state of his kingdom.

A large cloud loomed in front of him and he sped up, spearing through it. Mist clung to him as he passed through and the cloud broke apart, scattering on the wind. He weaved and dived, playing along the breeze and the clouds. The landscape zoomed along beneath him, and his serpentine shadow snaked over the trees, hills, and lakes. Occasionally he'd pass over a rice patty, and farmers would stop their work to tilt their heads back and watch him pass overhead. They'd convince themselves it was a trick of their eye or they'd think it was the wind or the clouds.

Humans were so slow to believe even when the truth was in front of their faces. *But there are still those who are hunting us.* For as long as he could remember, he had thought of humans as nothing more than harmless insects, far below his notice. But as he passed through lands he had once known, domains which had once teamed with yokai a few centuries before, he found human farms and human towns. And

"

no matter how much he searched, he could not find his kind. Not anywhere.

As Kaito continued his lazy journey across the countryside, he felt a flicker of power close by. It was enough that he slowed his progress to better pinpoint it. But as quickly as he had sensed it, it disappeared. Could there still be powerful yokai left in Akatsuki? There were those who had the ability to cloak their power. Kaito doubled back, trying to find the source of the power, even the smallest hint would have been a comfort. But after several fruitless minutes of searching, he found nothing.

Hana had said many of the big and powerful yokai had gone into hiding in recent centuries. Whoever it was, they didn't want to be found. The brush against that power reminded him of the purpose for his journey. All the dragons had set out to contact his former allies, and he was on his way to meet with one of the descendants of his old general. He only hoped the son maintained the same loyalty as his old friend. Ai's offer of marriage had to be a last resort. Everything he had, he'd gotten on his own. And he wasn't ready to shackle his life to another's to get what was lost.

The landscape grew more rugged as he approached his destination, and as he was preparing to glide over a mountain peak, he felt a brush of that same power again. Just a glimpse, enough to let him know it was there.

Kaito reached the peak of the mountain and wrapped his serpentine body around it so he could survey the landscape. The clouds hung around the top of the mountain concealing him from view. The feeling was gone. But he was certain he had been followed. Perhaps they were not as benign as he had thought. Kaito spread out his senses, searching for a hint of them, but found nothing. They had to be powerful indeed to disguise themselves this well. He waited a few more moments for them to attack, but when they didn't he continued onward.

For the rest of the journey Kaito was waiting for their attack, his eyes scanning all around him, above and below. But no attack came. He reached the mountain ranges of his destination, where the thick forest cloaked the outside world. Snow peaked the mountaintops and coated the ground. Even Kaito, who breathed ice, felt the chill of this place. The land was wild and devoid of humans. In fact, Kaito had not seen any humans in hours.

This was one of the last strongholds of the yokai. He could feel it in the air—the energy of his kind crackled all around him. It was as if no time had changed at all, this was how the world used to be. When the forest became too thick to see where he was going, he transformed into his more humanoid form and walked up a stone pathway. The yokai palace was a massive structure in the center of the forest, hewn from the rock itself. There was no real artifice to the place. It was a palace of function. A stronghold. The walls were made of stone and manned by massive oni. Their thick arms were corded with muscle and they possessed massive swords that were almost twice Kaito's size.

Walking up to the gate, Kaito had to tilt his head back to see the top of it.

Two massive oni were on the top of the gate and leered down at him. They had large underbites, and fangs protruding from their lips. Their skin was a mottled blue and green. And strapped to their backs were weapons that would cleave Kaito in two.

"State your business," the oni said in a booming voice.

Kaito cupped his hands together to shout up to them. "I am the great dragon, come to see your leader," he said. "My messengers should have sent word of my arrival."

Kaito had expected such a greeting. It was in their nature. He waited patiently, hands at his side. If he posed any threat at all, they would attack first and ask questions later. The oni who had shouted down to him disappeared and Kaito occupied himself by gazing at the scenery. On the rest of the island winter was not far off, but it had already gotten its icy grip on the landscape here high in the mountains.

After a few minutes the gate opened with a thundering creak and the oni was standing there waiting for Kaito.

"This way," he said, gesturing for Kaito to follow him. The courtyard was brimming with oni. They were practicing their swordplay, using their massive two-handed blades to bash into one another. Their footsteps rattled the floor beneath them as they thundered toward each other.

Kaito was led up the main steps into the building beyond. There was a long hall which appeared to be a simple room where more oni were gathered drinking and gambling together. They did not even bother to glance at him as he walked among them. Their leader sat, not at the head of the room, but gambling with a group of oni. Kaito only knew him by the enormous blade strapped to his back, which was bigger than any he had seen before.

Kaito was left standing there, waiting for acknowledgment from the leader, while he placed bets. After a time long enough to be an insult, the oni turned to Kaito at last. He had the look of his father. Long, thick, black hair fell over his brow and from his forehead protruded a single twisted horn. His skin was a green, bordering on black, his arms were corded with thick muscles, and a thick gut hung over the edge of his animal-hide pants. He wore several animal pelts tied together over his torso with the neck exposed and a necklace made of bones the size of human femurs. There was something in his keen eyes, which made him stand out against his more brutish and stupid underlings.

"You are far from home, dragon." The oni gave him a quick once over, dismissing him with a glance before turning back to his game.

It irked Kaito's pride and he shot an icy spear at him. The ice grazed the oni leader's cheek, sheering off a forelock. A chunk of the oni's dark hair fell onto the floor beside him.

Every oni in the room leaped to their feet at once, grabbing their weapons as they did. Only the leader remained sitting. He stared at the hair which had fallen onto the ground.

"You are bold to disrespect me in my own domain."

Kaito laughed, giving him a chilly smile in return. "You are the one who has not shown the proper respect to the ruler of Akatsuki."

He turned toward Kaito, his amber eyes glittering with amusement.

"No one has ruled Akatsuki for five hundred years."

"I admit I overslept a bit," Kaito said, flashing razor-sharp canines at the oni.

"Do you think you're the first dragon to come here claiming to be the great dragon? Everyone knows he died five hundred years ago, and with him a unified Akatsuki."

"Oh? I guess I didn't get the message."

A smile curled the yokai's lips. "I let you come because I wanted to get a look at you. But you're no different than all the rest. Leave now before I take your display as a real threat." He waved his hand and turned his attention back to the game. The other oni had not sat down however.

"Your father would be ashamed to see you grow so lax," Kaito taunted.

He rose up this time, drawing his massive weapon as he did so. "You pretend to know my father? I should strike your head from your shoulders for that."

"Try," Kaito said, holding out his hands palm up.

The oni pulled back his blade and swung backward. Had it hit Kaito it would have sent him flying, but the weapon was overlarge and bulky and he had plenty of time to dodge before it struck.

It collided with a nearby pillar, splintering it as he pulled it out. He stalked closer toward Kaito, who was dancing just outside of his reach.

"You're much slower than your father, perhaps it's that massive blade."

"Are you saying I cannot wield Tetsuyama?"

Kaito laughed. "That is not Tetsuyama." He remembered clearly the blade his friend had wielded, more an extension of himself than anything else. This blunt object was not that legendary sword.

"Do not waste my time. I grow weary of it." He swung his massive sword once more and Kaito dodged it again.

The son was a capable fighter, but with a sword whose only benefit was brute strength he was no match for his father's skill.

"What happened to his sword?" Kaito taunted as he continued to dance just outside his reach.

The oni was chasing after him, swinging his too heavy blade and destroying his own hall, without landing a strike upon Kaito. His men stomped their feet and cheered for their leader. But it was no use,

Kaito came up behind him and placed a quick hit to the back of his neck.

The oni's knees crumpled beneath him as he fell to the floor and as he crashed dust burst up around him. Kaito stood over his defeated opponent with a hand on his hips.

The oni that had been circling around him closed in but before they could lay a hand on him, the leader rose up and held out his hand to halt them.

Tears welled up in his eyes. "It *is* you. You've returned from the dead."

Kaito walked over, offering a hand to the son of the man he had known so well.

"I am and I have a request to make of you."

IN THE TYPICAL ONI STYLE, TALKS WERE DONE OVER DRINKS AND A MEAL. ONI brought out massive platters of whole roasted deer, mounds of rice, and miles and miles of side dishes. The oni ate greedily, grasping with their hands. The sake was poured from large jugs and the oni drank deeply, getting louder as the drinks flowed.

Kaito sat beside the leader of the oni, Katsumi.

"My father would have been so happy to see you returned to your place. He spoke highly of you," he said, wrapping his arm around Kaito's shoulder. There were still a few stray tears in his eyes. He was so much like his father.

"Your father was a good man." Kaito held up his sake to cheer with the younger oni.

"An even better fighter," said another yokai, continuing the cheers. They all drank.

"A superb leader," said another.

They drank again. There were several more rounds of drinking, and Kaito was starting to feel the effects of the drinks upon him.

"I never thought he'd fall in battle. It wasn't until that bastard came around," the oni said, slamming his fist onto the table.

"Who was it that he fought? Akio? Goro? Shinobi?" Kaito asked.

The man nodded his head. "A half-breed."

Kaito tilted his head. "Your father was killed by a half-breed?"

The man puffed up his chest, as if he needed to defend the honor of the dead. "He wasn't just any hanyou. He was unnatural. They say he had control of both human and yokai ancestry. It was said he could take any shape he wished and wielded spiritual power as a priest. He was something the likes of which we've never seen before."

"How long has it been since your father has fallen?"

The yokai lord had tears rolling down his face. "It has been almost two hundred years now." He dissolved into tears and large drops poured out of him. Kaito patted his back, trying to give him comfort.

"There was no fighter who rivaled your father and with Tetsuyama in his hand, he was unstoppable. How did this happen?"

"It was a trap. That bastard made us believe you'd woken again, my father went to you. And when he arrived he was slain. He took Tetsuyama!" he howled and pounded his fists onto the table.

What would a half-breed want with a yokai sword? And he had taken Kaito's image. If he ever found the man, he'd gut him for the offense but that was a concern for a later time.

Kaito stood up to face the crowd around him. "You have suffered loss, but I am here to tell you I am going to bring back Akatsuki to its former glory. I will find the bastard who took Testsuyama and bring it back home!"

There were cheers all around as the oni stomped their feet.

SEVENTEEN

Light had just barely started to filter through the cracks in her door when Suzume was awoken by the sound of footsteps approaching her. She laid immobile on her futon, her eyes screwed shut while her fingers inched toward the staff she left hidden under her blankets. A hand came down on her shoulder and Suzume bolted upright, parrying her staff toward her attacker. A frightened maid stumbled backward, knocking over a tray of tea and cakes that she had set down not far from Suzume's bed. The tea spill spread across the floor.

Suzume lowered her staff, but not entirely. She'd already been tricked by one maid. There was no telling if this was just another yokai in disguise.

"What are you doing here?"

"My lady, I brought you breakfast," she stuttered and hurriedly put herself into a kneeling position on the floor.

Her entire body was shaking, so either she was an expert of disguise or Suzume had truly terrified her.

The spilled tea spread out soaking what had been her breakfast. It dawned on Suzume that this was exactly as it appeared. The woman had only brought her breakfast as was her duty, not everyone was out to kill or kidnap her.

Suzume lowered her weapon to her side.

"Don't sneak up on me like that," she said and turned away from the servant, too embarrassed to admit she'd forgotten what it was like to live in the palace. She'd grown accustomed to fighting for her life. That, coupled with the recent attack, had left her on edge.

The servant cleaned up the spill, and the only sound in the room was the chink of the china as she scooped it off the floor.

"Am I interrupting something?" Suzume turned around to see Ryuu standing in the middle of her room. Once more she was much too underdressed to be receiving guests.

"What are you doing here?" she snapped.

"We have training, or have you forgotten already?"

Suzume flushed. She hadn't forgotten, in fact she'd spent a restless night thinking about how she was going to slip his notice.

"You didn't have to come and remind me," she snapped back at him.

He smirked at her and there was something familiar about that smile. "Well, I'll leave you to get dressed then and we shall head to the temple together."

The prospect of journeying to the temple with him was less than pleasant, but she knew there was no room for argument. She had to play the emperor's game if she wanted to free her friends.

The servant returned, noticeably shaken and Suzume did her best to try and be kind to her. But it felt as if gentleness was a trait she would always lack. Her clothes were not the opulent multi-layered style of a court lady, but something closer to what she'd worn as a priest—a hakama and hoari in muted grays. When the clothes were on she felt the most at ease she had felt since she'd returned to the palace. *I can move in these clothes.*

Ryuu escorted her out, and the halls were empty but for a few servants bustling about. No one would be out and about until much later. Suzume didn't notice the palanquin waiting for them. It had been such a long time since she had ridden in one that it did not even occur to her that she would ride in one now.

"Where are you going?" Ryuu asked as he stood by the open door of the palanquin.

"To the temple." She gestured to the distant outline of the temple on the horizon.

"It's much too far to walk." He pointed to the palanquin.

"Of course." She coughed, realizing too late her mistake as she hurriedly got into the palanquin and took her seat beside Ryuu.

The ride there was uncomfortable to say the least. Ryuu's presence seemed to fill the space and whenever she tried to avert her gaze, her eyes were constantly drawn back to him. There was something about him that was almost familiar and strange at the same time. As if she'd known him her entire life but she'd only just met him. She'd never seen him before and yet he moved about the palace as if he'd always been there. She still hadn't ruled out the possibility that he was working with Hisato. It could not just be a coincidence that twice he'd been nearby to rescue her from potential kidnapping.

"Why have I never seen you around the palace before and yet now you're everywhere."

He raised his eyebrows in question. "I've kept mostly to the temple. And other places. I do not care for politics."

"But now you do?"

"Things have changed," he said without elaborating. Suzume frowned. She knew asking him more would yield no results.

When they arrived at the temple, the sun was just starting to peek out over the horizon. It bathed the buildings in a yellow glow.

A group of priests were waiting for them as they pulled up. An ancient man with a long beard stood at the front of the group. They were all dressed in the same way Hikaru, then known as Makato, had been when they'd first met. The thought filled her with shame. As far as she knew, he was still locked in the prison, hopefully alive. She dashed the thought away. She would save him.

Ryuu climbed out of the palanquin first and then Suzume followed right after. The group of warrior priests bowed to her as she approached.

"We have been waiting for you, princess," said the Head Priest once he raised his head. "I am The Head Priest and you've met my second,

Ryuu."

"It is a pleasure to meet you," Suzume said, affecting the tone she would have had if she'd been greeting a royal official.

The priest seemed pleased by this and gestured for her to go up the stairs. She walked beside the Head Priest, Ryuu, and the others just behind them. Though the priest was old, he climbed the steps with ease. While Suzume was trying not to visibly pant as the stairs became steeper toward the top.

The priest prattled on, "You will be coming here several times a week. We hope to help you master your powers and better harness them. I hear you have a lot of raw power." The priest gave her a sly smile.

Suzume distracted by trying to breathe panted, "Uh, yes."

They reached the top of the steps, onto a large compound of buildings. In the center courtyard was a large gingko tree. Its enormous branches spread outward and cast shade over much of the courtyard. Priests in identical uniforms walked back and forth about their duties.

Though she had not spent long at the mountain shrine, the place had the same feeling of quiet, overall stifled control. She wasn't sure she was going to fit in here.

"Ryuu will be in charge of your training, but I shall check on you from time to time." The old man bowed and left her alone with Ryuu before she could even voice a protest.

"Shall we?" Ryuu said.

"Does it have to be you?" she asked, arms crossed over her chest.

He laughed. "I'm afraid so. Emperor's orders, remember?"

"Let's get this over with then," she said, strutting forward. She went a few steps before realizing she had no idea where she was going.

Ryuu was already at her side. "That eager, I see."

She glared in reply.

Ryuu led her across the courtyard toward a secluded area of the compound. Here the sounds of clashing wooden weapons and the grunts of men sparring filled the air. This was not a place of quiet reflection, but a battleground. Idle priests gathered around a sparring two, who were fighting bare-handed using a complicated series of moves to disarm the other.

They watched as one man pinned another to the ground. When the match was called the winner helped the loser stand up much to the cheering and condolences of his comrades.

Ryuu had disappeared during the fight but returned with a wooden sword which he threw at Suzume.

She caught it after a quick fumble.

"What's this for?"

"I want to see what you're capable of."

Despite her hopes that with the previous fight done the crowd would disperse, the men remained gathered around. Suzume felt their eyes on her and thinking about her own limited ability with fighting, she feared making a complete fool of herself.

"I don't fight with a sword. I use my staff." She gestured to the staff strapped to her back.

"The staff has greater reach than a sword. I want you on equal ground with your opponent."

"What opponent?" She squawked. He wasn't going to spar with her, was he? She could already imagine the rumors that would fly if she was flattened by Ryuu.

Just holding the wooden sword felt awkward. There was no way she could beat him with it.

"Haruto," Ryuu called out to the group of men hanging around. One scrawny young man stepped forward. He had the barest hint of fuzz on his upper lip. He couldn't be older than Suzume, and he might be even younger.

"I want you to fight him."

"She's a girl," the youth complained.

Suzume shot him a dirty look.

"Are you insinuating it would be embarrassing to be beaten by a girl? Or were you thinking of holding back because of her gender?"

The young man stared at the ground while his companions snickered behind him.

"Why don't you spar with her first and then we'll see who's the more capable fighter."

Suzume glared at Ryuu. He'd just set her up. Now this young man would be determined to beat her. It wasn't like it was going to be hard. She'd never won a sparring match, ever. She had to get out of this.

"You want me to fight a little boy?" she asked.

"I'm a man," he said as his voice cracked, making him look even more juvenile.

"Don't worry about getting hurt. It's just sparring," Ryuu countered.

She glared at him but couldn't think of a way to wiggle out of this situation without taking a blow to her pride. At least if she fought him she'd have a chance of winning. *I've fought yokai that could snap him like a twig.*

Now that she was fired up, Suzume took her position facing the man but she could not find a comfortable way to hold the wooden sword.

"Wait." Ryuu came up and gently pushed her hands into place and turned her shoulders slightly.

"I know my form is not perfect. I don't fight with a sword, remember?" she said, stopping his critiques before they happened.

"Your form could be improved, but overall it seems like you have the basics." Then to her surprise he went to the young man and made adjustments to his grip and stance.

She blinked after him. Kaito or Tsuki had always criticized her lack of ability. But here it seemed she wasn't the only one who wasn't perfect.

Ryuu stepped back and the skirmish began. The two circled one another. Suzume found herself running through all of Tsuki's teaching, and what she'd learned from fighting yokai. The young man moved quickly but his swing was slow. His first blow hit her hard on the arm and she almost dropped her sword.

But when he came in and swung at her in the exact same way as before, she was able to anticipate his blow and countered. She tried her own offensive move but found it missed the mark. The next couple minutes was a lot of trial and error. She struck, he struck. It was like dancing in slow motion. But she could also see he was getting tired. His movements were slower, sloppier. Though her breathing was heavy, she found that she could still move with some agility.

When one of his too slow swings came toward her, Suzume struck his forearm. He yelped and dropped his weapon to the ground. He grasped his arm, while his friends hissed or jeered at him.

Suzume stood staring at the wooden sword on the ground for several minutes.

"I did it," she said, gasping. Sweat was rolling down her face. She'd sparred countless times with Tsuki and she'd never been able to disarm him or make any progress at all. She'd never felt so powerful before.

The young man's friends merged around him, giving condolences and teasing.

Ryuu stepped up. "You've lost. Show your respect," he said to the young man.

He grudgingly bowed his head before he and his friends scurried away.

"Your form needs work, and you're too quick to attack. You should watch your opponent first."

"I won, didn't I?"

Ryuu handed her a cup of water in response. At first she considered refusing it but she was too thirsty to really consider it. She gulped it down and came up gasping for air. Ryuu watched her silently all the while.

"You won because they are untrained, just as you are."

"I'm not untrained." Well sort of trained. Up until now she'd only ever fought against yokai.

"You've got the advantage of experience but you lack discipline. That's the sort of thing that will get you killed."

Suzume sipped on her water and peered at him from the corner of her eye. Was he trying to make her angry? All the excitement from winning her match had been deflated.

"I think we've done enough training for today," Ryuu said.

Suzume leaped up. She didn't have to be told twice. "Great." She headed for the exit.

"I can show you out."

"No, I know the way." She waved at him as she casually strolled toward the exit. She waited to make sure he was gone before making a sharp turn to investigate the temple grounds. It was likely she wouldn't find anything at all, but who knew when this sort of opportunity would come up again.

She skimmed around buildings and down a corridor. *Now if I was going to keep yokai trapped in stones, where would I store them?*

As Suzume searched she felt something—a distant tingle on the back of her neck, as if an invisible hand was guiding her. She decided to follow her gut and found a room. The door wasn't locked but a barrier shimmered around it. This had to be it. She held her breath as she passed through the barrier.

Inside was not her friends as she had hoped, but the neko who'd tried to kidnap her.

Eighteen

Suzume drew her weapon and stood in a defensive position, her staff across her body. The yokai was lounging on the futon in the middle of the room, his eyes half closed, as he casually glanced over his shoulder in her direction.

"Put that down, girl, before you hurt yourself," the neko said with a bored drawl. He closed his eyes before laying back down on the futon.

"What are you doing here?"

"Trying to sleep. If you don't mind someone burned me badly recently and I need to recover." He peered at her through one narrowed, golden eye. He might pretend to be relaxed but Suzume could feel his spiritual energy uncoiling from him. It reacted with her own fire which crackled in her defense.

"I meant what are you doing here in the temple? How did a yokai enter this place?"

The neko sighed in exasperation and sat up to face her, his paw-like hands placed on his knees. Bare patches of pink skin healed around his eyes where she had burned him.

"You're the one snooping in my master's room. Perhaps I should be the one asking the questions."

He stood up, his body elongating in an exaggerated stretch. Suzume made a quick glance toward the door. She could make a run for it but that would also mean leaving her back exposed to a potential enemy—one she'd only just barely managed to escape the last time.

"Don't come close or I'll burn you again." Suzume held up her flaming hand in warning.

The neko chuckled. "The only reason I let you burn me the first time was because Ryuu ordered it."

The neko stalked closer and the flames rose up along Suzume's flesh, Kazue's defense coming to her aid. But she didn't run away. The neko's words had intrigued her.

"Ryuu ordered you?" she asked. *I knew there was something suspicious about him.*

"You ask too many questions." He extended his claws in a threatening manner. Suzume backed up and held up her staff.

"Stay back."

The neko only smiled as he lunged for her. Suzume swung her staff upward, catching the cat yokai on the chin. It knocked him backward and she took her chance to head for the door. But when she spun around to escape, she found the doorway filled.

"Why am I not surprised to find you here," Ryuu said. He did not approach her, nor did he move from the doorway.

"The girl came sneaking into your room, master," the neko said.

"And she got in because you were napping."

The neko flicked his double blue, flame-tipped tails behind his back, not answering his master's inquiry.

Suzume held her staff up as if the thin piece of wood would be enough to defend her. She had seen him fight, and even if she had beat that warrior priest in training, she doubted she was any match for the master. She was the mouse caught in their trap.

She did the only logical thing she could think to do. Confront him. "You tried to kidnap me!" She pointed at him with her staff.

"That's not how I would put it," Ryuu said, his blue eyes raking over her body.

"Then maybe it was attempted murder." She hated the way his gaze seemed to pierce right through her, as if he knew exactly what she was thinking and he was already five steps ahead.

"I'm not your enemy, Suzume," Ryuu said as he held his hand out to her like she was a wild animal he was trying to tame. And a part of her felt like a cornered beast. Her heart was racing and the flame churned in her gut, begging her to unleash it, to burn her way out of here.

"Like I'm going to believe that when your pet tried to murder me."

"I'm no pet," the neko hissed and leaned toward her. She swiveled in his direction, thrusting her burning staff toward him as a warning to stay back.

The neko stood back, his cat ears turned backward and his tails twitching even faster behind him.

The combination of yokai energy and Ryuu's immense spiritual presence was too much for her and she felt her own fear rising, along with the power inside her growing to protect her from the threat. *Not now. I will not lose control.* Her power was not willing to listen to her orders, and unfortunately sparks danced along her skin and the panic only grew.

"I sent him to rescue you," Ryuu said.

Suzume, distracted by her powers going haywire, looked at him in confusion. That was a first.

"Rescue me from what? You were the one attacking me!"

"You need to leave the palace."

"I don't know if you've forgotten, but you were the one who captured me and my friends." She threw her arms out. Had this man lost his mind or did he really have two different personalities?

"It was the only way I could protect you from him."

"Him who..." Suzume asked slowly.

"The emperor." Ryuu's words seemed to ring out through the room. She'd suspected her father was a danger to her from the beginning, but even if that was true Ryuu was still behind the attack at the onsen and here at the palace. She wasn't about to believe him either.

She forced a laugh. "What danger could the emperor hold against me?"

"I think you already know."

Suzume searched his expression, searching for any small hint of his intention. "You serve the emperor."

The neko's laughter broke the tense silence.

Ryuu shot him a look, real anger on his face. It was a peek behind the mask. She'd hit close to home, she suspected.

The neko's laughter died away and Suzume smiled, deciding now was her chance to stress the point.

"What are you really planning? Who do you work for?" She'd already deduced he wasn't Hisato, but perhaps he was one of his allies.

"I have no designs for the throne or the responsibility of ruling if that's what you're asking."

"But you're trying to tell me my own father has some sort of plan to hurt me?"

The neko chortled and Suzume resisted the urge to glare at him. Instead she glared at Ryuu. Back in the palace garden, he had been talking with her mother's allies. He was searching for Izume.

Ryuu turned his back to her and peeked his head out the door before turning back inside. "You should leave this place before the others see you here."

"I'm not going anywhere until you answer me," Suzume said, digging in her heels even as he started tugging her toward the door.

The yokai came up behind her and gave her a shove. Suzume spun around and threatened to slap the neko with a flaming hand.

"Maybe I didn't burn you bad enough the first time?" she growled.

The neko appeared unamused and flexed his clawed hand. "If you'd like to try a real fight, I'd be happy to oblige," he said. His eyes shifted in color and his body grew in size. Thick patches of hair grew all over his body, and his front teeth elongated.

"Enough," Ryuu snapped. There were a pop and a puff of smoke and where the neko had been was now just an ordinary cat. Suzume was so stunned that she forgot for a moment that Ryuu was trying to shove her out the door without answering her questions. The cat glared at the pair of them, his tail twitching back and forth in agitation.

"How did you do that?" Suzume asked.

Ryuu sighed as he pinched the bridge of his nose. "We are bonded. I hate doing that to him. He's going to give me hell for this," Ryuu said. The cat knocked over a sword propped against the nearby wall, and then jumped onto the nearest dresser and proceeded to knock everything onto the ground. The sounds of shattering objects filled the room.

Ryuu turned away from them as if it did not matter at all. She had so many questions about bonding. Thinking back to how she had commanded Kaito to stay away made her curious. Was the command permanent? Were they forced to listen? But she wasn't about to ask Ryuu that.

Suzume shook her head. "What is my father planning? Can't you tell me that?"

"You're woefully stubborn," he sighed and crossed his arms over his chest. His eyes flickered to the cat who was tearing apart the room. Perhaps it was because the dragon had been at the top of her mind, but his posture reminded her of Kaito when she was being stubborn. *Now is not the time to think about him.*

"I've been told that before."

The cat knocked over a large painted vase and pieces of ceramic shattered onto the ground. The cat had perched on the highest ledge in the room and stared down at the pair of them scornfully. Ryuu looked at the shattered pieces before turning to Suzume once more. "He wants to use your power for himself."

She scoffed. "I know. He's asked me already."

Ryuu shook his head. "Not in the way you think."

"Then how?" She rolled her eyes. It sounded like he had his own plans.

"I cannot answer that here." He glanced over his shoulder as if he expected someone to interrupt them at any moment.

She rolled her eyes. "Clever, and I should just leave the palace with you and you'll answer all my questions then."

He grabbed her by both shoulders, shocking her and for a stunned moment she stared up into his face. "This isn't a game. You are in real danger."

Suzume felt a cold chill run down her spine but she wasn't going to fall for his tricks. She knocked his hands aside.

"I've heard that before."

He shook his head as he grabbed her by the upper arm and pulled her out the door.

She fought against him to no avail. He seemed impervious to her flames. He ushered her out into the hall and slammed the door shut behind them. As if being out in public would silence her.

"Do you think I'm going to let this go just because we're in the hall?" she asked.

Just then a pair of priests came walking toward them—the Head Priest and to Suzume's surprise, Hikaru, who walked behind him like a dark shadow.

Ryuu bowed his head to the Head Priest, who stopped in front of them smiling.

"I hope your training is going well," he said to Suzume, smiling.

"Great," Suzume said distractedly as she tried to ask Hikaru with her eyes how exactly he'd gotten free.

Hikaru gave a small shake of his head, telling her to not make a scene.

"She was just leaving," Ryuu said, and gestured for Suzume to walk before him. She ignored his cue and said to the Head Priest, "I was hoping I could get a tour of the temple grounds." She smiled.

"I can do that, princess," Ryuu said.

"The emperor has requested an audience with you," the Head Priest said to Ryuu.

"But I am to protect the princess." Ryuu nodded toward Suzume who could hardly hold in her disdain.

The old priest waved away his concern. "There will be no attacks here on the temple ground."

The old man smiled at Suzume in a way that was likely meant to be reassuring. Then he said to Hikaru, "Show the princess around, would you?"

Hikaru bowed deeply to the Head Priest. "This way," he said, gesturing with his arm for Suzume to join him before Ryuu could give further protest.

Suzume didn't even give him a further glance as she followed Hikaru out of sight. She tried to keep her face calm, and pretend as if they were perfect strangers.

Once they were out of earshot and sight, Suzume pulled Hikaru aside. "How did you break free?"

"The emperor let me go in exchange for helping him stop Hisato." He looked around, just in case anyone was eavesdropping. "But I am forbidden from leaving the palace grounds."

"What about the others?"

"They're not here. I don't know where the emperor has taken them."

"Then he is really using me for my power."

Hikaru placed his hand on her shoulder. "There's something not right going on here. I'm trying to learn more."

Which reminded Suzume. "Ryuu is keeping a yokai in his rooms!"

"What? Are you sure?" He seemed nervous, like there was something he wasn't telling her.

"I just saw it with my own eyes."

Hikaru frowned as he considered her words.

"What do you know about Ryuu?" Suzume pressed. Surely there was something she could learn about him.

He hesitated before answering. "He's powerful, and he's been away from the palace for a long time..."

Footsteps approached and their conversation was cut short. There were no more chances to conspire together. As they toured the temple grounds, Hikaru droned on about the history of the place and the fortifications which were designed to keep yokai out. It wasn't until the end of the tour that Hikaru could say one last thing.

"I've been trying to get access to the temple records, find out who brought me here. But I'm being watched. If we can find those records maybe we can figure out how we ended up this way."

And figure out who was working with Hisato.

"Don't worry. I have a plan."

NINETEEN

The White Palace kept meticulous records—every birth, death, marriage, and likely each grain of rice the country produced was written down and stored in the archives. There were many scholars who kept the records on more things than Suzume could wrap her mind around. Her position at court had never required her to care or be interested. She'd met her fair share of scholars, mostly a string of learned men who taught her younger brother everything a young noble would need to learn. She'd never bothered to visit the records room before and only had the vaguest idea where it was. But Hikaru seemed to think there were answers there.

As she was hurrying out the door, having just finished dressing, she almost collided with Ryuu who was waiting outside.

He bowed to her. "Good morning, Lady Suzume."

Was he really going to pretend yesterday hadn't happened? She had a few choice remarks to make to him if that was the case. But as he straightened and met her gaze, he made the slightest shake of his head. Suzume glanced back at her maid who was standing just behind her, head bowed. *Is my maid a spy? Or is he using her as an excuse to not talk about it?* Given her position at court, she decided to keep her mouth shut.

She tossed her hair and headed down the hall. She'd forgotten the emperor had ordered Ryuu to follow her. It would make her errand a little more difficult. As she marched along, she started to formulate a plan.

The records room was actually just outside the main palace building. But since Ryuu was shadowing her, she had no trouble getting out of the main palace this time. Ryuu didn't question her or try to stop her from going where she willed. It was easy to pretend he wasn't there at all.

The records room was a small building without much adornment. While the rest of the palace slept, the scholars who maintained the records were already busy at work. They hurried past Suzume and Ryuu, arms overladen with scrolls and stacks of documents. They didn't even bother to glance their way.

Inside the building an ancient old man was sitting at a table, a sheet of paper covered in tiny cramped writing in front of him. His fingertips were stained black and his beard was trimmed neatly but it still brushed against the paper which he was bent over writing on.

Suzume approached the old man. "Excuse me," she said in a tone that was meant to be polite.

But the man did not seem to hear her. He dipped his pen into the ink and then continued to write.

She cleared her throat delicately, hoping he would catch the hint.

The old man continued on, oblivious. Suzume, losing her patience, slammed her hand down on the table. Startled by the sound, the man made a dark slash across his document.

"Look what you've done!" he shouted as he stood. "Now I will have to start all over." He did not lift his gaze from the ruined document.

Suzume glared at him with hands on hips.

"The emperor sent me to speak with you," Suzume lied.

"What is it, boy? I'm very busy."

Suzume blushed and couldn't help but peer in Ryuu's direction. There was a faint hint of a smile on his face. She was fortunate he didn't expose her lies.

Suzume sputtered in embarrassment. She could admit she wasn't at her best lately but to call her a boy! "I am not a boy. If you would look at me that would be clear!" she snapped, just barely holding back some choice insults of her own.

The old man lifted his head for the first time, his dark eyes scanning her up and down before returning to his parchment. "So you're not. This is no place for a woman, be gone with you."

Suzume growled low in her throat before taking a few calming breaths. Perhaps that's why Ryuu hadn't stopped her from coming here. Maybe he knew the head scholar wouldn't want to let her in. Well, she had a trick left up her sleeve.

Suzume jutted out her seal in front of the old man's nose, forcing him to look at it. As his eyes rested on the emperor's seal, they grew wide.

He dropped the ruined paper which fluttered onto the desk and he bowed deeply to Suzume. "How can I help you, my lady?" he said in a groveling tone.

That's more like it. Suzume preened.

"I would like to see the records."

The old man continued to stare at his feet. "Which records?"

"The ones that..." She trailed off. Hikaru had not been very specific with his instructions and she didn't want Ryuu to know what she was up to either. "That is not for you to know. Show me the way and I will find what I am searching for."

"There are hundreds of years' worth of records in the archives of all kinds. If you are more specific I can direct you toward what you're looking for?"

Ryuu was watching her very intently now. She had to think quickly.

She covered her face with her hand as if she were embarrassed, and gestured for the old man to come closer.

"You see, there's this young man..." She let the old man fill in the blanks.

The old man glanced up at her and frowned, perhaps puzzling out the nature of her request. "This is not a place to flirt," the scholar said, presumably getting annoyed.

Ever the actress, Suzume made a distressed expression in Ryuu's direction. "I'm not here to flirt!" She turned away from the both of them and peeked from the corner of her eye at the old man and Ryuu. The old man appeared to be very confused, but Ryuu was watching her, his expression impossible to read.

Suzume made a dramatic sigh. "There is a young man whose family genealogy I hoped to research," she said, meeting the old man's gaze.

His eyes grew wide with understanding of her fake request. He coughed, his eyes averted. "Of course. As you wish, my lady." Then he turned quickly to his left. "Akihito, show her to the hall of genealogy." A young acolyte who Suzume had not seen before leaped up from his desk at the far side of the room. There was a smear of ink on his cheek that didn't quite hide the pockmarked skin of his age. He wouldn't meet her gaze as he gestured for her to follow him down a long hall.

Ryuu motioned to follow her, but she turned around to face him. "I'll be safe enough with Akihito."

The youth blushed crimson. Ryuu did not seem amused by the notion. "I am to guard you at all times."

"It's just down the hall, and if I get a papercut I'll be sure to shout for you."

They stared at one another for a moment, neither willing to budge, before Ryuu nodded his head in consent. "I'll be waiting here."

The threat was plain enough in his posture. There would be no chance for an escape. The acolyte led her down a hall lined with doors. There were markings on each door to indicate what was within. She passed by the door to the temple records, but she didn't get a chance to linger long beside it before the acolyte was opening the door to the genealogy room. Inside, shelves reached up to the ceiling with stacks and stacks of bound paper.

Suzume's neck swiveled from one way to the other, gazing at all the paper.

"There's so much of it."

"Everyone who's ever lived and worked in the palace is recorded here," the young man said, his voice cracking.

He paused, likely embarrassed by his changing voice. Suzume pretended not to notice. "How does it all fit in here?"

The boy flushed. "To tell you the truth, we lost a lot in the fire seventeen years ago."

He pointed to a scorched shelf with papers whose edges were black and curled.

Suzume nodded. She'd remembered hearing about the fire but she'd been too young at the time to remember much about the actual event. They say it burned most of the main palace. This young man could not have even been born at that time.

After a few more minutes they stopped at a row of documents. "This is the royal genealogy," he said, motioning toward the papers.

Suzume picked up the closest one, it was perhaps a hundred years old. She flipped through the lists of names. It listed empresses and emperors, and from a quick glance she saw her mother's family name, Kaedemori, mentioned at least three different times throughout the generations.

The young man stood hovering nearby. She watched him from the corner of her eye. Could she trust him to get her to what she was really searching for?

Suzume strolled down the aisle, hand tracing over the faded dates on the spines of the documents. *Genealogy. I could have at least pretended to be looking for something a little more interesting.*

Since she was here, she decided to peruse for the year she was born. She skimmed backward from ancient years and the founding of the empire toward more recent years. But as she approached the year of her birth there was a five year gap. Files were missing. *Maybe I skipped them.* She went to the other side, but these were different records. She looked for the year of her birth and found the two years prior missing, as well as the year of her birth. *What is this?*

Suzume scanned three different rows. Every single document for the year of her birth was missing. There were archives missing in gaps ranging anywhere from ten to fifty years. But in every case the year after she was born, the documentation resumed. *Why is that year missing?*

"What caused the fire?" Suzume asked the acolyte.

He almost jumped out of his skin when she turned to face him and a blush burned up his face.

"I-i-it," he stuttered. She gave him an encouraging smile and he looked away from her and down at his feet before saying in a rush, "It was reported as an accident."

Suzume rolled her eyes. "I wouldn't have thought it was arson," Suzume said, taking a step closer to him.

She ran along a few more shelves and in every case, the year of her birth was gone. Could it be a coincidence? Or was there more to the story? The young man seemed very hesitant to talk about it. He was hiding something.

The young scholar was wringing his hands. She took a step toward him and his eyes shot up toward her. She leaned in close to his ear to whisper, "It isn't a nobleman I'm trying to learn more about." He visibly gulped. She had him right where she wanted him. "Can you help me?"

He nodded his head slowly.

"I need to see the temple records."

He stumbled back a step, his back slamming into a shelf which rocked dangerously. He spun around to balance the shelf, and as he had his back to her he said, "That's not possible. They're locked in that room." He gestured down the hall.

"You must know where the key is."

"Only the captain of the warrior priests has access."

Ryuu had the key. Why was she not surprised? She had to see those records. She doubted she could steal the key from him, not with a yokai protecting his room. And it wasn't as if she could just ask him for it. But one thing was for certain, the answer to why she was this way was within those documents. She just had to figure out how to find a way in.

TWENTY

Suzume picked at her breakfast, tearing apart the baked fish without bringing a morsel to her mouth. All this time in the palace and all she'd managed to do was to find out... well, nothing. Her friends remained imprisoned and with Ryuu guarding over her every move, she had trapped herself in a gilded cage. The answer to why she was this way was somewhere in the palace. She could feel it. If only she could figure out how to find it. Plus, there was the added concern of Hisato. She'd spent too many sleepless nights clutching her staff and waiting for an attack.

When the door to her chamber slid open, and footsteps came thundering in, Suzume leaped up to reach for her staff. She spun around to face the intruder, pointing her staff at the throat of a servant. He stared down at the end of her weapon with wide, terrified eyes.

Her replacement maid rushed in behind him and she too stared at Suzume as if she were a wild animal who had just barged into the palace.

"What are you doing here?"

The man swallowed past a lump in his throat. "A m-message." With shaking hands, he held out a letter.

Suzume lowered her weapon, realizing too late her overreaction. There was no use trying to cover it up and she kept her head held high.

"Well, read it," she said.

The man glanced around the room, to the scattered breakfast dishes that lay at her feet and then back to Suzume.

"It is from the emperor. I am not permitted to read it," he said in a shaking voice.

They were caught in a stalemate of sorts. She didn't want to lower her weapon, just in case, and he couldn't break court protocol. Since she already looked like a maniac, she said to her maid, "Bring the letter to me."

The maid very cautiously took the letter from his hands and brought it over to Suzume. She couldn't open it one-handed since she was still holding onto the staff with her right hand.

"Open it." She didn't like how imperious she sounded but she was too afraid to let go of her staff.

The maid bobbed her head and did as Suzume commanded, breaking the seal and holding up the open letter to Suzume. It all seemed a bit excessive, when the emperor could just as easily come and talk to her as he had before. Not that she was making it any easier by holding these two servants captive. She took the document from the woman's hand and read it over quickly.

'Come to the throne room.'

She stared at the letter, and sudden fear gripped her throat. Perhaps he'd tired of playing the doting father and he was about to imprison her.

There was only response she could give. "Tell him I shall be there within the hour."

"He said you are to come straight away." He seemed hesitant to tell her, as if he feared she would strike him with her staff if he did.

A knot twisted in her stomach.

"Is it something urgent?" she asked, her mouth felt very dry all of the sudden.

"The emperor did not tell me." The servant bowed in apology.

Her heart was pounding in her chest. "I'll be just a moment."

She turned and walked into her bedchamber, just out of view of the servant. Her staff was still held loosely in her hand. She paced back and forth a few moments. She only had to keep a cool head. Perhaps it was nothing at all. Or Ryuu had told the emperor he'd caught her snooping and she was going to be tried for treason. But if he wanted to imprison her, he would have sent a guard and not a servant with a message. Memories of her exile ran through her head and she found it difficult to breathe all of the sudden.

It took her a few minutes but she righted her nerves and walked out head held high. She left her staff behind, though her hands itched to feel its comforting weight. The servant seemed to have composed himself as well, or perhaps it was because she'd left the weapon behind. He escorted her to the audience hall.

A pair of guards stood outside the door, and as she approached they each reached to open one side of the double doors. The large audience chamber yawned open before her. It was by far one of the largest rooms in the main palace. It was filled with columns painted red and accented with gold. Normally the emperor met with his counselors and governors in this place. But today it was empty and eerily quiet.

Light poured in from windows along the edge of the ceiling, filling the space with alternating shafts of golden light and dark shadows. At the end of the room was a raised dais higher than Suzume's head with stairs leading up to it on either side. That was where the emperor sat.

Taking a calming breath, Suzume stepped into the throne room. As soon as she went through the double doors, they were slammed shut behind her. The sound echoed through the empty room. It took some convincing to guide her footsteps forward toward the dais.

As she got closer, she saw the emperor sitting atop his golden throne. At the foot of it, in the place where the council normally stood, Ryuu stood with his back toward her. Suzume kept her face blank of any expression and approached the throne, bowing deeply as was expected of her.

"Thank you for coming," the emperor said. His voice boomed with authority.

There was no doubt in her mind now that this was official business. She remained bowed low, and until the emperor gave his command she would not even so much as dare look at him. It was strange to think how much fear a mortal struck into her heart, when she'd faced far more dangerous yokai.

"My daughter, please rise," the emperor said in a softer tone.

Hearing his address, she was filled with relief and she raised her head. Ryuu remained one step in front of her, his back turned toward her and his head bowed.

"I brought you here to speak with you of grave matters that affect our kingdom." He paused, perhaps to let the weight of his words sink in. Suzume resisted the urge to fidget as the moment dragged out. "A threat has arisen that I think you are best suited to deal with."

From the moment she had agreed to work for the emperor, she'd feared this moment. But she couldn't leave the palace, not yet. Not when she hadn't learned anything, not when she hadn't freed her friends.

"Are you sure I'm ready?" she blurted without thinking. Her desire to stop the emperor overrode her better judgment.

"Ryuu has informed me you are more than capable," the emperor replied.

Suzume gave a sideways glance toward Ryuu. He did, did he? Was he trying to get her killed? Or was this part of his plot to get her out of the palace? Was that his plan then, get her away from the palace and the answers she sought?

"He is too kind, your majesty, but I think I would benefit from more training."

"You are strong and fierce like your mother. I have faith that you can complete this mission. Besides, you'll have Ryuu with you."

Further protests were on the tip of her tongue. But if she pushed back too hard, then the emperor might suspect her motives.

"I will do my best to serve you," she said mechanically, though there were a few other choice words she'd like to say instead.

"Is that what you think? That I only wish for you to serve me?" the emperor asked. His tone was sharp but not angry. It was almost sad. Suzume had been cautious of looking at him directly, but she chanced it now. His expression was hurt, almost sad. He looked down for a moment, and if she was a bit more naive she might think it was to pretend he was embarrassed. "I have not been a good father to you and for that I am sorry. If our need was not great, I would not ask."

"Why ask me at all? What can I possibly do for the empire?"

It was Ryuu who spoke. "You have more knowledge of yokai than most. You know their weaknesses and their strengths." His gaze almost challenged her to refute it.

She glared back at him and for a moment she considered exposing him to the emperor. But the emperor seemed to trust Ryuu's word. And accusing him might backfire and make her seem like the villain.

"There must be others, like the priest Makato. He is much more knowledgeable." She stared at Ryuu, challenging him without words. *I know you have something to do with Hikaru and me.*

The emperor stood and both Suzume and Ryuu fell into deep bows.

"Ryuu, leave us."

Ryuu stood up without a word and slipped out the back door. Suzume remained kneeling on the ground as the emperor walked down the steps from his high place and came to stand in front of her.

"You do not need to keep your eyes averted when we are alone," he said, in the voice of not a ruler but a father.

Suzume stood up and meeting her father's eyes, accepting the challenge of facing him as an equal.

"You have every reason to hate me. All your life I have shown only my cold and unfeeling side. But I did it to keep you safe."

Suzume suppressed the urge to roll her eyes. He'd ignored her up until now because he had no need of her until he realized what power she had. "I am sure you love all your children." She bowed her head to him, in an almost mocking way.

"I am sorry. I have done you and your mother wrong."

Just the mention of her mother brought back all the bad memories, the lifetime lived as second-rate, second best. She could not think of anything to say that was not embittered and instead she kept her mouth shut.

The emperor searched her face. "You do look so much like your mother."

Suzume couldn't stand to look at him and turned her head away. It was as much an insult as she could manage.

"I loved her, but circumstances made it that we were kept apart."

"I understand," she said. Love in the White Palace didn't exist. Perhaps it didn't exist at all. It was a pretty lie that people told to justify their selfish behavior. The allusion of love only made you miserable. Without meaning to, her own thoughts drifted to Kaito and she shoved the memories down.

"I would do anything to make up for the wrongs I've done you."

"Then let my friends go," she said without thinking, gazing into the emperor's eyes and daring him to deny her request. Because once he did, it would confirm everything she believed, that he did not really love her. That she was just a pawn in his game. She braced herself for his rejection.

"If that will please you, then I will grant you this request."

Suzume blinked a few times before she processed his words.

"What? Are you sure? But they're yokai."

The emperor smiled. "If you believe them to be trustworthy, then I am willing to put my faith in your judgment." He bowed his head slightly toward Suzume.

Her head was swimming. She didn't even have the awareness to thank him.

The emperor placed his hands on her shoulders. "All I ask for in return is you take on this mission. Protect our people."

Of course there was a price to pay, but she couldn't pass up this chance to help the others escape.

"As you wish." She bowed her head to the emperor.

The emperor smiled as he dropped his hands to his side. "I will let Ryuu fill you in on the details of your mission. Please bear in mind, you can tell no one of what you are about to do."

She bowed her head to indicate she understood. The emperor returned to his dais and then with a wave of his hand, Suzume was excused. She kept her gait steady as she headed for the door, but once she was past the guards she almost sprinted on her way back to her room. She'd done it, she'd set them free.

When she returned to her room, she found Ryuu standing in the entryway, facing the garden beyond open doors. All of her excitement drained out of her as she looked to her staff on the other side of the room. And Ryuu between the two of them.

He turned to face her. "I'm not here to fight you."

"Says the man who's trying to kidnap me. What did you have to tell the emperor to get me out of the palace?"

"I only told him the truth."

She crossed her arms over her chest but her eyes kept straying to her staff. "I'm sure."

"I will not force you to leave. But you have to know the longer you stay here the more dangerous it becomes for you."

She scoffed. "You're really scaring me."

"You should be. This isn't courtier games. You think of yourself as a spy, but I see right through you. I know you're trying to get to the temple records. But there are some things better left in the past." There was a dark shadow in his gaze, one that terrified Suzume more than she'd like to admit.

"What are you doing here? Are you trying to scare me?"

He shook his head. "I made a promise to protect you. And I'm doing what I said I would do."

It took all of her power not to let her shock show on her face. Perhaps he was working with Hisato, maybe not. But she was more certain than ever he was connected to everything that had happened to her.

"Who did you make that promise to?"

A small smile crossed his lips as he stalked over toward her.

Suzume backed away, hands held up in front of her. "If you try and touch me, I will burn you." Her hands sparked faintly.

He leaned in to whisper in her ear. "There are ears everywhere here. We will talk soon though."

He pulled away from her and in a loud clear voice said. "I shall meet you in the morning, come prepared. It's going to be a long journey."

He headed for the door, and as soon as he did her maid reappeared. Then her maid was a spy, but who did she report to? She shook her head. Ryuu was starting to get into her head. She had to keep her guard up before it was too late.

Twenty-One

Ryuu arrived at first morning light to escort her out of the palace. Suzume and the court at large were told she was going on a journey to the country estate of the emperor. It was a popular destination for relaxation, complete with hot springs or so she'd been told. Suzume had never been there before, and a part of her wished she was going there instead on this mysterious mission the emperor was sending her on. Ryuu was stiff and formal, nothing in his face gave away a hint of his subversion.

Ever since their last encounter Suzume had been wondering if her maid was listening in on her. So when she had offered to join Suzume on her trip, she had been adamant about not bringing her along. Ryuu was going to be supplying her replacement.

They entered the main courtyard, where servants were lined up prepared to see them off. A gilded palanquin prepared to whisk Suzume away. Her eyes didn't linger long on it, but on the people standing beside it. She had almost not recognized Rin with ebony hair and no fox ears, and in a maid's uniform. But when she saw Suzume she raised her head from a bow to give her a mischievous smile.

She realized the guards standing beside the palanquin door were Naoki and Tsuki. Suzume struggled to keep her face composed as she bowed her head, dipping into the palanquin.

Tsuki closed the door to the palanquin and grinned at her as he did so. "Good job," he said.

Suzume pressed a finger to her lips to indicate he should be silent. She wasn't sure if Ryuu was aware of the replacements or not. And she did not want it to complicate their freedom if that were the case.

Once Suzume was situated, Ryuu shouted, "Move out."

The palanquin was raised up and moved jerkily at first before falling into a steady cadence. Suzume kept the curtains drawn as they left the palace, fearing she would be too tempted to talk to her friends before it was safe to do so. It was early yet and with the days of terrible sleep and the rocking motion, Suzume found herself lulled to sleep.

She woke when they came to a sudden halt. She stretched and pushed the curtain back. Ryuu's back was to her, speaking with the soldiers who had escorted them this far. Suddenly, Tsuki's face filled the window as he crouched down beside her window.

"Have you gotten heavier since I was sealed? Because my back is killing me." He rolled his shoulder as if to work out a kink in his neck.

Suzume swiped at him playfully through the open window. She was too relieved to see them free and whole to really be mad.

"It's not too late to put you back in the stone," she said.

He chuckled, and for a moment, Akira's face came to the surface. "Thank you for freeing us."

Suzume smiled back at her, puffing her chest up with pride. She had been rather clever to trick the emperor into freeing them.

"It was nothing really."

Just then Ryuu approached and Tsuki leaped back up to his feet.

"You'll need to get out now, my lady," Ryuu said.

The door was opened and Ryuu held out his hand to help her stand, but Suzume snubbed his offer and climbed out on her own.

It appeared they'd come to some sort of port. There were several ships moored up against a pier. And a small city around them. People of all classes hurrying by, none even bothering to glance at the woman and the fancy palanquin.

"Where are we?" she asked.

"A port town not far from the palace. From here, we take the river to the coast."

Seeing the ships on the river made her stomach turn. She hadn't forgotten her last disastrous ride in a ship.

"You'll need to change. Your maid as well." Ryuu shoved a bundle of clothes toward Rin, who took them without comment.

"When are you going to tell me what's going on?" Suzume asked, hands on her hips.

Ryuu ignored her question in favor of going to speak with the men who were loitering about. She recognized a few from her training session at the temple. She wouldn't be surprised if they were all warrior priests. This wasn't the ideal situation; all of these people were Ryuu's men.

Rin nodded toward the palanquin where they both squeezed inside to change. The space was hardly big enough for the both of them and they had to take turns changing out of their clothes or one of them would put an elbow in the other one's eyes or stomach.

As Suzume struggled to free herself from the layers of kimono, Rin came behind her to help. Her hands moved with assurance and were rather gentle.

"Is Hikaru..." she left the question dangling, perhaps fearing the worst.

Suzume kept her voice low just in case someone was listening. "He's alive but is still a prisoner of sorts. He's serving at the temple, but he's forbidden from leaving."

Rin gave an audible sigh of relief.

"We'll get him out," Suzume promised.

The kitsune put her hands on both of Suzume's shoulders and squeezed. "You helped us get out. I believe you can save Hikaru."

The weight of her belief fell heavy on Suzume. She'd never had anyone believe in her before, but lately it seemed everyone was putting all their hopes on her. She shook her head. Better to not think too much about what that meant.

When they were finished changing, they both stepped out. They wore matching clothes—plain back hoari and hakama. The clothes were a tight fit, but not so much that it would be unseemly. The group was gathered at the edge of the pier, talking with what appeared to be a boat's captain and goods were being put onto the ship.

Ryuu saw them exit and came to greet them. "How do we know this thing is safe?" Suzume asked as she eyed the dingy.

"Are you afraid of a little ship?"

She lifted her chin in a haughty glance. "Of course not. Perhaps if you told me more about what your plans are and what it is they're carrying onto the boat." She nodded her head toward the barrels and boxes being transported onto the ship.

Ryuu watched the soldiers carrying the items on board. "Gifts for the governor of the southern town we are visiting."

Suzume rose a brow in question. "Is this a mission or a political envoy?"

"Both." He smiled faintly, but she wasn't going to fall for his bait.

"You and your 'maid' will have to pretend to be commoners as to not pose too many questions as we travel. At least until we arrive at our destination."

Suzume eyed him. Rin was staring at him as if she had questions for him as well. Perhaps they had talked before Suzume had joined the group. She would need to ask the kitsune about it when they were alone again. He gestured for them to go ahead onto the ship. Suzume eyed the boat dubiously, but she didn't want to lose face in front of Ryuu and marched onto the boat.

There was a single gangplank leading from the dock onto the boat, which wobbled unpleasantly as she crossed. And the moment she got onto the boat it swayed in a way that evoked memories of her near drowning. A boat passed by on its way out into open waters and the boat swayed even more. In a panic, she grabbed the sides, screwing her eyes shut and preparing for the whole thing to tip over.

When it didn't happen, she opened her eyes to see the sailors and warriors watching her with mockery in their eyes.

"If you need someone to hold onto, I'm here," Tsuki teased, coming to stand beside her.

"I can burn you. Maybe that will make me feel better."

He chuckled in response.

As the rest of the packages were loaded onto the boat, Suzume did her best to seem unaffected, keeping her head turned away and her posture upright, while inside she was screaming. She hated boats. She'd sworn she'd never get on one again. Why had she agreed to this damn mission? Oh, that's right, because she had wanted to free her friends.

The boat pushed off from the pier and it knocked against the dock several times, making terrifying thumping noises before they were into open water. Suzume clung onto the side, prepared for sea spray and rocking waves. But once they were in the current of the river, they glided forward gently, so slowly it was difficult to tell they were moving at all. It took a few minutes before Suzume felt confident enough to open her eyes and peer over the side. Water lapped against the side but the sound was more soothing than terrifying. Naoki, perhaps sensing her unease, came to stand silently at her side. At least someone was on her side.

"River boats are much smoother sailing," Naoki said, knowing without words her deep fear of boats.

She gave him a faint smile of thanks.

The boat was much too small to have private conversations with her friends, though she could see there were questions in their eyes. And Rin kept watching Ryuu, who stood at the front of the ship. Probably wondering what he'd done with her husband. She had questions for them too, namely how had they agreed to masquerade as part of the emperor's army. Suzume entertained herself by watching the country-side drift by. They slid by farms and farmers tilling in ankle-deep water as they harvested rice, backs bent.

They stopped to watch them go. Not with suspicion but smiling and waving. The sailors called out to friends, asking after their families. Suzume leaned over the edge of the boat. She'd been all over the coun-tryside now, but she'd never taken the time to appreciate the quiet beauty of it.

Tsuki leaned over the side of the boat but when he spoke in a hushed voice it was Akira. "That man, the one who freed us, he's the same one who sealed us isn't he?" she asked.

She couldn't take over control of the body she shared with her brother, not with so many people around. Suzume glanced over her shoulder toward Ryuu before nodding her head. "He is."

"First chance we get, we should escape," Akira said.

"But what about Hikaru?" Suzume said, voicing the concern before even Rin could.

Akira shrugged.

Rin who was nearby, scowled at Akira. "I am not leaving him behind," she said in a hiss.

Akira did not even bother to glance in Rin's direction. "That man is not human."

"I figured as much," Suzume replied, fighting the urge to look at Ryuu. It would only draw attention to them.

"He's not yokai either."

"What is he?" Suzume asked.

"A hanyou, a half yokai," she said.

Suzume did jerk her head backward to look at him this time. And when she did, Ryuu met her gaze as if he had known they were talking about him. Maybe he'd overheard their conversation.

She turned to the water again.

"We should talk more later," Suzume said.

Akira nodded her head, understanding without words that now was not a safe time to talk.

Someone at the front of the ship shouted and Suzume was knocked to the ground by Naoki, just as a shard of ice pierced through the sail of the ship and impaled onto the ground where Suzume had just been standing. A moment after that, a wave rose up rolling over the ship, drenching them all.

She struggled to lift up her head and see who was attacking. The clouds overhead had turned a dark, stormy gray where it had been a bright, sunny day before. The once calm river was rocking with enormous waves which were spilling over the sides of the ship.

"What was that?" Suzume shouted, but her voice was overpowered by the howl of the wind.

Lightning flashed in the sky, and Suzume caught a brief glimpse of a serpentine body flying through the sky. It couldn't be. *Kaito?*

"Everyone to your stations," Ryuu shouted, his voice barely a thread over the crash of the storm. Waves continued to wash over the ship's sides. "We've found the dragon who attacked the village."

TWENTY-TWO

The priests scattered to do as ordered while Suzume struggled to keep her feet beneath the rocking of the ship. Panic gripped her in that moment, not only as old fears of drowning surfaced, but as the horrible realization struck her. If she couldn't stop this, the priests might kill Kaito. Clinging to the side of the ship, Suzume dragged herself toward the front of the boat where Ryuu was shouting orders.

"You have to stop." She had to shout because the wind was howling so fiercely that she could barely hear herself speak.

"Stand down. We've got this," Ryuu said, not hearing what she had said.

Suzume tilted her head toward the sky, and she saw another flash of the serpentine body, blue scales flashing against the gray sky. How could she get a message to Kaito in time?

The priests were lining up, preparing to shoot holy arrows at Kaito. There was no use trying to convince them to stop. Suzume knew she had only one choice. The fire came hot and quick to her hands. The crackle of energy drew forth her power with ease. She went to the front of the ship, and concentrating all her power in her hands, she created a ball of flame. She took aim and shot the fire toward the dragon. Her aim, never very good, sailed past the dragon and fell in a large arc before it burst apart on the other side of the shore.

The dragon reeled away from her shot, which hadn't come close enough to actually strike him. At least it had gotten his attention. *It's me! Run away before it's too late.* She waved her arms up and down, trying to catch his attention.

But instead of turning the dragon away, it seemed to narrow in on her. Shards of ice came raining down from the sky, and she was saved from being impaled by Naoki lunging out of nowhere and taking her out of the pathway of the deadly projectiles. The ocean was getting rougher and the two of them tumbled backward as the ship rocked. Without warning something burst out from the river beside her. A second dragon rose up out of the water, spilling water on them as it joined the first in the sky.

"Prepare to fire," Ryuu's voice shouted.

Two dragons? Suzume didn't have time to think about what it meant. She had to stop them from killing Kaito.

The dragon rained ice from the sky, and hundreds of projectiles pierced the ground. One unlucky priest was struck in the head and fell to the floor of the ship bleeding.

"Fire!" Ryuu shouted. The remaining priests did not even have time to take care of their fallen comrade. A barrage of projectiles were shot into the air toward the dragons.

The dragons seemed unafraid, dodging the arrows with ease as they weaved their way around their attacks and came in closer to send another counter-attack. A barrage of ice washed over the ship, crusting everything over in ice.

Suzume shivered at the feeling of the cold and the immense spiritual pressure from the dragons drew closer. She felt the fire inside her grow stronger. Using her flames had only awakened her thirst and knowing there was powerful yokai nearby only made the craving stronger.

Ryuu was guiding his men, pointing and shouting as they scurried to keep the boat on top of the water despite multiple attacks.

Suzume grabbed onto Naoki's arm. "Can I command him?" she shouted.

Naoki shook his head, either she couldn't do it or he couldn't hear what she was saying. She didn't know how the power of control worked, if the words needed to be heard or if her intention would do anything.

A cluster of priests took position in the middle of the ship and they started to sing. Their voices rose together as one. Their song wove together a barrier around their ship just moments before another deadly attack rained down upon them. Suzume could feel it shudder through the entire ship. Once the barrier was in place, everything went very still.

Outside the storm continued to rage, the water rocked their boat slightly, but the rain that had pelted them and even the crack of thunder was kept out by the barrier. The priests continued chanting their song. It was the only thing keeping the barrier in place. For a moment, she got lost in the song. The power reverberating from them drew her to them. She was stopped by Naoki's hand on her shoulder.

"I need everyone to take positions. We're going to have to take them out together," Ryuu roared to his soldiers.

The spell of power broken, Suzume seized her chance, and ran toward Ryuu once more. "You can't attack them. I know that dragon."

Ryuu looked at her as if she'd just sprouted another head. "They're trying to kill us."

"Just give me a chance to talk to him," she pleaded.

"Those monsters slaughtered a village." Ryuu pointed toward the sky. "We're not going to talk to them."

Suzume froze. Kaito wouldn't kill humans. There had to be some mistake.

"Listen, it couldn't have been him. He wouldn't have done that."

But Ryuu turned away from her, ignoring her pleas. He was no different than the others. She tilted her head up, searching for Kaito in the sky, but he was nowhere to be seen. Perhaps he was escaping, maybe not. But she couldn't risk the priests attacking.

She searched for her friends. She couldn't do this alone.

"We have to stop them," Suzume said.

"The only way we're stopping this is if we fight the priests," Rin said.

"If that's what it takes, that's what we'll have to do."

There was no hesitation in the eyes of her friends. But just then, there was a roar overhead. The dragons had not retreated as she had hoped. The archers drew their bows, they only awaited Ryuu's order.

"Lower the barrier," Ryuu shouted.

The rain pelted down upon them, decreasing visibility. Suzume gave the signal and a moment before the archers could loosen their bows, they launched their retaliation. Rin had transformed into her true kitsune form, her body almost too big for the tiny ship. She ran up to the priests who'd created the barrier and knocked them aside, scattering them.

Naoki and Tsuki attacked the archers, taking out a few of them before they turned and fumbled for swords. Suzume joined them, swinging her staff. The priests fought, not only with weapons, but with their spiritual powers as well. And as the energy flowed around her, try as she might to fight its influence, the fire inside her had been awoken and it pulled from the priests around her. She took their energy into herself, making her stronger until she hummed with power. Suzume's vision faded in and out, even as she fought. She had to struggle to remain conscious to maintain control over her body.

One of the dragons came close to the ship, knocking into the side, perhaps using the temporary chaos to its advantage. The boat tipped almost completely over. Several people were thrown from the ship, including Rin who was unable to keep her footing and she was thrown into the water.

The only thing that kept Suzume from falling was clinging onto the side railing. Her legs kicked in the air, before the ship righted itself once more.

Between the attack from within and the attack that continued from above, the entire ship was chaos. The priests picked their battles, fighting who they could. Suzume kept one ear toward the sky, prepared for the dragon's next attack as she plowed through her opponents, twirling and striking with abandon. Then from the front of the ship, Ryuu came toward her. His eyes were glowing blue, and she felt the power inside him.

He drew his blade. When it was at his side it appeared to be of normal size, but when they faced off it was horrifying and massive.

"Stop this madness," he said.

"I can't," she shouted.

The sparred together, his sword slicing through the air gracefully, and her attacks fumbled. His power wrapped around the pair of them and even her fire was no match for it. He simply outclassed her. He pushed her back, further and further toward the railing until he pinned her in place. Her arms shook as she tried to use her staff to hold him back. There was nowhere to go other than in the water and Suzume couldn't swim. His power was intoxicating and Suzume felt that swirling sensation, the out of body experience that meant she was losing control.

He swung his sword, which glimmered with inhuman light, ready to separate her head from her body and as he did, Kazue awoke inside her. Suzume slipped into darkness.

Kazue awoke in flame. Danger. Fire. The man before her swung his blade, but before he could land the killing blow she raised up her staff and blocked his attack. Their eyes met and his went wide.

She used his surprise to her advantage, pushing him backward and away from her. He stumbled. There was power around her, so many different streams of energy. It was all tugging at her to the point of madness. But her first task was to stop the attack. The man recovered from his initial surprise and rushed her once more. But it took only a few more strikes before he was on the ground again, the end of her staff pressed against his throat.

"Watch out!" he shouted.

Kazue would not have believed his warning had it not been for the intense spiritual energy she sensed behind her. She spun in place, moments before an icy projectile would have pierced her through her spine. She spun, slicing downwards and broke the ice in half. It clattered into pieces on each side of her.

Above her, a pair of dragons circled. The pair was writhing in and around one another, drawing closer every moment. She summoned the fire from within her. She brought forth all the power at her disposal, pulling from the spiritual energy of those around her, and even from the lightning cracking in the sky until she was vibrating with power. And then she unleashed it upon the creatures in front of her.

One of them managed to miss her attack, but the second was not so lucky. The flames caught the end of his tail, but once the fire caught it would continue to burn. It spread across his body, while he writhed to free himself of it. But there was no use fighting. The fire would consume him. He lost altitude after that, coming crashing into the ground on the shore nearby.

She gave only a quick glance in the direction of the burning monster as its pained screams filled the air. The second dragon, seeing its partner's fate, fled.

When Kazue turned, the man who had been fighting her stared at her with large blue eyes. She knew that gaze, though she could not say from where.

"Suzume?" he said, speaking an unfamiliar name.

"Who is Suzume? I'm Kazue."

The others left on the ship all gathered around, loosely holding their weapons. She held up her staff, prepared to defend herself. They closed in around her and Kazue reached for her spiritual energy, but found only flame which she had depleted to attack the dragon.

She turned to face them, her mouth opened to sing a song meant to drain them all. But as soon as she tried, a counter song was sung, one that bound her limbs to her side and froze her tongue in her mouth.

"Let her go," the man said as he approached her.

Kazue's gaze burned as she stared at him. Those eyes were so familiar and yet so foreign.

I know you, but how?

She fought against his spell, unbinding herself from the inside. He was approaching her, hand outstretched. And those eyes kept boring into her, with sadness. When he got close, she burst from the binding, striking at him, knocking him backward.

The others swarmed forward, trying to attack but with a wave her hand they were all knocked backward by the force of her power.

The pair of them faced off with one another.

"This body is not yours."

She circled him. His power rivaled her own, but how was that possible? No one had the power she had.

"Who are you?"

The man did not answer her question and instead shot something like an icy blast into her chest. Ice froze her from the inside, reaching down to the very core of her spiritual being. The blow sent her falling backward. She clutched her chest and everything she had been faded back into the dark abyss from where she had come from.

Twenty-Three

Ai poured the tea, assuming the role of hostess as if she were his wife already. The very idea put him in a foul mood, but now more than ever he needed to keep his wits about him. Ai had not lied when she said she had powerful allies. The two yokai who sat before him represented the best of their kind, and were true first children like Ai and himself.

The man had been a supplicant of the Lady of the Forest. And it showed, the Lady of the Forest had been known for her great beauty and all those who served her were beautiful as well. The man wore his hair very long; it brushed against the ground even when he was standing. Right now, as he sat across from Kaito, his hair pooled around him, and half of it was tied up. There were flowers woven into his locks, and his hoari was a deep forest green, embroidered with thousands of pink sakura blossoms so lifelike they looked like he had just been walking beneath a sakura tree and the blossoms had come to rest upon him. His face was androgynous. In fact, he was more beautiful than any woman Kaito had ever met.

The lady was the opposite, her face was all hard lines and a stern expression. Her hair was worn in a high ponytail on top of her head. Her arms, corded with muscles, were crossed over her chest, which was covered in armor embossed with the sun emblem. Like Naoki, she was one of the legendary warriors created by the Sun Emperor—the deity who ruled over all others. And like all of his warriors, scattered centuries before, she served a different master now. She served this last remnant of the Lady of the Forest's court. Kaito glanced them over, learning all of this without their need for explanation.

Ai finished pouring the tea, and took a seat beside Kaito. The lord sipped his tea, watching Kaito with dark eyes, while the warrior glugged hers down without taking a breath. It was to be expected of someone of her rank. Her eyes continued to scan the room, as if waiting for someone to leap out at any moment and attack them.

These sorts of negotiations had never been something Kaito relished in. When he'd controlled all of Akatsuki, he'd often left it to his trusted advisers. But there were none among the dragons he trusted enough to handle such a delicate situation. And if he left it to Ai, she would not negotiate in his favor.

"I'm glad to see the rumors that you were killed by a human woman were not true," the lord said as he sipped his tea. He gave Kaito a sly smile over the rim of his teacup.

Kaito had his measure right away, cunning and ruthless. He kept the legendary warrior to intimidate, but also to weave into the illusion that he was not powerful himself. If anything, this lord was stronger than the warrior. They were equal in strength he determined, or perhaps Kaito was a bit stronger. Not that it would ever come to blows between them. This creature would rather use his words rather than dirty his hands in a fight. Which would be the real reason he walked around with this muscle.

"Why did you draw us here?" the woman asked. Her hands were balled into fists at her side. Her distrust and rage reminded him painfully of Suzume, but he pushed down those thoughts.

"I thought my intent was clear. I plan to reunite Akatsuki."

"Many have tried, and all have failed. What makes you think you're special?" the man said, setting down his cup.

"I ruled Akatsuki before," Kaito said, flashing them a smile revealing his canines to let them know he meant business.

"With the support of the eight." The Lord glanced around the rundown chamber. Unfortunately, this was the best he had to offer for entertaining. "Given the circumstances, I fear it would be an almost impossible task."

"I do not need the eight to rule."

The lord's smile was slippery as an eel. "I was speaking of your long absence. How can the people of Akatsuki believe in a ruler who abandoned them to the mercy of humans?"

Kaito had to hold onto his anger. Once again, the humans were brought into the argument. From the corner of his eye, he felt Ai's gaze upon him.

He ignored Ai's knowing look and said, "I am not concerned with a few humans."

"They are no longer few, dragon," the lord said in a drawl. "They number in the thousands, and they grow more powerful with each generation. There are those with exceptional power who can purify us. I have not seen the like since their creation."

"It's because our kind has bred with them. They're more like that abomination!" the warrior said. She was holding so tight onto her teacup Kaito thought it would shatter to pieces in her hand.

"Please, do not get her started," the lord said with a heavy sigh. But he made no move to silence her.

"How can you let this go? Our kind have been hunted by him for centuries now. He killed all of my comrades!"

Kaito frowned at her statement. This was the second time he'd come across this same story. "Who is this half-breed?"

The woman was shaking with anger, her rage flared in her eyes like flickering flames. The legendary swordsmen were unrivaled in battle. He should know, he'd fought Naoki enough times. But unlike this warrior, Naoki was always in control of his emotions. Was this what it looked like when he lost control? He could only imagine how a powerful being unconstrained by rage might be on the battlefield.

"The rumors say he is the spawn of a powerful priestess and a dragon," the lord said, meeting Kaito's gaze, pinning him in place.

They couldn't know about the half-breed bastard Kazue had borne, very few knew of his existence. Was it possible his son had been the one causing havoc all this time?

"I saw him. He exuded yokai energy, but he purified yokai energy with spiritual power of a human. He had combined the power of both, and it made him unstoppable." She slammed her hand onto the table. "If you can find and kill that bastard, I would swear myself to you right here and now."

The lord's expression was unreadable. It was one thing for her to swear herself to Kaito, but it was another matter entirely for him to. And what was one legendary warrior? He needed an army.

"And what is your price?" Kaito asked him.

"You must know I have the backing of the Lady's subjects," he said, preening by brushing away imaginary dust from his clothing.

Kaito glared at him, impatient with these games.

"What would I want?" He tapped his chin in thought, though Kaito knew he'd had his price the moment he'd walked into this room. After an overlong, dramatic pause he said, "I want to rule the western provinces."

It wasn't unexpected. And it wasn't so high a price that he wouldn't pay. Without someone like this lord, he would never get control over the other warring clans. And yet Kaito hesitated.

Ai looked at Kaito with a pleased smile, perhaps sensing her triumph. She had brought him a powerful ally, just as she had promised. But it wasn't just his promise of marriage to her that kept him from making such an alliance. The western province was heavily populated by the humans and the White Palace was there. And if he was being honest, if it was Kazue's bastard that was causing this trouble, Kaito wasn't sure he could face him. Because he was certain now that was who had caused all this trouble in the first place. This fight meant going against two things he had hoped never to do, fight the humans and Kazue's son.

The man was watching him, assessing, and perhaps trying to have Kaito expose his weakness. He'd chosen this for the purpose of wounding him, just as he'd brought the warrior, to open old wounds. He could be a powerful ally. He needed someone cunning on his side. Someone who could sway people with words. But at what price?

Before he could form an answer, the door at the back of the room flew open and Jirou stormed in. Kaito rose up from his seat as his guest turned toward the interruption with a knowing smile. Kaito strode over to him, stopping him before he could make a scene.

"What are you doing here?" Kaito snarled at him, grabbing onto his shoulder and turning him away.

Jirou wriggled out of his grip, throwing his arms out. "There's been another attack," he said, not bothering to keep his voice down.

Kaito glanced back at his guests, before trying to direct his brother out of the room with a hand to his back.

"I will attend to it shortly."

"You should be dealing with it now! Our patrol went out and they were attacked by priests again. Arata was burned." His brother was seething. This was no play act, not anymore.

That caught Kaito's attention. "Burned?"

"A priestess among them had control of fire and she burned Arata. All he was doing was patrolling as you ordered."

Kaito balled his hands into fists. It couldn't be Suzume. It had to be Hisato's idea of a trick, trying to lure him out. *This is exactly why you need their help.* If he had an army at his back, Hisato could not stand against him.

"Tell the men to keep an eye out. We are not to engage."

Anger flashed in his brother's eyes. "Would you have us sit inside the palace like children and wait for them to come knocking on our door?"

Kaito grit his teeth, trying to keep his temper under control.

"I gave an order," he said through gritted teeth.

"You care more about humans than us."

Kaito lost control of his temper and punched him hard enough to send him sprawling on the ground.

His brother wiped blood away from his lip.

"Do not question me," Kaito snarled.

His brother rose to his feet, head bowed but hardly defeated. "If you won't protect our people I will." He left in a fury.

Kaito turned toward Ai. "Follow him. Keep him from doing anything stupid." She nodded her head and followed his brother down the hall.

For a moment, Kaito watched the pair of them go. If it was up to him, he'd go and chase his brother down to beat some sense into him. But he couldn't expose his weakness, not during these negotiations.

"Problem?" the lord asked.

"Nothing that I cannot handle." Kaito turned around with a forced smile.

"Your brother is right to be concerned! The attacks have been increasing. The humans are growing bolder all the time," the warrior said, half rising out of her seat as if she would go join Jirou in his revenge.

"So I've heard," Kaito said as he took a seat across from them. "Now I am willing to negotiate on territory lines. I will be ruler over all and if you wish to govern the west-"

"As leader of Akatsuki, it should be you who is squashing this insurgence," the lord said calmly. But Kaito saw the accusation in his eyes.

"I have things well at hand," he said past gritted teeth.

"Do you? I heard that the dragon who fathered that half-breed menace was you."

The warrior did leap up this time, almost toppling over the table between them in the process. Her eyes were practically bulging out of her skull as she reached for her sword. The only thing that kept her from drawing it was a lazy hand in the air from the lord. "Is this true?" she asked.

Kaito glared at the man across from him who returned with a look of challenge, daring him to refute it.

"Believe me when I say I have no attachment to humans, whatsoever."

"Then you will have no concern with ridding us of him and the humans who rise up against their betters," the lord said, a small smile pulling at the corner of his mouth.

"I will handle that if it comes to it."

The man laughed, mockingly. "It has come to that now. With that half-breed leading them-"

"What?" Kaito interrupted him.

"The half-breed. He's their emperor."

Everything slowed around Kaito for a moment. The leader of the humans, the emperor, Suzume's father, was his son?

AFTER LEAVING HIS GUESTS, KAITO SCOURED EVERY INCH OF THE PALACE FOR his brother. But after tearing the place apart in his search, and half terrifying the dragons who were milling around the palace, he realized he wasn't there. Kaito flew into the air, searching out his brother by spreading out his senses and looking for a trace of his spiritual power.

He found him flying toward the village. Of course he had gone there. It was the closest human dwelling and the easiest place for his brother to exact his revenge for the attack. As Kaito pursued his brother however, he felt an immediate desire to turn the other way. He ignored the feeling, keeping his sights trained on his brother. But as he attempted to get closer to the village it went from a suggestion to a command. As if invisible hands were turning him, he was directed away from the village. He had to go anywhere but there. He could not get close even if he wanted to and any attempt to approach only resulted in extreme pain.

Despite that, he was closing in on his brother. They collided together in the sky, and he knocked him down from the air. They fell into the ocean together and dived down beneath the tossing waves, clawing and each wrestling for the advantage. The waves pushed them closer toward the village, and each inch closer pain shot through his body.

The pain grew so intense it forced him to let go and Jirou flew into the sky, and beyond his reach toward the village. He wanted to chase him but no matter what he did, he couldn't get his body to move. *What is this?*

Then it hit him like a ton of bricks. There was only one thing that could keep him away. The command Suzume had put on him. Which meant his blood-thirsty brother was heading straight for Suzume.

TWENTY-FOUR

Suzume awoke in an unfamiliar bed with a pounding headache. *This is getting really old.* The room was a fine one, with murals painted on the walls depicting mountains hung with heavy cloud cover and sweeping valleys. This wasn't just any room, it had to belong to someone of importance. This sort of thing happened to her so often she didn't even question it anymore. She shrugged off the silken blankets and stood up. Her legs were shaking beneath her but she managed to make her way into the next room.

An old man was sitting at a desk in the next room. He glanced up as she entered.

"You're awake then?" He stood up, his joints audibly cracking as he did so. "I was afraid I wouldn't have use of my bed tonight." He gave her a smile.

But Suzume wasn't in a smiling mood.

"Who are you?" She'd felt this sort of pain before, this aching fatigue. She tried to rack her brain to remember where she was, but the last thing she remembered was the dragon attack. Everything after that was a blank. Which could mean only one thing.

"Why don't you sit down." He gestured to a seat across from him.

Suzume's legs were trembling beneath her and she decided it wouldn't hurt to sit down.

"I am the governor of Osaka. But you can call me Souta. And you I am told are Princess Suzume."

The governor of Osaka had been the noble they were on their way to see when they'd been attacked. It seemed they had made it to their destination despite the attack, but that didn't explain why she'd woken up here. "What am I doing in your room?" she asked.

"After your little incident on the boat, Ryuu wanted to lock you up, but I thought we should talk first."

She'd almost forgotten she'd attacked the warrior priests in her attempt to protect Kaito. Suzume rubbed her throbbing head. "And I suppose you want me to thank you for that." Maybe she should be locked up. Just the slightest threat and she'd lost control again.

The old man smiled. "Not at all. But I thought I would understand your position better than most."

She snorted. "I doubt it."

"Are you sure about that?"

Suzume had been distracted but now met the man's gaze. His eyes were the most peculiar color, gray like a storm. And there was this strange feeling when she looked into his eyes, as if they'd known each other their entire lives. But she was certain she'd never laid eyes on him before.

"Do I know you?"

"We haven't had the pleasure. If you don't mind, I wanted to ask you a few questions."

She narrowed her eyes at him. Questions had their own sort of danger. "What do you want to know?"

"Has this happened to you before?" he asked.

"Losing consciousness? More often than I'd like." She rubbed her throbbing head and looked around the room to avoid meeting his gaze.

All laughter and humor were wiped from his storm-gray eyes. "I meant losing control of your body."

Suzume shrugged in a dismissive way. She didn't know who he was but she wasn't going to expose that part of herself to him.

"I'll take that as a yes." He sighed heavily.

"What do you know about it?" she challenged.

His gaze pierced her to the core, but he did not answer.

It occurred to Suzume this could very well be Hisato's trap and she leaped to her feet. "How do you know anything about me?"

"Please, sit down, there's more we need to talk about."

"How did you know me?"

He sighed again and then with a low whistle, the wind picked up around her, ruffling her clothes and her hair. Suzume felt the power as it unfurled from within him. That deep-down ache was familiar, that sensation of finding a missing piece.

She covered her mouth with her hand. "You can't be."

The wind died down as quickly as it had appeared. "As I said, Ryuu brought you to me."

"Who are you?" Her fingers were flickering with flame now, she couldn't control it.

"I am the wind of Kazue's soul."

She could only blink in surprise for several moments. "But you're so old!" she blurted at last.

The old man chuckled and shook his head. "And a man, but I suppose that doesn't surprise you."

He knows about Hikaru.

"Did you make me this way?"

The old man blinked at her for a moment. "Ryuu said you were as fiery as your personality."

Suzume crossed her arms over her chest. "Answer the question."

The old man chuckled again. "No, I did not put Kazue's soul inside you."

She relaxed, but only a little. "What does Ryuu have to do with all of this?"

The old man met her gaze. "That's his story to tell."

There was no use asking him questions about Ryuu, clearly they were allies. "Why did he bring me here?" she demanded.

"He brought you to me so I could help you get control of your powers. If you don't master it soon she will consume you."

"Don't you think I've tried?" Suzume shouted.

"I tried as well. For years it was as if I was two people. Until I stopped being two and became one."

Suzume's eyes scanned over his face. It was hard to look at him and think Kazue was staring out through those eyes. It was her worst fear confirmed as well. What if Kazue consumed her next?

"Then are you Kazue?"

The old man shook his head. "I am neither of the people I used to be but also both of them."

"How is that possible? You're either one or the other."

"I have all of both their memories, their attachments..."

Meaning Kaito. Suzume placed her hand over her heart. There was a longing part of her that still wanted to see Kaito, and that part of her was what had gone to such lengths to save him. It's part of why she'd run away, because she was so terrified of letting Kazue's feelings take hold of her.

"How do I stop it?" Suzume asked, her voice little more than a whisper.

"There is no way to stop it, only delay it."

A cold chill ran down Suzume's spine. "Are you saying I will be doomed to become her?"

"For you it may be different, you were born with Kazue inside you. It could mean-"

"That I was Kazue all along."

Suzume felt as if she were going to be ill. It was as if someone had taken her very identity and with the stroke of a brush taken it away.

"I'm not Kazue." She shook her head as if her adamant denial would change anything.

"For you there's a chance you can escape that fate. I can train you."

"To do what? To slow the inevitable of becoming her? I'd rather have my power sealed away than become her."

The old man continued to stare at her, while Suzume's entire body trembled. This was not the answer she had hoped to find.

"Your power was sealed your entire life. It didn't make a difference. She is a part of you, and you either must learn to control it or give into her."

Rage bubbled up inside her, rising up so hot and fast she had little control over it.

"So that's it. I'm stuck with this fate? Why am I this way, can you tell me that at least?"

"I'm sorry." He dropped his head.

"You've basically told me I am going to die and that's all you can say?"

"I know it's hard to accept."

She shook her head. "I will not accept it. I refuse to!"

Flames burst from her fingers as she threw her arm out toward the nearby wall, where it caught and spread upward.

The old man gave a shout of alarm and while he was preoccupied by the fire scorching his wall, Suzume stormed out of the room. A pair of soldiers were guarding the door, but when they saw Suzume encased in flame, they were too afraid to approach her.

She marched down the hall, her footsteps scorching the ground as she walked. The anger was all-consuming, it took over all her thoughts and feelings. There was no escaping this destiny. She and Kazue were inseparable, it seemed. Fate had led her here and she could not undo it.

When she reached the courtyard, Ryuu was there, his weapon drawn and his blue eyes blazing. There was something about his eyes that was so familiar but the rage in her wouldn't allow her to make the connection.

"Get out of my way," she growled at him.

"Where are you going?"

"It doesn't concern you."

He took a step forward to stop her, but Suzume was prepared for that and she launched a ball of flame in his direction. He dodged her attack with ease, running toward her. She swung her arm, planning on hitting him with her flaming hand but he ducked beneath that attack as well. She had no weapon but the flames at her fingertips, so he threw his sword aside and punched her just beside her collarbone. Her arm fell dead at her side.

"Don't try and stop me," she said through gritted teeth, as she attempted to use her unaffected arm to swing at him with fire. He caught her wrist in his hand and held it above his head.

"You have a choice."

She laughed mockingly in his face. "You mean either I die, or yeah, I die. Great choices." She wrenched her arm away from him and tried to send another counter-attack. But the sweep of his leg sent her tumbling backward, landing on her back.

She glared up at him as he pressed his foot to her chest, to keep her pinned in place.

"You cannot change how you were born. Either continue to fight against a fate you cannot change, or make a difference for once."

She glared up at him, anger blazing in her eyes.

"It's easy for you to say. You aren't like me."

"We're more alike than you think."

His blue eyes stared into her soul. It was all useless. Suzume slumped backward, all the energy draining from her.

"Fine, lock me up for attacking you. See if I care."

Ryuu eased off her, and reached out a hand for Suzume to take. She stared at his outstretched appendage, not willing to trust him.

"I know why you did what you did."

"How could you?"

"Because I'm doing the same for those I love."

She hated the compassion she saw in his gaze. He stretched his hand toward her, begging her to take it. After a moment of studying it she took his hand.

"We don't have to be enemies," Ryuu said.

"That's yet to be seen," Suzume said as he helped her to her feet.

He laughed and she scowled back at him. "Is that funny?"

His smile faded but only just barely. "You're very much like your mother."

Before she could ask him to explain, there was a crash that echoed all around them. Ryuu turned his attention to the sky and Suzume followed his gaze. Overhead, the sky was rippling, as if an invisible barrier encircled the town. Then a second shuddering ripple shook the barrier.

"The barrier will hold," Souta said, standing on the steps a few feet away.

"Who is attacking?" Suzume said, watching the ripples that were forming all over the barrier.

"The dragons are attacking the city," Ryuu said, his blue gaze focused on the horizon.

Suzume's stomach clenched with fear, was Kaito trying to rescue her? But that wasn't possible, she'd forbade him to search for her which meant this was some other dragon.

The barrier trembled once more and Suzume felt a ripple of energy as the entire sky erupted into sparks and several dragons came through, spraying the city with icy projectiles. The barrier had broken.

Twenty-Five

Ryuu shouted commands to his men. The warrior priests leaped to attention, moving with a clean efficiency of long practice. Suzume stood frozen in the center of the chaos. Warrior priests and regular soldiers rushed around her like the river around a stone as she stared at the sky. Three dragons, similar in appearance to Kaito but varying in color and size, were destroying the city. Her power could stop them, she felt it deep down. But what happened if she used Kazue's power, or worse got lost to her again? What if she never woke again as herself? That seemed a fate worse than death.

A hand rested on her shoulder and Suzume almost leaped out of her skin with fright. She turned to see the old man, Souta, smiling at her.

"You do not need to fear the power."

Suzume's hands were trembling as he placed her staff in them.

"Kazue is not your enemy."

"That's easy for you to say, she's already taken over your body." But the protests felt weak coming from her lips. All she had done for as long as she could remember was run away and she was sick of running.

"Would you choose your own life over that of thousands of innocents?" he asked. Suzume glared at him. What sort of question was that?

"I can't even control the power. What can I possibly do to help?"

"You have more control than you think."

He smiled at her before striding across the courtyard and toward the dragon that was attacking. He had no weapons at all, but there was an undeniable confidence to his stride. He seemed to be a man half his age. And Suzume realized what she was seeing was Kazue's spiritual energy emanating from him. Kazue had been the most powerful priestess in living memory. And Suzume could harness it, she'd proved that already. She looked down at her staff in her hand. Ever since she'd almost killed Kaito she'd been terrified of the power that dwelled within her. She was even more terrified of becoming Kazue. But the old man was right. The entire city was in danger, not just her. And she could try and do something at least.

"Where did the dragons come from?" Tsuki asked as he strolled over to her, his arms slung behind his back. He casually watched the priests running to grab weapons. Naoki and Rin were a few steps behind him.

She clenched her staff tighter. Her mind was made up. "I think they're the same dragons who attacked us on the river," Suzume said.

She didn't want to consider what a fool she'd been before. Of course it wasn't Kaito. He wanted nothing to do with her. If she hadn't interfered during the earlier attack, then the city wouldn't be in danger now. But she could fix this.

Rin had already transformed into her massive kitsune form. "Are we certain it isn't Kaito?"

"It isn't," Naoki said, his eyes turned up toward the sky.

Ryuu stopped giving commands to walk over to them. In his hand he was gripping his sword. When it was close to Suzume she could feel the spiritual energy radiating off of it. This was not some manmade blade, which only reinforced her belief that he was not what he appeared. But questions of that nature would have to be for another time.

He seemed at ease despite the chaos around him, and he looked over Tsuki, Naoki and Rin. "I don't remember letting you free."

"We heard there was a fight. We thought it might be fun." Tsuki flashed him a smile.

Ryuu's expression didn't change and she feared that he would try and seal them again.

She stepped between her friends and Ryuu, her arms outstretched to draw attention to herself. "They attacked you because I asked. If you want to punish anyone, then punish me."

Ryuu's stared at her for a moment, and she got the sensation that he was seeing into her soul. She stared back at him, not willing to back down.

"Can I trust you to not turn on me this time?"

"I think this time we're on the same side," she replied, with a defiant tilt of her head.

It seemed to be enough for Ryuu, for now. He nodded. "They can join the ground forces." He pointed to Naoki and Tsuki. "You and Rin follow me."

Suzume nodded to Naoki and Tsuki and then chased after a battalion of soldiers who were going out into the city, presumably to stop the stampede of people who were shouting and fleeing from the attack of the dragons. Every few minutes they heard a crash as ice was flung at a building or a roof collapsed under the weight of an attack.

Ryuu led their group out of the courtyard and down the winding city streets. The town was like a maze in itself, and with the additional chaos of the attack, they had to navigate around panicked villagers trying to escape. Suzume would have gotten lost straight away without Ryuu to guide them.

He led them to a nearby hilltop, where they could see the village sprawl from above. The dragons were moving through the village, destroying with abandon. Watching the devastation from a distance, Suzume felt suddenly helpless. What could they do against these agents of chaos? Then Suzume heard a song drifting on the wind. She didn't so much hear it as she felt it. The energy was alive, blowing across the entire village. The waves along the coast were crashing against the shore and the clouds gathered overhead were crackling with energy that flashed against the gray sky. The hairs on her arms stood on end just to hear it. At the same time, it awoke the craving within her. She wanted the power. To breathe in the wind and let it fill her. She wanted that power to complete the part of her that wasn't quite whole.

The overwhelming desire became so great, Suzume had to cover her ears with her hands just to block it out. But her eyes were hungry to find the source, and she scoured the horizon until they came to rest upon the old man. He was perched on the eve of a house, his robes flapping around him in the center of the maelstrom. His gray hair flowing like a banner behind him. And the wind seemed to circle outward from him.

The power within him spoke to her. The song called forth the wind and it buffeted against the dragons who were being drawn toward them, directed by the current of the strong wind they could not escape. Instead of fighting it, the dragons rode the wind, on a collision course with Suzume and the priests.

Lightning cracked through the sky and the clouds opened up. Rain poured down upon her and the feeling of overwhelming flames within her calmed. Her clothes were quickly soaked but she couldn't help but smile. Because with the rain she could think clearer. *I can do this, I can control the power.*

The dragons were almost close enough now that she could see the whites of their eyes. *I can control it*, she chanted in her head. The rain was already starting to let up and in a few moments she would unleash the full fury of her flames.

"Get ready." Ryuu raised his hand, telling them to hold. The priests notched their arrows.

Flames sparked to life on her palms, and a ball of fire formed there just from her command. The old man was right, she could control it. And then she heard it, that familiar laughter.

Do you think you can control her? Hisato's voice taunted in her head.

She shook away the thought. It was just her own self-doubt. He couldn't be here.

I am a part of you, Suzume, or have you forgotten? She felt it, the brush of a hand inside her skull. Her pupils dilated. When she had taken Hisato's power inside of her, a part of him had remained. She'd been able to forget about it until now. But he had chosen the worst possible moment to reveal himself.

"Now!" Ryuu shouted.

The warrior priests unleashed their holy arrows, firing them at the dragons who weaved out of the way. The arrows flew in a useless arc past them. Rin shot her own fiery balls at the dragons, but they retaliated with their ice. Suzume was frozen in place, too afraid to move.

You are only meant to destroy. Embrace it. Hisato's voice purred inside her head.

Suzume tried to put out the flame in her hand, but she couldn't stop it. It was as if an invisible string was pulling her along. The dragons were upon them now and one of their icy projectiles was headed straight for her. The flames burst out of her, from every inch of her, creating a flaming barrier which repelled even her companions. It melted the ice before it could even touch her, and the dragons reeled away from her, afraid of her fire.

Hisato had control of her now and it wasn't like when Kazue took control of her body. She was aware of each step she took toward the edge of the hillside. She was putting herself in clear view of the dragons.

"Suzume get back," Ryuu shouted at her.

But she could not heed his call. Hisato used her like a puppet and used her flames to shoot several quick blows at the dragons, taking no concern for the homes nearby. The dragons dodged most of them, and her fire caught onto the roofs of nearby buildings and trees. The city would be in a blaze if she couldn't get control soon.

The dragons circled, ignoring even the holy arrows which the priests continued to fire. One dragon in particular came barreling toward her. She shot her flame at him, and though he tried to avoid her fire he couldn't get away fast enough and the flames leaped along his side. Another came to his aid as he lost altitude, but that second one was hit as well. They came crashing to the ground.

Suzume struggled against Hisato's control. She screamed futilely inside her head. She may as well be paralyzed as he marched her toward the fallen dragon. It stared up at her with horrified eyes. And then with a flick of her fingers he erupted into flames. His agonized screams shook her to the core as she was forced to watch him writhing on the ground as the fire consumed him.

The dragon she had partially burned came toward her, and Suzume turned to face him with hands raised as if she would embrace him. Before he could land a blow, she shot another fiery projectile at him. He rolled out the way, but just barely.

"Give my message to The Dragon," Suzume said, her voice booming with power. "Tell him if he comes near me again, he will suffer the same fate as this creature." She pointed to the burning dragon who'd been reduced to nothing more than a smoldering carcass. This was the true strength of her power.

The dragon signaled to his companion and the two of them flew away together.

Why are you doing this? Suzume said to Hisato.

Hisato laughed inside her head. *You ran away, but you still want him to save you. Either you destroy the dragon or I will for you.*

And then just as quickly as he had appeared, Hisato was no longer inside her head. Suzume collapsed to her knees. Rin rushed to her side, but kept back. The fire was dying away from Suzume's body as the rain fell from up above. The priests and even Ryuu hovered around her in a circle as if they were all afraid to touch her. The stink of burning flesh mixed with wet earth and made her want to gag.

"Kazue, what have you done?" Rin asked her. She did not disguise the horror from her voice.

Suzume's fingers clawed into the earth. They thought Kazue had taken over her again. And perhaps it was better if they thought that. Because she had done this to herself by taking in Hisato's power. By being greedy to be stronger. She'd been trying to run away from it for so long, but there was nowhere she could run that Hisato couldn't find her. He was a part of her. At least when Kazue took control of her, she could blame her actions on her.

What would they think if they knew Hisato could take over her body? They'd never trust her again. This would have to be a secret she kept to herself until she could find a way to break his control over her.

Wet footsteps on the grass approached her. Suzume did not even want to raise her head to look at them. But she could feel his presence. A part of her cried out to him, aching to be reunited. She stared at him through the wet curtain of her hair. The old man held his hand out to her.

"Come, it's time."

Suzume took his outstretched hand. It was time. Either she learned how to control it or either Kazue or Hisato would consume her.

Twenty-Six

When Kaito landed in the courtyard of his palace, he found several of his dragons waiting for him. They ran toward him as he landed. He'd watched the fight from afar, until the storm had made visibility impossible. The only consolation was if he still could not approach the village, that meant Suzume yet lived. But he didn't know how much longer she would be. His brother was out for blood and Suzume wasn't strong enough to fight him. He needed reinforcements and now.

"All of you go to the village and stop this foolish attack." Kaito threw his arm out toward the village, as he strode over to them. There were probably a few more dragons loitering around the palace. He'd need them all to stop Jirou and the others who had joined him.

The pair who'd run toward him lowered their heads in shame. He was already in a dark mood, and being disobeyed only made his anger greater.

"What is this? I gave an order!" he roared. Thunder rumbled overhead as he spoke. But it wasn't his thunder, he could sense that. Something else had called down this storm. But he didn't have time to investigate, nor did he care.

The two dragons shared a look as if goading one another into speaking.

The younger of the two dragons, Kenji, spoke. He tried to give Kaito a defiant look, but Kaito's glare forced him to drop his gaze to the ground as he spoke. "Why are you trying to stop the attack? The village has been nothing but trouble lately." His face was burned from forehead to neck, where holy fire had struck him.

Though Jirou would never admit it, Kaito knew that he had instigated the attack which had gotten Kenji burned. And yet the young dragon still blamed the humans. Kaito had underestimated their loyalty to Jirou. At first he had thought it just a few outliers, but as the two continued to stand before him ignoring his command, he realized he was losing control—if he'd ever had it at all.

He should tear them apart limb by limb for their insubordination, just to make an example of what happened to those who disobeyed him. Before he could punish them, however, two dragons came careening into the courtyard still in their dragon form. At their head was Jirou. There was a burn along his side, and he stank of spiritual energy. It served him right, but seeing the extent of his injuries it was difficult to believe Suzume had done such a thing.

The other dragons rushed to Jirou's aid, but Kaito's snarl stopped them in their tracks. They hovered over him and his companion, the she-dragon, Chihiro, instead. They stared wide-eyed at the burns covering both their bodies. Chihiro collapsed onto the ground and could not move.

"See to her." Kaito nodded to Kenji and the other dragon and they rushed forward to check her wounds.

"What have you done?" Kaito growled, coming to stand before his brother.

"I did what you wouldn't," his brother spat. He could not maintain a human visage and remained in dragon form. Even though his true form was ten times Kaito's current size, he couldn't help but think how small Jirou seemed. A petty, vain creature who'd put the lives of those who trusted him at risk, all to make Kaito appear the fool.

"You nearly got yourself killed, as I said you would."

"She killed Kenta," Jirou growled and tried to rise up to look imposing, but he couldn't even keep himself upright. Rage burned in Jirou's gaze. A part of Kaito wanted to ask what happened to the priestess, but that would reveal too much. It seemed impossible that Suzume could do such a thing, but he couldn't deny she was close by. There was no other explanation as to why he couldn't approach the village.

"This is why I told you not to go." Kaito raised his hand as if he would strike his brother. To his credit Jirou glared up at him, braced for a blow. Kaito didn't strike him, but his anger had made him lose control of his form, and his scales came to the surface, his hands were tipped with claws.

Striking him out of anger would prove nothing, and he turned to walk away. Where was Ai? She was supposed to stop Jirou. He would have to find her and get the answers from her mouth.

"How many more of your men must die before you see the truth?" his brother called after him.

Kaito rounded on him and walked up to his brother bearing teeth like a ferocious beast. "I see perfectly. My brother cannot grasp the order of things and you got one of our own killed."

"It is you who is blinded by your love of that woman."

There was an audible gasp from the dragons around the courtyard. More had come from within the palace, perhaps sensing the rising tension of Kaito and Jirou's spiritual energy. His brother rose up off the ground, still in dragon form. Kaito froze, anger turning his skin to ice. In fact, ice was radiating out from where he stood, freezing over the entire courtyard, his brother included who, in his weakened state, could do little to fight the ice which was slowly encasing him and would suffocate him. He should kill him now, where he stood, and end this insubordination. Before Kaito was sealed, he wouldn't have questioned it even for a moment. But there were so few of the first children left, it felt like a crime to kill his own kin.

"You let one woman trick you and now you're letting your love for another blind you," Jirou hissed. He was testing Kaito's mercy.

Kaito tightened his grip and the ice encasing Jirou was covering everything but his brother's nostrils. A few more inches and he'd lose all of his air supply. All the eyes in the courtyard were on him, holding their breath, waiting to see what he would choose. He could not decide what was worse, letting him live and let him challenge him or the guilt of having killed his kin.

In the end he let go of the ice strangling his brother. The ice broke apart around him and Jirou fell onto the ground, no longer able to keep himself upright.

"I have no love for humans," Kaito said and gazed at everyone around him, to make certain they understood his words.

"Prove it and kill that woman," Jirou said. His voice was raw and hoarse, and still he taunted Kaito.

Kaito glared at him. He couldn't kill Suzume even if he wanted to. But if they knew she had command over him, then it really would be over.

"I will not make your fool's mistake and attack unprepared." Kaito gestured to the half-repaired courtyard, and the meager few dragons who would stand as his army. Surely all of them would have witnessed the threat the humans caused. And as the injuries and deaths mounted, Kaito could see this wasn't a problem he could ignore anymore. "I will not risk more lives. We must plan. We need a strategy."

"Don't use your words to twist your true intent. You want to spare her. But I looked into her eyes, she wants you dead."

This had to be his brother's trick, to seed more doubt. "Enough!" Kaito roared.

But Jirou would not listen. "She gave me a message for you. She said if you come near her again, she'll destroy you."

Kaito balled his hand into a fist at his side. He didn't want to expose his anger and hatred to them. The message brought him back to the moment she'd placed this damn spell upon him, banishing him from her sight. Was it not enough that she had sent him away? But now she made threats as well. In the past when she'd run her mouth, he thought it only boasting. But ever since she'd banished him, he'd seen a different side to her. It was written in the skin of his men. They were not just threats anymore, and she had power that might even rival Kazue's. Perhaps she had it all along and he'd been the one who was deceived. Once again, he'd fallen for the wiles of a human, given into their spell.

"You must choose a side," Jirou said, at last returning to a more human visage. "Either the yokai or humans."

From his dragons to the visiting lord, all of them were watching him, waiting for his answer. He'd let humans make him soft, and he'd been protecting them only for them to turn on him. Even now his people were dwindling because of Kazue, because of her son, and because of Suzume. Well, that ended now, it ended here.

"I will say this before all of you here. I am the Great Dragon, blessed by the eight, and chosen to rule over Akatsuki." His voice echoed like thunder across the courtyard as he unfurled the full strength of his power. "Our kingdom is infested with the menace known as humans, but today I swear to you, yokai will rise again. Even if it means we must wipe humanity from this island."

The dragons all cheered and stamped their feet. Despite their vocal support, Kaito felt hollow inside. He turned to walk away, but turned back around toward his brother. He hadn't forgotten his transgressions.

"You are grounded until further notice. If you leave these palace walls, I will kill you myself."

His brother bowed his head in subservience. Kaito had done as he wanted, he'd declared war on the humans. But this was only the beginning. As he exited the courtyard, he passed the visiting pair. There was an infuriating smirk on the lord's face.

"Bring your army to me, and spread the word to yokai great and small —I have returned and those who do not bow to me will pay the price."

The warrior gave him the deepest bow. Her eyes shone with excitement. She lusted for the bloodshed, and perhaps for vengeance. The lord gave a shallow bow, his eyes trained on Kaito. He would need to keep an eye on him, he had not won his loyalty.

"As you wish, my lord," said the man.

Kaito stormed past them. There was one last item left to take care of. He found Ai sitting beside a pond in one of the gardens, it had only recently been restored. Stepping into the garden was like going back in time, to when his palace had been an oasis. But despite the newly planted greenery, and the fresh paint on the veranda that surrounded it, everything felt gray to him. He thought his kingdom was all he wanted. Before he had never delighted in war but he found it a necessary evil. Now he wondered if it was all worth the cost.

Ai looked up at him shyly as he entered the garden. Her hand, half submerged in the pond, was creating ripples along the surface. Multicolored fish swam up to her fingers to nibble upon the tips of her digits. Seated beside the pool of water, she appeared more childlike than ever. And despite the rage that was bubbling up inside him, when she stared at him with her large eyes, he could not bring himself to unleash his full fury upon her.

"You were supposed to follow him," he said.

She tilted her head to the side. "Ai did."

"You were supposed to stop him."

She shrugged as she traced the surface of the pond, making lazy circles. The fish followed her finger in a rainbow-colored school. "He's too strong."

"You lie."

Ai turned to him, and all the childlike softness disappeared from her face. Sitting before him now was the powerful lady he had once served. "It had to be done, to make you see the truth."

Kaito swung and punched a nearby pillar, which shook with the force of his blow. His anger crept out of him in the form of ice, encrusting the shattered pillar with ice. She'd entrapped him. From the moment she'd suggested marriage, he should have known this was the outcome. Ai always got what she wanted.

"Ai has brought you an army. Now all you must do is take your kingdom back."

"And if I refuse to marry you, then they will scatter like the wind." It wasn't a question. That had been her plan all along. She and Jirou had likely been plotting behind his back this entire time.

Ai fluttered her eyelashes. Kaito shouted and punched at the pillar again, hard enough to snap it in half. Red splinters of wood flew through the air, but Ai did not so much as flinch.

"I would give you anything you wanted, rule of the entire north, if you wished."

Ai stood up and came over to him. She hardly came up to his waist in her current form. She was trapped in a child's body, but her eyes were ancient and full of power. Even now she was only half as powerful as she had been and yet still his equal. She grabbed his hand.

"I want you, Kai."

He yanked his hand away. "You want to control me as you once did."

She balled her hands into fists at her sides and her face scrunched up like a child told they couldn't have candy. "She has betrayed you. It's time to forget about her."

"You set this up, didn't you? You let that lord feed me lies so I would run into your arms."

"He told no lies. Your son became emperor of Akatsuki. Which means she is your descendant. Would you give up not only on your kind but do something so wrong?" She crinkled her nose.

Before he'd found out Suzume was his grandchild, it had been over between them. It was over before it even started. She had cast him aside, rejected his protection. He'd been blind to think there was anything between them, and now the very thought sickened him. Any offspring of that abomination Kazue had borne mattered nothing to him. He tried to tell himself these things, but his fear for Suzume still choked at him, made him desperate to lay eyes on her just once and make certain she was safe.

"I'm going to her." Kaito walked away.

"If you walk away now, you must give up your kingdom."

He stopped mid-stride.

Ai spoke to his turned back, "If you leave now, even if you return, I will withdraw all my support. You will be left with nothing but the crumbling remains of your castle."

The ice froze over the entire courtyard, the pond included, and the tiny rainbow fish were frozen in place. That was his choice—his kingdom or a woman—a woman he could not even have, for so many reasons. It was no choice at all. Kaito slumped against the pillar. Ai came and rested her hand on his back.

"It will be different than before. We are equals in this."

Kaito knocked her hand away. "I will marry you only because I have no choice. But do not mistake me, I will never love you."

He strode away, ice coating each step he took.

TWENTY-SEVEN

They returned to the White Palace and Suzume was blessedly saved from having to report to the emperor. On her first night back, she went straight to bed and would have slept the next day through had Ryuu not been there early the next morning, dragging her out of bed for training. She fought against him for as long as she could, because the very idea of using her power and potentially opening herself up not only to Kazue but also Hisato terrified her. But as he loved to remind her, it was the emperor's orders that she should train and so she went to the temple with him.

When she arrived at the temple, the old man, Souta was waiting to greet her. She was surprised to see him there, he'd come with them to the palace, she knew, but he wasn't alone either and he looked nothing like the infirmed old man she had first met. He stood upright and had the physique of a man a quarter of his age. From his confident stance, she would have mistaken him for a man closer to her own age, if not for the gray hair which he had tied in a top knot. Standing just behind him was Hikaru, also wearing the sparring clothes.

Being this close to two other pieces of Kazue's soul left Suzume with a buzzing feeling in her skin, as if every sense was alive. Hikaru must have felt it too, because he met her gaze and she saw concern there. Ashamed of her own lack of control, she turned away from him.

"I hope you're ready to work," the old man said with a smile. Either he did not feel what they did, or he was ignoring it.

"What are you doing here?" Suzume asked, before glancing sidelong at Ryuu.

"I thought I told you when we first met, I'm going to train you how to better control your powers."

"Then why is Hikaru here?"

"Master Souta thinks I need some additional training as well." Hikaru rubbed the back of his neck as if he was embarrassed. Unlike Suzume, who'd only discovered her power recently, Hikaru had been training at the White Temple for the past twenty years and before that he'd been a traveling exorcist with his wife, Rin, for centuries. If the old man thought he needed training, what did he think of Suzume's failed attempts to control her power?

"But Hikaru can control his powers," Suzume said, looking with suspicion between the three of them. Hikaru's gaze was wandering, and the old man was smiling in a knowing way. As if there was some secret all of them shared that she wasn't in on.

"His problem is he's too quick to sacrifice himself." The old man pointed at Hikaru with a long, knobby finger.

Hikaru lowered his head as if chastised.

Then the old man pointed at Suzume. "Your problem is you take too much."

"Hey!" Suzume snapped.

The old man turned his back to them and started walking away, ignoring Suzume's glare. "It is the nature of your elements to balance one another. Earth feeds fire. But wind guides both."

Suzume rolled her eyes. "Very poetic."

She couldn't see the old man's face but she thought she saw a little spring in his step at her comment. "Today begins your lessons. Both of you must learn to control your elements and work in harmony." He led them to the sparring circle where she'd first faced off with the other acolytes. He stood in the center of the circle. "This isn't going to be easy. For people like us, we have an excess of an element, which gives us greater control but also the worst attributes of our element.

You can be unmoving as the mountain." He said to Hikaru and then to Suzume he said. "Or as temperamental as fire."

"As flighty as the wind," Suzume countered.

The old man only smiled. "It is true, I do not stay still for long. As you will see." He clapped his hands together. "Today we start with sparring."

Suzume reached for her staff, which she had strapped to her back. She wasn't crazy about the idea of using her power. What if she lost control? What if Hisato took over her body again? Ryuu was watching her, not commenting, and not wanting to seem suspicious, she drew her staff. But as soon as she drew it a gust of wind blew her staff from her hand and it clattered onto the ground a few feet away.

"I thought you wanted us to fight?" She scowled at the old man.

"Not with your weapons. But with your elements."

Sudden fear clutched at her chest. Using her fire would definitely not end well.

"Are you crazy? What if Kazue takes over my body and hurts someone?"

The old man smiled. "That is your lesson, to learn how to control her. Harness the power within you and do not let it consume you."

Hikaru assumed the position while Suzume crossed her arms over her chest. She didn't like this one bit, at least when she had the staff in her hand she felt some semblance of control. It helped her channel her power.

"What are you waiting for?" the old man asked.

They held each other's gazes, Suzume not willing to admit to her fear, and the old man not willing to back down. After several seconds, she caved under the intensity of his stare.

"Fine, but if I burn down the shrine, that's on you."

She reluctantly took position on the opposite end of Hikaru. Before the bout started, Hikaru bowed and Suzume followed up with her own hasty bow. Despite her fear and hesitation, her body seemed eager for a fight. Hikaru unleashed his power, and she felt it all around her, like hundreds of little pinpricks racing over her skin. It awoke the fire in her and her own hands sparked with flame.

But she wasn't sure how she could fight Hikaru, if she struck him with her fire it would only burn her too. There was no way they could do this without hurting each other.

"Wait, how do we-" before she could finish her question, Hikaru attacked. The sand beneath her feet started to shift and move and Suzume sunk into the ground. While she was trying to get her feet free, vines shot out of the ground and wrapped around her wrists.

"Hey, that's not fair."

"Those are the rules," the old man shouted. "Use your fire to stop him."

The vines continued to tangle around her, and across from her Hikaru was focusing his gaze on the ground. If she could distract him, she could break the vines. Focusing all her energy onto her hand, she formed a ball of fire. With the limited movement she had, she flung it toward Hikaru.

The flames had the desired effect. Hikaru's concentration broke and Suzume freed herself from the tangle of his vines. But knowing what he could do, she realized she couldn't stay still for long or his vines would grab her again. They circled one another. His vines kept shooting out of the ground trying to tangle her up, and each time she threw her flames at them, scorching them and burning them to ash, before they could touch her. Around and around they went, until Suzume was left panting and grasping her knees and Hikaru's face was drenched in sweat.

"Again." The old man clapped his hands.

"Are you crazy? I'm going to collapse from exhaustion," Suzume said between panting breaths.

"But you haven't yet."

She scowled at him again and they resumed positions. Again she leaped out of the reach of his vines but as she got tired, her steps became sloppier. Hikaru's vines wrapped around her and she fell to the ground. The vines wrapped around every inch of her body. She tried to focus her flames on burning them but they were growing too fast for her to keep up. If she wasn't quick, they were going to suffocate her. But the more she panicked the harder it was to control her fire. The spiraling sensation came over her again and the edges of her vision started to go black.

Then next thing she knew she was standing over Hikaru, who was flat on his back and there were scorch marks on the ground. Seeing the fire and the terror in his eyes, she knew she'd lost control again. Suzume stumbled backward and headed for the edge of the sparring ring.

"Where are you going?" the old man asked, blocking her way.

"Can't you see? I lost control again." She pointed back toward Hikaru, who was climbing back to his feet.

"And so?"

"What if I hurt him?"

"I won't let that happen. If you give up now, she will consume you. But if you keep on fighting, you'll be stronger for it."

She scowled at him. This wasn't just about Kazue. Hisato could take her over at any time too. What if for all her effort she still failed and Hisato used their connection to hurt people? For some reason she felt compelled to look at Ryuu. He was standing at the edge of the circle, arms crossed over his chest. He gave a single nod and she turned away from him. She didn't need his approval.

"I'm ok," Hikaru said from behind her. "We won't let you hurt us."

I have to learn, or someone else is going to get hurt. Like Kaito. She mentally shook herself and turned back to face the others. "One more time."

They squared off once more. The fire came quick to her hand but Suzume hesitated to throw it at him this time. They continued to circle. When she wouldn't attack, Hikaru took the initiative and came toward her. In a panic she flung a fireball toward his face. He dodged and rolled, coming up and they circled once more.

"Don't hold back," the old man shouted.

There was a drumming in her ears, a pain that she couldn't quite part from. Kazue was so close to the surface. She had to do this, to learn how to control her power. She flinched and then lunged into her attack, flinging balls of flame at Hikaru. He dodged her attack and used his vines to shield himself.

"Embrace your power," the old man shouted at Hikaru.

Then the old man started to sing, and with the combination of his and Hikaru's power and the close proximity, it was almost overwhelming. Suzume felt it tingle against her skin and she was so distracted she didn't see Hikaru's vine shooting toward her. It slammed into her leg and sent her flying backward. The combination of his strike and the power that floated around her, unlocked something within her and she came up swinging. She flung her fireball at Hikaru, and this time she didn't bother to try and avoid him. She was out for blood. Her limbs moved without her command and she lunged for Hikaru.

The next thing she remembered she was lying on her back staring up at the sky. The old man was squatting above her, shaking his head.

"You gave into her, again."

Suzume sat up and scowled at him. "I told you that's what happens."

The old man shook his head again. "You've given her too much power."

"I didn't give it to her. It was hers to start with."

He flicked her across the forehead with thumb and forefinger. "And that's your problem. You control the power, not a woman five hundred years dead. Do it again."

And so they sparred again and again and again. Each time she blacked out only to be revived by the old man, standing over her shaking his head as she was the greatest fool who ever lived.

"I think that's enough for today," the old man said after what felt like her hundredth failure.

Suzume snatched up her staff and headed for the exit. She'd been an idiot to think there was some solution to losing herself to Kazue. They'd trained all day and it hadn't made any difference at all.

As she marched away, Hikaru chased after her. "Wait for me!" he said.

She pretended like she hadn't heard him. She kept on walking, but as she approached the temple gates she saw a group of priests talking together. Because she didn't want rumors of her temper to get spread around, she made a quick turn and went toward the temple garden. There was a bench beneath a large gingko tree. She sat down and turned away from the path where Hikaru was still following her. She crossed her arms over her chest.

He stood nearby. "I know you're frustrated, but this won't happen overnight."

"I don't have time to waste," Suzume growled.

Hikaru was silent for a few minutes. He knew her fears, but could he really understand them? He'd lost his memories but he'd gotten them back. She wasn't even sure who she was anymore. And besides that Hisato could take control of her at any moment.

"I've been looking into the records, like you asked." Suzume turned to face him, desperate for a change of subject. She hadn't had a chance to talk to him about it before now. And she still hoped finding out who brought Hikaru to the temple would lead to answers as to who had put Kazue's soul inside him. And by extension, Suzume.

"Oh." There were still secrets he was keeping. But she was keeping her own.

"Ryuu's the one who has the key to the records we need."

"Don't worry about it," Hikaru said. He picked up a fallen gingko leaf and twirled it between his fingers.

"What do you mean, don't worry about it? We're trying to find out why we're like this!"

"Ryuu doesn't have anything to do with it. I'm certain."

"How can you be? Is there something you're not telling me?" Suzume tilted her head, trying to catch Hikaru's eye but he turned away from her.

He rubbed the back of his neck. "He asked me to not tell you."

"You've talked to him?" She couldn't keep the accusation from her voice. What else was he keeping from her?

He turned to face her and seemed on the verge of telling her more when Ryuu walked into the garden.

"It's time to go back to the palace," he said. His gaze flickered to Hikaru for a moment.

"Are you two keeping secrets?" Suzume asked, looking between the two of them.

Hikaru laughed, but it was high and forced. He might as well have had a sign on his forehead that read, 'I'm lying.'

"Now is not the place," Ryuu said.

"You keep telling me to trust you, but how can I trust you when all you do is lie?"

"Just wait a while longer." Hikaru held up his hands in a placating gesture.

She scowled at the both of them. "Whose side are you on?"

Hikaru wouldn't meet her gaze. It was all the confirmation she needed. She got up and marched up to Ryuu. "I'm going to find out the truth, and when I do..."

"You'll what?"

Suzume scrunched up her face. "You'll see."

Twenty-Eight

It had been a week of training with the old man and she'd made little improvement. Each night Suzume stumbled back into her chamber, full of bone-deep fatigue, and she would collapse on her bed and sleep until morning. Then she'd have to start all over again. Hikaru was making great progress. It was harder and harder for her to pull energy from him. But Kazue seemed determined to take control of Suzume's body at the slightest provocation. She didn't have the energy to worry about Ryuu or wonder what he had to do with Kazue's soul being inside her. Maybe that was his plan all along, keep her preoccupied.

After another particularly brutal training session, Suzume was heading back to her chamber, with Ryuu shadowing her as he always did. She was sweaty and probably smelled like fermented vegetables. She did not even bother to go the long way to avoid being seen, as she had been up until now. Before she didn't want anyone to see her in her training clothes, and see her in such a disarray, but fatigue won out to vanity.

Half delirious with fatigue, she did not see the empress and her entourage coming her direction until they were upon her. Suzume, too tired from her sparring, did not even bother bowing her head at the empress as was expected and she kept on stumbling past them, almost knocking into the empress herself.

"What do you think you're doing?" the empress said, scandalized.

Suzume came to a shuffling stop and turned around to face the empress. She squinted as the empress swam in and out of focus.

"Oh," she said and bowed her head before stumbling forward again.

The empress's usual entourage surrounded her and as Suzume tried to make her way through them, they buzzed about like a hive of angry bees.

"Show the empress some respect," said one of her ladies.

Suzume turned once again, blinked but couldn't quite put them into focus. "Is there something you need from me?" she asked, not caring if she came across as crass.

"Your outfit," the empress said as she turned her nose up at it. She covered her face with her fan, perhaps to shield herself from the smell of sweat. "It is not appropriate for a lady of your station."

"I'll go change then." Suzume stumbled a few steps.

"I have not excused you." There was a frantic note in the empress's tone. No one had ever openly defied her before. Under normal circumstances, Suzume wouldn't have. The empress could be vicious when she wanted to. And given the history between her mother and her, she imagined she'd use the opportunity to make Suzume miserable. But as tired as she was, Suzume wasn't thinking about any of that. She turned toward the empress and spread out her hands in a gesture of 'what else do you want.'

The ladies who surrounded the empress shared looks, clearly not sure how to react to Suzume's impertinence. "Your majesty must have so much free time," Suzume said without thinking. There was no filter left between her thoughts and her mouth.

Behind her Ryuu coughed, and Suzume glanced over her shoulder at him, remembering he was there. She scowled at him. *Why did he have to follow her around? She never got a moment to breathe.*

"What was that?" the empress said through gritted teeth. Suzume could practically hear her teeth grinding together.

Ryuu came to her rescue. "Your lady is generous to take an interest in Princess Suzume, who lacks common sense and manners."

"Hey!" Suzume attempted a swing at Ryuu but he caught her quickly and forced her into a deep bow before the empress.

"You are fortunate the emperor has placed Ryuu to watch over you, otherwise I'd have to teach you a lesson." And then with a quick cough she said, "We are having a gathering this evening, I would be pleased if you were there." The last portion was spoken as if it physically pained her to extend such an invitation.

Even as sleep deprived as Suzume was, it was clear the emperor had forced her to extend the invitation to Suzume.

"I will have to see if I have time in my schedule." Suzume bowed her head again and scooted out of Ryuu's reach before he could force her into an even more humiliating position. She had no real interest in going whatsoever and would avoid it as best she could.

"The emperor wished I remind you, that as your mother is absent from court, it is important you attend," the empress said.

Now she had her attention. There was a smirk on her lips. It wasn't an invitation but a command.

"I will attend if it pleases you," Suzume said to the ground. Though she had to grit the words out.

The empress only laughed. "I see your tune has changed. How like Izume you are. You even have Ryuu following you around like a lost dog."

Suzume looked up on impulse and by the devious smile on her face, the empress knew she'd caught Suzume in her web. She glanced at Ryuu, but his expression gave nothing away.

"You served my mother?" she asked Ryuu.

He stared forward without answer.

It was the empress who replied, "I thought you knew." Her ladies all twittered as she smiled. Suzume only glared at her, not hiding her anger. "Come tonight, and I will tell you."

Suzume was dismissed, and she went back to her rooms. She didn't bother trying to pull the information from Ryuu. He wouldn't tell her. Tsuki was lying on her bed when she entered, while Naoki stood guard. She thought about kicking Tsuki off her futon, but no matter how tired her body was, the empress's taunts had piqued her curiosity and she wouldn't be able to rest. Her maid, that is, Rin, who was pretending to be her maid, prepared a bath for her, and she soaked in the hot water considering everything she'd learned.

By the time she got out of the bath, she hadn't made any progress. But her mind had been made up. When she'd returned from her first mission, the emperor had gifted her with a gorgeous kimono. Rin helped her dress and style her hair. She was rather skilled at it. She hadn't told them about Ryuu and her mother, partly because this was her concern. Half the court knew every last scandalous detail of her family's lives. And she didn't want them knowing the same.

"Are you sure you don't want us coming with you?" Rin asked as she fastened a pin into Suzume's hair. It was still too short to be fashion-able, but the decorative comb she wore sparkled with gems. And the kimono fell in such beautiful ways she knew no one would be able to keep their eyes off her.

"No, it would be too hard to explain so many people around me."

"I'm going to die of boredom here," Tsuki said, lying on the ground and staring at the ceiling.

"You could always investigate Ryuu for me," she said, mostly teasing. With Ryuu's spiritual sensitivity, he'd sense them before they got any answers.

"No!" Rin said, a little too hastily.

Suzume met her gaze, waiting for her to elaborate. Rin pretended to need to fix the fold of Suzume's kimono. "We don't want to get in trouble. It's better if we keep a low profile," she said. Suzume glared at her. So she was in on whatever secret Hikaru was hiding as well.

THE PARTY WAS BEING HELD IN THE GARDEN. IT WOULD LIKELY BE THE LAST OF the season as the winter winds were already settling on the palace. Suzume wore a cloak over her kimono. In the garden many braziers had been lit to keep the space warmer and candles were set to float in the garden pool. The party was focused around the covered pagodas that surrounded the pools. She was one of the last ones to arrive and as she got closer she heard the music and laughter that floated out toward her.

In the second largest pagoda, the empress held court, sitting at the head of her circle of onlookers. Suzume searched for Ryuu. He hadn't come to escort her to the party. Perhaps he felt there was no real risk of her being attacked here. *And there wouldn't be when he's the one who sent his yokai after me.* As she scanned the garden, he was nowhere to be seen. A large pagoda housed the emperor and his court, but when Suzume glanced inside it, she did not see him there either. Not that it mattered. It would be a more pleasant evening if she didn't see him at all. But then, unfortunately, she saw him across the courtyard talking with a few courtiers. His back was to her but as she approached, he turned to her.

His gaze slid up and down her, and she felt a blush rush to her cheeks. It was silly, of course. It wasn't as if she were attracted to him. But it had been a long time since a man had given her any attention. But his glance was brief and he soon turned back to his companions as if he hadn't seen her at all. *How dare he!* Suzume, not one to be ignored, tried to march over to him but when she got close, he disappeared around a corner. Suzume went to give chase, but as she did, a servant stepped into her path. She was about to tell him to get out of her way when he spoke.

"The empress wishes to dine with you," he said.

She looked back toward the empress who was waiting for her, perhaps to turn down the invitation. She'd only come here because she'd been ordered to do so. But the temptation of learning Ryuu's relationship with her mother was too much. She followed the servant into the empress's pagoda.

She entered the crowded space, head held high. Whispers stopped as she entered as if they'd all been talking about her moments before. A space was set aside beside the empress. Normally this would have been an honor but Suzume could sense the trap for what it was.

"Welcome, Princess Suzume." The empress greeted her with a smile that did not reach her eyes. A musician sat in the corner, plucking the strings of his instrument as the two of them sized one another up.

Suzume went to sit down beside the empress. Food was served and everything was going as it would be expected. Whatever trap the empress planned to spring, it would be drawn out, likely to cause Suzume the most pain.

A courtier whom she had at times flirted with before she'd been exiled stood up.

"I would read a poem I wrote for the empress," he said.

She nodded her head for him to read it. Suzume was only listening with half an ear. It was the typical sort of thing, talking about the weather and the flowers, changing of seasons. It was nothing she hadn't heard before. Everything was allegory for the beauty of the empress. Suzume had similar poems written about her. And then the poem took a turn.

"Her rival's vile plans..." he said. The accompanying music turned more sinister. And Suzume turned her attention to the poet.

As he spun out the poem in flowery words, it was clear who he was speaking about. It was about her mother, and more than that, it painted her mother as an adulterer, who'd stolen the emperor's heart only to betray him with someone close to him, while his faithful first wife was left to pick up all the pieces. So this had been her plan all along, to shame Suzume. Well, it wasn't going to be enough to stop her. She'd heard the rumors enough to have grown hardened to it.

"It was quite beautiful," the empress said once he had finished.

Suzume stood up. "I have my own poem."

The empress narrowed her eyes but she didn't tell Suzume no. And so Suzume gave her reply in her own poem. It wasn't very long, just a few carefully chosen words that were not polite to repeat. When Suzume was finished she bowed to them, before storming out of the empress's pagoda.

She'd tired of the palace games. She should just corner Ryuu and demand answers. But as she went to go and search for him, another servant stopped in front of her.

"My lady," he said. This wasn't the empress's man, but the emperor's. "The emperor wishes to speak with you."

I'm rather popular tonight. The emperor must have heard the uproar from the empress's pagoda and had likely made the connection for the cause. She shouldn't have said anything. It wasn't anything that hadn't already been said about her mother. But it bothered her more than before. Everyone seemed to know more about Izume than her.

The emperor's pagoda was cleared of all hangers-on when she entered, all except for Ryuu who was standing at the emperor's right hand. Suzume bowed low to the emperor. "You asked for me, your majesty?"

The emperor said, "Rise, child."

Suzume did. She didn't want to face him after the embarrassment of the empress's trick.

"There is a lot of commotion coming from the empress's pagoda," he said, looking across the twinkling garden where the empress was wailing dramatically. Suzume did not back down.

"She insulted my mother, your majesty." She bowed her head in apology. But she wouldn't make the words leave her lips.

The emperor chuckled. "You are as full of fire as always." His eyes sparkled in the light from the brazier.

Suzume chanced a glance at Ryuu but his expression was blank.

"Don't let her get to you. She has always been jealous of Izume. And with her gone, now you have become the target of her ire."

"I won't let it bother me." She nodded her head to acknowledge him.

"There are things I thought you should know about your mother and I-" he started to say but held himself back. "It will be better for another time." He gestured to the seat beside him. "Please sit."

Suzume did as he commanded, and the emperor waited until she was seated before saying. "I have another mission for you."

Her stomach clenched, were there more yokai attacks? "What is it?" she asked, her chest tight with worry.

"I want you to visit your grandfather."

"What?" She asked, her eyebrows shooting up toward her hairline.

Her father chuckled.

"When your mother disappeared, he went back to his province. I need you to go to him, find out what he knows about your mother's disappearance."

"Why me?"

"Because I trust you." Not because of her power or because of who she had been born but her as a person. It warmed her more than she thought it would.

"I will do this for you, father." She bowed her head toward him.

He brushed the hair from her face. "You look beautiful tonight. Your mother would have been proud."

A sudden emotion welled up in her. Her throat was thick with words unspoken. "Thank you, father," she managed in a strangled voice.

Twenty-Nine

Ryuu must have been a master of avoidance. Despite being on the road together for nearly a day, she had not found a chance to speak with him even once. Not that anything he could say wouldn't sound suspect at this point. She rode in a palanquin, only this time it wasn't subterfuge. She was not one of the emperor's warrior priests, but as a granddaughter visiting her grandfather. She'd sent a letter ahead of her arrival announcing her visit to her grandfather. His reply had been less than warm, but he had not turned her down either—he couldn't when it was the emperor's command.

As was fitting her station, Suzume had a contingent of guards. Mostly warrior priests from the temple, but Naoki and Tsuki joined them as well, along with Hikaru and Rin, who continued pretending to be her maid. Suzume had begged the emperor to set Hikaru free and to her surprise he had granted her request. Normally she would be suspicious of the emperor's generosity, but he had not asked her for anything in return. It seemed he was doing it all out of a genuine sense of remorse. Being the emperor's favorite certainty had its perks.

Suzume had never been to the ancestral home of her mother's family, though she'd heard stories about it from cousins and other relatives on her Kaedemori clan. Her grandfather, the head of the clan, was known for his strong-armed rule. But he was also well loved among his contemporaries. He was famous for his parties, and many a courtier had fought for his favor. Her grandfather's generosity with his allies was only a small part of the appeal. The Kaedemori's were the most influential family in Akatsuki, rivaled only by the royal family. It was said that her grandfather had more influence, money, and land than even the emperor.

Suzume read over the instructions her father had given her, recounting what she already knew about her mother's family. According to this, her grandfather had retired from his council seat and returned to the country home. It seemed strange to her that he would do such a thing. Everything she remembered about her grandfather had painted him as a man hungry for power. Coupled with his disappearance around the time of her own exile, it seemed very strange indeed. Suzume folded up the document and tucked it away as the palace came into view.

The palace was as grand as her cousins had made it out to be. It sat atop a hill overlooking rolling hills and farms. They arrived at sunset, and the golden light gave the landscape a shimmering glow. The gates were open, awaiting their arrival and guards stood at either side, their faces stoic. The inner courtyard, where guests were received, was swept clean and the household stood waiting to greet them.

At the far end of the courtyard was a flight of stairs that led into the inner ring of the palace. Her grandfather stood at the top of the steps, as austere as she remembered him. His beard was long and white, and atop his head he wore the traditional black hat of a councilman. His eyes were as sharp as obsidian.

Suzume closed her curtain to not be seen peeking. Just seeing him standing there reminded her of his strict punishments and his love of rules and proper etiquette. Seeing him again, she recalled a time when she had been a child and she had let her quick tongue get away with her. He had her beat for her insolence and left her kneeling in the courtyard well into the night for it. A phantom pain echoed on her backside and she sat up a little straighter in her seat. *I'm not that little girl anymore.* Naoki opened her door, and he nodded his head as if he could see the fear on her face. She climbed out of the carriage, keeping her face the perfect mask of indifference. The old man didn't scare her. As she approached her grandfather, she made sure to keep her head held high like the princess she was.

"I hope you have been well, grandfather," Suzume said, bowing her head to him. "Thank you for your hospitality."

The old man's gaze swept over her and toward the guards assembled behind her.

"I did not have much choice, did I?" he asked before he turned his back on her and walked into the palace proper.

"I guess that's as warm of a greeting as I can expect," Suzume said under her breath.

Tsuki chuckled. "I can see where you get your temperament from."

Suzume shot him a look, but he was not scared of her death glares and only grinned in reply. Servants showed them to their rooms and Suzume was given a bath to wash off the travel grit from her skin. When she got out of the bath, Hikaru and Rin were standing close together speaking in hushed whispers. She scrutinized the pair of them as if she could divine what they were hiding from her by the backs of their heads.

When they saw Suzume, they turned toward her with guilty expressions on their faces. Suzume glanced between them but before she could ask what they'd been talking about, Hikaru spoke first.

"This place hasn't changed in years," he said, admiring the room.

Any other questions flew from her mind as her brain froze on his statement. "You've been here before?"

Hikaru laughed a bit sheepishly, running his fingers through his hair. "I was born here."

Suzume frowned. "But you're like old, really old."

"And a Kaedemori, though I have not called myself one in many years."

"We're related?"

He smiled. "Very distantly. You would be my brother's granddaughter, many generations removed."

Suzume shook her head. She knew her family had a long history, but Hikaru was her great uncle? That seemed absurd, despite everything else she had learned recently. It was just another connection that tied them together.

"Is the old man my relative too?"

"No, he isn't. I asked him already."

It was worth asking, she supposed. "As far as we can tell the only link we have to one another is the White Palace," Suzume said, considering the evidence.

"Don't worry about that now. You have a dinner party to prepare for." Rin put her hands on Suzume's shoulders, assuming the role of maid once again. She noticed the quick change of subject, but decided not to ask more. They would only find more clever ways to keep the truth from her.

"Don't you have anything for us to do?" Tsuki said as he plopped down on a seat beside Suzume.

"Please find something for him to do," Akira drawled. "He hasn't been this restless since we were left at that shrine."

Suzume considered this for a moment. The emperor wanted her to find any hint of her mother, and considering Tsuki, Akira, and Naoki could move about without being seen, perhaps they could investigate while she was at dinner.

"Why not do a bit of snooping? See if you can find any signs of where my mother went."

Tsuki gave her a deep bow. "Consider it done, my lady."

Naoki lingered a moment longer. "There is a strange energy about this place. Be careful."

"I will. Keep an eye out for me." Naoki bowed and went out into the garden, disappearing onto the rooftops without a sound.

Rin finished styling Suzume's hair and she and Hikaru made an excuse to leave as well. She wanted to follow them and see what they were up to, but it was almost dinner and seeing as she was guest of honor, her absence would be noted.

The dining hall was packed full of her many distant cousins, uncles, aunts, and other members of far-flung branches of the enormous Kaedemori family at the evening meal. To her surprise, she was given a place far away from her grandfather while Ryuu, however, was placed right next to him. *I'm his closest relative here. I should be sitting beside him.* Suzume scowled toward her grandfather's empty seat. Not that she particularly wanted to be close to him. Ryuu did his best to avoid eye contact with her by chatting with one of her great uncles that sat to his right.

A musician played as the dishes were served. Her grandfather remained conspicuously absent. Suzume made polite conversation with her third cousin, about nothing of real particular interest, while her eyes drifted toward Ryuu ever so often. Then halfway through the second course, her grandfather came in. He had a scowl on his face as he sat down. Ryuu leaned across and said something to him but the old man shook his head. *What's Ryuu's connection to the family?* She couldn't help but wonder. The empress had hinted as much. But at the time Suzume thought it was just to goad her.

When dinner was over, the guests slowly drifted out of the room. Suzume kept her eye on Ryuu, waiting and watching for him to leave. He seemed in no hurry to leave and was drinking with the other people in the room. Her grandfather had eaten and left. She considered following him, but given his cold welcome she knew she could not speak without being summoned first.

One of her cousins was talking to her with animation and knocked over a glass on her tray. Liquid was spilled on Suzume, and she took her eyes off Ryuu for just a moment.

When she looked up again, he was gone. *How does he move so quickly?* She wondered. She swiveled her head around, searching for him. He was exiting the hall on the far end away from her. Without even apologizing to her cousin, Suzume leaped up to chase after him. She wanted to see what he was up to.

She weaved her way through the crowd of people in the hall. Only after making her way over, she saw no sign of Ryuu. It was as if he had disappeared in a puff of smoke. Just when she was about to give up, a hand shot out and snatched her. Suzume was pulled into a nearby room.

A hand pressed over her mouth. Flames shot along her body, but a pressure point was pressed into her middle back and the flames died away in an instant. Suzume wriggled around and turned to see Ryuu staring down at her, his blue eyes illuminated softly in the dark room. He pressed his finger to his lips, telling her to be quiet.

She frowned at him, but he let her go and gestured for her to follow him. The room they were in was one that had a fold back door which could make the room larger.

Ryuu crept along the wall and pressed his ear up against the folding door. Suzume frowned after him, was about to ask questions when she heard her grandfather speak on the other side.

"Do we know why they've come?" he asked.

"We have not discovered that yet, my lord," said the second voice.

"The emperor must have sent Izume's daughter to test me."

The servant made no reply, perhaps it was not meant to give anything away.

"Just in case, send warning."

"Yes, my lord." The servant bowed. They listened as the footsteps receded. After a few heartbeats they heard nothing more. Perhaps they had both left.

Ryuu yanked Suzume by the arm and brought her out into the hall again. He kept on pulling her behind him, and it wasn't until they were in a palace garden far away from where they had been that he unclamped his hand off her mouth.

"What was that?"

"I thought you liked eavesdropping," he said.

Suzume only scowled in response.

"If he heard you stomping outside the room, you would have given me away. Not that he revealed much," Ryuu sighed.

"You did that on purpose. Why?"

"Why do you think?" he said with a crooked smile.

She was so frustrated with him. Why did he try to kidnap her and then introduce her to someone else like her? Why did everyone around her trust him, when all he did was confuse her? Why was he so maddening?

"What do you want from me?" she asked out of sheer frustration.

He crossed his arms over his chest and studied her for a moment. "You're much more like Izume than I thought."

She glared right back. "Don't try to change the subject."

His expression turned more serious. "If I could, I would tell you everything. But even now his eyes are on us. It was a risk just bringing in Souta."

"Who's watching us? Can you tell me that?"

"Who do you think?"

They were in her grandfather's home. Was that what Ryuu had been trying to tell her all this time? But what did he have to do with anything?

Before she could question him further however, Ryuu grabbed her and pulled her into the shadows of the nearby awning.

"What are you doing?"

"Shh," he clamped his hand over her mouth. Up above on top of the nearby building, something was leaping from roof to roof. Suzume felt the prickle of warning. There was a yokai in the palace and it was headed straight for her grandfather's room. Suzume and Ryuu shared a single look before they both went running after it.

Thirty

Suzume ran down the hall, with Ryuu just a few feet in front of her. They sprinted through a courtyard, past a few servants who were almost bowled over by their pursuit. The shadows of three yokai leaped from roof to roof. They were headed straight for the inner rings of the palace and straight toward her grandfather. As they approached the inner rings of the palace where her grandfather's rooms were, the yokai dropped down from the rooftops and onto the ground.

Before she could get closer, Ryuu held out his hand to stop her and placed his finger against his lips to tell her to remain quiet. They watched from the shadows as the yokai approached her grandfather's door. One of the group looked around. He was human-like in appearance, with shaggy brown hair, pointed ears, and a wolf pelt tied around his waist. For a moment Suzume thought he had spotted them watching from the shadows, but his eyes glided over them before sneaking inside. The other two yokai followed after him. Suzume and Ryuu waited a few heartbeats before creeping closer to the door.

Ryuu leaned in close to the door to listen in on the conversation. But there were no hushed conspiratorial whispers, only shouts rang out from within. Ryuu threw open the door, and Suzume followed him inside. Her grandfather stood in the center of the room, his long white hair down around his shoulders, and swinging a sword like a madman. The yokai circled around him, weapons drawn. But when they saw Ryuu and Suzume enter they turned their attention to them instead.

She hadn't been expecting an attack here, and she'd left her staff in her room. The only thing she had to fight with was her flame. As the yokai came barreling toward her, she hesitated to attack, running away from him to the far end of the room. *I can't just run away.* She glanced over her shoulder toward the monkey-like yokai who chased her, his long canines gleaming in the dim light of the chamber. *But if I use my flame now, the old man isn't here to help bring me back.* Despite her hesitation, flames sparked along her hands. As usual the flame of Kazue's soul had other ideas. Suzume turned to face the yokai.

She concentrated her fire to her hands, forming a ball of flame. She flung it at her attacker, and the smile was wiped from his face as the fire struck his torso and the flame caught onto his clothes. The yokai screamed before falling onto the floor, thrashing about and trying to put out the fire. While Suzume had taken care of that one, Ryuu had knocked out the second. A third had taken a hold of her grandfather and had a blade pressed to his throat.

"Don't move or I'll kill the old man," the yokai said.

Ryuu was not fazed by the threat and sang a song. Suzume felt the power of it reverberate on her skin. The fire on her body rose higher as if it would reach out and pluck the energy from the very air. But through sheer force of will, she was able to curb her desire to take the power for herself.

The song had no effect on the man holding her grandfather hostage but the yokai on the ground writhed in pain, backs arched as if someone was burning them alive from the inside.

The yokai holding her grandfather watched as his friends were tortured with wide eyes.

"Make all the threats that you want, everything you do to Lord Kaede-mori I will do tenfold to your men," Ryuu said. There was a fierceness to his voice she had never heard before.

The yokai looked back at Ryuu, his eyes wide. "I know you, you're-" The yokai snarled but he was cut off by Ryuu.

"If you know who I am, let's cut to the chase," Ryuu said coldly. "What do you want with Lord Kaedemori?"

He had yet to let go of her grandfather and stared at his men on the floor. "Akio wanted to give him a message." His eyes drifted toward Suzume. "Give me what I am owed."

There was a sinking sensation in Suzume's gut. She didn't like the way the yokai's gaze settled on her.

"Let him go and we can make a deal," Ryuu said.

"We're not making deals with yokai," her grandfather said through gritted teeth. The wolf yokai only smiled and held the blade closer to his throat, just tight enough where if her grandfather breathed too hard the blade would scrape his throat.

Lord Kaedemori held his breath.

"It's too late for that. The deal has already been struck," the yokai said.

Ryuu sang again, and his song was drowned out by the screams of the yokai on the floor. The yokai's grip on her grandfather loosened as his gaze was focused entirely on his comrades.

Suzume saw her chance and took it. While the wolf was distracted, she lunged for him. She shoved her shoulder into his free arm and her grandfather took that same opportunity to slide just out of his grip. The wolf turned toward Suzume with a snarl, and she held up her flaming hands. The pair of them circled one another, and she grabbed onto his forearm with a flaming hand. He pulled back just in time to sweep his leg and knock her onto the ground. Before he could pounce onto her though Ryuu sang another song, different than the first. It caught the wolf yokai in his trap and it was frozen in place. His eyes glared at all of them.

Suzume got back up, panting for breath.

"So you're not completely useless," her grandfather said to her as he rubbed the spot on his neck where the blade had been inches from ending his life.

"Thanks," Suzume replied snidely.

"You've got quicker responses than my men."

Her grandfather looked past Suzume to see several guards who had just arrived. The soldiers did not seem surprised to see the incapacitated yokai lying on the ground. "Take these things away," her grandfather said with an imperious wave of his hand. The guards hurried into the room and gathered up the incapacitated yokai dragging them from the room. Suzume watched them go, shaking her head. *Was everyone keeping yokai from me my entire life?*

"This isn't the first time, is it?" Ryuu asked Lord Kaedemori.

The old man glared at him for a moment, and for a second Suzume thought he was not going to answer at all.

"No, it is not. Come." He gestured for them to follow him.

He led them into the adjoining chamber. His audience chamber was lined with empty armor. The voids of darkness in the helmets seemed to be staring at them as her grandfather led them to a table at the far end of the room. Everyone sat down, and Suzume looked around at the dreary room. A servant came in and when he saw the disheveled state of Lord Kaedemori he tutted.

"They were back again," the servant said. "At least let me dress you, my lord."

"Do something useful and bring us tea," Lord Kaedemori snapped.

The servant only shook his head and left to fulfill the command.

It felt strange to be in her grandfather's personal chambers. He appeared to be dressed for bed, his hair unbound from its typical top knot. She could see how his hairline receded at the temples and he seemed so much older and shrunken in his night clothes.

The servant returned with the tea. He poured each of them a glass before backing out of the room, leaving them alone. No one said anything as they drank their tea.

It was Ryuu who spoke first. "You have some explaining to do."

Her grandfather sighed and set down his teacup. "This goes back generations. Our clan owes all our success and power to the blessing of the forest guardian, Akio."

"And what price have you paid for that?" He looked away toward the empty suits of armor on the wall.

"Nothing important. We honor him with offerings just as one would any other deity."

"And then what changed?" Ryuu prompted.

Her grandfather pursed his lips. "Several years ago someone of my house made a deal with him, for power. The agreed payment was not made and he's started causing problems. It is nothing that we cannot handle."

"What sort of deal did you make?"

Lord Kaedemori turned those dangerous obsidian eyes toward Ryuu. "It wasn't me who made the deal, but my daughter, Izume."

Suzume felt her entire body go cold. "What sort of deal did she make?" Suzume asked.

"You'd have to ask her that."

"You know, don't you?" Suzume slammed her hands down on the table. She was sick of secrets. Anger burst out of her like fire.

The old man glared at her for a moment. "Izume was never forthcoming with me. But she is my daughter. Not long after she disappeared into the forest, she was chosen as a candidate for the emperor's bride."

"She made a deal with this yokai to become empress."

Her grandfather did not answer but continued to stare at Suzume.

"Where is Izume?" Ryuu asked.

Her grandfather looked away from Suzume to focus on Ryuu. "No one knows for certain. She disappeared without leaving a trace and she took her son with her."

It stung her to hear that. Had her mother cared so little for her that she cast her aside?

"The emperor knows you're communicating with her," Ryuu said.

"Does he now?"

"Either you can cooperate or you will be arrested for treason. Those are the terms the emperor has set."

Her grandfather smiled as he leaned forward. "I will make you a deal. Help me with this problem I'm having and I will tell the emperor everything I know."

"We don't need to make a deal."

"Oh, but you do, because once I am gone, it will be her the guardian tries to collect from." He nodded toward Suzume.

"I'll do it." Suzume stood up and both men stared up at her. Her grandfather had a small smile pulling at the corner of his mouth.

"What?" Ryuu swiveled toward her. "Are you insane?"

"You want to find my mother, don't you? Well, so do I. I have some questions for her."

"Are you certain you are up to the task? Akio is nothing to be trifled with," her grandfather said, his hands were folded on the table in front of him, his dark eyes intent on her.

"You don't know what I am capable of."

Her grandfather inclined his head. "Then stop this yokai and I will tell you everything I know."

Suzume bowed and walked out of the room. Ryuu came chasing after her. He grabbed her by the elbow before she could storm away. "You don't need to do this."

"It may not matter to you, but I need to find out why I am this way."

She yanked her arm free and was turning to walk away when Ryuu said to her retreating back, "Your mother asked me to watch out for you."

Suzume turned to face him, eyes wide. "What?"

"I sent you to that shrine for your own protection."

Suzume felt as if the ground was swaying beneath her feet. "Who are you to her?"

She could already see him shutting her out. He hadn't meant to say that much. But she'd had enough of the secrets. She grabbed him by the arm, forcing him to turn around and face her.

"Why are you looking for my mother?" She demanded, meeting his gaze with a steely resolve.

Ryuu sighed heavily. "I've known your mother her entire life. I met her when she was very young."

"And?"

He rubbed the back of his neck not meeting her gaze. "I didn't think you should know."

"Know what?"

He turned to face her at last. "We were lovers."

The word sent a ripple through her. The rumors were true then, this was the man her mother had cheated on the emperor with.

"So, it was you," Suzume said. It was difficult to look at him, staring into the face of the man who had ruined her life. "And when you were caught, you just decided to hide me away in a shrine? Why?"

He reached for her, a tender gesture, but Suzume knocked his hand away before he could touch her. He recoiled, dropping his hand to his side.

"The palace is a dangerous place; your grandfather is a dangerous man. If he found out what you are-"

She shook her head, no one had ever consulted her, so it shouldn't have come as such a surprise.

"I thought she was better than this. I thought..." I thought she cared more about her position as the emperor's wife than to just throw it all away. *She threw me away when I was no use to her.*

She turned to walk away from Ryuu but he grabbed onto her shoulder.

"I love your mother. I will always love her."

Suzume shook him off. "The two of you ruined my life with your selfishness."

"If you'd let me explain."

"I don't want to hear it." She marched away from him.

THIRTY-ONE

Rin crept down the hall, keeping to the shadows. She turned both ways, making sure she wasn't seen. When she knew the way was safe, she slid into the chamber. The old shrine had been painted in recent years and the ofuda plastered to the walls were new. As soon as she approached them they sparked with spiritual energy. This wouldn't be as easy as she had hoped.

The three yokai captives were seated around the open courtyard. It would seem they could leave any time they wished. But a barrier sparked all around the space, and if any of them got too close it would burn them to a crisp. It would be the same for Rin if she got too close. Two of the space's occupants glanced up as she approached. The monkey yokai and the boar yokai watched her warily. The wolf yokai kept his back to her, but she saw how he straightened up as she approached. He had sensed her as she got closer.

"What are you doing here?" the monkey yokai asked as he stood up, and Rin saw the hopeful expression.

"I'm setting you free if you keep quiet." Incapacitating the guards had been easy. With her fox magic she could transform into anything and they hadn't even thought to question one of their own. She'd knocked them out before they knew what was coming. But they wouldn't sleep forever and there was always the risk of someone discovering their unconscious bodies.

"I know you. You work with that exorcist." The boar yokai pointed his hoof at Rin.

"Would you rather die in here?" Rin snapped at them.

The wolf yokai had yet to look at her, but she knew he was listening to every word. The other two yokai watched her but kept their mouths blissfully shut. Rin paced the length of the barrier, searching for the seal which locked them in. Fortunately, it was not an overly complicated one. She could burn it with her fox-fire and destroy it but there was always the risk of starting a fire that would burn out of control. As she puzzled over what she was going to do, a figure approached from the shadows. Rin spun around to face them, her hands up in a defensive pose.

"I should have known I'd find you here," Hikaru said as he stepped out of the shadows.

Rin relaxed to see her husband. She hadn't told him where she was going because he was practical and would have stopped her. But she should have known he would have noticed her missing from their bed. "Do you mind?" She nodded toward the charms on the posts which were sealing the yokai in.

"How are we going to explain when the prisoners are found missing?"

She looked to the prisoners and Hikaru followed her gaze. The wolf had yet to lift his head, but Rin could see the collar around his neck gleaming in the moonlight. It had been hundreds of years since she had seen the face of her old friend. She hated to have their reunion be this way, but they didn't have much other choice. She didn't know much about this generation of Kaedemori, but from what she'd seen since she'd been here, there was no doubt they would kill these yokai. And she couldn't stand by and let that happen.

Hikaru sighed. He knew the history that lay between Rin and the wolf better than anyone else. And because of that he would override his better judgment and help her. He walked up to the charms on the wall and pulled them off with ease. The barrier flickered and fell. The two yokai rushed toward the door and to freedom without a backward glance toward the okami, who remained seated on the ground with his head down.

As far as she could tell, he wasn't injured.

"The barrier is down." Rin took a step toward him but she couldn't bring herself to get any closer. It hurt to see him collared, knowing it was her fault.

"Just go," the wolf said, his voice low but full of intent.

"Enough of this, Shin," she burst out, no longer able to hold back or pretend they were strangers.

He lifted his head, his golden eyes meeting hers for the first time in hundreds of years. The last time she had stood face to face with him, he had exchanged his life for hers, becoming the eternally bound servant of Akio.

Tears pricked her eyes but she refused to let them fall. She took a step toward him and he growled like a feral dog. She held her ground, glaring at him.

"Does your pride know no bounds?" she snapped.

Hikaru came and put a hand on her shoulder. Shin's eyes flickered toward Hikaru, and she saw that same sadness cross over his gaze.

"You found him again." He lowered his gaze back to the ground.

"Do you think either of us like seeing you this way?" Hikaru asked. He was normally stoic, but there were frustration and anger reflected in his eyes. "I wouldn't have let this happen if I knew this is how you'd live your life."

Shin's eyes snapped up to Hikaru. "I hoped neither of you would ever have to gaze upon on this pathetic form again. Do you think I'm happy being reduced to this?" He snatched at the collar as he stood and glared at the both of them.

But the fire died out him and he sank to the ground again. "I'm tired of fighting. Leave me to the humans, at least then I'll be at peace."

Rin marched up to him and slapped him hard across the face. Hard enough that he almost fell backward.

"I hate seeing you this way."

"If it was my choice, you'd never see me again." He reached for the collar and then his hand dropped to his side.

"It's not the collar," Rin sighed in exasperation. "All the light has died from your eyes. Now more than ever, I need you."

She saw a glimmer of hope there in his expression. "What can I do bound to Akio?"

"The dragon is regaining power and he needs you by his side."

Shin balled his hand into a fist. "I can't do anything for him."

"You were his eyes. You were his right hand once."

For the first time she saw real hope shining through. "Akio will not let me go easily."

Rin nodded. "I know, but if I cannot be with him, someone has to be there that he can trust."

Shin did not question her or ask her why she had left the dragon behind. But as he had sent her to the dragon, so it was her to turn to send him to their former master.

Shin stood up, and there was a ghost of the old him in his expression. But it was quickly wiped away and replaced by a snarl. Rin felt the energy and she turned slowly.

Ryuu stood in the doorway. His presence seemed to fill the space.

"I found the guards in the hall." He said it calmly. There was no accusation in his tone.

"You," Shin growled, and stepped in front of Rin and Hikaru.

Ryuu held up his hand. "I have no intention of raising the alarm."

Rin reached for Shin, trying to hold him back. "Don't." She shook her head.

Shin looked at her as if she'd lost your mind. "You know who he is, don't you?"

Hikaru stared at Ryuu. "We know exactly who he is."

"Then let's end this here." Shin growled again.

"I'd rather not fight you," Ryuu said blandly and rested his hand on the pommel of his blade. Shin's gaze flickered toward it.

They could all feel the weight of the blade. It was not human forged, but a great yokai blade. Blades like that could only be wielded by the strongest yokai, and by all rights he never should have been able to lift it, let alone wear it with ease. But there were many things about him that made no sense at all.

Ryuu said to them, "I wanted to speak with you, but the timing wasn't right."

Rin wanted to burst out laughing but this wasn't funny. Not even a little bit. "Did you really think we wouldn't recognize you?"

Ryuu lowered his head as if chastised. "I suppose not. Thank you for keeping my secret."

"It wasn't for your benefit," Rin snapped.

Hikaru grabbed onto her. She could feel herself losing control. Now was not the time or place and even if she wanted to tear him apart, piece by piece, it wouldn't change anything.

"If you let me explain."

"There's nothing you need to explain," Hikaru said calmly. He stood between Rin and Ryuu now.

"Only one thing matters now. Will you let us go?"

Ryuu stepped aside. "I was never going to stop you. But if you would do me a favor, don't tell Suzume about this."

"Why should I keep it from her?" Rin challenged him.

"Because I want to explain everything to her. It's the least I can do."

There were so many things she wanted to say. So many questions, but now was not the time or the place. And that was why Ryuu had chosen now, when she was trying to free Shin. This was the price for her secrecy. And she would have to pay it.

"Tell her soon, before I do," Rin said.

He nodded his head. "I promise."

He bowed to them and then walked away. Shin watched him go, mouth half open. "Are you going to let him go?"

Hikaru and Rin shared a look, their thoughts were the same on the matter. "Even if we tried to stop him, he could defeat all three of us with ease. We're no match for him." But that was only half the truth. She could tell Shin, who at one time had been her closest friend. It was her fault Ryuu was this way and now he was too strong for her to stop him.

Thirty-Two

Early the next morning they headed into the forest. Suzume's eyes were heavy from lack of sleep and she'd woken to even more bad news. The yokai they'd captured the night before had escaped. Everyone was on edge as they traveled. Fortunately, Rin and Hikaru knew this area well. As it turned out, they had lived and tended to a shrine in the foothills of the mountains into which they were journeying. But the pair of them had been hesitant to go into the forest. According to them, the guardian of the forest was a dangerous yokai one known for his mercurial temper. But after some serious wheedling on Suzume's behalf, she wore down Hikaru and he agreed to guide them.

Finding her mother could put her one step closer to figuring out why she had a piece of Kazue's soul inside her. If Suzume had been born with it as the old man claimed, then her mother had to know something and she had a feeling this forest guardian knew how it had happened too.

They made their way through the forest by foot. Sunlight could hardly permeate the thick canopy of foliage overhead and as a result, the forest was left in a dim twilight. Fog collected, making visibility limited. The entire forest prickled with spiritual energy, making the hairs on the back of her neck rise up on end. At the head of the group was Ryuu, followed by six of the warrior priests they'd brought. Suzume had been avoiding him since the night before. There was no excuse he could make that would let her forgive him.

Between her mother and him, they'd ruined her life. If he'd never suggested she go to the shrine, Suzume would have continued living in the palace with her father. The emperor had already proved his willingness to protect her. He was the only one who really cared for her.

Something screeched in the mist and Suzume was yanked from her thoughts. The flames leaped to her skin in her defense and she reached for her staff as she scanned her surroundings. She expected some monster to leap out of the forest at any moment. But a lone bird flew past their heads. Suzume relaxed, as did all of the warriors around her.

Naoki, who stood to her left, was the only one who remained alert, scanning the forest.

"Do you sense something?" Suzume asked him.

Naoki didn't take his eyes off the impenetrable fog, as if he was seeing beyond what everyone else could see.

"We're being watched," he said.

Suzume swung her head around, as if eyes would materialize out of the mist, but she couldn't see anything.

At the head of the group Ryuu shouted, "Everyone keep close, we don't want to get separated."

"He'll already know we're here," Rin said. She'd taken her true kitsune form, and her flickering tails gave them dim light in the fog and darkness of the forest.

Hikaru was gripping his bow and arrow tightly and his eyes were illuminated green in the dim light.

Suzume drew her staff and crept along after the others. She jumped at the slightest sound. Tsuki stepped on a twig and she leaped into the air, swinging her staff, and would have knocked Naoki upside the head if he didn't have quick reflexes. He caught the staff before it could strike him, and gave Suzume a look that said, 'calm down.'

She tried deep breathing to calm her nerves, but this place was like a twisted maze of trees and fog. A white blur zoomed past, and Suzume saw only a flash of it from the corner of her eye. On closer inspection there was nothing but a fallen tree, thick with moss. *I'm starting to see things.*

As they went deeper, all light ceased to break through the trees and though it should have been early morning, the forest was dark as night. There was a definite chill in the air. That's when she heard a howl in the distance. Everyone drew their weapons and they moved into a circle, waiting for an attack.

"Hold," Ryuu said, putting up his hands. He scanned the forest.

There was no sound, just wind blowing through the trees and the faint echo of their breathing. Then very faintly at first, Suzume felt it, a rumbling just beneath her feet. She looked around to see if anyone else had felt it and that's when the massive beast burst from the nearby forest. It was twice the height of Rin in her true form. Suzume stared at the boar that was both animal and something made of foliage. Its thick hide was covered in moss, and its eyes were hollow like a skeleton's. Its tusks were the entire length of Suzume's body and were hung with vines.

"Run!" Ryuu shouted.

Everyone scattered. Suzume did not even bother to try and stand up to such a horrifying monster. She ran heedlessly through the forest. As she ran branches reached out, grabbing a hold of her clothes, tearing into her. Suzume felt the flames rising up in response to her fear, illuminating her and making her the perfect target for the beast. It turned and its thundering footsteps followed after her.

A root jumped up out of nowhere and caught her foot. She tripped and collided with the ground, landing hard on her right arm. She rolled a few feet before coming to a stop. When she did, she grasped her arm. Pain bloomed from her shoulder, shooting down to her elbow. It might be broken. There wasn't much time to assess the damage because the creature was closing in now, but her staff had been knocked out of her hand. She struggled to get to her feet, unable to put weight on her arm. She fell back onto her back.

The tusks were inches away from impaling her when she held up her hand and shot a fiery blast toward the creature. The flames caught on the moss, which covered its entire hide, and began spreading fast. The creature had reacted just a moment too late and began thrashing around in the forest—bucking and smashing into trees, trying to put out the flames.

Suzume rolled out of the way of its crashing feet, found her staff, and kept on running in the opposite direction away from the monster. Her injured arm dangled at her side. She kept on running until she was certain she'd gotten far enough away—where it could not find her again. Only then did she stop to catch her breath, by leaning against a tree. Her shoulder was throbbing painfully and she could not quite raise it up. *I definitely broke it.*

Behind her a branch snapped. Suzume turned to see where the sound was coming from. She thought she saw that white shadow again. Unthinking, she reached for her weapon but pain shot up her arm as she tried to raise it. After a few tense moments, nothing came out of the mist to kill her, but that didn't change the fact that she was in the middle of the spooky forest, surrounded by trees, with no way of knowing from which way she had come. *Just great.* She chose a direction at random and started walking. She figured eventually she'd stumble into someone or figure out where she was going.

She had only gone a few feet when a giant white wolf stepped out of the shadows and in front of her. His fur was pristine as fallen snow and he was twice her height. Suzume stared up at it as it bared pointed teeth.

Suzume channeled her fire, thinking the flames would deter the creature that was slowly creeping closer to her with every second. But the animal seemed unafraid of the flames. Even a yokai should have feared the holy flame, or at least she would have hoped. It couldn't know she wouldn't use the full extent of her power for fear of losing control again.

"Stay back," she said, waving her flaming hands at the creature.

"You shouldn't be here," he said.

"I'm warning you."

The wolf lunged for her and Suzume stumbled out of the way. She tripped over a nearby branch and went falling to the ground, rolling over just as the wolf pinned her in place.

"Humans are not allowed in the guardian's forest. Get out of here before it's too late."

It was a risk but Suzume tried something. "I'm here to see the guardian."

"You're a fool to even tempt him. Leave before it's too late." He stepped off her and backed away.

She climbed to her feet the best she could with an apparently broken arm. And the two of them faced off. The giant white wolf was blocking the way, but even if she hadn't broken her arm, she didn't think she'd be any match against this wolf. That massive boar had been just dumb luck. Well, maybe not so lucky since she broke her arm for her trouble.

"Go!" he roared, his voice echoing over her. Suzume almost stumbled backward, but before she could fall over she was caught from behind.

She turned around to see Naoki holding onto her.

"Bring her to Akio. I think he'll want to see her," Naoki said, his voice even.

"That's exactly why I'm not bringing her there," the wolf said.

"This is outside of your control."

"You're free of him. You don't have to serve him anymore."

Naoki made no comment and only stared at the wolf. Suzume's head swiveled between the two of them. "Anyone care to explain what's going on here?"

The wolf transformed from the white wolf to a more human visage. It was the same yokai who had attacked the night before. His shaggy, brown hair was tied at the nape of his neck and his kosode was open to reveal a tanned chest, leading down to a wolf pelt tied around his waist.

"Like what you see?" he said with a wolfish grin at Suzume after catching her assessing him.

Suzume scoffed. "Hardly."

The wolf laughed, but sobered quickly. "Are you sure about this, Naoki?"

The legendary swordsman nodded his head. "She made me promise."

The wolf sighed heavily and then ran his hands through his hair before turning around. "Come. I will bring you to Akio."

Suzume hesitated to follow the wolf. "What's going on? You know him."

"We used to serve the same master."

"You mean he served Kazue too?" Were there any yokai she hadn't enslaved?

"No, we both served Akio, the forest guardian, until she bought me from him."

"She bought you?"

But Naoki was no longer in the mood for sharing and he silently followed the wolf, forcing Suzume to join or be left behind. They took a winding pathway through the forest. Both of them seemed to know the way and Suzume struggled to keep up with them. After a few minutes they reached a large bridge over a canyon, and beyond she could see high walls of a palace. She had not expected the place to be so large.

"This is it?"

"What were you expecting?"

"I thought guardians of the forest lived more naturally..." In truth she didn't know anything about forest guardians, but this one lived in a palace, just like the kami had. Was he some sort of kami? Her grandfather spoke of him like he was a god.

"Akio is not like other forest guardians," the wolf replied.

He led the way across the bridge, on which Suzume resisted the urge to peer over the side. From the way their footsteps echoed, it was a long way down. They entered a courtyard with a massive tree, the roots of it weaving into the gaps between cobblestones.

At the top of the stairs leading out of the courtyard, a pair of servants with the heads of deer were waiting.

"Prepare the lady to meet with Akio," the wolf barked.

As the maids came closer to her, Suzume felt her defenses flare. There was something about this place that put her on edge. The sooner she could talk to the guardian and get out of here the better. When the maids reached for her, she knocked their hands away. "I'm not here to waste time. Take me to this guardian."

"He will not see you unless you are properly attired," the okami said.

He glanced down at her muddy clothes. Suzume flushed, embarrassed by her disheveled appearance.

"What's wrong with my clothes?"

The wolf only raised an eyebrow without comment.

The servants gestured for her to follow, and Suzume sighed before letting them lead her down a series of twisting hallways. Naoki stayed close to her, but it was only a small comfort. She was starting to question whether she made the right decision coming here. Once Suzume peeked behind her, trying to get her bearings on where they were in case she needed to escape, only to find the hallways had changed entirely.

"The palace shifts all the time," Naoki said.

Suzume felt a chill down her spine. What had she gotten herself into?

She was brought to a room that rivaled what she had at the White Palace. There servants dressed and changed her into a kimono with a pattern of sakura blossoms. The servants bowed and left her and Naoki alone. When they were alone she turned on him, pointing her finger.

"You have some explaining to do."

The legendary swordsman was leaning against the wall, staring at the garden beyond her room. A tree grew in the center of the garden with giant white blossoms which floated gently on the breeze before landing on the ground.

"I was given to Akio as punishment for betraying my creator," he said, not facing her. His voice was even and without emotion. "And then Kazue made a deal with Akio. She traded the dragon for me." He turned to face her. His gaze was direct, without conflict. He merely stated the facts.

"Kazue sealed Kaito to protect her child." Suzume felt compelled to defend her, perhaps because a part of her was Kazue.

"That is what she told you. Kazue wanted power. By the time she sealed the dragon, she had already started amassing more power than any human before her. She wanted to be equal in power to the dragon. And it made her enemies, so she needed me. But to get me, she had to pay the price."

Suzume's hands trembled and she started pacing the floor to quell her restlessness. "Then why did you want me to come here?"

"Because you have to make the same deal."

Suzume rounded on Naoki suddenly. "What?"

"You have to destroy the dragon."

THIRTY-THREE

Suzume stared at the legendary swordsman. It felt as if her entire body had turned to ice. Kill Kaito? That just wasn't possible, even if she was strong enough. She never wanted to see him again, sure, but she didn't want him dead either. She shook herself. She couldn't even consider it. Naoki was watching her with a slight smirk on his normally expressionless face. And then it hit her.

"You're not Naoki."

The corners of his lips turned upward in a maniac's smile. How had she not seen it straight away? Naoki was sworn to protect her. He would never have lured her into this sort of trap. It could only be one person.

"You're losing your touch, Suzume," Hisato said as he revealed himself, transforming into the form she was most familiar with.

Suzume backed up and reached for her staff with her broken arm. Shooting pain traveled up and down her arm and it fell uselessly at her side. Even under normal circumstances she was no match against Hisato, but in this condition she was practically helpless. Hisato stalked closer to her and Suzume backed away, never letting her eyes leave his face.

"I haven't lost my touch, you're just getting sloppier. I knew it was you the entire time," she lied.

Hisato threw his head back and laughed, his voice echoing off the ceiling and even inside her head. His lips didn't move, but she could feel his words slithering around inside her.

You cannot lie to me, Suzume. I know you too well.

Knowing he was inside her head and in front of her, Suzume panicked and ran for the door. But before she could even reach it, he cut her off, smiling in that insane disjointed way of his. Fire bloomed along her fingertips and she lifted it up to shield herself. Maybe if she could burn him enough to disable him for a little while, she could escape.

But before the flames even came to life they were extinguished and Suzume was frozen in place. She couldn't even move her fingers.

"Each time you use your power, I get stronger. Just as it did in Kazue." He reached out, cupping her face in his hand. "But you knew that, didn't you? The darkness calls to you, just as it did Kazue."

Never!

"What I said before, it was the truth. Kazue betrayed the dragon to his greatest enemy in exchange for Naoki. She will pretend she wants you to destroy me but in reality, she wants to consume you. If I am gone she can be reborn truly immortal.

And you want the same, Suzume thought, as she mentally struggled against whatever spell Hisato had put her under.

"I can see it in your eyes. You think I am no different than Kazue, that I will absorb you to make myself stronger. But that is not true. I merely want to give you the life you deserve." He pushed her hair behind her ear in a mockery of a loving gesture. There was nothing about Hisato that was affectionate. Everything he did was calculated to make her believe his poisonous lies.

He dipped down as if to press his lips against her, but it was then that the flame inside her sparked and burst out, burning both her and Hisato's face. He reeled backward and clutched at his burned lips.

To her surprise Suzume found her voice and she could move again. She leaped backward away from him. "You can spin all the stories you like, but I know you for what you are—you're a murderer." She jabbed her pointer finger in his direction.

"Quite the opposite, actually. I am giving back what Kazue took." Already the burned flesh on his lip was healing.

Suzume laughed mockingly. This was just more of his tricks. Despite her show of confidence, inside she was terrified.

"I knew you would not believe me. That's why I brought you here, so you could see what I've been working on." Hisato turned to walk toward the door, and she found her feet forced to follow. Whatever escape she'd made from his hold on her had been temporary. Maybe he'd only allowed her momentary freedom so she'd feel like she had a choice.

Hisato led her down the twisted corridors of the palace. Despite the ever-changing nature of the path and the confusing, curving hallways, he moved about with ease as if he'd spent his entire life here. Suzume once again tried to memorize their route, still planning an escape. It was an exercise in futility. She was going to have to play along with Hisato's games for now. They stopped in front of a pair of double doors where two yokai stood guard.

When Hisato approached the yokai bowed and allowed them to enter. The room beyond was enormous, rivaling the size of the emperor's throne room. Columns lined the edges of the space and inside were hundreds of yokai, most of them strange mixtures of humans and animals. There was a man with the body of a boar wearing human clothes. While a woman with a deer's head and a woman's body carried a tray. There were all manner of forest animals, foxes, raccoons, all in human clothes and standing upright. But towering over the heads of a few of them were monstrous oni—the same dumb, brutish creatures she'd fought before. They watched her with hungry eyes as she followed Hisato to the front.

At the far end of the room was a massive boar. His bulk consumed the space. Beautiful women yokai held up platters of food from which he ate greedily, spilling crumbs on the heads of his servants, who barely came up to his middle. He wore hakama and hoari, vaguely in the court style, but even with human clothing it did not disguise his pig-like face or the hoof-like hands. He drank heavily from a bowl and liquid dribbled over his snout and down his neck, staining the collar of his hoari. Had Suzume the ability, she would have crinkled her nose at the sight of him.

As they approached the throne, Hisato bowed deeply to the creature and Suzume, like a puppet controlled by Hisato, did the same.

The creature dropped a giant thigh bone picked clean of meat onto a platter held by one of the nearby servants and then turned his beady black eyes on Suzume.

"You are her, then." The creature scanned her up and down. "Not much to look at. I would say I was cheated in my trade."

Not much? If I had control, I'd burn him to a crisp right here. As if the flames were summoned by her thoughts, her fingers sparked faintly but unlike the last time her power had taken over, she did not regain control over her body. Hisato's hold on her was too strong.

"Her appearance can be deceiving," Hisato said.

The boar sniffed. "She has the look of that woman."

"Kazue?" Hisato asked with a sidelong glance at Suzume. That was for her benefit, she could tell. Hisato already knew everything.

The boar shook his massive head, his tusks gleaming in the light. "The Kaedemori brat, the woman who sold her firstborn to woo the emperor."

Then what my grandfather said is true. My mother made some sort of deal with this monster.

"Then if she matters so little, you will not mind giving her to me," Hisato said.

The boar narrowed his eyes at the pair of them, roving over Suzume in a way that made her skin crawl. "Don't think I will give her up so easily. The dragon has returned, and I'll be needing someone powerful to protect me."

As if I would ever serve you! Suzume screamed inside her head, to no avail. She could only stay still, head bowed, listening.

"Then I can be of some service. I have an even better prize for you, if you will give me her." Hisato gestured toward Suzume.

The boar leaned forward. "Show me."

Hisato waved his hand. "Bring him in."

The doors at the end of the room were opened. One of the warrior priests who had been traveling in the forest was brought into the room. He walked in with his head held high, his gaze trained on them. When he saw Suzume his eyes widened only for a moment, before he was forced to kneel on the ground in front of the boar.

"You have trespassed upon my land, human, and the price for such a transgression is death. How do you plead?"

The man glared back at him without speaking.

"I had to still his tongue, lest he try to chant and free himself," Hisato said.

"It matters little. Do what you will with him."

He strolled over toward the man and knelt before him. A small stone appeared in his hand and he held it out to the young man.

"I can spare your life. All that you must do is consume this stone."

The man eyed the stone dubiously, his gaze flickering toward Hisato before he reached out with shaking hands to take it. *Don't do it, you fool!* But no one could hear her pleas, except perhaps Hisato. Very slowly the priest brought the stone to his lips. Suzume watched powerlessly as the man swallowed the stone. There was a deadly hush throughout the room. Nothing happened, and even the man appeared visibly relieved.

Then Hisato stood and turned toward Suzume. "Now sing."

With every ounce of willpower she had, she tried to keep her lips sealed. The command Hisato gave her pulled at her lips, yanking them back over her teeth which she clamped closed. But in the end she could not disobey, and when Suzume's mouth opened an unfamiliar song poured out of her, weaving through the air. Power prickled all over her body and as she sang, the man fell over in convulsions. Try as she might she couldn't stop the song which was torturing the man. The power continued to pour out of her and slam into the young man's body in waves. His face changed colors first, and then hair started to sprout all over his body. Horns burst from his forehead. The man pitched forward, screaming in agony as his entire body contorted. His bones cracked and his entire body turned into a glob of jelly. The song died away, and the unformed mass stretched and contorted as new limbs were reformed from the wreckage.

Suzume could not tear her eyes away even after the song finished and there was nothing left of the priest but a panting pile of fur and torn clothes. For a moment she thought she had killed him. And then slowly, he rose, monstrous in appearance. Not quite man, but not quite human either. His arms were covered in coarse fur. It was his eyes that were the most disturbing—they glowed red. The same as her spiritual aura.

Hisato turned with a flourish to Akio. He was leaning forward, examining the creature with intense pleasure gleaming in his eyes.

"What is it?" the boar asked.

"This is a new breed of life. Both human and yokai, with the ability of both." Hisato pointed at the monster. The yokai around the room muttered to themselves, gazing in horror at the creature. At the front of the room, she spotted the wolf, the same who'd come to attack her grandfather and found her in the forest. Of everyone in the room, he was the only one watching her. As if she were the monster, because it had been her power which created it.

"Will it be able to defeat the dragon though?" Akio asked.

"Watch." Hisato gestured. "Kill him." He pointed to one of the oni, whose body was covered in mottled blue skin. It was perhaps twice the height of the creature Suzume had created, and he wielded a club stained suspiciously with what looked like blood.

"That abomination will not be able to destroy me," the oni said as he pushed his way to the front of the crowd. He came thundering toward it. The creature kept its head lowered, as if it was ashamed of its own existence.

The oni swung his club, but before he could land a blow the monster lifted his head, its bright red eyes trained upon its attacker. A song rippled out from him, and Suzume felt the power brush against her skin and was repulsed by it. It was like spiritual energy but different, almost as if it was rotted from the inside.

A blast of red light slammed into the oni, burning a hole through his chest. He fell over with a wet thump, dead before he even landed. His club clattered on the ground beside him.

There was a deadly hush throughout the room as everyone stared at the fallen oni, and then the monster who had killed him.

"I have hundreds more at my disposal. Give me the girl and you will have what you wanted, destruction of the dragon."

"And it is her who has the power to make these?" The boar's eyes gleamed. "Why would I give you her for a mere copy when I can use her and make my own army?"

Hisato had another trick up his sleeve. Her eyes darted around the room. If only she could break free.

"We made a deal," Hisato said, and as he spoke the yokai around the room started to close in around Suzume and him.

"Oh, we did, but I've decided the deal is off." And then to the okami, who had transformed into a massive white wolf, he said, "Take her."

Kill them all, Hisato said, giving a silent command inside her head that could not be disobeyed.

THIRTY-FOUR

The yokai crowded around her. Fire was already rising to the surface, surrounding her in flames. As soon as the yokai saw the holy fire which haloed her, they took a step back. Only the white wolf seemed unafraid of her flames and he lunged toward her. Suzume swung swiping at his body, but he rolled out of the way. The flames brushed against him, hardly singeing his fur.

A boar wielding a long spear jabbed it toward Suzume. She dodged the blow by spinning out of the way. And came up behind the creature and sliced him across the back. It fell to the ground. As she did this another yokai came up behind her, attempting to catch her unaware, swinging with his sword. She turned one hand, sending a fiery blast toward him, that burned hot and fast. It would reduce him to ashes in a matter of moments.

The monstrosity she had helped Hisato create was also beating back the yokai, using the power of his spiritual energy to blow through the crowd. All the while Hisato's manic laughter floated on the air. Suzume watched it all, trapped within her own mind as the drama unfolded.

The wolf continued to hound her, attempting to scratch and claw at her. They were equally matched it seemed because neither of them could successfully land a debilitating blow.

That's enough for now. I think he's learned his lesson, Hisato said.

The creature made an opening for them to escape and Hisato took a hold of Suzume, pulling her along as if tethered to him by an invisible string. They made their way down the twisting corridors of the boar's palace with Hisato leading the way, the monster covering the rear, and the boar's guards chasing after them. The creature stopped to hold them off as they turned the corner. The shouts and clash of weapons competed with the song the monster tried to use against them. But the sheer numbers of yokai overwhelmed the monster and his pained screams drowned out all other sound as he was killed.

She could not even turn her head to see what had happened.

"Don't worry, we can make more."

It wasn't a comforting thought. They found an empty room and Hisato pulled her inside. They listened as the boar's men ran past. Once he was confident they were safe, he turned to her.

"I appreciate your role in this charade, Suzume. It won't be long before everyone learns of your power to corrupt humans—to make them more powerful than yokai."

I will destroy you, she thought. He stepped closer to her, so her entire vision was taken up by him.

"I gave you the choice to come to me, Suzume. But now you've forced my hand. I will not take you with me, not yet. I have one more job left for you. You must kill the dragon."

As if I would do that.

"You can try to fight it, but just as you control the dragon, so I control you. We are connected because I am a part of you and you will do as I say."

Pain rippled through her as if she were being stabbed by thousands of white-hot needles. Her legs buckled and she fell to the ground. Though she wanted to curl in a ball, she was not even afforded that luxury.

"You are forbidden from telling anyone what you must do. If you try to interfere in any way, I will know and I will punish you for it."

He grabbed her by the chin, forcing her to meet his gaze. Staring up at him, she knew there was no hope of fighting. It was her selfishness that had gotten her here, and now she would pay the price.

"Now go, return to your friends."

She stood up and started walking, her steps automatic. Hisato had opened a portal in the nearby wall. Try as she might to fight against his command, she marched through the portal anyway. Walking through it felt like stepping through an icy waterfall. She felt all the hairs on her arms and neck stand on end. There was a strange disorienting sensation, as if she couldn't figure out what way was up and what was down. After a few seconds it was over and she was standing in the middle of the forest, not far from where she had disappeared.

A quick test revealed she had control of her limbs once more. It wasn't until then that she realized the arm she had thought broken had healed. *How is that possible?*

There wasn't much time to consider it because Tsuki and Naoki came bursting from the nearby brush. When they saw Suzume standing in the middle of the forest staring at her hand, they both came up short.

"Well this might be the easiest rescue we've ever done," Tsuki said, sheathing his weapon.

Naoki handed Suzume her staff which she'd dropped when she fell and broken her arm.

"His-" she started to say, but the words dried up in her throat. So, it was true, she couldn't tell them anything. "Do-" she tried again. No matter how she tried to form the sentence it was impossible.

"As much as I'd love to chat, we need to get you out of here," Tsuki said. "Ryuu has called a retreat. The guardian isn't going to let us get anywhere near his palace today."

They don't know where I've been. Perhaps a few hours had elapsed, long enough for them to believe she had merely been lost in the woods. And it wasn't as if she could tell them different. Naoki was watching her, his expression impossible to read. Suzume hesitated, thinking about how Hisato had used his form to deceive her. Would she ever be able to trust anyone again? She couldn't even trust herself anymore.

THEY REJOINED RYUU AND THE OTHER PRIESTS WHERE THEY WERE congregated in the forest. As she approached with Tsuki and Naoki, Ryuu met her gaze. Her guilt made her turn away from him. There was something about the way he looked at her, it felt as if he could see right through her.

"Are we missing anyone else?" Ryuu asked the group.

"Just Touma."

Suzume cringed. That had to be the name of the priest Hisato had forced her into transforming. And how was it possible she could do such a thing? If only she could speak up and say something, but as it was, her tongue was glued to the roof of her mouth. None of them would ever know the fate of this man. His death would forever be her secret shame.

"Let's get the princess out of here. The rest of you keep searching for Touma." Ryuu, seeing Suzume's pained expression, misread it and said, "We'll find another way to get the information about your mother," Ryuu said, placing his hand on her shoulder.

She had almost forgotten that was the reason she'd gone into this forest. Once again her impulsive nature had put everyone around her in danger. *Don't worry about finding her. I need to figure out how to stop Hisato from using me to kill Kaito.*

But she couldn't say that. All she could manage was a nod.

They returned to her grandfather's palace and she and Ryuu were shown to his personal chambers once more. Tea was served. Suzume would have rather been anywhere but there. She needed to figure out how to break from Hisato's control over her, not wasting time on politics. Even if her mother knew how she had gotten this way, it wouldn't change anything. She could see that now. She'd been so obsessed with the past that she couldn't see what was right in front of her.

"You've done it. I'm impressed," her grandfather said.

Suzume's head shot up. *What is he talking about? All I did was turn a man into a monster before getting him killed.*

"But, my lord, we never made it to the guardian's palace," Ryuu said, clearly just as confused as Suzume.

Lord Kaedemori shrugged his shoulders. "Whatever you did it made an impression. I received a visitor." He said the word with hardly veiled disgust. "Who informed me Izume's debt has been paid."

Suzume stared at her grandfather. Was this Hisato's trick? Had he taken her grandfather's form to deceive her? But why would he do that? Her head hurt just going through the possibilities.

"As for my end of the bargain." He slid a map across a table toward them. "I've marked the location where she is hidden."

Ryuu took the paper and bowed his head.

Suzume thought of all she had seen—the man who had died, Hisato's spell over her. None of it was fair. Not to her and not to the innocent who had died. And then a thought occurred to her, what if this had been her grandfather's plot all along? According to Souta she had been born with the power. Her grandfather controlled every aspect of the family. It would not surprise her if he knew exactly how she'd gotten this way.

"You knew," Suzume said to her grandfather.

"I knew your mother made a deal with that creature to become empress. But the fool didn't realize there are still many who oppose us. And she still ended up as second wife."

Suzume gripped the table hard. "Don't pretend it wasn't your idea from the start. That's why that monster was after you. But when she didn't become empress you had to make a different plan."

All the pieces were starting to fall into place. He had to be the one. There was no other explanation.

"I do not know what you're talking about."

"You did this to me." Suzume slammed her hands onto the table in front of her, singeing the wood. Her grandfather stared at the burn marks then to her.

"Pity you weren't born a boy, then you might have been useful to us."

In a flash she lost her temper and a ball of fire came to her hand. She flung it toward his head, missing just by a few inches. The flames caught on the wall behind him. Her grandfather leaped up, shouting to put out the fire as Suzume turned and stormed out of the room. Servants rushed in to put out the fire she had started.

She stormed away and started heading to her room. But she couldn't look into their eyes knowing that she was going to kill Kaito and didn't know how to stop it. Besides, her grandfather was going to have her kicked out soon anyway. She headed for the door outside instead, storming through the courtyard past the confused guards. She'd almost made it to the gate when someone grabbed a hold of her arm.

She spun around to face Ryuu, whose eyes were glowing blue. It reminded her too much of Kaito.

"Go away." She gnashed her teeth, like the monster she was.

"We need to talk," Ryuu said.

"I have nothing to say to you." She flung a fiery ball at him, but he knocked it aside as if it was nothing. The fire dispersed into sparks that faded into the night.

"Well, that's good, because I just need you to listen."

"You're right to be mad at your grandfather. He's a grasping, power-hungry man. And you are correct, he did make a deal with the forest guardian to make Izume empress."

Suzume scoffed.

"But she didn't become empress because I convinced the emperor not to choose her."

Suzume's eyes widened.

"Why?"

"Because I loved your mother."

Suzume threw her head back and laughed. "Well thank you for being honest about how you've ruined my life." She turned to walk away but he stepped in front of her, blocking her path.

"I'm not telling you this to make you angry. I'm telling you because it wasn't your grandfather who put Kazue's soul inside you. It was me."

THIRTY-FIVE

There were a hundred different questions she could have asked. A thousand different feelings burning up inside her. But none of them were good enough. There weren't words that could express what she felt.

"Why?" she croaked.

He took a step toward her as if he would reach out to her, try and comfort her. She stepped away from him.

"Don't touch me." Her emotions were unchecked and flames erupted along her body.

He didn't seem to be bothered by this fact and continued to stare at her, pleading with her eyes for her to understand.

"I thought my seal would hold. I never knew the powers would manifest," he said.

Suzume let go a bitter laugh. "Is that your excuse? You really expect me to believe it? You sent me to that shrine and I awakened the dragon. Was that your plan all along? Were you and my grandfather plotting to bring the dragon to your side? To help you take over the throne?"

"Just let me explain."

She shook her head. It all made sense now. He had brought her to Souta. He was second-in-command of the temple where Hikaru had served, and he had been her mother's lover. She laughed again. It was a mad disjointed sound, and for a moment she felt as if she were floating outside her body. As if Hisato had taken her over once more. But it wasn't that. She was just numb to it all now. Ryuu watched her as she slowly unraveled, not saying a word.

When Suzume's laughter faded away she shook her head and said, "On second thought, don't tell me why. Whatever your motivation was I don't really care. But the least you can do is take this from me." She slammed her hand against her chest.

Ryuu glanced over his shoulder, as if making sure there was no one who could overhear them. The only people around were the guards, but they were too far away to hear anything they said.

"I'm sorry-" Ryuu started to say. Suzume shook her head. She should have known.

"Don't lie to me!" she shouted, her voice echoing back at her bouncing off the walls. The guards turned in her direction now, and Ryuu stood up straighter, scanning the horizon.

"Please, if you'd just let me." He tried to grab her again, but she shot a flaming ball at him. He dodged it, but it caught onto the nearby building.

"Fire!" the guards shouted as they rushed to put it out. The flames caught quickly, spreading up the side of the building but neither Suzume or Ryuu moved. They were locked in place. Orange light and long shadows blanketed them both. Dark and light played against one another as Suzume's anger manifested in the flames she had created.

"I can't take her away. It would kill you."

She scoffed softly. "I should have known. If it doesn't help your purposes, then you won't do it. Well I'll find my own way to be free of your curse."

She turned and ran out the gates before her grandfather's men could stop her. She was never going to be free of this curse, it was obvious now. Kazue would eventually consume her or Hisato would use her. There was no escaping it, no matter how far she ran—through the fields of rice, toward the forest, or along the road. Distance and movement used to give her some sense of peace. She could fool herself into believing it made a difference.

Maybe if she kept on running, she could run all the way back to the palace. But even that didn't feel like home anymore. She was trapped between worlds now. She belonged nowhere. Still she kept on running, though she had no real direction in mind. She just wanted to be away. Running was what she was best at and maybe if she ran for long enough she wouldn't be under Hisato's control, maybe she could fight his command to kill Kaito. Suzume tripped and stumbled onto the ground. She caught herself from face-planting with her hands, but scraped her palms. She didn't even care.

She stayed like that for a moment, beating her hands on the ground until they were bloody.

She felt Naoki approach from behind without having to lift her head. Her spiritual perception was getting stronger. Just as the cuts on her hands were already scabbing over and in a few minutes would be gone as if they never existed. She was getting stronger, but she was also losing her humanity.

"Do you enjoy seeing me this way?" she asked the ground.

Naoki didn't answer. Suzume stood up and flung a flame in his direction. He dodged it with ease, and the fire burst apart in sparks on the night air. The light it created dispersed into darkness in an instant.

Out of desperation she asked, "How can a bond be broken?" She wasn't even sure what bond she meant anymore. The one that forced Kaito to do her bidding? The one that Hisato was using to make her his puppet? Or the one she despised most—her connection to Kazue, which was slowly eating away at her, turning her into something else entirely.

He didn't answer straight away as usual. The wind rustled through the trees and night animals called out to one another.

"Tell me!" she said.

"I assume this has something to do with Kaito?"

She clawed her nails into the earth. She couldn't even say it. It was as if Hisato's command forbade her from even speaking his name. She tried to nod her head but her neck remained stubbornly stiff.

"A bond is formed when a yokai's true name is invoked. And then it can only be broken if the holder of the name returns it to the yokai. Or if the other dies."

She gave a bitter laugh. *Of course. I cannot be free unless I'm dead.*

"How do you return a name?" It hurt to force the words out, as if Hisato was there choking her, trying to still her tongue.

"In the same way it was taken—the holder speaks the name and orders them to be free."

"Is that how Kazue captured you, by learning your name?"

"I was given to Kazue," Naoki replied. He so rarely showed any emotion, but she could see his discomfort. It was subtle, a small tightness around his lips.

Then Hisato had told the truth, Kazue really had traded Kaito for Naoki. But what was so special about the swordsman that she'd trade love for him?

"Why did Kazue need you?"

"I served the gods and she hoped to make herself into one."

"Could I free you?" She did not want to keep him bound to her anymore. What if Hisato forced her to use him against Kaito?

Naoki shook his head. "For you it is different. Our bond is unique. All yokai have a name given to them at their creation, known only to them and their creator. To have that name binds them to those who hold onto it. Kazue knew my true name, you do not."

"But I don't know Kai-" her throat closed up on his name and she corrected herself saying, "I don't know his true name. Which means we shouldn't be bound at all." Perhaps there was hope she could avoid him forever.

"What you share is different. When you absorbed his energy, a part of him fused with you. It is not so much a bond as you are imposing your will on him. He could fight it if he chose."

It has to be the same with Hisato. I just have to fight his command. I don't have to obey! But how do I do that exactly? It was a small spark of hope in an otherwise dismal situation, but she was willing to cling to it if there was a chance.

They headed back to her grandfather's palace together. When they returned, her grandfather's guards were waiting outside for her with Ryuu at their head.

Suzume braced herself for the confrontation she knew was coming. She'd set fire to her grandfather's palace after all. Naoki stepped in front of her to protect her. But she wasn't going to run away from what she had done.

"Are you going to arrest me for starting the fire?" Suzume asked him, tilting her head defiantly.

"Your grandfather was livid, but I managed to convince him to let you go," Ryuu said.

She scoffed. "Do you think I'll forgive you just for that?"

"I don't deserve your forgiveness, Suzume."

"I guess we agree on one thing at least."

"We're leaving tonight. It would seem we've worn out our welcome here." Ryuu looked around at the crowd of soldiers and Suzume's distant relatives. All of them were staring and whispering. She held her head high. Let them gossip, it didn't make a difference to her.

"Good and when we get back to the palace, I'm going to talk to the emperor about getting you removed as my guardian."

"Do as you wish, but first we must go find Izume."

"I'm not going anywhere with you."

"It is the emperor's order. You have no choice."

Had the emperor really sent her here to find her mother, or was this Ryuu's plot? She had no further reason to stay at the palace now that she knew it was impossible to remove Kazue.

"I don't take anyone's orders."

"Help me and I will teach you how to stop Kazue from taking control over you."

She narrowed her gaze at him. She couldn't trust him, could she? But he controlled a yokai and maybe there was something he could teach her that could stop her from killing Kaito.

"I'll do this, but it doesn't mean I trust you."

He bowed his head. "It's all I can ask for."

SUZUME AND THE REST OF HER FRIENDS CLIMBED INTO THE PALANQUIN AND headed out in search of Izume. Suzume dozed intermittently throughout the night, her dreams haunted by visions of what she had seen in the forest guardian's palace. She awoke with a start come morning by a knock at her palanquin door. She rubbed the sleep out of her eyes, and saw Tsuki smiling at her.

"Morning, sleepyhead."

Suzume gave him a dirty look before climbing out of the palanquin and giving a stretch. The soldiers had made a fire and were cooking their breakfast. The scent of cooking meat wafted toward her, but it only made her stomach turn.

"We were talking while you were asleep," Tsuki announced. "We think it's time to leave the palace. We've learned all we can for now."

Suzume froze. She couldn't tell her friends she needed to get back to the White Palace to train more with Ryuu to fight Hisato's influence.

All she could manage in reply was, "What?"

Hikaru rubbed the back of his neck. "I should have told you this before, but Ryuu was the one who brought me to the White Palace and I have reason to believe that he's the one who made us this way."

She stared at him. She wasn't really mad he was keeping secrets from her, she was keeping her own, but her tone was accusatory just the same.

"And you didn't tell me."

"We weren't certain." Rin came to his defense.

Suzume waved it away. "Well I'm not going anywhere."

"We know why we are this way, but it hasn't told us how we can stop Hisato. I think it's time to focus on how we can defeat Hisato," Hikaru said.

It was the logical next step, but Suzume couldn't defeat Hisato when he had control of her.

"Not yet. I need more time at the palace."

"For what?" Akira asked. "We know why you are this way, and even with you and Hikaru it's not enough to change us back to how we were. Souta tried as well. For now, we need to focus on improving your ability. That's how we're going to set everything right."

"We can do that at the palace," Suzume replied.

"It can be done anywhere."

"We have to find my mother."

"Your mother doesn't make a difference." Akira's voice rose with impatience.

"It's my decision." Suzume stamped her foot on the ground. Her friends all saw her as a spoiled child.

"Is this because the emperor is favoring you? You have everything you've ever wanted and now you don't want to go back."

"That's not it, I-" but she choked on the words.

"I thought you were better than this," Akira said.

"Just give me more time, I promise we'll go and look for the last piece soon."

Akira shook her head, disappearing from view, and leaving Tsuki in her place. He did not seem impressed.

"I'm going to sharpen my blade." He turned to walk away.

Rin did not disguise her displeasure. "I thought you were serious about this. You left Kaito behind because you wanted to learn to control your powers. But all we've been doing is running errands for the emperor. Do you care about anyone other than yourself?"

"Of course I do!" Suzume snapped. "Do any of you care about me, and what I might be going through?"

"All we do is for you," Rin said. Hikaru placed his hand on her shoulder and they too left her behind.

Suzume crossed her arms over her chest. Let them think she was selfish. She didn't need them to stop Hisato. She'd learn how to control her power and then she'd show them all.

Naoki watched her. Though he knew a portion of the truth, he had not spoken up in her defense. She wanted to be angry with him, but it wouldn't change anything. Suzume climbed back into the palanquin and slammed the door shut. She didn't care what any of them thought. Really. She didn't. She would solve this problem on her own, as she always did.

Thirty-Six

According to the map, the place where her mother was hidden was less than a day from the palace in a nearby valley. There was a road that led most of the way there, but the road ended and beyond that was nothing but forest. It was a little after midday when they were getting closer to the place marked on the map. As they did, Suzume started to feel strange. The closer they got, the more her head started to spin. They had to take more breaks because she became tired easily. The fire seemed to be close to the surface as well. Rin could not maintain her humanoid form and reverted to her true kitsune form.

Tsuki and Akira were unstable, their form settling on a mixture of both their features—Tsuki's stubble, with Akira's lips and eyes. When they spoke, it was a combination of their voices overlapping one another.

"We cannot go any further," they said, leaning against a tree.

Naoki was the only one who seemed unaffected. "There are strong enchantments here. Yokai cannot get any closer." His eyes scanned the horizon.

"I think I've heard of this place," Hikaru said as he massaged his temple. "There is a hidden shrine, tended only by priestesses. I think the closer we get, the harder it will be."

Hikaru's face appeared to be bleached of all color. While Suzume felt a little light-headed, she seemed to be faring better than the others. The warrior priests and even Ryuu were not faring much better.

She would have to go on alone it seemed.

"I'll go on. You can follow if you're able," she told the group. The sooner they finished this, the sooner she could get Ryuu to teach her how to stop Hisato's commands.

"Are you sure?" Rin was panting for breath, her tongue lolling out of her jaws.

Ryuu stumbled forward and his footsteps were sluggish. "Be careful," he said.

She tilted her head up as she turned away from him. "Don't you forget your promise once we're out of here."

As she went deeper into the forest the tingling sensation only began to grow. Everything around her vibrated with power. Even the leaves on the trees seemed to be greener, and more flowers bloomed. The fragrant air smelt of earth and flowers. A river ran through a fork between two of the hills that made up the valley, and Suzume followed its twisting path to its source, which marked the shrine where her mother was supposed to be.

A thick mist rolled in and obscured her vision. Suzume had to rely on the sound of the river to find her way. After wandering around practically blind for what felt like an eternity, she emerged at the river's shore.

The shrine was on the other side of the river. Torii arches guarded a bridge which separated the valley entrance from one side, while high walls encircled it. From a distance, the temple seemed to be equivalent in size to that of the White Palace temple, which was surprising, considering this was in the middle of the forest. As Suzume started to cross the bridge, two women bearing spears stepped out from thin air to block her path.

They wore the clothes of a priestess with armor overlaying it.

"What is your business here, woman?"

Suzume sized up the two women. She could feel their spiritual energy crackling off of them, like fire. It drew her like a moth to a flame and she had to suppress the desire to take the power from them. She might be able to beat them in a fight if she wanted, but she decided the peaceful route might be better for now.

Suzume approached the women, her hands up to show she was harmless.

"I'm looking for my mother, Izume," Suzume replied.

The women shared a look. It was clear from their expressions her mother was here.

"Come with us." They gestured for her to follow across the bridge. As soon as she passed under the torri arches she felt a tingle of power.

One of the warrior priestesses nodded her head. "You were not lying."

"Of course not," Suzume said indignantly.

"If you had, the barrier would have sent you flying," the second warrior priestess replied.

She was led into the courtyard of the temple where an old woman was waiting for them. Priestesses hurrying about their chores stopped to stare. She imagined it was like the temple shrine she had been briefly training at. They probably rarely had outsiders here.

One of the warrior priestesses went up to the old woman and whispered in her ear. The old woman's hair was completely white, and she wore it in the traditional way of the priestess with a single white tie. She watched Suzume as the priestess whispered in her ear.

"So, you are Izume's daughter."

"I am, and I would like to see her."

"You will, but that is not how things are done here. There are impurities on you. Before you can enter the inner shrine, you must be cleansed."

"Are you saying I'm dirty?"

The old woman turned to walk away, while another priestess came and directed Suzume to a nearby building where a large trough of water awaited. Suzume was stripped down to her underclothes despite her protests and then dumped with icy cold water.

"Was that really necessary?"

The priestess who'd done the dousing made no comment as she handed Suzume clean priestess garb to change into. With her only privacy being the priestess's back turned, Suzume changed her clothes.

Once she was purified, Suzume walked through a second torri arch into an open garden beyond. A large tree dominated the center of the space and seated beneath it, wearing the clothes of a priestess, was her mother. Izume glanced up at her. As Suzume approached, her expression was perfectly serene. Knowing she was here hadn't prepared Suzume for their reunion. She hadn't seen her mother since her selfish actions had banished her. And meeting Ryuu, knowing what she did, it only made her hatred of her mother grow.

"What are you doing here?" Izume asked.

"That's all you have to say after you've ruined my life?" Suzume spat after her.

"What would you have me say?" Her words cut through her like a hot knife. There was no caring or affection in her tone. Not like her father who she'd been ripped from by this woman.

"Maybe you could show the least bit of concern for your child? Or do you only think of yourself?"

Her mother stood and strode toward her, hand raised to slap her for her insolence, but before she could the fire erupted along Suzume's skin.

Izume stared at the flames that were engulfing her oldest child. "Then it's true. You've broken the seal."

"Then it's true you knew all along." It only fueled her anger further. A part of her had been hoping Ryuu lied and that her mother had been innocent in everything.

"Of course I knew," Izume said with a shake of her head, as if Suzume was the world's greatest fool. And maybe she was for holding onto any faith in her mother.

"Did you and Ryuu plan this together? Were you hoping I'd be born a son and you could put me on the throne?" Now she could see every horrible thing said about her had been true. Her mother was nothing but a power-hungry, selfish monster.

"How do you know that name?" Izume's eyes were wide from fear. It was the first time Suzume had actually seen her mother afraid.

"I came to bring you back." She threw out her hands, fire erupting from her digits. A crowd of priestesses had come to watch. They whispered behind their hands to one another. Izume watched them from the corner of her eyes.

"Let's speak alone," Izume said.

"There's nothing to say. Let's go."

"There are some things we must talk about first," Izume said.

"There's nothing you can say to try and redeem yourself," Suzume said, glaring at her mother, daring her to try and fight her on this point.

"Don't make that face. It's ugly," her mother hissed.

Suzume only scrunched her face up more to spite her mother, who only rolled her eyes in response.

"I did what I had to protect you," her mother said in exasperation.

"Protect me from what?"

"Your power. It was never meant for you."

"What is that supposed to mean?"

"It was meant for me."

There was a murmur from the crowd, and Suzume glanced at them. She should have known her mother would have turned this into a performance. She was always good at entertaining a crowd. But it was too late to make their conversation private.

Izume lowered her gaze, her expression wistful. "I met Ryuu when I was a girl. He was sent by the emperor to serve my father. It was love at first sight, for me at least. I was a scrawny girl, prone to falling over my own two feet. I doubt he knew I even existed at first."

Suzume scoffed. "Is this really time for a story?"

The priestesses had drawn in closer to better hear Izume's story, standing back only just enough to leave Suzume and her mother in the center of the circle. If Izume was anything like how she had been at the palace, she'd likely wooed all of these women to love her—perhaps by telling them stories of love. Suzume shook her head. They were all fools.

"I convinced him that I wanted to learn swordsmanship in an attempt to get closer to him. I was miserable at it, and we both knew it. But he was patient and never gave up on me. Little by little my skill improved, much to my father's chagrin." She smiled to herself. It was an alluring gesture, one that Suzume had seen her use before. Izume was a master of manipulation. She was drawing them all in with her tale, with her sly glances. But Suzume wasn't going to fall for it. This was her way of buying time. She didn't want to leave and Suzume needed to find out why.

She kept her arms crossed over her chest and glowered. "Are you done with your sob story?"

Izume continued on, ignoring her daughter. "I told myself on the day I beat him in a sparring match, I would confess my feelings for him. But the day never came. Your grandfather had other plans for me—the crown prince, your father." Izume was trying to win her over.

But Suzume only rolled her eyes in response. There was no stopping her it seemed. She should have known Izume would make a scene.

"He was looking for a wife and I was put forth as a candidate. You see, once you become a candidate you belong to no one else." She said this for the benefit of the priestesses who practically had hearts in their eyes. They were all hanging on her every word. Then to Suzume she said, "Your grandfather thought that I would be made empress. Oh, how I fought him on that." She shook her head.

"Fate is cruel because in the end, I lost both the man I loved and the crown, becoming the emperor's second wife."

The girls murmured their disappointment to one another. Izume stopped, giving her story dramatic pause, letting the listeners feel her sorrow, her lowest moment.

"What does this have to do with me?" Suzume asked, impatient with her mother's sad love story. She may have swayed these girls, children really, but Suzume knew her real intent, Izume was painting herself as the victim of fate.

Izume waved off her temper. "I was getting to that." She smoothed out the imaginary wrinkles in her hoari before continuing. "Though I was second wife, I found a second chance at love with the emperor. During the competition to become empress we'd drawn closer. And as the years went by our bond became only closer. But the empress was jealous of us and when I became pregnant with you, Suzume." She nodded toward her, "At first she spread a rumor that the child was not the emperor's. But I had been with no other man. When the emperor refused to believe that, she took more drastic measures."

The priestesses had moved very close now, any sense of propriety forgotten as they crowded around Izume bumping against Suzume's shoulders. She shoved a girl who glared at her before turning to Izume to hear the next part. They were devouring her every word as if it were a rare delicacy. The fools.

"The empress bribed a servant to put poison in my food. As a result, my labor pains came too soon. I labored for over a day, making no progress. I began to bleed and they feared I would die." She took a shuddering breath. "I can still see it all when I close my eyes." She closed her eyes as she said this. "And then as I lay dying, Ryuu came to me. My beloved. He had a stone in his hand which glowed with spiritual energy.

"'If I give this to you, it will save your life, but you may lose the child,' he'd said. I refused. I'd rather die that you should live." Her voice rose with dramatic emphasis and a false motherly affection. Suzume couldn't meet her gaze and turned away from her. She wasn't going to fall for her lies. Never again. "But he insisted that if I did not take it we both would die. He forced me to swallow the stone, it fused with my body and I was on fire. I was a living inferno, blazing with heat." She clutched at her chest, reliving those phantom pains before them all. Then her hand slowly fell to her side, and her eyes were closed. "But as quick as it had come, the fire passed through me and in a few more moments you were brought into the world. Screaming and kicking, full of passion." She reached out to brush Suzume's hair behind her ear. Suzume moved out of her reach and Izume's hand fell to her side once more.

"For the first year of your life everything was wonderful. The empress had a second son, but it did not matter to me. I had my beautiful girl and I was happy. But around the time of your first birthday, things took a turn. The true nature of the stone revealed itself." She turned her head to the sky. "One night, I woke to the smell of smoke. The palace was on fire. I tried to reach you but the flames were too high. I was forced out into the night and watched as the fire burned. I wept, thinking I had lost you." She placed her head in her hands as if she were reliving the memories.

It wasn't until Ryuu came out with you in his arms that I realized he was not human, and you were different as well." She met Suzume's gaze. "That was when Ryuu told me that the flame stone he had used to save our lives had fused with your soul and unless we bound your power, you would continue to destroy unchecked. I feared for your life, so what else could I do? I let him bind you. And from there on out, you were as a normal child should be. At times I forgot that you were any different."

There was a hush that fell over everyone as Izume finished her story.

Suzume clenched her hands into fists. "And you never thought to tell me any of this before?"

"What difference would it have made?" she asked, her voice rising with accusation.

"All the difference. At least I would have known why I am this way! Is that why you sent me away, because you couldn't stand the sight of me anymore?"

Izume shook her head. "It's not like that. Things were changing at the palace. I had to protect you."

"Protect me how?"

Anger blazed on her beautiful face. The priestesses were whispering to one another. Her illusion of a loving mother shattered. "You are as ungrateful as ever. I gave up everything to keep you safe."

"You never cared for me at all. That entire story was to paint you as a loving mother. But all you wanted was your own happiness. I know you traded me to Akio to win the emperor's heart."

Izume froze, caught in her lie. "I did, but I would never have given you to him."

She shook her head. "Why was Ryuu there? The night of the fire?"

Izume's face lost some of its color.

"You were together, weren't you?"

"I hardly see how that matters."

Suzume's flames erupted from her body. "It matters because your affair ruined my life. And have you once apologized for it?"

"Please, you have to understand. I love Ryuu."

She shook her head. "I don't need your excuses."

Suzume turned and ran away from her mother. Everything that had happened to her was because of her mother's own selfishness. She'd known it all along but it didn't hurt any less.

THIRTY-SEVEN

The temple was an interconnected series of buildings. There were barracks where the priestesses lived, meeting rooms where they congregated to meditate, and a place where they cooked and ate their meals. There were also gardens where they grew their own food. And at the center of the temple, a shrine. She was so distracted by being angry at her mother, she'd almost forgotten why she'd come there at all. And if her mother's melodramatic tale was any indication, she would likely not be leaving willingly. Instead Suzume walked around, hoping her temper would cool enough that she could reason with her mother. Eventually she found herself standing outside the shrine. The entire place vibrated with power, and being this close to the center of the shrine, and the heart of power here, Suzume found herself drawn to it. Kazue, as always, was seeking more power.

As a general rule, she stayed away from temples or shrines. She had too many unpleasant experiences at any place of power. Suzume turned to leave, but as she did, she felt like something was calling out to her, leading her into the temple. Curious, she walked up the steps to the shrine.

The outer-most room was empty but for a young girl who was bent over polishing the floor. When Suzume entered she stopped her cleaning. The girl appeared to be close to Suzume's own age, maybe a bit younger. But there was something in her gaze; her eyes were ancient and powerful. Perhaps it was a trick of the shrine, or the lingering power of the gods who dwelled here, but Suzume found herself drawn to the girl.

"Have you come to pay your respects to the kami?" she asked.

From her time at the mountain shrine, she knew how seriously priestesses took their worship of deities. If she refused she'd insult her. *I guess it couldn't hurt to at least pretend to pray.*

"Uh—sure."

The girl set aside her rag and stepped aside so Suzume could approach the inner sanctum. The inner sanctum was separated by doors which folded back. Unlike most other shrines Suzume had visited there were eight effigies depicted. Eight paintings on the wall. It seemed strange that there would be a shrine dedicated to so many kami.

"Who do you worship at this temple?" Suzume asked.

The girl gazed lovingly at the eight portraits of the gods on the wall. "The Eight."

"I thought the gods were jealous of one another. I've never heard of them sharing a shrine before."

The girl laughed, and it was a sweet sound. "Perhaps if they knew they would not be pleased."

Suzume raised her eyebrows in question. At the mountain shrine where Suzume had briefly served, the priestesses there were devout believers that the god of the mountain dwelled in their shrine. Suzume, though not necessarily a religious person, assumed all priestesses thought the kami to be present in their shrines.

"What do you mean they don't know?"

The girl turned to Suzume. "The Eight were defeated by our founder, Fujikawa Kazue. They no longer walk this earth but we pay our respects to them here."

The paintings depicted the first eight gods. They were the most powerful and those that Kazue had captured in her quest to become immortal.

"We believe she will return to us someday, and lead our people once more." The girl pressed her hands together and bowed her head in prayer toward the kami.

Suzume scoffed. If only Kazue could come back and clean up this mess.

Her face was so young but when she looked at Suzume it was if she could see more than the surface of things.

"Sorry. I have something in my throat," Suzume lied. There was something about this young priestess that put her ill at ease.

She seemed appeased and walked up to a small pedestal beneath a painting of an imposing man. She'd seen him depicted before, the Lord of the Sea, Kaito's creator and Ai's father. Waves burst from the ocean beneath his feet, and his expression was fierce and thunderous. The girl filled the basin beneath his painting with a pitcher of water that had been set down on the ground.

"You do not believe and yet you are touched by the divine," the girl said as she filled the basin.

The painting in front of Suzume had caught her attention. Though she had never seen her face before, she knew who it was meant to be straight away. The kami depicted in the painting was serene yet powerful, flames burst from her hands, and her bright crimson hair seemed to burn. The Lady of Flame, the goddess whom Kazue had bound the flame of her soul with. Her power was within Suzume, along with Kazue's soul.

The girl lit a stick of incense beneath the painting.

"It's not that I don't believe. I just wonder what she would do if she came back," Suzume replied.

The girl continued to fill the different bowls with offerings like fruit and meat. The final painting depicted a dark figure. Almost his entire face was obscured in shadows and only his eyes were visible as two glowing orbs. The priestess placed bones in his basin. The darkness of that painting made her think of Hisato. A cold chill ran down her spine. She knew she shouldn't have come into this shrine.

The girl finished placing her offerings and then bowed her head, her hands pressed together. Even though Suzume knew the gods were no longer among them, she still felt a touch of power in this place. Perhaps Kazue had imbued it with her power before she left, because Suzume felt her body crying out for it.

"I think she would want to heal the world," the girl said after she finished her prayer.

Suzume scoffed again.

"You doubt that as well."

She shouldn't destroy this woman's beliefs. It wasn't her place. But she was feeling bitter about her situation lately and she said, "Kazue only craved power. If she were to return, I am certain she would continue on her quest to become immortal."

"There are many facets to every person. What you see is only one side of the story from your own perspective."

Suzume rolled her eyes. She was being lectured by a child. "Sure."

"You should give your mother a chance. She does not show it but her heart aches over what she has done to you."

Suzume stood up. "Thanks for your advice, but you don't know anything about me and my mother."

"I may not know Izume well, but I am gifted at seeing people's hearts. And I can tell both you and she carry many wounds that together you could heal."

Suzume crossed her arms over her chest as if she could stop the girl from peering into her soul by doing so. "Any wounds I have she inflicted upon me! You want me to feel sorry for her?" She forced a laugh. "You're insane."

"And so her father did to her. The expectations of our parents can weigh heavy on the child."

"Did my mother put you up to this?"

The girl shook her head slowly. "I saw your heart was hurting and I wanted to help you heal."

"You can't heal me. I'm too broken to fix." The ugly truth spilled from her mouth without her meaning to. This went beyond her mother's selfishness, that was only a part of it. She was terrified of the power inside her that she could not be freed from and the fate she couldn't escape.

There was a long silence, and then the priestess said with a sigh, "Humans are flawed. It is what makes them beautiful. Once you see that your mother and you are more alike than you think, you will understand. She has lost much as well."

"I won't ever see her as anything other than a selfish monster."

"You don't mean that."

"I do." Suzume stamped her foot and flames erupted. But before her fire could catch flame, spiritual energy poured out of the girl, both calming and familiar. It wrapped around Suzume like an embrace, extinguishing both her flame and her anger. She was left staring at the singed floor. There was a momentary confusion in her expression. But she shook it off quickly.

"I'm sorry. The Head Priestess tells me I shouldn't use my power in that way, but I-"

Suzume shook her head. "No, I'm glad you did it." If she hadn't Suzume would have lost control entirely.

"I should go." She turned to walk away, but it turned into a run. She didn't want to face what the girl had said, or the truths about herself she had uncovered. As she fled the temple, however, she found Izume where she had left her, sitting under a large tree with her head tilted up watching the leaves fall gently downward. It would be easier to walk away and ignore what the priestess had said but she needed Izume to leave with her.

She marched up to her mother, who tore her gaze away from the tree. There were tears along her lashes and she turned away to discreetly wipe them.

"Ah, Suzume, I was coming to find you."

"Spare me the theatrics. I came here to bring you back to the White Palace, so let's go."

She shook her head. "I cannot go back there."

"Why not?"

Izume faced the river, which was burbling just on the far end of the garden. "Your grandfather is trying to make your brother emperor. He'll kill the emperor to have his way. If I go back he'll use me to find your brother and carry out his plans. Hiding was the only way to stop him."

Ryuu had said that her grandfather was ambitious, and she knew he'd made the deal with the yokai and likely Hisato. Maybe it was due to what the priestess had said, but she wanted to believe her this time.

"What about the rumors about your affair, are they true?"

"Don't be crude."

"That's the least you could do for me after everything that's happened."

"Yes." She wouldn't meet Suzume's gaze.

"Is the emperor even my father?"

Izume stood up and smacked her hard against the face. Suzume reeled backward from the blow.

"What do you think I am?" Izume's face was flushed with anger as she balled her hand into a fist at her side. As her mother glared at her, Suzume saw her own anger reflected back at her. She'd always thought her cold and detached, but she realized now that had not been the case. It was all a mask behind which she hid her true feelings. Maybe the priestess was right and they were not so different.

Suzume scowled at her. "What else can I think?"

There was a flush on Izume's pale skin. "It is not possible. He is sterile."

It gave her some small relief. At least the emperor really was her father. But it didn't change the fact that her mother had lied to her her entire life.

"Then what you said before, it's true?"

Some of the color had left Izume's cheeks as she nodded her head. "It is."

"Why didn't you ever tell me?"

"How could I? The fewer people that knew, the better. If you grandfather had known what power you had he would have used you as well. I was trying to spare you." Her voice rose.

"Why didn't you take me with you?" She hated how hurt and upset she sounded. It had never been about the lies. The least her mother could have done was kept the family together.

A leaf fell down from the tree and landed on Izume's shoulder. She plucked it off her clothes and rolled it between her thumb and forefinger.

"Does it matter what my reasons were?"

"How could it not? I thought my father didn't love me and I had been exiled. I was left feeling completely abandoned."

Izume reached for Suzume, but stopped when Suzume stepped out of reach.

"I would rather you told me the truth. I wanted to be with you."

Izume's hand fell to her side. "I wish I had been better to you."

They held each other's gazes for a moment. Scars remained, and it would take time to heal. But for the first time since she'd left the White Palace she felt she could understand her mother.

"Then do better. What is it he's done? Who is he working with?"

Izume shook her head. "I can't. If he finds me-"

"He won't. If you can help me, I'll find a way to protect you from my grandfather."

"How could you possibly?"

"I have the emperor's seal. I'll beg him for your protection." Suzume removed the seal from where she'd kept it hidden in her pocket.

"You're not a child anymore, are you?" This time when Izume reached to cup Suzume's cheek she let her and she took comfort from the gesture. For so long she'd been deprived of her mother's love. But now that everything was out in the open, she felt as if they could move forward together.

"Right before we left the palace, your grandfather was approached by a strange man. He asked for you." Izume looked at her daughter. "In exchange for you, he would help your brother become emperor. That's all your grandfather wanted."

"Hisato." Suzume clenched her hand into a fist.

Izume nodded her head. "That was the man, but how did you know?"

It was all coming into place now. Her grandfather had been working with Hisato all along. Which meant her father was in danger. She had to get back and stop him.

THIRTY-EIGHT

Yokai were arriving at the palace by droves. Each day it felt more and more like the palace of his memories. But despite that, Kaito felt as if there was an empty void inside him. One that no matter what he did, he could not quite fill it. The yokai were drawn here, not only by his command, but the promise of a wedding. His marriage to Ai was to be the symbol of the new age. It would not only bind Ai, the daughter of one of the eight, with Kaito, the chosen leader appointed by the eight, but also signify Kaito's devotion to yokai.

The rumors had been floating around the palace, and everyone knew the story. The once great dragon brought low by his love for a human woman. If he wanted to take control of his kingdom then he would have to marry a yokai, and someone as powerful as Ai would only lend strength to his own image. Though he did not delight in marrying Ai, his rise in power should have been some comfort. His newly repaired barracks were swelling with willing soldiers. The halls were restored to their previous splendor and everywhere there was music and laughter. At times it felt as if no time had passed at all. Those centuries trapped in stone were nothing but a nightmare.

But instead of glorying in the return of his previous position, Kaito most often skulked around the palace, avoiding the groveling atten-tion of the courtiers, and more often dodging Ai as she tried to drag him into wedding plans.

There remained only a small part of the palace which had not been repaired. And it was here he escaped. The ocean had reclaimed most of it. The walls crumbled into the sea, and crabs and barnacles clung to the rocks beneath his feet. Kaito stared out to the horizon, watching the white tips crash against the far distant shore. From here he could see the human village. He'd tried going to the town and found he could reach it with ease. Suzume was gone. And perhaps it was the best. Caring about her, even thinking about her, was dangerous. She was his blood, even considering it was an abomination.

Footsteps approached from behind. He thought he had found a place to himself but it would seem he had thought wrong.

"Leave me now before I rip open your guts and choke you with them," he said.

"I see your temper hasn't improved," the intruder said.

A familiar face strode toward him. He blinked for a moment, because he could not believe it was real.

"Shin?" he asked.

"It's been that long that you've forgotten my face?" The okami smiled, revealing his pointed canines.

Kaito rushed forward and the two of them embraced.

"What are you doing here?" Kaito said as they broke apart. In all the centuries, there was no one he had trusted as he trusted Shin. To have him back was like a dream. He had not realized how much he needed him until he was standing in front of him once more.

Shin grinned back at him. "I thought since you've finally woken, I'd pay a visit."

Kaito shook his head in wonder, and then his gaze fell on the metal collar around the wolf's neck. Seeing that had the same effect as a bucket of cold water being dumped over his head. Things could not go back to how they were. Everything had changed. And despite his friend's teasing, he was not here for a social call. He'd been sent by that bastard Akio. The guardian of the forest had been summoned to the palace just like all the others who served him. But unlike the others, he had not made an appearance.

Even before Kaito had been sealed in stone, Akio had been defiant. He was a constant thorn in Kaito's side. Now that he was back, Akio was no different. He supposed it was some comfort that some things never changed.

"It's good to see you, even if I know it was not by your own choice," Kaito said, trying to force some levity into his tone.

Shin nodded his head. "Akio thought it would be poetic to send me as a messenger." There was a bitter note in his voice.

It was to mock them both—Kaito, who had once struck fear into the hearts of everyone on the island, and Shin, one of his four great generals and the person Kaito trusted above all others. He'd been the first to swear himself to Kaito, before the eight had even chosen him to rule Akatsuki. They'd been through everything together, and only a cruel twist of fate had separated them. Now the most brilliant, strategic mind and loyal friend had been reduced to a mere messenger.

If Kaito saw Akio, he would tear his head from his neck. Once he had his army, he would make sure Akio paid and Shin was freed.

"I know that look. Don't get carried away," Shin said, placing his hand on Kaito's shoulder, as if reading his thoughts.

"You think I'll stand for this insult? I never should have let you go to him in the first place."

Shin only shook his head. "I made my choice."

Kaito bared his teeth at his friend in a mostly playful gesture. "Well I need you here. These men I have now are incompetent, none could stand up to you."

Shin chuckled. "You flatter me, my friend."

They were silent for a few minutes as they stared out at the ocean together.

"I'm assuming Akio sent you with some excuse as to why he's not coming."

Shin nodded. "There is trouble with the humans near his domain. He cannot leave right now because of it."

Kaito has expected as much, and he would deal with Akio in time. But for now, it was good to have Shin here to help him. Perhaps this was what he was missing, having someone close to him that he could trust.

"When do you have to be back?"

"I can't stay long. He'll grow suspicious if I linger."

"I'm not worried about him." Kaito waved his hand to dismiss the idea Akio could be any threat. "I'll send my own messenger telling him I've held you captive."

Shin shook his head. "As much as I appreciate the offer, I don't think it's wise. He's made allies with some powerful beings."

"I may have been gone five hundred years, but I'm not weak." Kaito laughed.

But this wasn't their usual banter. Shin's expression was sober.

"Who?" Though Kaito asked, he suspected he already knew.

"There were talks with a man. I don't know how to describe him. He wasn't human, but he wasn't yokai either."

"Kazue's son," Kaito said.

Shin shook his head. "No, not him. This thing was different. He had a priestess with him. She did something to a man, made him into a monster..."

"A priestess?"

Shin wouldn't meet his gaze, and Kaito grabbed his shoulder and squeezed. "Tell me."

"It's that priestess you were traveling with before. She used a song and it turned a man into a monster. He felt like a yokai, but he could use spiritual powers like a priest."

Just like Kazue's son.

Kaito turned and paced away from Shin. This couldn't be a coincidence. But all accounts of that half-breed had been he fought like a yokai, and could wield spiritual power like a human. Could it be he was trying to make more like him? And using Suzume to do it?

He stopped pacing and turned to face Shin. "Where are they now?"

"I don't think you should go to her."

Normally he would have taken Shin's advice, but there were too many questions he needed answered. Suzume had sent him away, and ever since then there had been nothing but strange rumors. She wasn't acting as she should. If he could face her then he could hear the truth from her own lips.

Kaito grabbed Shin's shoulder and squeezed. "Help me find her. I promise I will not make the same mistake again."

Shin shook his head. "I must be a fool for doing this. But she's northeast of here, heading back toward the human capital. Whatever you do, don't get too close to the capital. The humans there are more powerful than they were in the past."

Kaito grinned. "I promise to be careful."

He transformed there and launched himself into the sky, leaving Shin behind. As soon as he set out, that feeling of unease coiled in his stomach. The command she had given him would prevent him from searching her out. But he could not sit still and wait for her to come to him any longer.

If he could see her face at least maybe he could prove to himself that she was not of his blood, that she was not betraying him. Perhaps he could continue on with his life as it should be. Maybe at last he would find peace.

The journey there took longer than it should have. If he let his guard down he found himself wandering off track and away from where he should have been. But as he got closer to the human dwellings, the pain intensified. Her power to hold him back was stronger than he thought it would be.

As he drew closer Kaito started to spread out his senses to search for her, and at first he found nothing. Then as if someone had lit a candle in the dark, he felt her close by. Kaito zoomed toward her, eager to be reunited once again. He saw her on the hilltop, the wind catching her hair and tossing it behind her. She seemed powerful and he had to admit, beautiful. Perhaps she'd come to her senses at last and that was why she had let him approach. Whatever her reason, he was glad for this chance.

But as he drew closer to her, she formed a ball of fire and shot it toward him. He swerved in time to miss it, and flew out of range to avoid her attack. He hovered overhead, watching as fire encased her. This wasn't right. This wasn't like her. It had to be Kazue who'd taken control over her body again.

He risked coming in closer, and this time she didn't attack him. Kaito landed and then slowly approached her. Flames crackled in her hands as she scowled at him.

"Enough of these games," he said. "It's time you came back to me."

She threw her head back and laughed. "Are you really such a fool? Isn't it obvious? I don't need you anymore. I've grown more powerful."

He felt her power. It radiated off her like the heat of her flames. Her eyes were strange—it wasn't Suzume, but reminded him instead of Kazue, in the moment just before she had sealed him.

Kaito stepped toward her. "This isn't you."

"You think you know me?"

"I do. Give up this game before you hurt yourself."

She laughed again. It was high and disjointed, not like Suzume at all. Then it struck him, the reason he could approach her at all. It wasn't because Suzume had welcomed him, it was because this wasn't Suzume.

"You're not Suzume."

Hisato assumed his own form. "You are correct, but she is mine."

"What have you done to her?" Kaito growled as he lunged for Hisato, but he only leaped out of the way.

Even taking that step forward filled him with pain. Kaito fell over to the ground as Suzume's command rippled through him, keeping him from getting closer. She was nearby. If he could only fight it, he could get to her.

"Come and find her, if you can." Hisato waved his hand behind him and a portal opened up. "Before it's too late."

Thirty-Nine

Suzume returned to the White Palace a woman on fire. As soon as she arrived, she did not even stop to wash the dirt off or change out of her travel clothes and instead went straight to the emperor. He had to be informed about her grandfather's intentions. Ryuu chased after Suzume as she hurried down the hall.

"You can't just rush in there," he said.

"You know what he's plotting and you'd try and stop me?" Suzume challenged him.

"It's not that I'm trying to stop you. There's an order to these things."

She yanked her arm free of his grip. "I'm not going to wait around. I've been playing by the palace rules all my life. The emperor needs to hear this."

She turned on her heel and continued down the hall. Ryuu didn't try to stop her now. When she reached the audience hall, there were guards at the doors holding their ornamental spears and they thrust them out to stop her from entering.

Suzume pulled out the seal her father had given her and flashed it in front of their faces. "I need to speak with the emperor now!" she shouted, her voice echoing off the chamber walls.

The guard closest to her glanced at the seal and nearly collided with his companion as he turned to open the door. The pair of them stumbled so much in their haste to open the door that their decorative spears got tangled up in one another. After they dislodged their weapons, together they opened the heavy double doors. Suzume waited only long enough for a space large enough for her to slip through before pushing past them.

Council was in session and the hall was filled with men. All of whom turned and watched as she marched toward the front of the room, her gaze fixed on her father who sat obscured by a screen. Her grandfather, who prior to her visit had retired from public life, had resumed his place at the top echelon of the emperor's counselors. Her grandfather raised one curious silver brow in question as she approached. He had likely started spreading rumors about how she'd set his palace on fire. Judging from the hushed, almost terrified way the courtiers all stared at her, they all knew. Not that it mattered. Her only concern was protecting her father.

"Princess Suzume." His voice was distant and imperious. For a brief moment it gave her pause. This was the father of her memories, not the warm man she'd come to know. "Why have you interrupted our council meeting?"

She bowed, realizing court protocol dictated it. The courtiers all whispered to one another, their voices like a low-level buzz.

"I apologize for my intrusion. There is an important matter I must speak with you about." Her head swiveled from her grandfather. Then back to the emperor. "Alone."

"A woman has no place here. How dare you," said one of the noblemen standing beside her grandfather. He was one of the minor lords who served her grandfather.

She glared in his direction, and the man visibly shrank.

"Lord Yamato is right. She had not even dressed properly," said another lord scornfully.

Fire prickled along her skin and it took all of Suzume's self-control to keep herself from bursting into flame in front of the entire court.

More men shouted out their disapproval until their voices overlapped one another into a collection of angry shouting. The emperor raised his hand, silencing them all with his gesture.

"Princess Suzume, I gave you my seal believing you would use it wisely. We will speak later." His tone was meant to be final.

There was a slight smirk on her grandfather's face. He thought he had won, but she wasn't going to let him get away with this. She would have her revenge for how he ruined her life.

She turned and pointed her finger at him. "Lord Kaedemori is plotting to overthrow the throne."

Utter silence followed her proclamation. No one moved, as if everyone feared the first to exhale would be executed. She could feel her grandfather's stare on her, but she kept her gaze fixed on her father. It was difficult to read his expression through the screen.

At last it was a member of the council who broke the silence. "We cannot be wasting time on the fantasy of a young girl." He too was another one her grandfather had in his pocket.

"This isn't a fantasy. He has plotted with yokai to-" Suzume tried to defend herself.

"Your majesty, send her away. She's clearly hysterical," shouted a counselor, cutting her off. "Yokai? These are nothing but fairy tales."

Suzume took a step closer to her father, and the guards at the foot of the throne held her back. "Father, you know this is true. I have proof." She pushed against the guards but no matter how she struggled she couldn't get any closer to her father.

"Enough." Her father's voice snapped across the room like a whip crack. Even Suzume ceased her struggle. The emperor pointed toward the door. "Take her out of here."

The guards grabbed her by the arms and dragged her from the room while Suzume kicked and flailed against them.

"Father, you can't do this. You're in danger!" she shouted. But her cries fell on deaf ears and she was deposited in the hall. The door slammed shut, keeping her from her father.

Suzume scowled at the guards, as if the force of her displeasure would move them. But in the end, she turned and walked away. She had not gone a few feet when she ran into Ryuu.

"I don't want to hear anything from you." She held up her hand before he could say something like he told her so.

"Come with me." He grabbed her by the wrist, dragging her after him.

She tried breaking free of his grip, but he was deceptively strong. He didn't stop walking until they were alone in a deserted garden. All the leaves had fallen off the trees and the wind blew over the desolate landscape. Winter wasn't far off now. But despite the chill in the air, Suzume was burning up.

Ryuu looked around the deserted garden before his gaze came to rest on her. "I imagine you saw the true strength of your grandfather."

"He's a greedy old man. My father will see reason."

Ryuu sighed. "I've told you to be careful, and now your grandfather knows about your power and he knows you're out to get him. You won't be safe in the palace. You should leave."

"You of all people have no right to tell me what to do." She turned to walk away but he caught her wrist.

"I swore to Izume to protect you, and I'm not going to let you get in the way of that."

She yanked her hand free. "And what about my father?"

He shook his head. "The emperor has men who can protect him. Who's going to protect you?"

She forced a laugh. He almost sounded like Kaito. "Don't you know? I'm more than capable of taking care of myself."

She walked away from him, not sparing him a second glance. It wasn't until she was back in her own room that Suzume exhaled, sliding against the wall. She hoped wrapped inside her old life she'd feel safe from Hisato's influence, but even as she tried to expose Lord Kaede-mori her thoughts were filled with concerns about Kaito, and how to break Hisato's hold on her. She'd rushed in to accuse her grandfather to protect herself from being ejected from the palace for being what she was. But her father had treated her so coldly. She might have made things worse. Now Ryuu even wanted to take her away, but she needed his help more than anyone else.

Suzume paced her room as she tried to think of how to ask for help without breaking Hisato's command and how to protect her father from her grandfather's plots. There were so many emergencies vying for her attention, she didn't know which one to worry about first. Tsuki and Akira, who were lounging in her room, assumed she was only worried about her grandfather's plots and called out unhelpful suggestions on how to capture him. They all wanted her to leave the palace behind, and saw her stubborn insistence on staying as her own selfishness. She wished she could explain her reasoning to them, but each time she tried the words dried up in her throat. Just when she thought she was going to wear a hole in the rug, a messenger arrived.

Her father had summoned her to speak with him. He was likely going to scold her for the scene she'd made earlier that day. She changed before she left, at the messenger's insistence, and she hurried ahead of the messenger to her father's chambers. The servants opened the doors and let her in.

Her father was seated beside a table where tea had been set out. He sipped casually as she burst into the room, her hair fluttering behind her in her haste. Her father glanced up at her dramatic entrance.

"I'm glad you could join me."

"How can you be so calm when your life is in danger?" Suzume threw her arms out to make her point. Her fear for him hadn't been feigned.

Her father set the teacup down on the table in front of him. "Every moment I've sat on my throne my life has been in danger. If I got worked up over every threat, I'd never be able to rest."

But she couldn't return the gesture. He wasn't taking her seriously. He thought she was being hysterical.

"This isn't some vague threat. Lord Kaedemori is partnering with yokai and plans to usurp you to put my younger brother on the throne," Suzume shouted as she lost control of her temper, flames shooting off her fingertips.

Her father gestured for her to sit. "We need to talk."

"We don't need to talk. You need to have him arrested right this minute."

"I received a letter this morning from your mother. She's disclosed where your brother is hidden. My most loyal men, including Ryuu, are on their way to retrieve him. Once we have my son, the threat will disappear."

"Have you arrested Lord Kaedemori?" Suzume asked.

"No."

"Then this isn't over. I think he's working with a dangerous monster called Hisato. He wants to-" she choked on the words. She couldn't reveal Hisato's plans.

Her father gestured for her to take a seat once more. "Please."

"Tell me you're at least trying to protect yourself." Hisato was dangerous, and she could only imagine what he was plotting against her father. It made her sick to think she could do nothing to protect him.

Her father only stared at her for a moment, and then with reluctance, she sat down across from him. Her father poured her a cup of tea. She held onto the glass but couldn't bring herself to drink.

"This is a delicate matter. Your grandfather is a powerful man, with many allies."

"But you're the emperor."

"And I can maintain my position with the support of my council. Of whom your grandfather has many in his pocket."

Suzume growled in frustration. "So, what, you're just going to let them kill you?"

Her father laughed. "No, I have not resigned myself to death quite yet. But before we can make a move against Lord Kaedemori, his guilt must be irrefutable. Do you have any proof?"

"My mother. She told me she will speak with the lords."

Her father sipped his tea. "Are you certain she would implicate her own father?"

"But she told you where my brother was. Shouldn't that prove she is loyal?"

He reached across the table and took Suzume's hand. "I love your mother. But we both know she thinks for herself before all others. She revealed where your brother was because she wanted to keep him safe. To confess against your grandfather, it would put her at risk."

Suzume growled. "This is madness. So, what, I should do nothing?"

"I appreciate your concern. I am doing everything in my power to make this right, but for now we must be patient. If we can prove his betrayal, then he can be tried. Until then, I will not risk causing unrest."

It wasn't a satisfactory answer. She'd find the proof herself if she had to. And she was about to tell her father just that when the room opened and a flushed guard came running in.

"Your majesty, the palace is under attack."

Suzume leaped to her feet, reaching for her staff which was not strapped to her back.

"What do you mean, under attack?" the emperor asked, his voice calm despite the dire situation.

"It's a dragon, your majesty. He's destroying the town."

Suzume's stomach clenched. It couldn't be. Why was he here? But even as she thought this, fear prickled along the back of her neck. A sinister laugh filled her ears.

"It's time to play your part, Suzume."

FORTY

Suzume watched as Kaito flew over the city from her place on the palace walls. Soldiers lined up all along it on either side of her. Warrior priests, all of them, as if the palace had been prepared for this all along. *I have to stop this.* By her command of the dragon, he could not come any closer. She caught sight of Ryuu further down the line, instructing the warrior priests. He spotted her and ran over.

"What are you doing here?"

Stop me. Don't let me do this. There hadn't been time to train or to prepare. She'd never gotten the chance to ask for his help.

But her body betrayed her and she knocked Ryuu backward with more force than should have been possible.

"Don't try and stop me. This ends now," she said, her voice sounding foreign to her own ears. Flames licked up from her feet, encasing her in fire as she leaped down from the wall, flying through the air and landing hard on the ground. A fall from that height should have broken every bone in her body. But it was becoming increasingly clear she was not quite human anymore.

Just outside the palace walls was a large space. A vacant lot separated the emperor's home from the surrounding town. She could see the dragon in the distance.

Now call him here.

Suzume clenched her hands into fists. *I will not do it.* Her lips were pressed shut and she used her sheer force of will to prevent his command.

Call him. Now.

Suzume gasped as pain shot through her. The only way to stop it was to do as she was told.

"Come save me!" Her order was ripped from her throat and echoed over the town. Instead of circling, Kaito changed directions and he was coming up fast; if he didn't stop soon, he would crash into her. She held her breath as he came to a sudden halt in front of her in dragon form, his body coiled around nearby buildings. She had to crane her neck to meet his gaze. He did not come to her as the man she had come to know. His spiritual energy unfurled from him, sparking against Suzume's skin.

"I knew you'd need me," he said as he transformed from dragon to man. He walked toward her.

Don't come any closer. Get away! But even as she shouted warnings in her head none of them passed her lips.

"What mess have you gotten yourself into?" Kaito watched the warrior priests lining the wall. With each step he came closer and she felt her hands twitch, the flames preparing to be unleashed.

She took a half a step back, but even doing that was a monumental struggle.

"You're being oddly quiet. Too ashamed that you needed me to rescue you?" He was inches away from her now. She could feel his spiritual energy wrapping around her. He thought she needed him to rescue her. But this was all a trap.

"You can thank me later." Kaito launched into the sky, flying toward the priests along the wall.

"Don-" she cried out, but it was strangled, as the priests unleashed a volley of spiritually imbued arrows. Kaito swerved away from them, spraying the priests with his deadly ice. Frost crept up the sides of the walls. He flew high up into the sky, preparing another attack, when she fired at him. It would have caught him dead on, but Suzume had managed to redirect her attack at the last moment.

He turned his attention to her and his eyes were an icy blue. *Run away. I don't want to kill you*, she shouted inside her mind. But no matter how she tried to fight against Hisato's influence, she couldn't break free.

"I told you I would destroy you," she said. Her voice was confident, arrogant. It was who she had been when she first met the dragon. He believed it. That's how everyone saw her, wasn't it? They thought she was still nothing but a spoiled princess.

The dragon laughed, and it sounded like more of a roar. "Do you think I'm going to fall for that?"

He flew high into the sky, out of her reach. Internally, Suzume gave a sigh of relief. If she was lucky, he'd leave and never come near her again.

The others arrived, weapons drawn and ready to defend, but when they saw Kaito flying overhead they all paused. The dragon dipped down low again, coming closer to them and Suzume ran toward him firing at him.

Rin cut her off before she could do any damage. "What are you doing?"

"Doing what Kazue could not," Suzume replied.

Hikaru joined his wife. "You don't really mean this. This isn't like you."

"You don't know me. This is what I must do if I want to stay here."

Hisato was clever. He was using her own past mistakes against her. And it was working, she could see the doubt gathering in their expressions.

"I can't let you do this." Rin transformed into her kitsune form, while Hikaru sang a song.

Please stop me before I kill him! Suzume shouted silently, but no one heard it.

In retaliation, Suzume tossed fiery flames toward both Rin and Hikaru, and a song rose to her lips that made the fire grow higher. It wasn't long before they were surrounded by the flames. Rin lunged for her, teeth bared, but before she could land a blow, Naoki was there, blade drawn and pushing her back.

No! Suzume wanted to scream.

"What are you doing, Naoki? We have to stop her," Rin said.

"I must protect her. Your intent was to kill."

Tsuki stood behind Suzume, his blade also drawn. *No, you can't stop them.* She wanted to shout, but they all believed her capable of killing the dragon. Of wanting to kill the dragon to stay at the White Palace. And because Naoki and Tsuki were bound to serve her, they wouldn't stop her no matter how much she wanted. Hisato had complete control of them as well, through her bond with them.

"Don't try and stop me."

Flames encircled her friends but Suzume could cross through with ease. For a moment, she thought Hisato was calling her away from the battle, but as she ran down the road she felt the tug of her spiritual power. The unspoken command was meant to bring Kaito down to her. Ice rained down upon her in response to her summons. Suzume waved her hand and before the ice could hit her she melted it with fire.

High above, Kaito weaved in and out of the clouds, using them for cover. But even hidden behind clouds she could sense him. When he was this close she could close her eyes and feel like he was right beside her. Hisato used this to his deadly advantage, and she aimed a fiery blast toward Kaito. He dodged it, but just barely. He was coming closer, his jaws open and power coalescing there. Before he could fire another attack, holy arrows flew from behind her. One caught Kaito along the side, and he roared as he was distracted. Suzume was forced to watch as more arrows landed in his hide. She turned to see Ryuu leading the warrior priests.

You have to stop this. Please. Before more people get hurt, Suzume pleaded to Hisato, but it was no use. His laughter filled her ears. He was reveling in her pain.

It is time the dragon met his end, Hisato purred in her mind.

Kaito blasted the priests with shards of ice in retaliation, and they scattered to avoid his blows. But not all escaped, one man had taken a blow to the throat. He slumped over on the ground, blood pouring out of his wound.

She'd seen him kill before, but never before had she felt her own life was at risk. That blow could just as easily hit her.

Suzume stared at the dead man. So this was Hisato's plan—turn them against one another. And he'd done it well. She was his tool of destruction.

Kaito lurched back as the pain of the arrows brought him to the ground. He collided with the ground, taking human form. He laid on the ground on all fours, and there was death in his gaze. Ryuu rushed forward to help her, but with a flick of her wrist a wall of flame separated her from everyone but Kaito. This was what Hisato wanted, just the two of them.

"You want to fight," Kaito said as he climbed to his feet. He yanked out the arrows embedded in his skin. Just touching them burned his flesh, and the stink of it filled the air as his hands smoked from contact. He tossed the broken arrows to one side. "Let's fight."

He rushed toward her, feigning to the left, and Suzume fell into the trap. He struck her hard along the side, knocking the wind from her and she stumbled backward. Kaito used his advantage and pressed her hard backward. Suzume stumbled and almost fell onto her back.

Suzume unleashed her flames and let them run up and down the staff, not wild and out of control, but focused and precise. As soon as the flames were unleashed, she saw what she most feared, horror in his eyes. To him she was a monster. Inhuman. Other.

Hisato used Kaito's momentary weakness and pushed him back. He stumbled only for a moment before regaining his feet and coming up swinging.

"You can fight this, Suzume. I know it's not you," he said.

In an instant, Kaito was behind her, his arm across her throat, choking her. He moved too quick for her to even see and she realized he had been toying with her the entire time. Even now, he underestimated her and she had thought him better than that. His hot breath was against her neck.

"That's where you're wrong. This is exactly what I wanted," Suzume said with a smirk he couldn't see.

Suzume swung her staff backward and smacked Kaito in the face. The action was so quick that he didn't even have time to shield with his ice before the fire burned his face.

Kaito snarled as he clutched his burning flesh and Suzume spun away from him. They turned to one another, and she could see the skin on his face was already starting to heal. All that remained was an angry, pink mark now.

He lunged for her and knocked the staff out of her hand. The pair of them fell to the ground and Kaito ended up on top of her, his hands pinning her to the ground.

"I let you run away. I told myself you'd come back to me. But I should have never left you alone. I knew you would only get in trouble," he said.

Flames erupted where his body touched hers and Suzume stared up into his dangerous icy blue gaze. "Your mistake was coming here."

With a sudden forced push, she knocked Kaito backward and he ended up sprawled on the ground. Suzume leaped up and pinned him to the ground as well.

"It's over for you." More than anything she wanted to close her eyes. But she stared into his face as the realization dawned, and the true depth of her betrayal sunk in. Perhaps up until that moment, he had hoped this was all a trick. But she watched as his hope died. He knocked her off him before she could complete the song.

She jumped backward, landing on her face. Suzume panted for breath, the fight having taken the wind out of her. Or maybe it was Hisato's way of making it seem more real.

"What are you doing?"

"I told you to stay away from me, but you wouldn't listen."

Kaito roared, transforming into the massive dragon again, and launched himself into the sky.

The song failed, but Hisato used her power over Kaito to try and bring him to the ground. The bond between them hummed like a taut string on an instrument—if plucked the right way, it would bring Kaito crashing down. As Suzume tugged on their bond however, Kaito pulled back and it resulted in a dangerous tug of war as they pulled on each other's energy.

His power traveled through their bond like an icy touch down her spine. Suzume shivered,and even her flames could not warm her. For a moment, it seemed he would break free and take over. Kaito thought so too, and for slightest moment eased up. It was then, with one last tug, Suzume brought Kaito crashing down to the ground. She ran toward where he'd fallen and she held her staff aloft. The song to seal him was on the tip of her tongue.

One of his blue eyes was full of pain and anger. This was it, she was going to kill Kaito. Inside her head, Hisato's voice echoed with laughter.

"Goodbye," he said.

Suzume, struck by his words, didn't even realize that one of his ice blades was coming toward her until it was too late.

It pierced through her and Suzume gasped as she lost her grip on her staff. It clattered onto the ground beside her. It was then, as blood pumped out of the wound, that she regained control of her body. Her hand reached for it.

"I'm so-" She choked on the word before collapsing to her knees.

FORTY-ONE

Suzume's eyes were wide as his ice pierced her through the heart. The stain spread across her chest, and her mouth opened in an 'o'. The horrifying realization of what he had done swept over him. As the stain spread she slumped forward onto the ground.

Kaito ran to her, kneeling at her side, but her eyes had fluttered closed. Her blood coated his hands, and he felt the life flicker out of her like a dying candle.

Kaito threw his head back in a pained roar. What had he done? What had he done?

"You stay away from her," Ryuu growled as he approached, baring teeth that were almost canine. As Suzume's life slowly slipped out of her, the flames which had kept everyone else back fell away.

And this creature, who he had previously assumed was a priest, was not human at all, but not yokai either.

"What are you?"

"Your destruction." The man rushed forward and Kaito could see the power and grace in his movements. At the same time, Kaito rushed forward and they clashed in the middle, meeting eye to eye for a moment.

"If you don't let me take her then she will die," Kaito snapped.

"What do you care when you tried to kill her?" the man said.

"Who are you to her?"

"Someone who can protect her better than you."

The man's eyes were an icy blue and the power that rolled off him was stronger than he'd ever before encountered in a human. Before he had any more time to consider the meaning of that the man rushed toward him, swinging his blade straight for Kaito's head. Kaito leaped away. He should let Suzume go. She had betrayed him. But his own traitorous heart wouldn't let him. The stain on her chest was growing, she was losing too much blood. If he could stop the bleeding he could save her. *And then what? It wouldn't change anything. She wanted me dead. She was about to seal me.* She'd threatened it before, but he could see this wasn't a game anymore.

The man rushed toward him again and Kaito, still weak from the spiritual arrows which had shot him, could only leap out of the way. When the man sliced at his head, he almost sliced Kaito's throat with it. There was something familiar about that icy gaze and the set of his jaw. And the sword in his hand, he knew it. Tetsuyama. *It cannot be.*

"You want to fight me?" Kaito said, his power fueled by his anger. He flexed his claws, half-transforming into a dragon. He sped toward the man faster than any mortal's eyes could trace. But when he reached where the man had been, he'd disappeared. Kaito spun just in time to find the man standing behind him, his sword poised for a strike.

Kaito caught the blade in his hand, but as soon as he touched the metal it burned his flesh. He jerked his hand away, glaring at the man. This very blade had been imbued with his spiritual energy. How was that possible? It was a yokai blade. This man was stronger than he could have imagined.

"You're as much as a bastard as I imagined you would be," the man said.

"Do I know you?" Kaito eyed the man up and down, even now trying to delay the truth which laid in front of him.

"No, but I've been waiting all my life for this chance."

The man's blade glowed with spiritual energy as he lunged for Kaito. He swung his sword and though Kaito tried to dodge it, the blow struck him along the side. The cut was not deep but the spiritual energy seeped into his flesh as if it were a poison.

Kaito clutched his wounded side for only a moment before the real anger started to pulse through him. This was his chance for real vengeance against all the yokai who'd been destroyed by his mistake. Kaito pushed forward but his anger only made him stupid, and it left him open to an attack from his opponent. The second strike hit across his chest, pulsed through him, and sent him staggering backward. The man turned from Kaito, perhaps thinking he'd done all he could, when Kaito threw himself around the man's middle and they end up on the ground, wrestling. The man rained punches down upon Kaito, his anger fueling his fists and Kaito, equally enraged, returned each one.

The air crackled with the clash of their spiritual energy. Each time they collided it created sparks in the air.

Kaito spun and got the upper hand in their fight. Rain pelted against his back. When he looked into his eyes, it felt like he was staring into a distorted mirror.

"Who are you?" Kaito asked. He needed a confirmation, because he couldn't bring himself to ask the real question.

The man answered by butting him in the head and sending Kaito careening backward. Before he could recover from the blow, the man had his weapon in his hand again and had it pressed against Kaito's throat. There was no escaping it, by now Suzume would have lost too much blood. She was surely dead. And he realized he too longed for the release of death.

"Do it!" Kaito roared.

But before the man could land the final blow, Kaito heard a roar from his side. Hot flames licked past them and for a fantastic moment, he thought Suzume had lived.

But when he turned it was not Suzume but Rin in kitsune form. She was growling, not at Kaito who had banished her, but at the man with the blade who was staring at her with a pained expression.

"I thought you were better than this, Takashi," Rin said.

The priest, Hikaru, was standing beside Rin, pointing his holy arrows at the man.

The man bowed his head, as if chastised. *Then it was true—this was his and Kazue's son.* But furthermore, Rin knew him. And judging from the way she spoke to him, they'd been close.

Kaito turned toward her. "You hid this from me?" he said.

Rin's golden eyes flickered in his direction. "I wanted to tell you. So many times, but-"

"You knew he was out there killing our kind, and you didn't tell me?" Kaito roared. The ground shook beneath his feet. He rushed toward Rin, but before he could attack her for her betrayal both his bastard and Hikaru stood in his way.

"Leave now," Hikaru said.

It should come as no surprise that Kazue would be protecting this abomination even beyond the grave. Perhaps that's why Suzume had left him too. In the end, it was this thing that stole all his joy.

"This isn't over," Kaito said before transforming and taking to the air.

KAITO RETURNED TO HIS PALACE AND FOR THREE DAYS HE REMAINED IN THE same spot, staring out at the crashing of waves in the crumbling portion of his palace. No one dared disturb him. It seemed everything ran perfectly without him. He did not matter. It wasn't until the sun set on the third day that anyone came for him. Ai approached from behind, her footsteps nearly silent.

"This is enough," she said.

Rage that had hardly been banked inside him over the past few days burst out of him, and he grabbed the nearest object, some stone debris, and smashed it on the ground. But it wasn't enough and Kaito picked up several more items which all ended up in fragments on the floor. He found himself standing in the center of the chaos, eyes glowing blue and a storm raging in the sky overhead.

"Will you be satisfied once you've smashed the entire palace to bits?" Ai asked.

Kaito swung a punch at her that stopped just inches from landing. Ai did not even flinch. And before he could land the blow he turned his back to her instead.

"Leave me."

"Your people need you," she said.

"Go!" he roared without turning to face her.

"You mourn for a woman who betrayed you? Who is working with the same monster who has been hunting us for centuries? Who within her holds the soul of the woman who sealed you?"

"Shut your damn mouth." Kaito turned to stalk toward her. This time he wasn't going to hold back. He would knock her through the wall.

"I have not been idle while you sulked. I have eyes everywhere and they have told me the truth. She belongs to the emperor and they are planning on destroying us."

"She's dead now, so what does it matter?"

She could not understand the pain inside him that threatened to shatter him into pieces. His brother was right, he was too soft on humans. He let his affection for them blind him time and time again. Perhaps even their meeting had been his son's way of getting revenge. In the same way he had plotted to use her, he had been used. What a cruel irony.

"Ai does not like to see you this way," Ai said, quietly, reverting to her more childish tone. She never could hold onto her former self for long. The tenderness of her words almost reached him, but not quite.

"Then get out," Kaito said, but with less venom than before. He was so very tired.

But Ai crept closer to him, kneeling down beside him and took his hand in hers. He wanted to shake her away, to growl, to bring ice down from the sky and flatten the entire island under his grief. Suzume was dead. Gone, killed by his own anger and fear. *She was going to seal you. You had no other choice.*

"It is better this way," Ai said, stroking his hand.

Kaito knocked her away. "Yes, it is better that I saw the truth before it was too late." Just thinking about the time he spent sealed in stone awakened his anger all over again. He should never have trusted Suzume. She had made threats since the beginning but he had thought them only that. Idle threats. How could he have been such a fool to not see it from the start? And Kazue's son, right there under his nose the entire time. Suzume's father.

He curled his hand into a fist. But Suzume was gone now. Dead. Just like Kazue. And with the both of them gone so was the piece of his heart that held onto the hope that humans might be of value, that they might bring him happiness and peace.

"I want to be alone," Kaito said.

This time Ai didn't argue and she slipped out of his chamber, leaving him in silence. Kaito stood by the window for a while longer, he wasn't sure how long. Time ceased to have meaning. When he finally turned away from the window, he went straight to the audience hall. He knew what must be done.

The dragons and the yokai who had gathered in the hall were more hushed than usual. There wasn't any of their usual revelry. Perhaps they all sensed the mood he was feeling and feared him. Well, good. There was no more doubt left in him now. There was only one way to return his kingdom to the way it had been.

When Kaito entered the audience chamber, they all turned toward him. He took his place at the front of the room, standing on the dais and gazing out across at the crowd.

"For too long the power of the yokai has been in the shadow of humans." His words rang out around him. All eyes were glued to him. "They have bred like vermin and slaughter our friends and loved ones. But that ends now."

There was a sudden hush, as if everyone was holding their collective breaths.

"I am going to kill the human emperor and extinguish all human life."

FORTY-TWO

The first thing she felt was pain—an intense, throbbing pain in her left shoulder. It pulsed down her entire arm and rippled through her upper body. It felt as if someone had torn open her chest cavity and scooped out what was inside. *If I could stop waking up battered that would be great.* Suzume groaned as she tried to sit up. What strange place would she wake up this time?

"Don't sit up, you'll reopen the wound." Suzume blinked and tilted her head toward the person sitting beside her bed.

The room's only light was a brazier burning in the corner. The person sitting by her bed was backlit and their face was hidden in shadows. Through the fog of waking and the lingering pain, she thought it might be Kaito. And that maybe the last thing she'd remembered was all a bad dream. For a brief second, she let herself indulge in a fantasy where she never left him behind, and she never went to the White Palace. None of it was real.

A gentle hand pushed her to lay back down, and as his face got closer, Suzume saw it was the emperor staring down at her with a concerned expression.

"The healer said you should not sit up yet."

Suzume stared wide-eyed up at the emperor, the ruler of Akatsuki, sitting at her bedside like a nursemaid. Suzume frowned as his words filtered through her mind in a hazy fog. If the pain in her shoulder was any indication, Kaito trying to kill her hadn't been a nightmare, but her reality.

"How did I get here?" she asked with a dry, cracked throat.

"Drink first." The emperor gave her a cup to drink from and Suzume gulped it down as if she had never drunk anything so delicious in her entire life. The emperor watched her drink from her cup for a few minutes. When she had drained the glass, he took it from her and set it to one side.

It was strange to see him perform actions that were more suited for a servant than the ruler of an entire country.

"There was a yokai attack and you were nearly killed," the emperor said. She didn't need that part recounted. The battle played out in her mind—vivid images of Kaito's eyes, the betrayal she saw in them when he pierced her chest with a shard of ice. Suzume pressed her hand to a hard lump on her chest. The wound was bandaged, a hole just above her heart. He'd almost killed her—he had intended to kill her. But by dumb luck she had survived. By all rights she should have been angry. The only emotion that was left within her, however, was an aching sense of helplessness. This wasn't over. Hisato wasn't done with her yet.

"We're lucky Ryuu got to you in time, otherwise you would not be with us now," the emperor continued.

"Ryuu saved me?" She wasn't sure why that surprised her so much.

The emperor nodded. "He would not want me to tell you, but he fought very hard to get you away from that beast." The emperor reached out to push a lock of hair behind Suzume's ear. "I thought I had lost you when you wouldn't wake. But Ryuu assured me that it would take time but you would come back to us."

The emperor looked at her with the concerned eyes of a father. It was strange to see him that way. Since she'd arrived at the palace she'd convinced herself that he wanted nothing but to use her and her power. But if that's all she meant to him, why would he be sitting by her bedside tending to her?

He grabbed Suzume's hand and squeezed. "You should rest."

He stood up as if he was about to walk away. Before he could, Suzume grabbed his wrist to stop him. "Thank you."

"Why are you thanking me?"

She wasn't sure how to express her feelings. At her darkest moment, when she'd been betrayed by someone she thought she trusted, it warmed her to know that her father cared. Suzume hesitated to put her thoughts into words. She'd never been good at expressing these sorts of sentimental feelings. "Just because."

The emperor leaned down and planted a kiss on her forehead. "Rest and get better soon."

THE FOLLOWING DAYS PROCEEDED MUCH THE SAME. A FUSSY HEALER WITH A long gray beard came to check on the progress of her healing. He smelled of incense and medicinal herbs. He snapped at the maid, ordering more blankets and to keep the room as warm as possible. He poked and prodded at Suzume, checking her pulse and feeling her forehead.

It had been several days since she had awoken and was bored to tears with bed rest. She'd started to look forward to the healer's visits. At least it interrupted the tedium of bed rest. Tsuki and Akira had done their best to keep her entertained but there was only so much she could do lying in bed other than sleep and read.

The healer came in blustering about this and that, but she'd learned to mostly ignore his diatribes.

"Well, sit up then. Let's change those bandages."

Moving in bed was getting easier with each passing day and Suzume scooted into a seated position. The room was toasty warm even without the layers of blankets. The healer had already chased out the others, demanding privacy for his patient. Suzume stripped down to almost nothing, leaving her bare shoulders exposed. The healer unwound the bandages around her chest. As he drew back the bandages, he paused and stared at her shoulder.

"What is it?" Suzume asked. That couldn't be a good sign.

The old man leaned in closer, his nose almost pressing against her skin. "I've never seen anything like it," he muttered to himself.

"What?" Suzume demanded, sudden fear gripping her. She couldn't see past the top of his head.

The old man pulled back, shaking his head and Suzume got her first glimpse of her wound. If it could be called that at all. The hole, which had pierced her through to her shoulder blade, was gone. All that remained was a faint scrape, as if she'd gotten a small scratch.

"The skin is healing well, but the insides will take longer," the old man said. He was still staring at her scabbed chest.

"Is this normal?"

The old man's dark eyes flickered up to her and then he turned away to fiddle with his bandages and poultices. "Perfectly normal." But she couldn't believe him. She wasn't an expert on serious battle wounds, but she thought something that had almost killed her would look a bit more gruesome. *How could I be healing this quickly?* It was just like her broken arm.

"You can sit up, but no leaving your bed."

"But I feel fine." Suzume lifted her arm to show her full range of motion had returned.

The old man looked away again. "Do not lift your arms above your head. You could do further damage."

Suzume lowered her arm to the bed once more. So this wasn't normal, but the healer wouldn't admit it. He gathered up his things in a hurry after that and scurried out of her room.

After the healer left, Akira came and sat down on the bed beside Suzume while she inspected her fingers which flexed with ease. In just a couple days she'd gone from the worst pain imaginable to the faintest twinge when she flexed.

"You're healing has been quick," Akira commented.

"I guess so." She kept her tone light and indifferent while on the inside panic had started to grip her.

Akira shook her head. "It isn't normal for a human to heal this quickly."

When Suzume didn't respond, Akira said, "You never healed this fast before. Has something changed?"

Suzume swallowed past a lump in her throat. She knew what had changed. Her body wasn't her own. Hisato needed her whole to kill Kaito. And perhaps she was slowly turning into that monster she had seen in the guardian's palace. Suzume shook her head. She wanted desperately to tell her the truth, but Hisato's spell was too strong. Instead lies poured out of her. "Nothing has changed, I've always healed quickly."

Akira stared at her for a moment, but didn't press her. How many more lies would she have to tell her friends? She had to find a way to escape Hisato's control.

It took several days of arguing with the healer before he would let her out of bed. By the time he had agreed, there was barely a sign she had been injured at all. Her victory was only half—the healer forbade her from leaving her chamber and she was forced to stalk around her bedroom while she puzzled through how to stop Hisato. It finally came down to asking the old man for help.

She couldn't ask Souta outright to help her, but she hoped if she wrote it down it might work as a sort of loophole. She requested a brush and parchment from a maid, and set out to write what was happening to her. But try as she might, Suzume couldn't get her arm to cooperate. All that resulted from her work was smeared streaks on parchment. Frustrated at her lack of control, she crumpled up the paper into a ball and flung it at the nearby wall.

"Did I come at a bad time?" Souta, the old man, asked. She hadn't even heard him enter.

"It's fine," she said through ground teeth. She was anything but fine. She knew that the time was coming closer. Any moment Hisato could take her body and use her to go and finish what she'd started.

"I heard you've been recovering well."

Suzume placed her hand on the shoulder which she had thrown the paper with. It was the same one she'd been stabbed through. She dropped her hand to her side.

"I'm making progress," she said with a lift of her chin, to stop any further questions.

The old man smiled in a conspiratorial way, before making himself comfortable across from her. *Did he know why she was healing so fast?* He groaned as he got comfortable and then after a few moments, he said, "I know you've completely healed."

She held his gaze. The truth was right there on the tip of her tongue.

"It means things are progressing faster than we thought."

Her stomach dropped. Was he working for Hisato too? Did he know what he'd ordered her to do? Flames erupted along her skin, sparking against her in response to her fear.

The old man eyed her burning hands and the sparks flying off her hair.

"What can I do, just kill the dragon?"

The old man grinned at her.

"Is this funny? I can't control my own body! He's using me to kill Kaito!"

"You seem to be in control right now."

It occurred to her she had fought against Hisato's command. "But how?"

"Nothing can be the darkness of Kazue's soul but Kazue. Those are the facts. She will not obey his command."

"How did you know?"

"Because he's come to me already. He tried drawing me to his side, but I saw him for what he was and I banished him. But he hasn't given up. I know he'll be back." The old man sighed.

"Tell me how I can stop him." Suzume fell onto her knees, practically begging the old man.

"There is only one way—you must embrace Kazue's power," the old man said.

"But that means I could lose myself to her. You're saying I have to die?" Suzume asked, her voice just barely above a whisper. What was worse, giving herself over to Kazue or Hisato?

"Don't think of it as dying. The person you are now may very well be the same you will be once you come into your power. You were born with the power after all."

Suzume clutched the edge of the table. She didn't like to think about that. What if she lost all her memories the way Hikaru did?

"I can't." She stood up and paced away from him. There had to be another way around it.

"I tried to fight it as well. But in the end, she took me."

"Why are you like this, did you choose it?" She pointed her finger at him.

He lowered his head. "I did choose this. I was dying and fearing death, and I asked Ryuu to save me." His gray eyes seemed ancient and foreign. It wasn't Souta who was stared back at her, but Kazue. "And I chose this life over death. You can make the same choice."

That was her choice. Kaito's life or her own. She didn't want to accept it. "Maybe if I learn how to control my powers?" she asked.

"No amount of control will save you from Hisato. He will never tire of you. Because you have what none of us have."

Suzume rested her hand over her chest. "Kazue's heart."

The fire was sparking all over her and she felt Kazue surrounding her, like a soft breeze. It had been Souta who healed her from Hisato's control. But already she could feel the power fading.

"I cannot protect you from it," Souta said, as the power receded from her. "Everything is in motion already; the emperor has declared war on the yokai."

"Why would he do that?" She got up and tried to run for the door, but her footsteps froze in place. "I have to-" she strangled on the rest of her words. *I have to stop him.* This was what Hisato wanted, a war between yokai and humans would give him everything he needed to create his monstrous army.

"Ryuu has done what he could to try and dissuade him, but the emperor is decided."

She had to stop them, but she couldn't seem to make her feet obey her.

"Can't you stop him?"

"It's not just the emperor. There have been attacks by yokai. The dragon has to be swayed as well."

What can I possibly do? She felt as if she were being torn in two, caught between two sides in which there was no winner.

FORTY-THREE

Suzume stared forward as her maid dressed her, her gaze fixed on nothing in particular. Her mind was racing. She'd tried over and over to speak with the emperor but she'd been blocked at every turn. Because of her outburst in the council, she was not allowed anywhere near council meetings. And at all her attempts to speak with the emperor in private she was turned away. Her last hope was having her mother speak with the emperor on her behalf.

To celebrate her return, Izume was having a party. It wasn't surprising knowing her mother. Suzume was expected to attend, but even as she prepared for the party, her mind was filled with more serious problems. It had been nearly a week since the attack, and she'd been trying to figure out how to summon Kazue to help her fight the compulsion of Hisato's commands. It was slow going. When she needed Kazue the most, she was absent. Suzume's maid finished adding the final layer to her ensemble. Rin, who continued to play the role of her maid, was assisting. She watched Suzume, her gaze boring into her.

They'd hardly spoken since Suzume had attacked Kaito and she knew the kitsune was mad at her. She assumed, like everyone else, that Suzume had taken it upon herself to kill Kaito. Suzume had tried several times to explain herself, but every time she tried Hisato twisted her words. But she had a plan. Maybe she couldn't subvert Hisato's order but she could find a way around it.

Rin handed the maid a pin for Suzume's hair and once it was placed, she held up a mirror for Suzume to look at herself. No makeup or fine clothes could hide her fatigue. There were circles under her eyes that could not be disguised, and it seemed she'd aged a hundred years in a short amount of time.

"Leave us," Suzume said to the maid.

The maid bowed in response, backing out of the room, leaving Suzume and Rin alone. The kitsune glared at Suzume. She'd been waiting on this scolding for a while, and until now had been able to avoid it. But if her plan was going to work, she was going to have to face Rin's ire.

"If you have something to say, just say it," Suzume said, assuming the defiant, headstrong role she was known for.

"What are you doing?" Rin asked.

More than anything she wished she could confess the truth to Rin, but there was no getting around it.

"Going to a party." Suzume smoothed imaginary wrinkles from her kimono.

"That's not what I mean and you know it. Why did you attack Kaito? Why are we wasting time here in the palace?"

Suzume's rolled her eyes. "He attacked me first." She headed for the door, but as Suzume expected Rin wasn't done with her. She leaped in front of Suzume before she could leave.

"You banished him. He should never have been able to come near you unless you summoned him."

"Do you have a point? We all know I'm not as strong as him." It hurt her pride to say the words out loud, but if she'd learned anything recently, it was that she was weak. Not only in strength but her character. If she hadn't tried to steal power to get stronger, she wouldn't be in this situation.

"Why are you doing this? It isn't like you." Rin's golden eyes searched Suzume's gaze, trying desperately to find the goodness inside her. It warmed Suzume to know Rin still believed in her, but if her plan was to work she had to push her away.

"The dragon almost killed me, and yet I'm the bad guy?"

"You're not answering the question," Rin pressed.

Suzume laughed, tossing her hair over her head. "You're a fool if you think I cared about Kaito. I've gotten what I wanted. I'm back home where I belong. I only attacked him to eliminate any possibility he'd come back and take it from me."

Rin shook her head, perhaps trying to deny it. But up until recently, all Suzume had wanted was to return to the White Palace, to resume the life she had. Suzume turned away from the kitsune so she wouldn't see her resolve starting to crumble.

"What about Hisato? You have to stop him."

Suzume shrugged. "I don't see how that concerns me."

Rin stared at Suzume in disbelief. "I thought you had changed."

"People never change." She pushed past Rin to leave the room but as she was about to exit, she stopped and turned to meet Rin's gaze. "If you don't like it, why don't you go back to the dragon?"

Rin's eyes widened, perhaps with realization. She hoped she knew what Suzume was trying to say but couldn't.

"Is that really how you feel?" Rin asked.

"I don't need you anymore. But-" the rest of her sentence tangled up in her throat. *Kaito needs you, go warn him.* As it was, she was playing a dangerous game. She'd already skirted too close to the truth.

"This isn't over, Suzume. You cannot change your destiny."

"I know."

She ended the conversation there. She wasn't sure if Hisato was watching her or if it was only his command that kept her from saying what she meant. But she didn't want Rin or anyone else to get hurt if he tried to use her again. If she was right, Rin would be gone by the time she returned from the party and Kaito would know what was coming next. Maybe with time, she could figure out a way to fight Hisato's control and stop the attack altogether.

These thoughts filled her mind as she headed out of the main palace where she'd been staying to the second wife's palace. It was within the compound of the palace and a short walk through the connecting garden. The secondary palace was where she had grown up and she hadn't been back since she returned. But as she walked up the familiar pathway, she was overcome with memories. There was the maple tree that dropped beautiful crimson leaves in fall. There was the place where she took her lessons. And around the side of the building was where she'd had her first kiss with a young courtier.

A servant greeted her and showed her inside. The main hall glittered with candles, and as she shed her outer coat, handing it to a servant, she heard the murmur of voices coming from the entertaining room. Throughout her childhood Izume had often thrown parties, trying to gain favor of powerful courtiers.

Hearing the sounds of a party and her mother's laughter, she felt as if she'd been transported back in time. Like everything that had happened up until now was nothing but a dream. Suzume made her way into the dining room, where her mother sat at the head of the table, restored to her former place. Like a flower blooming in the winter, she was a burst of color against a drab landscape. She sat at the center of half a dozen courtiers, all council members to the emperor.

A part of her wanted to be mad that her mother had gone right back to her old habits—scheming and politicking. But it was good that she was, if Suzume could get her mother on her side. As Suzume entered her mother made a loud exclamation and leaped up to greet her. All eyes turned toward Suzume.

"There you are. Come sit with me at the head of the room." She took Suzume's hand and led her to the head of the table. "This looks beautiful on you," Izume said, admiring the very kimono she'd gifted Suzume and requested she wear to the party.

The guests greeted Suzume before everyone settled in for their meal. Among the older council members was a young courtier who was unsurprisingly placed beside Suzume. Likely with the intention of having them get to know one another. Since her marriage to Daiki had been absolved, no doubt, her mother was already planning a marital alliance. It was strange, before her mother had never taken much interest in Suzume's hunt for a husband. But she supposed things had changed since the exile. She should take it as a sign their relationship was being repaired.

The nobleman flattered Suzume all through dinner, but she used her fan to hide her bored expression. Before she would have reveled in his attention. He was young and handsome, the heir to a powerful family. He was an ideal match, but all she could think about was Rin, hoping she would get to Kaito in time to warn him. Which would inevitably lead her to thinking about how she could avoid killing him.

After the meal was served, Izume stood up. The room fell silent and everyone turned to her expectantly, as if they'd all been waiting for this moment. But this wasn't part of her usual routine.

"I am very happy to be back among friends at the palace." She smiled as the courtiers laughed, as if they were all sharing in some joke. Izume waited for the laughter to die away before continuing. "But I am twice blessed to have not only my daughter, Suzume, here with me, but my son, as well."

She gestured to the back of the room and door which led toward the private quarters of the house. Suzume's younger brother, Ryouta, stepped through the door. He'd grown since she'd last seen him. His dumpling cheeks had thinned and he was almost as tall as her now. Suzume blinked in surprise to see him. At first she hadn't recognized him at all. Though he was not quite a man, it was clear he was on the cusp of manhood. The ghost of a mustache was on his lips. Even before she had been exiled, they'd hardly seen one another. When he was still a child, he'd been sent away to study.

"Now let us toast to the dawning of a new era in Akatsuki." Everyone lifted their glasses before taking a drink. Suzume tore her gaze away from her little brother, who kept his head lowered, to her mother who was smiling and exalting in the attention of her guests.

When the toast was finished, her brother took his seat on the other side of her mother. The men around the table complimented him, inquiring after his studies. All questions he answered with shy, quick answers. Suzume had to have misunderstood what her mother had said. It was Lord Kaedemori who was the one plotting against the throne. Suzume had been the one to make the accusation.

There was no chance to ask her mother what she meant, as the party continued to flow around them. After a while the guests left one by one, until only the three of them remained. A servant came and poured them tea, and Izume picked up the steaming cup, inhaling the aroma. She gave a contended sigh.

"It is good to be back together," she said as she set her cup back down. She reached out to touch her brother's hand, squeezing it gently. Suzume pretended not to notice the snub. That didn't matter right now. She was concentrating very hard on trying to summon Kazue, so she could ask her mother for help.

Izume noticed her intense concentration and said, "What's the matter, darling?"

"You should be more careful with your words. People might get the wrong impression," Suzume scolded her mother, her tongue automatically changing the subject.

"These are our most trusted allies. We have nothing to worry about from them."

"But if the emperor hears rumors that you are plotting to take the throne, where will that put us?"

Izume shook her head and laughed. "Suzume, don't be so naive."

She bristled at her mother's insult. "I'm being realistic. The court is watching our family."

Izume shook her head. "I have given my account to the court today. Your grandfather and the Kaedemoris have all been shamed."

"What? Why didn't you tell me sooner?"

"Because we are not Kaedemoris, we are the emperor's family."

Perhaps she'd given Izume too much credit. Was it a mistake to bring her back here? It made her sick to her stomach.

"What are you planning?"

"I only want to make your life better, my dear."

"What are you planning?" Suzume asked again, her voice rising. Kazue's flames came burning to the surface. Ryouta and her mother both stared at her with wide eyes.

"You know what I want, Suzume."

"You said it was my grandfather who wanted to put him on the throne."

Izume laughed. "You believed that?"

Suzume clenched her hand into a fist. She'd been an idiot to ever trust her mother. She'd fallen for her charms, just like all the others. Perhaps that priestess had even been part of the deception.

"You can't do this. You'll put the whole kingdom in danger!"

"That's exactly what I want. While your father fights a pointless war against storybook monsters, we will grow more powerful."

"No."

Izume petted her son's cheek. "It's all thanks to you. You have won the emperor over better than I ever could have. You even brought me back."

"I won't let you get away with this. I'll tell the emperor."

"No, you won't," a voice said, and Suzume felt a cold chill down her spine. It couldn't be. Suzume's entire body froze in place. It had to be a dream. But even if she wanted to shut her eyes and pretend it wasn't happening, it wouldn't change the truth. She turned to face Hisato.

Izume rose to greet her guest, and Hisato bowed to her and then to her brother.

"I'm sorry, did I miss the party?" Hisato asked Izume who embraced him in a way that was much too familiar.

"What are you doing here?" Suzume said.

"Don't be rude to our guest," Izume scolded.

Suzume ignored her mother and faced Hisato. "Why are you here?" Fire came to her fingertips. She could fight him now. Kazue's power was coursing through her.

"Don't bother. You'll only hurt yourself," Izume said, in a casual, off-handed way.

Suzume turned wide-eyed to her mother. "How do you know that?"

"Haven't you figured it out yet? Izume is the one who freed me."

"You're lying." Suzume took a step back, but she collided with Ryouta who grabbed her arms. She didn't want to hurt him. He was only doing their mother's bidding. "Why did you do this, mother?" Suzume spat.

"None of this would have been necessary if you'd been born a boy as you should have." Izume brushed her hand against his cheek. "Or if Ryuu could bear his own children."

"What does Ryuu have to do with any of this?" Suzume stammered. It felt like her heart was in her throat.

"Ryuu is the first emperor, the true emperor. If I could have had his child, it would have ruled without question." She shrugged. "So I decided if I could not have a true born heir, I would make the most powerful heir."

Suzume shook her head. "I thought you loved him!"

Izume laughed, her voice ringing off the ceiling. "Oh, you have become a fool, daughter."

"Then is my brother like me?" She felt none of the power radiating off him. He seemed an ordinary human. But she had thought the same about herself before she'd awoken Kaito.

"Not yet, but once you bring me the dragon, we will change that."

"I won't!" Suzume shouted. "I'm don't have to obey you, Hisato, not if I have Kazue's power to protect me."

"Get on your knees."

Despite the fire that was burning up inside her, Suzume did as he commanded.

"I let you think you could defeat me." His shape transformed and he took on Souta's face and he smiled at the dawning horror on her expression. "I needed you to lure out the dragon, and you sent the perfect bait. Someone he trusts."

She tried to pull away, to fight his stare. But what was the use. It was impossible to fight his control.

"When Souta finds out, he'll try to stop you." She hoped, she didn't really know where his allegiance laid, or Ryuu's.

Hisato squatted down in front of her, grabbing onto her chin. "Accept it Suzume, you're alone. There's no one who can stop this."

He'd played her for a fool, let her believe and then taken it all away. She dropped her head, what was the use? Hisato had won, and she would have to kill the dragon.

FORTY-FOUR

Going back to Kaito's palace was not difficult. She and Hikaru had dodged all the patrols of which there were many. It was clear Kaito was on guard, which should have been a relief. But instead Rin had this sinking feeling in her gut. Ever since Suzume and Kaito had fought, she'd known something was wrong. It wasn't until their fight that she realized exactly what it was. Kaito had to be warned Hisato was up to something, but if he'd infiltrated even at the heart of their group what could have been done to Kaito?

Hikaru and Rin were able to stay together until they were standing along the shore. She could see the palace in the distance. Memories of long ago flooded back to her, happy times, and some sad. When she'd left it had been without regret, it had been to start a life with Hikaru. But now returning after how she and Kaito had last parted, she feared what her reception would be.

Hikaru squeezed her hand. "I'll be waiting for you in the village nearby."

Rin wrapped her arms around him, holding him close. The beating of his heart brought her comfort. He couldn't go with her into Kaito's domain. According to the rumors, Kaito was declaring war on humans. She wouldn't bring Hikaru there, not when his life would be at risk. But how many more partings would they have to endure before they'd be happy again? It was easy to fear the future when everything seemed so uncertain.

"You'll be fine. This is Kaito we're talking about."

She laughed. "I know, that's what I'm worried about."

"Be strong, my heart, and if you're not back by sunset tomorrow, I'll storm the castle to rescue you."

She laughed and rested her forehead against his, feeling the warmth of his body, the comforting presence of his spiritual energy. She could do this. It had to be done. Suzume had trusted her with this message.

She let go of his hand reluctantly and walked the pathway which led into the dragon's palace. It was a single strip of land that connected the shore with the island palace. To the mundane human, it would appear as nothing but ocean. Torri arches guided the way, and Rin took her time admiring the familiar landscape.

A pair of yokai in mismatched armor guarded the entrance. One wore ancient armor, damaged by time and rust, with Kaito's old insignia freshly painted on the breastplate, while the other wore the symbol of the Lady of the Forest.

"State your business," they said as she approached.

Rin straightened her back as she said, "I've come to see the dragon."

"If you're here to swear loyalty, you'll have to wait until morning," they said, already losing interest in her.

Beyond the entrance, the courtyard was bustling with activity. It seemed many had come to the palace. Rin considered insisting she be brought to the dragon straight away, but considering his temper, and the fact that he had banished her last time they'd been together, he might not be willing to see her even if she insisted. She would have to find another way to get close to him.

"I am here to pledge my loyalty."

"Find the neko in green, she'll tell you what to do," the guard in Kaito's insignia said in a bored drawl.

Rin bowed her head in thanks and entered the courtyard. She met the harried neko, who hastily showed her to the barracks where the surplus of would-be supplicants were gathered. The place was packed full of futons, and Rin, seeing a pair of yokai fight over a bed, decided to make herself comfortable, lest she be sleeping on the floor that night.

It seemed strange to see so many yokai had gathered here. And what were they preparing for? More importantly, what would she say to the dragon? How could she explain something she was not entirely certain of? There was a part of her that wanted to turn around and try and talk some sense into Suzume. She knew she was prone to selfishness, but Rin never thought she'd actually kill Kaito, and even though she hadn't spoken the words out loud, she felt certain she was trying to ask her to warn him.

Rin sighed. This wasn't just about Suzume, there were other things she had to warn him about. Secrets she had kept too long from her old friend. Rin flopped herself back on the futon. Maybe she should stop being a coward and just go talk to him, instead of using this excuse to stall. A pair of tanuki walked in, chattering amongst themselves.

"Are you going to stay for the wedding?" One asked another.

"It was the only reason I came!" They laughed.

"It's a shame that he'll be off the market. I caught a glimpse of him sparring with the others." She fanned herself.

"Excuse me." She interrupted their conversation, and the duo eyed her with suspicion. Seeing the hostile air between yokai in the barracks, she didn't blame them.

"I couldn't help but overhear what you were saying. Who is getting married?"

The two of them shared a look before bursting into peals of laughter. Rin blinked at them, waiting for them to calm themselves.

"Do you really not know?" one of them asked.

"The Dragon is taking a bride."

"If you came here with hopes of wooing the dragon, you're out of luck," the second tanuki said.

Rin wanted to laugh away their assumptions but she never imagined Kaito would marry, not after Kazue. This was a strange development. Perhaps it had something to do with Suzume's odd behavior.

"Who is he marrying?"

"The daughter of the Lord of the Sea. Where have you been living, under a rock?"

They laughed before walking away. *Kaito is marrying Ai?* Has the entire world turned upside down? Maybe it was better if she didn't delay in trying to talk to him.

Rin got up and went to talk to one of the servants hurrying through the yard.

"Excuse me," she said.

The servant carrying piles of clothes and armor regarded her with raised brows.

"Can I help you? I'm very busy."

"I need to speak with the dragon."

"You and every other yokai here." He turned to walk away. Rin tried to catch his attention but it was to no avail.

After several more unsuccessful attempts, Rin resigned herself to waiting until morning when the dragon would be holding his audience.

The following morning the group Rin was a part of was led into the audience hall. It had been recently remodeled but it still held some of the old grandeur that she remembered. Many of the yokai gazed around in awe at the high ceiling and the columns. The group filed in and took their places, bowing before the throne. Rin prepared herself for the confrontation that was going to come. But it wasn't Kaito sitting on the throne, but Ai.

"You've all come to swear your loyalty to the dragon. And we welcome you." Ai's gaze drifted over the group and came to rest on Rin. They held one another's gaze for a moment before Ai skimmed past her as if not seeing her at all. "We have an important task before us. The humans have grown too numerous and have killed our kind, but that time has ended. We are rising up against them. Those of you who stand here have a choice, join the fight or perish. What do you choose?"

"We serve," the group called out together.

Ai nodded, seemingly pleased with the turnout. "Go out and you will be given your uniforms and start your training." She turned, dismissing them all. The group started to file out. The tanuki girls grumbled that they hadn't gotten the chance to see the dragon. Rin did not follow the group and instead chased after Ai. She was nearly out the rear door when Rin caught her.

"I need to see the dragon," Rin said.

Ai stopped mid-stride, and then turned to Rin. "You gave up that right when you betrayed him."

"I never betrayed him." Rin shook herself, now was not the time to defend her actions. "There's something he needs to know."

"No one sees the dragon and he will especially not want to see you."

"Ai, you know me."

"Do I? Ai has met many kitsune."

"A little desperate, don't you think," one of the tanuki whispered.

She had not realized it but the yokai had gathered at the exit to watch their exchange. Rin turned toward them with a death glare. The pair of tanuki were giggling at her behind their hands. Rin ignored them, turning back toward Ai.

"I'm not some mere kitsune and you know it. Tell Kaito that Rin was here, and I have something urgent to tell him."

Ai harrumphed and stormed out of the room. Rin tried to follow, but guards blocked her way. And after a slight struggle, she was removed to the courtyard with the others. Fighting them would only get her evicted for certain. So she decided to play along. If she stayed, eventually there would be a chance to slip out and find Kaito.

She and the others were given uniforms to wear, and then introduced to a large oni who was training them in combat. The day passed by and she couldn't find an opportunity to talk with Kaito. Ai must have told the guards to keep an eye on her, because any time she tried to get away she was stopped. As the day wore on, Rin had another problem. Hikaru had said he'd come for her by sunset today. He tried to play it off like a joke, but she knew he'd been serious. If she couldn't talk to Kaito, she'd need to at least tell Hikaru what was going on.

Just before sunset she headed for the exit, but when she tried to leave her way was blocked by the guards.

"No one leaves without the dragon's permission."

"Then go and ask him, because I need to leave." Rin stood her ground, considering transforming into her full form and fighting her way to freedom.

"The Dragon is not to be disturbed."

Rin frowned. This wasn't like Kaito. He never forced people behind walls. Everyone came and went as they pleased from his court. Which could only mean this was Ai's influence?

"What is going on here?"

Rin turned as Kaito strode through the courtyard. Ai was right behind him, attempting to pull him away. When he met Rin's gaze he paused. Everyone bowed to Kaito except Rin.

"What are you doing, kitsune? Bow before the ruler of Akatsuki," Ai hissed.

Rin lowered her head slightly toward the dragon.

He kept on staring. And then after a moment, he strolled toward her. Rin felt every eye on them. Kaito stopped a few feet from her.

"What are you doing here?"

"We need to talk."

Kaito looked at the people gathered around them, realizing this was not the place to do so.

"Come with me."

She followed him down old familiar corridors, until they were alone in an abandoned part of the palace. No repairs had been done here, and the walls had crumbled into the sea.

"Go." He pointed to the ocean.

"You want me to leave?"

"Go before I force you to leave."

"We were friends once." She didn't regret choosing Hikaru over Kaito. If it came down to it again, she'd choose him a thousand more times. But she wished the dragon had a more forgiving heart. Hikaru had sealed Kaito to protect her, and Kaito could not forgive him for it.

"You chose that traitor over me," Kaito said.

"It doesn't have to be like this."

"Don't," Kaito said, turning to face her.

She shrunk back. It was too presumptuous of her. There were wounds that remained between them.

"I'm not leaving until you hear me out."

"On whose behalf?"

"Yours."

He forced a laugh. "Do you think I'm going to believe anything you say? How do I know this isn't a trap set by Hisato and your man?"

Rin sighed heavily. "I'm not asking for forgiveness. I only want to warn you." She wrapped her arms across her chest.

"What is this about?" It was gruff, but she'd take her chance.

"It's about Suzume."

"She's dead. I don't want to hear her name ever again."

"She's not." Rin watched as hope and anger battled in his features. He turned his head skyward as if he would fly off and go find her.

Rin reached out to stop him, but he knocked her hand away before she could even touch him. She recoiled.

"You can't go to her. It's too dangerous."

"Who said I wanted anything to do with her?"

"I can see it in your eyes."

He bared his teeth at her in a snarl. "Did you come here to taunt me?"

"I came here to tell you Suzume is not herself and..." she trailed off.

"And what?"

"There are things I should have told you a long time ago. But I didn't have the right words."

"About what?"

"About your son." She held his gaze, daring him to challenge her on that fact.

He was silent for a very long time, and she thought he would expel her from the palace before she could get the truth out.

"I raised him."

"So you came here to twist the knife in your betrayal?"

"I came here to tell you about him, so you can make your own decision."

"I know what he's done. I've seen what he's capable of."

"But you can save Suzume from him."

"What does she have to do with him?"

Rin took a deep breath turning toward the ocean. She couldn't face Kaito while she said it. "Kazue gave birth to Takashi at our temple. Since Hikaru and I couldn't have children of our own, we raised him as ours. But when he got old enough, he started asking questions. About Kazue and about you." She peeked at him, but Kaito wasn't looking at her. He was staring at the sky which was turning gray overhead.

He would pretend not to care, but she knew he was listening.

"We did the best we could, but he grew restless, and insisted on learning about the world for himself. We tried to hold onto him, but he disappeared. Years later we started hearing the rumors, of a man who could wield both yokai and spiritual energy. A new powerful creature, both human and not. We spent centuries searching for him, but we never saw him again. It wasn't until we realized he was at the human palace that I learned he was the one who found Kazue's soul pieces. He made Suzume and Hikaru this way. And he freed Hisato."

Kaito half turned toward her. "Why are you telling me this?"

Rin gave a ragged sigh. She didn't want to believe it, but she could find no other explanation since the attack. "I believe he has Suzume under his control. He's using her and her control over you to get his revenge."

"What do you want me to do?"

"Save her."

"She doesn't want me to help her."

"Sometimes we don't know what's best for us. Or we can't say what we need, but she sent me here to warn you. And right now she needs your help."

Kaito turned to walk away. "Go back to your man."

"Are you going to save her?" Rin asked his retreating back.

"She can save herself."

FORTY-FIVE

Dawn broke over the horizon, painting the sky pink and orange. Long shadows were cast over the garden Suzume's room overlooked. Fingers of darkness crept toward her where she stood, half in shadows herself. It would have been a beautiful morning had she not been on her way to kill Kaito. Her last hope was that Rin could warn him in time. Hopefully by the time she reached her destination he would have gone into hiding. She scoffed at her own thoughts. Knowing the dragon, he was probably already on his way here to try and save her from herself. That's what Hisato had wanted, to force them together. If she was lucky, he'd kill her for certain this time.

Her maid came in and Suzume turned away from the window and the growing light of day. She donned the warrior priest attire, wearing all black with her staff strapped to her back. By the emperor's decree she was to go and kill the dragon—who Izume and Hisato had led him to believe was a threat to the kingdom. If only she could get close to the emperor and explain the truth to him. But Izume had made sure Suzume couldn't get near him. Not that she could break Hisato's command anyway.

"Up already?" Tsuki asked with a yawn and a stretch as he entered her room.

Suzume clenched her mouth shut. She didn't want the lies to spill out of her. Hisato's orders had been clear—tell no one where you're going.

"I-" she started to say. *No, I won't do it.*

Tsuki frowned as he got closer to her.

"What's wrong with you?"

You can do this. Fight him. "We-" she started again but all that came out was a strangled growl.

She swung at the wall, punching it hard, as she'd seen Kaito do when he got angry. Pain rippled up her arm, radiating outward and flames flickered there. Kazue had taken her self-harm as an indication Suzume was in danger. If only her power could burn up the bond between her and Kaito.

Akira shifted into view, taking Suzume's hand in hers. "What is the matter with you?" She touched Suzume's bloody knuckles. The wounds were already starting to heal, just more proof that Suzume was no longer human.

"Don't let me-" she started to say, but her mouth clamped shut. Kazue's fire had given her only a few seconds of control.

The pain was only a momentary distraction. But it wasn't enough. She'd have to bash her head into the wall to get more time, but she might lose consciousness before she could warn her friends too. What was the use? Even if she warned them Hisato would use that against her too. He had won. Every moment had been orchestrated by Hisato. Even the people she thought she could trust betrayed her. She slumped to her knees, collapsing beneath the weight of her realization. There was no way she could stop Hisato. He would always be two steps ahead.

"The emperor has sent us on another mission," Suzume replied.

"You said, 'don't let you?'" Akira frowned.

"I misspoke," Suzume said in a hollow, defeated voice.

"What are you not telling us?" Akira said, her voice more authoritative.

"It's not the mission," she lied again. "I just don't want to leave the palace."

"You're not acting like yourself."

They've begun to suspect. If they are going to be an obstacle, then they must be removed, Hisato's voice cooed inside her mind. Suzume's head shot up.

"No!" Suzume cried out.

"Suzume?" Akira reached out for her, but as she approached her, Suzume leaped to her feet.

The first notes of the song of binding poured out of Suzume. Tsuki took control of the body he shared with his sister but not quickly enough. The song wove around him, freezing him in place. His betrayed expression cut her deep.

I don't want this. Why are you doing this?

Hisato's laughter filled her ears in reply. *This is who you are, Suzume. Embrace it.*

Naoki rushed in just as the stone Tsuki was sealed in clattered to the floor. He swerved around the room, moving quicker than her eyes could trace. She raised her hand, flinging flames in his direction. He dodged and came up behind her, ready to knock her unconscious. But as he prepared to land a blow, she held up her hand. "Stop."

Naoki froze in place. "Suzume, this is not you," he said.

I wish I could stop this. Flames crackled in the palm of her hand.

Do it, Hisato urged her. She imagined him watching her, smiling with glee as she betrayed her friends.

"I can't," She croaked, as she flung the fiery ball at Naoki straight into the center of his chest. It sent him flying backward, crashing into the painted screen at the back of her room. Before he could take even a moment to recover, she sang the song of binding. As the last notes of the song faded away into the emptiness of the room, she fell to her knees and stared at the place where Naoki had been. All that remained was the shattered remains of the screen. *You belong to me now.*

She was well and truly on her own now. If only she had been stronger, then none of this would have happened. The door opened and Suzume did not even raise her head as Hisato strode in.

"I see you're ready." He reached out to cup her cheek. "I must thank you for helping me. By sending the kitsune, you've perfected my trap.

He will be wary of you for certain, but the dragon cannot resist rescuing you."

She stood up and followed Hisato out to the courtyard where her escorts were waiting. Several warrior priests were among them—ones she had gone on other missions with. Thankfully Ryuu wasn't there. She wasn't sure what she would have done if she had to face him again. This had been her fault, for even daring to trust him. It was obvious now. He'd been working for Hisato all along. He had led her to Izume, so they could bring her back here where she could continue influencing the emperor.

The journey to Kaito's palace would not take long. They took the same route they had when she had gone to Osaka. Hisato joined them up until they got to the docks.

"I shall join you at sunset with my army," he said.

Before the day was out, one way or another, she and Kaito would fight and this time one of them would die.

Suzume got onto the ferry boat and watched as the countryside rolled by. A few miles downriver the waters became rough. The calm river should not have had tossing waves, but the wind picked up and blew everything around on deck. Suzume stood, clinging to the railing to keep from being tossed overboard. She half expected to see Kaito but though the sky overhead was a bleak gray, and thunder cracked, there was no sign of the dragon.

Instead the crew and priests had all focused their attention to the shore, where two figures stood. The breeze carried with it a familiar power. Hope sparked inside her as she got closer to the edge.

"Spread out. Keep the princess safe," the leader shouted.

Warriors pulled her back from the side of the boat, but not before she caught a glimpse of Souta whose arms were outstretched as he sang to the wind. Ryuu, beside him, glowed with power, his eyes flashing through the storm. Souta's wind was bringing them closer to shore.

Kill Ryuu, but spare Souta, Hisato commanded her. She thought Ryuu was on Hisato's side, but perhaps she'd been wrong. If allies remained to her, then there might still be hope.

Souta's wind knocked back the soldiers as the boat was pulled closer and closer to shore. Suzume raised her hand and a fiery ball appeared there. She could see the pupils of Ryuu's eyes, so she was close enough where her flame would destroy him. But she hesitated, seeing them there had given her hope to continue fighting, hope that this wasn't over yet.

The boat crashed against the shore and still she held her power. The soldiers got back to their feet and rushed over the side of the boat to attack Souta and Ryuu.

"Do it now!" Hisato shouted inside her head.

Suzume let go of the flame, closing her eyes as to not watch her last hope die. Souta shot a torrent of wind toward her fire which combined with it and swirled together to become a flaming tornado. Guided by his song, the flames were doused in the river where they could do no harm.

The soldiers surrounded Ryuu, who fought them all off single-handedly. Souta's song changed melodies, awakening a powerful longing inside her and it ignited a blaze within. The inferno was rekindled, fed by Souta's wind. It gave Suzume freedom, but Hisato wasn't done with her.

You think you can escape? Hisato taunted.

Inside her two sides warred—Kazue stirred deep within her, just as her body fought the compulsion to do as Hisato commanded. She froze in place.

Unfortunately, while Suzume was immobilized, the soldiers had regrouped and were attacking Souta and Ryuu. Ryuu drew his sword and was fighting off three at a time, trying to shield Souta who was still singing and keeping Suzume immobilized. One of them got past him, however, and attacked Souta, breaking his song and with it Suzume's war.

Hisato regained control of her body, to the point where she felt as if she were floating outside it entirely. *Kill him. Now.*

She leaped forward, her body moving with skill she did not have, heading straight for Ryuu and Souta. As she attempted to attack Souta and stop his song for good, Ryuu blocked her, stopping her staff's strike from hitting him with his blade.

The blade pulsed with yokai energy, and while she was disconnected, she still felt the call of it from both Souta and Ryuu.

"Fight it Suzume. I know you can," Ryuu shouted.

Without warning, Souta's energy slammed into her chest. Not an attack, but him sharing his power with her in the same way she had done with Hikaru in the past. It knocked her backward and she lay sprawled on the ground, clutching her head which felt ready to burst apart. She wasn't sure who was in control anymore—her, Hisato, Kazue. There were a thousand voices chattering away inside her head, all of them overlapping into an unrecognizable hum. But slowly, coming through the noise was a song, one she'd never heard before and yet seemed so familiar. It filled her with that same aching feeling that she couldn't explain.

Suzume blinked and stared up at the blue sky. The only sound was Souta's song. It was the song she'd heard through all the other noise. The notes died away, until the only sound that remained was the rustle of wind through the trees. Suzume held up her hand, once more in her control.

"I've pushed him out, for now," Souta said as he knelt down beside her, offering her a hand. "But it is not a permanent fix. He's not going to give up easily."

She took his hand and stood, gazing at the unconscious soldiers who surrounded them. "How did you know?"

"I knew he was plotting something, but I never thought the darkness would have this kind of power. Had I known, I would have sealed you sooner. He's getting stronger."

She shook her head. "It's my fault. I took his power inside me and it bound us together."

The old man patted her head. "The darkness is inside all of us. We cannot be separated from it. All he's done is manipulate the doubt in your heart to his own ends. You can fight it."

"I don't think I'm strong enough."

"You are." Ryuu spoke for the first time. He handed her the stones in which she had sealed Tsuki, Akira, and Naoki.

Suzume's hand closed like a fist around them. "All I've ever done is hurt those around me. I can't control this power. I wasn't meant for it."

"You're right," Ryuu said.

His brutal honesty stung, but at the same time, he was the first person to ever say that to her.

Ryuu grabbed her by both shoulders. She met his blue eyes, which reminded her so much of Kaito that she had to look away. "It's true that the power was not originally intended for you. But despite it all you're still fighting to save your friends. If you're anything, Suzume, it's a fighter."

"Maybe before, but what's the use? I can't get it right. I'm better off living with Kazue sealed."

"Right now you have a choice. I will take you away from here, hide you from Hisato. Or..."

"Or?" Suzume asked.

"You fight."

She looked at the stones in her hand. All she had been doing was running away and it hadn't fixed anything. If anything, it had made things worse. Maybe Ryuu could hide her away for a while, but Hisato would find her in the end. But she realized it wasn't the offer he was making that made the difference. She'd chosen to fight before because she felt like it had been her destiny. He was giving her the option. She could walk away now, no questions asked.

"I need time to think," she said.

"We have until sunset," Ryuu said, pointing to the sky which had just reached its peak.

There wasn't much time to decide on her fate. Naoki, Akira, and Tsuki were freed from the seal by Souta and Ryuu and after explaining the situation, they were surprisingly forgiving. With Souta's seal Suzume was cut off from her power, but it also kept Hisato from controlling her. It could always be like this. She could go back to the way things were.

But walking away meant putting everyone she'd come to care for in danger. And for the first time, she couldn't just think of what was best for her, but those she loved as well. Her father who'd fall prey to her mother's plot, her brother caught up in her ambition, and Kaito who would fight a war because of her.

"I've made my decision," Suzume said.

"I'm ready to fight. I want to end this for good."

FORTY-SIX

They journeyed to Osaka, where they were reunited with Rin and Hikaru. There wasn't much time to explain, but Suzume had a plan. The sun was starting to sink on the horizon and Suzume saw Hisato's army approaching. She watched from the far shore. The only relief was Kaito had not come to rescue her. It hurt to think he had given up on her, but in the end it was for the best. She didn't want to put him at risk. Even with Souta's seal, she felt Hisato nearby. He knew that she had found a way around his orders, and he would be coming for her soon. But she planned on going to him first.

Hisato's army lined up along the shore, preparing for their attack. She had to get to Hisato before the yokai were drawn into the battle. As they drew onto the shore, there was a brief moment of silence. The thunder of the ocean rolling echoed the hammering of her heart.

"Are we ready?" Hikaru asked her as he came to stand beside her.

Suzume nodded. Souta and Hikaru had both unleashed their power and it prickled against her skin, making her sick with wanting. The seal Souta had put on her soul pressed against the inside of her chest, making it difficult to breathe. When he'd cut off Hisato, he'd also divorced Suzume from her powers. Part of their plan meant she'd have to rush in relying on her friends' protection until they got close enough. They couldn't risk Hisato taking control of her again. With Souta and Hikaru's support she could fight it by awakening Kazue.

Suzume took a deep breath.

"Let's go."

They slipped down the shore, using the long shadows cast by the forest and the trees to hide them. Hisato would not be near the front-lines but hidden away from the fighting, and that's where she had to go. They were almost upon the army when a high shriek and a roar filled the air.

The group turned to see hundreds of yokai pouring out of the ocean, bursting up from the floor of the sea. The warriors shot arrows at them. The first line of yokai fell, just as many humans were torn apart by yokai claws.

"No!" Suzume shouted.

The combination of yokai energy and spiritual energy was almost overpowering. Suzume's stomach churned as she felt Kazue push against the confines of Souta's seal. Their plan would be ruined. With the yokai attacking they were all in danger. Hisato would use them to create more of those hybrid monsters.

She motioned to go join the fighting to try and stop it, but Ryuu grabbed her arm, stopping her. "The only way we're going to stop the fighting is by destroying Hisato."

He was right of course, but it made her sick to think of all the inno-cents who would die. They resumed their quest, heading toward Hisato. But as the battle raged on, the seal continued to flake away, like old paint.

A group of yokai found them, stopping them in their tracks. They gnashed their dagger-like teeth together trying to intimidate them. Kazue, sensing Suzume in danger, sent sparks flying from Suzume's fingertips.

"I'll handle them. Get her out of here!" Ryuu shouted.

This left Suzume and the others to continue onward without him. And the further into the battle they went, the more dangerous it became. They were attacked by one of Hisato's hybrid monsters, a fierce beast that wore torn clothes and had green, scaly skin and a human face.

"Keep going," Tsuki said, smiling with glee. "Me and my father will take care of this brute."

They lured the monster away, leaving Suzume, Hikaru, and Souta on their own. Everywhere was chaos. They had to fight their way through yokai and soldiers and with each successive battle, they were pulled further apart.

As they moved together, fighting their way through the crowd, one of the monsters leaped in front of Suzume. It had the height of an oni and one single bloodshot eye bulging in its socket, but the arm on one side was underdeveloped. As she approached it, she used her staff to hit its underdeveloped arm. Souta and Hikaru were on the other side, fighting their own battles.

She reeled backward, trying to escape. As she turned to run away, another monster cornered her. This one was of average size and height, but when he grinned a snake-like tongue came out. He exuded immense energy, and when he sang it froze her in place. Suzume wriggled against his control to no avail.

There was no one to help her. She would either have to use Kazue's power now or die before she had the chance. As she reached down to break the already weakened seal, one of the monsters gave a pained grunt before slumping over. She spun her head toward the creature that had frozen her in place to find it was glaring at Kaito. Joy and terror warred within her. The last person she wanted to find on this battlefield was him.

Kaito took out the snake-hybrid with ease before coming toward her. She stepped back and away from him. Even now she felt Hisato's orders burning at the back of her mind.

"What are you doing here?" she asked, backing away from him.

"I think you should be saying, 'thank you.'"

It was as if nothing had happened between them. It was just like old times.

"Thanks." She shook her head.

"Don't mention it." He grinned.

There wasn't time for much else, because another monster attacked. Kaito handled it and she returned to her search for Hisato. She spotted Souta across the battlefield, his wind knocking aside the warriors, while in another direction Hikaru was using his vines to capture more of the soldiers. They were all slowly making their way toward the front. She had to get away from Kaito. After the battle there would be more time to explain. Even being near him was making the seal fall apart piece by piece, but Hisato hadn't taken control of her again. Not yet.

Then she spotted Hisato a few feet away, his arms raised as he threw his head back in laughter, delighting in the carnage. Where yokai fell he sang, and they and the humans near them rose up as grotesque monsters. She had to stop him. She started to make her way toward him when an icy projectile nearly cut off her arm. She leaped back and away, and looked up to see who had shot her. At first she thought it was Kaito who had shot at her, but he was busy fighting three hybrids, so whoever had shot her was another dragon, likely thinking she was the enemy.

She swerved away from the line of fire, taking cover beneath the trees, hoping he'd go for easier targets. But even as she moved out of sight, the dragon seemed intent on targeting her. When she could not be attacked from the sky, the dragon came down to her. She ran as fast as she could, using the forest as cover.

Fear and the surrounding energy made the impulse to lose herself to Kazue that much stronger. She had to resist if she was going to defeat Hisato. She used the tools Souta had given her to try and visualize her power, tame and control it. But then the dragon came crashing down in front of her. He resumed a more human form with bright colored hair and a dangerous look in his eyes.

"I'm not your enemy. I'm fighting on the same side as you," she said, holding up her hands in surrender.

He circled her like a predator. "You're no ally of mine. You're the priestess who killed Kenta."

"I don't know what you're talking about."

He moved closer to her, and the fire was just beneath the surface. The seal would soon be broken entirely. But if she didn't protect herself she'd die.

"Do you think I'm going to believe that? You're going to pay for your crimes."

He launched himself toward her, claws extended. She used her staff to defend herself, blocking his attack and swinging it upward to strike him hard in the gut. It didn't slow him down much but it gave her a chance to run. He was much faster than her and he blocked off her escape before she could get very far.

"It's over," he said as he drew a blade.

She swung wildly, trying to buy herself more time, but he knocked her staff from her hand. Suzume backed away, her shoulder blades colliding with a nearby tree. He stalked toward her and pressed his blade to her chest, just over her heart. There was no other choice. She reached for the flame deep within her, preparing to break the seal. But before she could take hold of the power, the blade was knocked away and Kaito collided with the other dragon.

The pair of them rolled around on the ground together, clawing, punching, and wrestling to get on top.

Suzume rushed over to help, but was almost kicked for her trouble. She stood by helplessly as they fought.

Blood trickled down the dragon's chin, and he bared his teeth at Kaito who'd managed to get on top. "Are you going to choose a human over your own kind? She killed one of ours!"

"It's not your place to pass judgment," Kaito said.

"You've gone soft. You can save her now, but you cannot protect her forever. I will have my revenge."

"It doesn't have to be this way."

The other dragon headbutted Kaito, knocking him aside. Kaito rolled over as the dragon launched himself at her. She held up her staff in an attempt to defend herself, but before he could strike her, he slowed and stumbled. Blood came to his lips, and he slowly turned around, revealing the bleeding wound on his back.

"So that is your choice?"

The other dragon slumped over onto the ground. His knees buckled at a weird angle and one of his arms got pinned under his body, while the other one was splayed, reaching out for Kaito.

Kaito stood over him, his hair tangled around his shoulders and his hand curled into a claw. It was drenched in blood and the gore dripped onto the ground beside him. She didn't know what to do or say. She'd seen him kill before. She knew he was capable. But there was a haunted look in his eyes that she could not tear herself away from.

Suzume walked over and placed her hand on his shoulder. He turned to her and the pain in his gaze was more than she'd ever seen from him before. Kaito collapsed to his knees, burying his face into her stomach, his hands bunching into the fabric on her back. For a moment she did not know what to do and held her hands up in the air.

"I killed my brother," he said, his voice raw. "He would have killed you if I hadn't."

Realization dawned on her—the weight of what he had done. She rested her hands on his shoulders, lowering her head to rest on top of his.

"I'm the last now," he said. "There are no more dragons like me."

She didn't have the right words to say and instead just stroked his head. All around them the battle raged. But for all she cared it might as well just be the two of them. She'd never seen this side of him before. He'd never seemed vulnerable. He was always strong, but he had killed his own brother to save her.

Now Suzume. Do it now. Hisato's command slipped through her consciousness like an eel.

Without realizing it, the seal had fallen away. And while she had held Kaito, her guard was down and now Hisato had her again. *I won't!* She raised her head, trying to find him. He was there at the edge of the tree line, his gaze focused on her, his eyes boring into her soul.

You can't make me. I don't have to listen to you. She reached for Kazue's flames, ready to use them against Hisato.

But try as she might to access her power, it was gone.

Did you really think you could outsmart me? I have you exactly where I want you.

"No." Suzume choked on the word.

"Suzume, what's wrong?"

Her hands, which had been stroking Kaito's head, slowly went to his shoulders. He tried to pull away but her grip held him tight. He stiffened as he met her gaze, just as the song of sealing burned along her tongue.

FORTY-SEVEN

The first notes of the song of binding rose from her lips, the sound deceptively sweet despite its dark purpose. Flames sparked in her hands. His ice was forming to protect himself from the power of her fire but other than that, he didn't try to break away from her. He grabbed a hold of her wrists. His touch was not icy, but warm and reassuring.

"You can fight this, Suzume. I know you can."

Hisato's laughter drifted over the battlefield. As the song started to take effect on Kaito he lurched forward, groaning as he fought against it. She tried everything to fight Hisato's influence, to stop this from happening, but this was the inevitable end. This is what Hisato had always wanted to do. All their clever plans meant nothing when Hisato was always two steps ahead of them. He would use her as his puppet to destroy Kaito, the same way Kazue had sealed Kaito to prevent him from stopping her from becoming immortal.

"Suzume, look at me," Kaito said, his voice pained. Veins bulged along his neck as he struggled to keep his head upright. The song continued to pour out of her. Another moment and he would be back inside the stone.

Kaito climbed to his feet, though his back was arched as if weighed down by thousands of pounds. He grabbed onto Suzume, pulling her close to him. She felt the power leaching out of him, draining away, making him smaller. But Kaito continued to fight. He placed both hands onto her cheeks, and his face filled her vision so she could see nothing else. Her song faltered.

"Finish it!" Hisato's voice vibrated through her, forcing her to obey.

But before she could finish the song, Kaito's lips were pressed against hers, silencing her.

The battle. Hisato. Everything melted away as his tongue parted her lips. Kaito absorbed her every thought and emotion. Every part of her was alive, on fire, hot and cold at the same time. The two of them were caught up in a swirling vortex of their powers, not in battle, but working together in harmony. It cocooned them both, protecting them not only from Hisato, but anything else that would want to hurt them. They were apart from the rest of the universe.

This wasn't just a kiss. It wasn't just his words telling her that he believed in her. Kaito was pouring his power into her. And she was burning up with it. The ice tempered the flame. Instead of Kazue consuming her, instead of Hisato commanding her, for the first time it was Suzume who had control.

As the last of his energy was absorbed into her, the sparkle of their combined energy faded away, leaving them in the center of a shower of sparks. Kaito held her, his gaze fixed on hers. There were so many things she wanted to say. Her eyes darted across his face, wanting to drink him in.

"Go." He stepped back out of her way. His hand held onto hers for a few more seconds before she was striding away, burning with a power so bright everyone around her turned to see. Soldiers shielded their eyes from it, and the hybrid monsters Hisato had created hissed and backed away, leaving a clear pathway toward him.

From her left and right, Hikaru and Souta joined her. She felt their power join hers, connecting them all, uniting them for one cause. The power pulsed through her and the echo of Kaito's heart beat in time with hers. He was with her.

As she walked, Suzume held her staff in front of her and it glowed with purple flames. Hikaru took out his bow and arrow and Souta raised the wind to guide them.

Hisato watched them, his eyes glowing, as he drew out his own dark blade. "You've gotten stronger, Suzume, but it won't change anything," he said mockingly.

"I'm the master of my own fate now."

She lunged for Hisato, using her staff to strike at him. Hisato parried and leaped out of the way. They circled one another and as they did, Hikaru shot arrows at him. Hisato knocked them away before they landed. While he was twirling away from the arrows, Souta's gust of wind pushed him backward to where Suzume was waiting for him. She struck at him with her staff, but before she could land her blow he moved out of the way again.

The three of them alternated their attacks, keeping Hisato moving, but he was too quick for them. Then Souta shot his wind at Hisato, and Hikaru used it to direct his arrow. It struck Hisato in the gut, and they all felt the ripple of pain echo through them. It knocked the air from Suzume's lungs and she doubled over in pain.

Hisato bent over, ripped the arrow from his gut and tossed it aside. "Your fight is futile. You cannot stand against me," he said.

Hisato waved his hand and a blast of dark energy was shot at all three of them. The pain rippled through her chest as visions of every wrong thing she had done, every jealous thought, every lie played before her eyes followed lastly by the monster she had created, and the face of the man's life she had destroyed.

"It will never end. Each of you has darkness in your heart. While you remain impure, I will continue to grow stronger."

The pain of the darkness brought all three of them to their knees. Hikaru clutched at his skull, while Souta was frozen in place. What horrid visions he saw, she could only imagine. As she was writhing in agony, Hisato stood over them gloating.

"Give in. All of you."

His triumph was cut short as Ryuu came up from behind him and slashed at him. Hisato leaped out of the way just in time to avoid having his head taken from his shoulders.

Hisato turned to face, Ryuu. "Ah. Ryuu, or should I say, Takashi."

"I suppose I should thank you," Hisato said.

Ryuu only glared at him.

Hisato lifted Suzume off the ground, wrapping her up in dark tentacles which came from his body. He suspended her in the air in front of Ryuu. The tortured visions had stopped, but Hisato was not done playing games with her yet.

"You've met Kazue's son, haven't you, Suzume?"

"Do you think that's going to change my mind? Ryuu already told me what he's done."

"Has he told you everything?" Hisato paced around Ryuu who seemed to be frozen in place, only his eyes followed Hisato. "The first emperor, and the man who gathered up Kazue's soul. The man who helped free me." Hisato stopped pacing to stand in front of Ryuu then slowly turned. "Is that what he told you?"

Suzume looked at Ryuu. "He's lying, isn't he?"

Ryuu bowed his head in shame.

"I thought I could trust you!" Suzume shouted.

Hisato's laughter surrounded them. Dark vines rose up, wrapping their way around Ryuu's body as he screamed, tortured by his own dark nightmares. "Darkness exists in all hearts. And Takashi has the darkest heart. He wanted more than anything to be as strong as his father. He will try and seal us, that is his real motive. He will destroy you all to make himself stronger."

Hisato dropped the binding that held Suzume in place. All her friends were caught in their own nightmares.

"Now that you know the whole truth, what will you choose? Life or death?"

Suzume looked between Hisato and Ryuu. There was only one obvious choice. She walked toward Hisato.

Hisato held out his arms. "Yes, come to me, Suzume. Let us restore balance to the world. You and me."

She took his hand, and he beamed at her. In his own way, Hisato did care for her. She could see that now.

"I knew you'd make the right choice in the end. Your life is more precious than anything else. You're just like Kazue. Power calls to power."

Suzume smiled at Hisato. "That's where you're wrong. I'm not Kazue."

The song of binding ripped out of her throat as she gripped onto Hisato. The power Kaito had given her burned bright, giving her what she needed to seal Hisato. But as she tried to seal him, a wall of darkness rose up around them, blocking out everything but the two of them, plunging them into absolute darkness. Hisato pulled away from her, leaving her alone in the abyss. The song faded from her lips. Where was she? Had he taken her into that alternate space he traveled through?

"My dear, Suzume." His voice echoed from all around her. She spun around, trying to find him. "That was clever. I almost believed it this time. But you cannot outsmart me."

"Come out and face me," she said.

"I am right here." He materialized in front of her, inches from her face. She swung for him, only to have him disappear once again.

She gripped her staff tight, her eyes searching through the endless darkness for a hint of him.

"I'm always with you, Suzume."

She swung in the dark, trying to hit him but it was no use. Out of the darkness, he sliced her across the shoulder. She gasped from the pain and fell onto her knees. The darkness was creeping in through the wound, trying to consume her, become her, the same way Kazue tried to take over her body, and so Hisato wanted too. The light of Kaito's power and her own flame were growing dim, smothered by the darkness that was Hisato. From the gloom Hisato came forward, standing over her with a smug expression.

"You fool. You cannot defeat me. You're not strong enough."

The wound on his shoulder that reflected her own was starting to heal. She thought she could do it all alone, that she didn't need anyone else to help her. She'd tried to get stronger on her own and had failed. She'd tried reversing what had been done, to change her own fate, but there was no changing it now. As she watched Hisato's wound repair itself, she saw him as her dark mirror, her opposite in every way. But one truth remained, he would never kill her because that meant killing himself.

"You're right. I'm not."

"So you've finally learned." He held out his hand for her to take.

"I can't do this alone, but I'm not alone. I have my friends."

Cracks formed in the dome of darkness that surrounded them—thousands of hairline cracks, which gradually widened. Hisato spun around, looking at the growing cracks. Then vines burst through, snaking their way toward them, followed by a fierce wind. Lightning cracked and thunder boomed as the darkness Hisato had surrounded them in was burst apart.

Hisato spun around, real fear and shock on his features.

Suzume climbed to her feet, and found the wound on her shoulder had healed as well. Together she, Hikaru and Souta stood together, three pieces of Kazue's soul united against one enemy. Hisato thought he knew her, that she would only ever try to fight him alone, but as they stood shoulder to shoulder, united in their determination, Hisato knew he didn't stand a chance.

The fear was quickly replaced by a smirk as Hisato said, "The whole family is together." He surveyed the group, "Oh, not quite, there's one more missing."

"It doesn't matter. This ends here," Suzume shouted at him.

Souta, Hikaru, and Ryuu all joined in her song, which flowed through her surrounding Hisato. As the song took effect, she felt a squeezing sensation on her chest, her arms, her neck, as if someone had their hands on her shoulders and was compressing her downward.

The pain Hisato was feeling was rippling through them all, and threatening to tear her body apart by the seams. Hisato struggled to free himself from her grip, but she held on tight. Because if she let go, then everything would fail.

Hisato was in a panic, his eyes wild and crazed. "You cannot do this!"

The pain was bright white, hot, blinding. And just as she thought it could not last another moment, she was flung backward. She collided with Souta and Hikaru, who had been standing behind her. The three of them landed in a pile and when they looked up Hisato was gone. Suzume crawled to the place where Hisato had been, hoping to find a stone. But there was nothing. He'd escaped again.

She beat her hand onto the ground. She'd failed again. Souta put his hand on her shoulder.

"It's not your fault," he said.

"We were so close," Suzume said.

Her friends all gathered around her. Ryuu had dirt and soot on his face. Rin limped toward them with Kaito supporting her. Naoki and Tsuki were both splattered with gore. The last battles were being fought, and the yokai had been triumphant. Those soldiers still alive had fled.

"But you did it," Kaito said as he came forward. "You stopped him. You banished him."

It was the first time he'd ever acknowledged her strength. And as much as it warmed her to hear, it wasn't the truth. All of them were battered from battle, all of them had fought for her cause.

"Not alone. We did it together."

FORTY-EIGHT

It was strange to have everyone gathered together in one place. It seemed their group kept expanding. In the aftermath of the battle, Kaito's allies came forward. It took some convincing to keep everyone from tearing each other apart. Kaito revealed that he had rallied his army to fight back against an oncoming human attack. But now that the battle was done, everyone had to make peace.

The groups eyed each other warily. There were yokai apart from the dragons who had joined Kaito in the fight. A large oni who wielded a sword bigger than Suzume's entire body eyed her with suspicion.

"I guess we have some introductions to make." Kaito laughed.

A line had been drawn in the sand. The priests on one side, and the yokai on the other did not seem too keen to intermingle. Now that Hisato was gone, the lines were drawn. For many of them, they had likely come out expecting to fight them.

It was Rin and Hikaru who stood in the middle.

Suzume started them off. "This is Souta, the wind of Kazue's soul."

The old man bowed his head to the dragon.

Kaito pointed at him. "You're the old man from the village!"

Souta grinned. "I could not resist seeing you again. Please pardon me for not introducing myself sooner."

"How-" Kaito started to say, but Suzume shook her head. That was a story for another time she decided. They went down the list as introductions were made on both sides, until all that remained was Kaito and Ryuu. The pair of them had been glaring at each other through the entire exchange.

"Come to finish what you started?" Kaito challenged Ryuu.

Ryuu's eyes were glowing blue and his sword crackled with power. The two were like mirror reflections of one another. Why had she never noticed before? How had she not realized before?

"I believe I already defeated you, father."

"Father? Are you saying-" the dragon Kaito had introduced as Hana said.

The yokai reached for their weapons, and Naoki moved closer to Suzume, preparing to guard her if there was an attack. She had forgotten that when Kaito had nearly killed her Ryuu had stepped in to save her.

"Did you think I would forget?" Kaito asked.

Ryuu held onto the hilt of his blade, but did not draw it. Suzume could almost see the sparks flying between the two men. This must be what it looked like when she fought Kaito. "I won't make excuses for what I did. You tried to hurt someone I care about," Ryuu said.

Kaito's gaze flickered toward Suzume, and she felt her gut clench. Had he really not gotten over his jealous streak?

"What is she to you?" Kaito asked Ryuu.

She held her breath, wondering what he would say. There hadn't been much time for them to resolve their relationship. He was her mother's former lover, and protector by extension, but with him coming to her rescue against her mother's orders, what did that make him?

"She is someone I will protect with my life," Ryuu replied.

Kaito eased back, and said, "Then I'm willing to hear you out at least."

Neither of them seemed completely at ease, but Suzume felt like she could breathe.

"What is it you want to know?"

"For starters, where did you get that blade?" Kaito nodded toward Ryuu's sword.

The giant oni just behind Kaito stirred. His attention suddenly focused on Ryuu, and Suzume saw the hunger in his gaze. Kaito wasn't making peace as she had hoped but stirring up trouble.

"I defeated its owner and the blade chose me as its new master," Ryuu said simply.

"Tetsuyama would never have gone to a half-breed." The oni pushed his way forward, raising his massive sword above his head. Ryuu did not move.

Suzume was about to step in and interfere but Kaito held up his hand to stop her. As the oni came barreling toward him, Ryuu held his ground. He was about to bring the giant blade crashing down on Ryuu, but before he could, Ryuu drew his own sword and blocked the oni's attack one-handed.

"You were never fit to wield Tetsuyama," Ryuu said, meeting the gaze of the oni. "And that is why it came to me. Your father challenged me because he feared my power. And I slayed him to protect my own life. Wouldn't you have done the same?"

The oni roared, and the ground beneath his feet shook. Veins pulsed on his forehead as he tried to grind Ryuu into the ground by the force of his strike. No matter how he tried however, he could not break through. Then with a flick of his wrist, Ryuu shoved him backward, and the oni went tumbling onto his back.

Ryuu stalked over to him and pointed the blade at the oni's throat. "Your father was a worthy opponent. Had I been given the choice I would have spared him."

The oni shouted, "I will have my revenge!"

"I shall wait for that day to come, but you will not defeat me with your current strength."

He stepped back and turned to walk away but as he did the oni leaped up to make a surprise attack. Before he could land the blow, Kaito intercepted him, grabbing onto his meaty wrist.

"What are you doing?" the oni said to Kaito.

"Your father would never have attacked an opponent when his back was turned. Perhaps this is why Tetsuyama abandoned you."

Kaito dropped the oni's hand and the large creature dropped his head in shame. Kaito turned back to Ryuu. "That explains that. But what about the others?"

"Why are you doing this?" Suzume asked Kaito. He glanced at her, and there was a softness in his expression she'd never seen before. Unwillingly their kiss came to mind and she felt a blush burn on her cheeks. Was he playing with her emotions already? They'd only just been reunited.

"He has done wrong against yokai and I would have him answer for his crimes."

"What does it matter? It's in the past," Suzume argued.

Ryuu placed his hand on her shoulder. "I don't mind." The Dragon pulled Suzume away from Ryuu. Even being that close to Kaito felt uncomfortable and she carefully extracted herself from his grip, an action Kaito noticed but said nothing.

"It wasn't my intention to destroy yokai. They found me." Rin and Hikaru held each other's hands, watching Ryuu with a mixture of affection and desperation.

"As you know, my mother left shortly after giving birth to me. She left me with a priest and his wife, Hikaru and Rin." He nodded toward them. "They raised me as their own. Because Hikaru was like me, a half-yokai, I believe she thought he would know how to best prepare me for a world which would always despise me." He paused, not meeting anyone's gaze. "I learned all about my spiritual powers from Hikaru and how to fight from Rin. But even from a young age, it was clear I was stronger than most and it caused...problems."

Ryuu cleared his throat and then continued. "To save my family from danger, I left them behind. It wasn't until I was on my own that I learned what my mother had done. I never wanted this cursed existence and I thought perhaps if I could find the pieces of her soul, I could-" He shook his head and sighed, "Bring her back." There was a pained expression on his face. "I did not know it until recently, but my attempts were unsuccessful because I did not have her heart. During my travels, I encountered many yokai, drawn to me by my spiritual power and looking to make themselves stronger by devouring me. I defeated many, befriended others. But my reputation grew out of control. And it suited me, I became something of a legend. I discarded my old name and assumed another—one as a man. And as fate would have it, I became the first emperor. As Hisato said."

"And that makes you Suzume's many times removed grandfather or father?" Kaito asked.

Suzume's head swiveled toward him. He had kissed her thinking that they were related. Then there was no denying it, it had been purely a means to give her power. Kaito didn't have feelings for her.

Ryuu laughed. "No, hanyou cannot have children. When my rule came to an end, I passed it on to my friend's child and it is his line who has ruled over Akatsuki and from whom you are descended."

"But how did Hikaru end up this way?" Suzume gestured toward him.

"The centuries passed, and I began to long for home and took a position in the household of Lord Kaedemori. Many times I almost went back home to Hikaru and Rin, but I did not want to put them in danger."

"You weren't putting us at risk," Rin interrupted.

"I can see that now. Had I not been a coward, perhaps things would have happened differently." He took a deep breath. "One night, I became very drunk and told Lord Kaedemori about the stones and their power. He stole them from me, and eager to test out what could be done, he kidnapped Hikaru and fused his soul with Kazue's, hoping to make more powerful soldiers.

"After what happened to Souta, I knew he would never be the same. So I made Hikaru forget, and brought him to the temple shrine. I told myself it was to protect Rin from watching her husband become a stranger. But in truth, I was ashamed for putting them at risk again."

Rin took a step toward Ryuu and grabbed his cheeks. "It wasn't your fault."

He gave Rin a tender smile, like a child to his mother. Then he continued to say, "After that, I served for many years in the temple shrine."

"And it was there you met my mother again," Suzume said as all the puzzle pieces fell into place.

Ryuu nodded slowly. "I thought she loved me, and despite my better judgment, we began an affair. She had learned about the stones from her father, and more than anything she wanted power."

"And she tricked you into giving it to her."

"She took poison, forcing me to choose to either lose her to death, or save her and give her an immortal life—one where she would never be as she was before."

In the end he chose her. It hurt to know her mother had manipulated Ryuu in that way.

"That's one missing," Suzume said. "Where's the last stone?"

"The final stone is missing. I have discovered there is another like you, Suzume, born with the power. But Izume has hidden her from me, and that's why I needed to find your mother. To find the missing piece so I could seal Kazue's soul once more."

"So we can defeat Hisato."

"Exactly. Izume will continue to fight to get the throne. More than that, she wants to become immortal as Kazue was. To make herself the immortal ruler."

"And Hisato will give her that." How had she fallen for her mother's lies? And her father and brother were trapped by her plots as well, all because she'd believed her mother's sad love story. She had to save them. It only proved what she already knew. Love was a dangerous game. It could cloud your judgment. How many times did she have to see that to know it was the truth?

"That's why I have to leave and find the last piece of Kazue's soul," Ryuu said finally.

Suzume's head shot up. "I'm coming with you."

Ryuu started to shake his head. "I can't put you in danger."

Kaito cut him off. "You must not know her very well. Suzume is more than capable of taking care of herself."

Their eyes met for a moment before she looked away. It was dangerous to even entertain the thought. There was no time for love, or romance, not when the fate of her family and the world was on the line. Besides, it wasn't like that kiss actually meant anything. It had been a good way to stop her song, and share his spiritual energy with her.

"He's right," Rin said. "We've all got a stake in this now."

"I'm the one who started it. Who taught her-"

Kaito held up his hand. "I'm the one who taught Kazue about this world. You've only echoed your father's mistakes. But you don't need to make all of my mistakes. Don't be a proud ass who can't see there are people here who care about you and want to help you."

Suzume stared at Kaito, mouth slack. Had he really just acknowledged Ryuu as his son?

"Including you?" he asked.

Kaito laughed. "Of course not."

Ryuu laughed as well and all the tension drained from the air. It was a start at least.

FORTY-NINE

Kaito returned to the palace with Suzume and the others. The courtyard was swarming with yokai. Not all of them had joined him to save Suzume, and there would be questions that needed answering. He hadn't been able to answer Hana and Arata when they asked where Jirou was. His death would remain etched onto his heart for a very long time. He didn't delight in killing him, and if he hadn't turned on Suzume, perhaps they could have found a way to understand each other. But there were no more chances now. He was dead and Kaito had to face his people.

As Kaito led the way through the courtyard, humans in tow, the yokai stepped aside to let them through. Perhaps they sensed the strength of the priest and priestess who flanked him. Or maybe it was the fierce look in his eyes. Whatever it was, he wasn't taking any chances and made sure to keep Suzume close by. Both to keep her safe and because it comforted him to be close to her. If it was up to him, he'd never let her out of his sight again. But it wasn't entirely up to him anymore. As much as it pained him to admit it, she had come back to him, but it didn't mean she was his, not yet.

The watching yokai whispered to one another. The old rumors about his love of humans were racing from ear to ear. Yokai were dashing off to inform their friends who hadn't witnessed his arrival. It would not take long before every yokai in the palace knew. It was just as well, he only wanted to say this once. Servants threw open the double doors which led into the audience hall.

Many yokai, anticipating his moves, were already gathered there. Unfortunately, seated on his throne was Ai, her head held high as if she were the ruler of Akatsuki. As they approached he saw Ai's gaze darken, turning entirely black, and her hair rose up behind her, twitching impatiently.

"What is the meaning of this?" Kaito roared.

"Ai has heard rumors of a human woman who you took as your lover, is this her?" Her words were meant to be indifferent, but her eyes narrowed as she spied Suzume behind him. She wanted to continue playing this game where she had control of him. And for a while, he'd let her. But he wasn't her plaything.

Kaito grabbed Suzume's hand and yanked her forward. "She is."

"I'm what?" Suzume started to bluster, as he knew she would.

Suzume's fervent denials were drowned out by the roar of the yokai around the room. Hundreds of them had followed them into the audience chamber, filling up the space, and those closest pressed in closer, snarling and grasping for Suzume. Those yokai who were loyal to him and had seen the hybrid monstrosities on the battlefield held them back. A secondary circle of their friends protected her from within.

"Are you trying to get me killed?" Suzume said to Kaito.

Kaito only grinned down at her. "Just play along."

It had been a while since he'd really embarrassed her. And this might not be the right time, but he couldn't resist the urge to do so. He pulled Suzume onto the dais with him, holding onto her hand. She gazed across the crowd of angry yokai and her face paled.

Kaito held up his free hand and a hush fell over the assembled crowd. All eyes were trained on him.

"I summoned you all here for a reason," Kaito said.

"To kill humans!" Someone shouted from the crowd.

Many took up the call with grunts and howls of agreement.

"Silence," Kaito roared.

Hungry gazes stared up at him. They had wanted a leader, they were desperate for a leader. Since he had gone, they'd all fallen into chaos, tearing out one another's throats. Feuds had toppled the greatest of the leaders, and greed the rest. It wasn't humans who had caused the fall of his kind, but a lack of leadership—not only his, but the guidance of the eight. That was why the eight had chosen him to lead in the first place, because left to their own devices, the yokai would tear one another apart.

"This is my woman, and she is a human."

There was a rumble of disagreement from the crowd. He kept speaking, shouting over their anger.

"The humans are not our enemies. I saw the face of the true enemy today on the battlefield—a monster who would use a war with the humans to wipe us all from existence. To use our own petty differences against us. Together we are strong, divided we are weak. If you walk away now, I can guarantee he will find you and he will destroy you. I will not force you to join me and I will not keep you here against your will. But if you dream of the Akatsuki of old, and wish to reunite the kingdom, then stay and help us rebuild. If not, there is the door."

There was a general grumbling and lack of movement from those assembled. And for a moment, he thought he had won them all over. Until Ai stepped in front of him.

Though small in stature, she had a commanding presence. "Your heart is being swayed by humans. It was them who started this war, they attacked us first. And now you would have us believe they are not the enemy? Are you suggesting they are our allies?"

"I am," Kaito said, his voice rumbling across the assembled masses, echoing off the ceiling.

"Your judgment is clouded. Let us hear from your brother, Jirou." Ai swept her arms out to welcome him on the stage.

Everyone whispered as they searched for a man who was not coming.

Arata turned to Kaito with accusation in his gaze. He would not make excuses for what he did.

"I killed him to protect the one I care about."

"He chose a human over a yokai?" Ai said, her voice rising with incredulity.

The yokai were feeding off her protests, and more voices shouted. She would turn the entire crowd against him if he wasn't careful.

"You cannot rule over the yokai while you have a human in your heart," Ai announced. "You've promised yourself to me, now you must choose. Her or me?"

And there was the true heart of it. Ai did not really despise humans. All she cared about was having him to herself. But he was done playing her game. He didn't need her anymore or those who followed her.

Kaito was prepared to declare his choice to the world. "I-"

"Don't!" Suzume shouted.

The crowd glared at Suzume, murmuring and perhaps wondering why a mere human would dare interrupt their lord and master.

She stepped forward, hands clenched into fists at her side. "I freed the dragon from the seal, and I want no harm to come to him."

The yokai's voices hummed. Some called out challenges, but many more seemed to believe her. She continued. "From the moment he was freed, he has thought of nothing but protecting his people, and returning Akatsuki to its former glory. I swear before all of you, I will not stand in the way of him ruling as he should."

Ai frowned as Suzume stepped back and the crowd murmured amongst themselves. It seemed Suzume had given his answer for him, though he did not like it one bit. Ai, meanwhile, was glaring daggers at the back of Suzume's head.

SHE WAS WILLING TO PUSH HIM AWAY IF IT MEANT PROTECTING THEM BOTH. He couldn't throw away his kingdom for her. If his army hadn't come and helped them fight Hisato she might not have been here. Besides, she knew that kiss and him claiming she was his woman didn't really mean anything. The crowd of yokai started to drift away, satisfied for now knowing that Kaito had chosen them over a human.

Kaito led the way out of the audience room and they had to push their way through the dispersing crowd as yokai vied for his attention. It seemed not everyone was appeased by her explanation, and a nearby neko swiped at Suzume's face as she passed. Naoki, Ryuu, and Tsuki surrounded her. The neko stared at the three warriors with wide eyes before bowing in apology and shrinking backward away from them. No one else tried to attack Suzume after that, but the group kept her and the other humans toward the center just in case. She couldn't stay here long in the palace, not if she wanted to stay alive. The idea of leaving Kaito was an unpleasant feeling and one she stuffed down for further analysis when she was alone.

Once they were in the corridor outside of the audience hall, the lack of voices and bodies was a welcome relief. She felt Kaito's stare on the back of her head. She'd probably wounded his pride by speaking out on his behalf. But she wasn't going to explain herself here, not in front of everyone. They were led down the hall by a very smug Ai, who clearly knew her way around.

Suzume supposed she should feel jealous. She had just forced Kaito into marrying her. But it was hard to feel that way when Ai was so childlike. It felt wrong to even think of them together. Any marriage Kaito had with her would be in name only, Suzume was certain of that.

They all entered a small private room, and once the door was closed and everyone was crammed inside.

"Our engagement is off," Kaito said to Ai.

Her iris disappeared and her hair rose up, undulating behind her.

"Are you trying to make a fool of me?" she asked.

"You may have brought me an army, but what good is an army I cannot control?"

Ai stamped her foot. "Don't be a fool, Kai. Don't you see? This is your chance to rise up, if you waste it now on her-" She pointed an accusatory finger in Suzume's direction. "Everything you wanted, everything you fought for will be lost."

"It has nothing to do with her."

"They've all heard the rumors," Ai pressed. "If they see another human at your side, they will continue to doubt no matter how many pretty speeches you make."

"Enough," Kaito roared. His voice shook like thunder. Everyone shared a look, not sure what to do. "I gave you your chance to leave with dignity. Now go!"

Ai wouldn't budge "Leave! All of you," he shouted as he pointed toward the door.

Everyone started to file out, including Suzume. But Kaito's sharp command stopped her in her tracks. "Not you."

Suzume turned around to face him. Now only the three of them remained.

"I said go," he snapped at Ai.

"You're making a mistake. When I leave, all my aid goes with it." Ai's shadow grew as her temper rose.

"I said, go."

She glared at both of them before turning and storming out of the room. As she left the room, the air seemed to be sucked out of it. Suzume and Kaito were left alone, with the memory of their kiss hanging between them like a weight. She had to clear up any misconceptions. She didn't want him to think she was an obstacle. His stare didn't make it easy to explain herself.

Kaito paced away from her while Suzume wrung her hands, trying to figure out what to say to break the silence.

When she couldn't take it anymore she said, "I know you're mad at me."

He stopped, turned, and stared at her.

"Mad at you?"

"I pushed you away, and then I tried to kill you... twice." She looked at the ground. "So, I'm sorry." The words fell from her lips and flopped on the floor like a dying fish.

Kaito stared at her for a moment. His expression was blank.

"I confessed my feelings for you in front a hoard of bloodthirsty, man-eating yokai and all you can say is 'sorry I almost killed you?'"

Suzume's mouth fell open and then she snapped it shut.

"But you didn't mean that," she stammered.

He took a step toward her and her breath hitched. This was just another one of his jokes. He didn't mean it, he never meant it.

"They wanted me to make a choice, but you made it for me."

She forced a laugh. "I wasn't going to let you humiliate me in front of all those people. I'd rather do it myself."

He shook his head and leaned in close to her. "It's not that simple."

She stared at his lips, remembering what it felt like to kiss him. She had to physically shake herself of those types of thoughts. *If he knew what that kiss meant to me, would he tease me like this?*

"Don't do that to me. It's not funny."

She turned to leave before she made a complete idiot of herself. But before she could walk away he grabbed her by the wrist and twirled her around to face him.

"I wasn't done talking." Her hands were against his chest, their faces inches apart.

"What else is there to say?"

"Don't you want to hear what my answer would have been?"

She pulled away from him. "I can't keep playing this game with you. I know that kiss meant nothing to you. And it didn't mean anything to me either," she added hastily, before she exposed that soft, vulnerable part of her heart.

Kaito's smile faded. "Is that how you feel?"

He didn't love her. He was in love with Kazue. And she didn't want love anyway—it would only lead to heartache.

"Yes."

He nodded as he turned away. "You should get some rest."

She shouldn't have taken it personally, but when he turned his back on her it felt like a punch to her stomach. She stared at his back for a moment, considering what she didn't know. It wasn't as if she wanted that sort of relationship with him. Did she? She ran for the door before she made a complete idiot of herself.

Outside, she was met by a yokai servant who was to escort her to her chamber. When she arrived at her room, the servant left her with a bow, and Suzume leaned against the door without entering. *I am the world's biggest idiot. Did you really think he could love anyone other than Kazue?* Suzume exhaled in frustration.

As she was opening the door, she felt a prickle along her spine. There was a yokai close by. *Of course, it's a palace of yokai.* But as she opened her door, pretending everything was normal, all her warning bells were screaming. And as subtly as she could, she reached for her staff. After that neko attacked her, she didn't doubt one of them had come to finish the job.

A whoosh of air brushed past her ear just seconds before she rolled out of the way. She didn't have time to grab her weapon as a tentacle wrapped around her neck and slammed her against the wall. Suzume's hands grasped and clawed at the tentacle which was cutting off her air flow.

"You've ruined it!" Ai screeched, her eyes black and without pupils. "Ai will not let you steal him. He belongs to Ai."

FIFTY

Kaito paced back and forth in his chamber. Suzume's words kept replaying in his mind. Had he been rejected? He stopped pacing.

"She turned me down?" He shook his head. "I was about to give up my kingdom for her!" He laughed bitterly as he shook his head.

He turned to the door. "Is she crazy?" He shook his head again and resumed pacing. Then after another moment's deliberation, he decided it wouldn't hurt just to make himself clear. Maybe the kiss hadn't been enough to make her understand his feelings.

He hurried down the hall, grabbing a servant who was passing by. "What room is the priestess staying in?"

"Ai requested she be put in the east wing," the servant said with a bow to Kaito.

If Ai had organized the rooms, then Suzume was in danger. He ran down the hall toward the east wing and rounded the corner just as Ai attacked, her tentacles wrapping around Suzume's neck. He yanked Ai off of Suzume, whose face had started to turn blue. Suzume fell to her knees, choking and gasping for air. He knelt beside her.

"Are you alright?"

Suzume coughed and hacked in response, at least she was breathing. But before he could inspect her for further injury, Ai beat on his back.

"Get out of my way, Kai," she said.

Kaito grabbed a hold of Ai's arm, almost dangling her off her feet.

"What do you think you're doing?" he said.

"Ai is doing what you cannot." She tried to pull herself free by flopping around against his grip. He knew for certain if he let her go, she'd attack Suzume again. Kaito blocked Suzume from Ai's view.

Suzume leaned against the nearby wall, gasping for air as she massaged her throat. It seemed she hadn't recovered her voice quite yet.

"I've been patient with you, but you've gone too far this time," Kaito said to Ai.

"Should I stand by while another human uses you? Wait until she turns on you and seals you for another five hundred years?"

"I don't need you to protect me. Suzume would never harm me."

She scoffed. "Even if she cares for you, they will never accept her."

She was right of course, but even if Suzume wouldn't have him, he had to think of another way to protect her. He wasn't going to let her go, not after getting her back again.

"Leave while I'm still patient." Kaito pointed at the door.

"If Ai cannot have you, then no one can." Ai's tentacles wrapped around Kaito quicker than he anticipated. They crushed his body. The pressure of her power smothered his spiritual energy as much as the air from his lungs. His eyes bulged in their sockets. If she kept on squeezing his guts were going to be painting the walls in a moment.

Then suddenly, she dropped him. Ai screeched as she clutched at her head, her tentacles writhing around her. Kaito looked from Ai to Suzume who was staring at Ai. Her entire body glowed with a power he'd never seen before.

"Be gone back to the underwater palace. Never show yourself before me again."

Ai screeched louder, her voice high enough to rupture eardrums. But she could scream all she liked, she could not resist Suzume's command. She headed for the door.

"You haven't won. Our kind will never accept your union."

"Not that it matters to you, but we're not together," Suzume called after Ai.

"You poor fool," Ai said to Kaito before storming out of the room. Leaving Suzume and Kaito alone at last.

"I don't know how I feel about being the one saved all the time," he said as he massaged his neck.

A bright purple bruise was starting to blossom on Suzume's neck, and seeing her injury, he forgot all about his own. He reached out to her but she backed away.

"You've been getting into trouble a lot." She laughed, but it sounded forced and she wouldn't meet his eyes.

Kaito took a step closer to her, but she took a step back. A part of him wanted to keep chasing her to force her to look at him like she used to, full of fire.

"I'm not going to give up my kingdom," he said, continuing the conversation from earlier.

She nodded her head. "I know. You don't have to keep saying it. I don't care what you do."

"And I'm not giving you up either."

Her head shot up to meet his gaze, and her lips were parted slightly as she searched his face. "What are you saying?"

Kaito tilted his head to regard her. "I thought a piece of me died when you did."

Her eyes widened. The space between them was growing smaller again. Kaito reached out to grab a hold of her, but held back at the last second. He didn't want to chase her away.

"I can't replace Kazue for you."

"This isn't about her, Suzume. I only want you. Your arrogance, your stubbornness, your smart mouth." He grinned at her.

"You're the arrogant one," she grumbled.

"Maybe we suit each other?"

She laughed. He took it as an invitation and tried to reach for her, but once again she backed away from him.

"We need to take this slow," she said, putting space between them and backing herself against a wall. "I don't know how I feel yet. And there's Hisato..."

Kaito leaned against the wall, hovering over her, forcing her to crane her neck up to meet his eyes. "I'm willing to be patient, but are you?"

"I am. Why wouldn't I be?"

"You'll see." He turned to stroll away without further explanation. He counted in his head, *one, two, three..*

"What does that mean?" she shouted but he didn't reply. He was glad his back was to her so she couldn't see the smirk on his face. He had really missed teasing her. For now, if she was by his side, that was enough.

"Fine. I don't care," she said and he could just imagine her crossing her arms and turning her back to him.

And then a moment passed. "Just tell me what you meant!"

FIFTY-ONE

The temple was difficult to find, hidden away in the valley as it was. The wayward merchant or careless hunter might stumble upon it, but anyone who they told of the idyllic valley would not believe them. Because any time they tried to find their way back there, it was as if the mountain pass they'd traveled through had been swallowed up by mist. Or the bridge over which they'd wandered had fallen into the river. No one could really recall how they got there, but all of them told the same story of a green valley and the shrine run by priestesses, the most beautiful and pure they'd ever seen.

The Head Priestess stared out her window into the garden. Their green valley had its first touch of frost. The maple tree, which had the most crimson leaves, now lay barren and hung with frost which sparkled in the early morning light. Three young priestesses in training gathered beneath the tree, their heads pressed together as they shared in a secret. They were likely talking of the mysterious stranger who'd arrived at the first light of day. He'd given a fright to the girl gone to fetch water from the well that morning.

Normally she would have scolded them for their idleness, but with a guest to entertain she could not leave. And, besides, it was not often someone found this place.

He wore a straw hat, the brim pulled down low to hide his face. His long, black hair was hanging around his shoulders. Strange that he wore it loose instead of a top knot like so many men. But that wasn't the strangest thing about him. He wore all black, just as he had the day she'd met him. Their first meeting had been so long ago, that she had thought it something out of a dream. If it hadn't been for the child he left behind, she would have convinced herself it was. From the little she could see of him, it seemed he had not aged at all. All she could see were his long-fingered hands, ageless. Her own hands, which had once been pale and smooth, were wrinkled and calloused.

"I had hoped you would never come," the head priestess said.

"But you knew I would," he replied.

The old woman turned back to lean on the windowsill. There was something about the man's presence that set her ill at ease. As she had when he first appeared in their valley over a decade ago, she tried to get a reading of his spiritual energy. And just as she had back then, she found nothing but emptiness when she peeked. Across the garden one of the girls laughed, covering her mouth with her hand. Her eyes sparkled. She was the picture of innocence.

"I am reluctant to let her go," the old woman said with her back to her guest, instead watching the young woman. "She shows great promise. She could be the greatest priestess since priestess Fujikawa Kazue herself."

"But she will."

The priestess turned back to the man. "Not if she does not complete her training."

"I will teach her what she needs to know."

"If you could just give us more time," the priestess pleaded.

He waggled his finger at her, as if she were the child.

"We had a deal."

She sighed. It had not seemed such a high price to pay at the time. But she had never expected to grow so attached to the child. It felt like giving up her own flesh and blood. She should feel that way about all these girls who had been left in her care for various reasons. But this one was different, she wasn't like the others.

There was no changing the past, she supposed. "You're right, but if you would be kind enough to give us a moment alone?"

The man bowed his head. "I will return in a few moments."

The man saw himself out of the room, and an acolyte who'd likely been spying at the door peeked around the corner as he slipped out.

When she realized she'd been caught spying, she froze. The head priestess, too tired to scold her, waved her hand. "Go and get her." The girl ran off to do her bidding, and she watched from the window as the acolyte went to fetch her. The girl rose up gracefully even before the acolyte spoke, as if she had been waiting her whole life for this moment. And perhaps she had. At times she seemed much older than her sixteen years.

She floated after the acolyte, and each movement she made was so precise. There really was no one who danced the holy rituals or sang as beautifully as her. It was such a shame that destiny was taking her away from the life of service she was meant for.

The old woman turned away from the window and back to the door, waiting for her entry. She took a seat, as to not alarm her. After a few moments there was a knock on the door, and she called her in.

The girl stood before her, head bowed. "You called for me, head Priestess?"

"Yes, child. The day has come you are to leave us."

Her eyes were wide but she did not protest. She was too obedient for that.

"May I ask where I am to go, Head Priestess?"

"I cannot say. That is for your father to tell you."

"My father?"

"The man who brought you here sixteen years ago. I knew from the start you would not stay here forever. You were to be trained for your duty and return to your father."

She gazed at the floor. "I don't want to go. This is my home."

The old woman rose up and went to take her hand. "My child, you were meant for great things. You and I both know that. Do not pretend you will miss this place. I can see the excitement in your eyes."

The girl's eyes sparkled with pleasure and she bowed her head to hide her smile. This small shrine could never contain her. She should have known that from the start.

The door at the back of the room slid open, and the high priestess glanced at the man who had returned. Even their goodbye had been too brief.

"It is nice to meet you." The girl bowed her head. "Father."

The priestess's stomach twisted. She didn't want to give her up to him. On impulse, she grabbed her hand. What would he use her exceptional power for? She'd sworn never to ask, but fear made her reckless.

"Child, you don't have to do this. You have a choice."

The girl shook her head. "I've known this day would come. It is my destiny. Isn't that why you named me Kazue, because I am her reincarnation?"

She let her hand go and took a step back, those ancient eyes stared back at her. She was not a girl, the priestess had to remind herself of that, but the rebirth of their mistress, Kazue.

ACKNOWLEDGMENTS

As I write this acknowledgment, I am overwhelmed by gratitude. The seeds that would bloom into the Dragon Saga germinated in high school. Though the final version looks nothing like the story I first envisioned, the earliest themes of elemental magic and a love that stretches across eons and tale of epic proportions remained. This book started out on Wattpad, where it gathered a small cult following of persistent, dedicated readers who spurned me to complete the first draft, which took me two years to write.

This series has been a decade in the making and I must heap praise upon my husband, Drew, whose always supported me as I've struggled with it giving me quiet encouragement and excitement over every story related triumph and comfort in the dark parts of the creative process. I also would be lost without my sounding board and best friend, Nicole, who is and will always be my biggest cheerleader.

This gorgeous edition you're holding in your hands wouldn't be possible without the support of my Kickstarter backers. I never thought I could see my words bound in such a beautiful fashion. Thank you a million times for helping me make my dreams a reality.

Also by Nicolette Andrews

<u>Moonlight Dragon</u>

Empress Ascending (Newsletter Exclusive)

Dragon's Deception

Dragon's Temptation

<u>Thornwood Series</u>

Fairy Ring (Free)

Pricked by Thorns (Free)

Heart of Thorns

Tangled in Thorns

Blood and Thorns

<u>World of Akatsuki</u>

The Dragon Saga

The Priestess and the Dragon (Free)

The Sea Stone

The Song of the Wind

The Fractured Soul

The Immortal Vow

Tales of Akatsuki

Kitsune: A Little Mermaid Retelling (Free)

Yuki: A Snow White Retelling

Okami: A Little Red Riding Hood Retelling

<u>Diviner's World</u>

Duchess (Free)

Sorcerer (Free)

Diviner's Prophecy

Diviner's Curse

Diviner's Fate

Princess

<u>Witch of the Lake Series</u>

Feast of the Mother

Fate of the Demon

Fall of the Reaper

About the Author

Nicolette is a native San Diegan with a passion for the world of make believe. From a young age, Nicolette was telling stories whether it be writing plays for her friends to act out or making a series of children's books that her mother still likes drag out to embarrass her with in front of company. She still lives in her imagination but in reality she resides in San Diego with her husband, children and a couple cats. She loves reading, attempting arts and crafts, and cooking.

You can visit her at her website: www.nicoletteandrews.com or at these places:

facebook.com/nicandfantasy

x.com/nicandfantasy

instagram.com/nicolette_andrews

amazon.com/author/nicoletteandrews

bookbub.com/authors/nicolette-andrews

goodreads.com/nicolette_andrews

pinterest.com/Nicandfantasy